Jonathan Sean Lyster

I0565513

JUDGMENT DAZE

ARMAGEDDON BOYS ⚡ BOOK ONE

Heuronic Books

All characters and events in this book are fictional.
Any similarity to persons living or dead is coincidental.

Also available in ebook format through Amazon.

Published by Heuronic Books
Copyright © 2018 Jonathan Sean Lyster

Cover design and art by Enodeer
https://99designs.com/profiles/enodeer

978-0-9937570-3-7

TABLE OF CONTENTS

The Book of
Seth

I

I grew a tail at the east end of the airport parking lot. An eggshell blue Mustang wagged three cars back all the way to the Rutherford Freeway. I wasn't about to lead the bastards to my brother, so I cut across four lanes of blasting horns and waving middle fingers to an off-ramp. The Mustang overshot.

My rental's GPS led me to the industrial park where Sharkey kept his lair. Fat little Sharkey waddled me down endless aisles of weaponry. I tooled up. Eight U.S. Marine grenades, just because. Two Kimber 9mm pistols. Extended magazines gave them nine shots each. A vintage World War Two Sten gun. Also 9mm to share ammunition. I gave the Sten a worried look. Sharkey insisted I could count on it despite its reputation. If he vouched for it, that worked for me. In his business, selling shoddy hardware meant the friends of the poor guy who'd bought it might show up and make things unpleasant.

Next stop: Tim's Diner. I parked a block down, dropped a Kimber in my jacket's inner pocket and headed in for a family get-together.

As I pushed the creaking door open, I came face-to-face with a tall guy in a suit, little round glasses on the end of his nose. He gave a condescending smile as I stepped to the side. "I recommend the breakfast special, eggs over easy with toast," and brushed past.

I looked around. Nathan rustled a newspaper while he ate, looking just like his online profile. Two studs in his left earlobe and a cynical face. He'd picked a table next to the windows, convenient for whoever had shot or blown up six of our half-brothers. His eyes looked Asian. Maybe his mother was Chinese. The shape of his cheekbones matched the rest of us. He had the usual skinny wiry build. The kind of frame that makes it easy to nail us to a post and lift it up.

I thumped the table. He bounced like a rubber ball.

"Back there." I pointed toward a table near the sign for the restrooms.

Nathan stared up, uncomprehending.

"Seth," I said.

"You really came all this way?" He rustled his newspaper again. "How have you been?"

"Not dead. Planning to stay that way."

His lip curled. "Where do you get the tough-guy dialogue?"

I strode to the back and dropped into a seat at the empty table. He looked around, slowly folding his newspaper. A man came to my table in greasy-spoon formal wear: grimy white apron, white cap.

"Menu?"

"Sure," I said. "And water. In a coffee cup."

He gave me a look but brought both as Nathan slid into the seat opposite me. I waited for "Tim" to leave, then laid my hand over the cup. The shift felt like a spark in my fingertips. Steam rose between my fingers, carrying the aroma of fresh coffee.

Nathan's mouth quirked. "Parlor tricks?"

"No one else brews it this good." I sipped. "Someone is rubbing out the brothers."

"Like I haven't heard. So?"

I almost spewed Sumatran dark roast with a pinch of cane sugar and cream. "That doesn't bother you?"

"I'm out of the game. It isn't my problem." He peered at me a moment. "How did you find me?"

"Adam. He told me you eat here every morning before work. With a big target on your chest. You could be next."

"I'm an avowed atheist now. I'm safe."

"An 'avowed' . . . how did you manage the kind of head trauma you'd need to believe that? Anyhow, Trent converted to Buddhism, Loren changed his name to Seeker-After-Truth and joined some sect back in Cove. Both are dead. Graeme would be too if I hadn't been using his crapper when his apartment blew up. What makes you think whoever is killing us will care that you're trying to swing for a different team?"

Nathan shrugged.

Tim showed up again. "Like something?"

"Sure." I held up the menu. "The special. Eggs over easy. Whole-wheat toast. And throw in some extra bacon."

He took the menu, scratched his butt with its left corner, and passed it to a couple of women at a table farther on. Nathan opened his newspaper to the entertainment section, pretending to ignore me.

"Someone shot Mel ten blocks from here last week," I said. "Did you hear about that?"

Nathan glanced at me over his newspaper. "Yes. Gay-bashers. Speaking of swinging for a different team."

"Gay-bashers bash up close and personal. Mel took one bullet through the head, sniper style. The bullet matched the gun that iced Loren back in Cove. So whoever is killing us has moved here."

Nathan flinched. "How do you know the bullets match? You're a bookstore clerk. You don't have connections like that."

"I do now. Where are the others?"

"I don't keep in touch with them. Not my brother's keeper and all that."

"You don't need to be beer buddies with them. I just want phone numbers."

"What if they don't want to talk to you?"

"That's up to them. I'll leave messages." I opened my jacket and reached into my shirt pocket for my day planner. My jacket gaped enough that Nathan saw the Kimber.

His eyes grew.

I thumbed my day planner to one of the notes pages in its back and slid it over his newspaper, a blue Bic lying next to the spiral in its center.

"Write. Last known addresses and phone numbers."

He started penning. I looked at the morning traffic drifting along, halting, I assumed, when the lights turned. A breeze had come up. Someone's snack trash pirouetted past the window. An eggshell-blue Mustang cruised by, slowing outside the glass.

My hand darted into my jacket and closed on the pistol grip. Nathan looked as if his eyes would fall out and roll across the table. I glanced at him and scowled, then watched the car until it rolled out of view.

I kept my eyes on the door. Tim slid one plate from his armload onto the table as he wandered past. I tugged Nathan's paper over and drew the pistol out, setting it down with the paper making a tent over it.

"Who are you expecting?" Nathan whispered. He finally had the decency to appear as if his knees were turning to goo.

"Keep writing."

I could see the butt of the Kimber under the newspaper. In particular, I saw the square black hole at the bottom of its handle. I'd left the ammunition clips in the trunk of my car. That, I thought as a chill crawled along my shoulder blades, saved me from learning how to handle a loaded gun.

"Someone followed me from the airport," I said.

"And you led them to me?"

"No. I lost them over on the south side. They found you on their own. Leave." I jutted my chin at an old wooden door marked *Employees Only*. "Go that way. Don't think it over; just run."

I slid my dayplanner into my shirt pocket. Then rammed the gun into the top of my pants. Not something I'd usually recommend, but there was no reason to worry about sending a slug through future Seth Juniors.

"I can help," Nathan said, gaze darting to the window.

"By stopping a bullet?"

His mouth opened and closed and opened and closed. Then he reached for my plate. "Yum. Extra bacon." Chewing like mad, he took out his wallet and dropped a twenty on the table. Apparently trying for nonchalance, he got to his feet, yawned, stretched, chewed some more, and sidled down the hall past the washrooms.

I headed out the front door as the Mustang pulled in across the street. Slipped into the alley across from a black dumpster, gasping at the stench of week-old food. Drawing my useless gun, I glanced around the corner.

A sound up the alley spun me around to see Nathan rabbiting away as a door swung shut. Swallowing the chunk of vital organ that had shot into my throat, I peered at the street again.

A tall woman in a black skirt cut off above the knees jaywalked toward me, ash blonde hair shining. I had expected someone pulled from the standard goon cast, not a cool, elegant hired gun. I did wonder why the assassin hadn't picked better work shoes; two-inch heels are lousy victim-chasing attire. The skirt wouldn't help her either. I waited, listening to the clip-clop as her heels neared.

When she stepped into view, I grabbed her collar and swung her around me to the wall. She whined through the whole orbit. I held up the gun. This got a reaction. Not the one I'd wanted. Hell descended in the form of a purse walloping my skull and a foot flying at my nuts. I deflected the kick. Somewhere amid the roaring in my head, I felt a thump against my arm. The pistol skittered across grimy concrete.

I went for it. So did she. As I said: heels are a bad idea in a fight. When I scooped the Kimber up she froze, hands out in mid reach.

Her voice might have sounded better if she weren't talking into a gun muzzle. It came out strangled. "I'll scream."

"I'll shoot. That's louder."

She took a step back toward the mouth of the alley.

"Uh-uh. Running gets you a bullet too. Why are you following me?"

"I'm not. I'm here to have coffee in the diner."

"You followed me from the airport. In that blue Mustang."

She shrugged. "I'm a journalist. You've probably seen me on Channel Forty-eight."

"I don't watch television."

Her purse lay nearby on the dirty concrete. I stooped for it.

She stepped toward me. "Hey."

I motioned with the pistol. "Back against the wall."

The woman rolled her eyes and stepped back, not quite to the wall. She put her fists on her hips superheroine style while I dug into her purse. Flipped her wallet open without dropping the gun. Barely. Business cards in with the cash read, *Kaylee Jerrel, Investigative Journalist. Channel 48: All News All Day!* in bold, blue letters, next to a little planet-Earth logo. The picture on the cards showed shorter hair forming a halo around her face.

I pulled out her digital recorder, thumbing the *Play* button.

"That's personal." Kaylee stepped from the wall. I motioned with the muzzle to back her off.

Dead air. The screen listed files. I nudged the back arrow and hit play again.

"October twenty-third," her voice said. "Seth Brown's arrived. He's renting a car. Wish I knew what he's doing here."

Today. I hopped the recorder farther back.

"October twenty-first. Seth Brown. Apartment nine-oh-one, one-seven-five Cranberry Lane, Cove City. Works in Wordwings Books. He's been asking questions about the Earl Munny disappearance. And Loren LeBron. Google has nothing on him. He's never put up a website. Keeps his social media accounts private. Bought a Wal-Air ticket to Summerton."

I clicked it off. "How do you know about Loren and Earl?"

Kaylee folded her arms together and raised her chin. "I have my sources."

"I have nine rounds." Technically true: they were hanging out in the trunk of my car.

Her eyes rolled again. "I know you came here to find others like you. All born in a certain week one April. Someone killed fourteen of you in the past year alone."

I knew of only six. I nudged the recorder back again.

"August thirtieth. Two more. Frank Charmer in Cove City and Tom Knightly from up north in Riley. Knightly vanished weeks ago. Charmer was gunned down last Friday. Whoever's doing this is getting more brazen."

I hit the button. Damn it. "How many more do you know about? I mean the ones who haven't been killed. Do you have their numbers? Addresses?"

She gave me an arch look and crossed her arms. I thumbed my pistol's hammer back.

Kaylee grinned. "I'll make you a deal. You tell me why someone would want to kill these men, and I'll tell you what I know. A straight exchange."

"How about I shoot your kneecap?"

"How about I shoot you with my finger? It might actually be loaded."

Blood leached into my cheeks. I glared at her, trying to figure out what to do next. When nothing came, I shrugged and tucked the gun in my pocket. Well, hell. "Someone is hunting them down. I need to warn them."

I tossed the purse. She caught it in one hand. "You're not used to handling a gun, are you?"

"Sure I am."

She gave me a look I couldn't decipher. "Okay. Tell me who is doing this."

"I haven't a clue. That's why I'm here."

"Are you part of some numerology cult?"

"No."

"A biker gang?"

"Not bikers."

"Something political then? Or a sex scandal? Did some politician have a lot of illegitimate children?"

Well hell, I thought. The truth. "No. I'm the next Savior of Mankind. So were all those who've been killed."

"Huh?"

"You know. The New Testament. Jesus Christ. Healing the sick, turning water into wine – or coffee."

A confused look rolled around on Kaylee's face. Then a grin spread across it. "A religious cult. That's great."

I eyed her thoughtfully. "Why are you following me?"

"A source said you were coming to see Nathan Filman."

"Who is your source?"

"What's in it for me?"

I considered saying, "Breathing." But it's tough to keep up the strong-arm facade when the woman you're threatening knows you forgot to put bullets in your gun. Besides, the ass-kicking had nearly gone very badly for me. I had to wonder if she'd decided not to thrash me all over this alley only because she knew she needn't bother.

"You want this story, you help me out," I said.

"I'm still not hearing anything worth trading for." She came to me and snatched her recorder out of my hand. Then she thumbed record and recited the date. "I'm with Seth Brown in an alley in Summerton. Okay, Seth, tell me about this cult. Are you a member?"

"Uh, yes."

"How did that happen?"

"I was born into it. Now tell me who you know and how I can find them. Then we'll talk. Otherwise I walk away, and you don't get your story."

Her brow creased. She glanced at the mouth of the alley then back at me.

I turned and started walking. "Guess it isn't all that important to you."

"Okay, damn it. My car."

At the street verge, she glanced right and left and minced across. A car honked in a perfunctory way. As we reached her Mustang she clicked the locks, reached in for a cheap red schoolkid's notebook, and laid it open on the hood of the car.

I looked at the list. Nine names. Four I didn't know. Phone numbers marked home, work, or cell. She ran her finger down the list. "This is the weird part. All of them were born within a few days of each other. Look: Emile, Loren, Mel on April third. Quentin, Nathan, Chase on April seventh." Kaylee glanced at me. "You were April eighth, right?"

"At eleven fifty-two PM. Mom says I ruined her sleep."

They say there are some events where you remember exactly where you were and what you were doing when they happened. JFK's death. The space shuttle *Challenger* blowing up. The Twin Towers.

I can tell you exactly what I was doing when Tim's Diner exploded: looking over Kaylee's shoulder, trying to concentrate on her neat handwriting while appreciating the view of her cleavage.

2

The charging-elephant percussion ensemble slammed into my chest and threw me against a concrete wall. Deceased journalist Kaylee Jerrel landed nearby, a shard of Tim's front door protruding from her.

I lay within silence. Pieces of menus and serviettes fell like snow. Gasping, I picked myself up. A huge quantity of blood had left Kaylee and ran in rivulets to the curb. I picked up her red notebook. The cover had been sprayed with darker crimson.

My hearing came back online. Someone bawled somewhere. A siren came closer. Kaylee knew more about the others here than I did and had contacts I didn't. She had to come along.

I walked around her car. Spiderweb cracks filled its side windows. Police cars, lights flashing blue, screeched into a blockade of the street in the direction her car faced. Carrying a body was going to be easier than getting her car through that.

I turned her on her back, put my shoe against her stomach, and pulled hard on the piece of door. The thing dragged bits of Kaylee as it came free. I gathered her up and felt a shocking warmth spread across my belly.

She'd lost weight, but I had time to wish she'd lost more as I carried her past dazed zombies cowering near walls or wandering about. I dumped her on the street between my rental and a UPS van and opened the Camry's trunk. Moving my weapons and clothes aside, I picked Kaylee up and dropped her in. She thumped like a sack of potatoes.

New sirens wailed. A fire truck followed an ambulance. I eased the car out, mulling over how to get Kaylee into my motel room. Someone might ask embarrassing questions if I turned up covered in blood and lugging a corpse. New plan: find somewhere else to take care of her, some place discreet.

As I headed across the river, it occurred to me that the corpse of honor lay in my trunk, already out of sight.

"Well, hell." I pushed the Resurrection Button.

On my fifth birthday Mom took me to a pet store and let me pick out a kitten. I chose a male with gray fur and a white lightning bolt wound around his tail. I wanted to name him Fuzznuts. Mom made an executive decision and christened him Zeus. A week after my seventh birthday, Zeus wandered out onto the street and under the wheels of a minivan that blew past the stop sign at the corner. I saw it all happen. When I reached him, he lay in a puddle of blood and snakelike intestines on the side of the street.

Zeus was my first resurrection, purely by accident.

Let's be clear about this. It isn't like any cheesy flick or TV show you've seen about people with psychic powers. You don't moan and gasp and break into a sweat, or chant something ridiculous like, "Rise. Rise, you bastard, ri-i-i-i-se!"

Picture a big red button marked Resurrection. Picture yourself pushing it. Then sit down and wait; it's out of your hands.

But don't wander too far from the body. I discovered this the next time I had to revive Zeus. He wasn't exactly a sage among felines. The resurrection moves out from you like waves in a pond after a stone hits the water. During Zeus's second return trip, I walked over to the cedar tree outside our house and sat down to wait. I'd forgotten about

Hammy, buried four years before under that tree. A few minutes after I launched the resurrection, Zeus still hadn't moved. Instead, the ground beside me began to churn, and up popped a very annoyed hamster. I picked him up, sucked my finger, caught him again, and marched back to Zeus. I pushed the Resurrection Button. Again. This time I sat on the curb beside him.

Hoo-hah! Mom threw a conniption. We'd finally sold Hammy's cage at a garage sale two weeks before.

The resurrection buzzed like static in the stale air of the car. Then it rolled from white noise into a single high-pitched squealing note; it had found someone or something dead. As I reached the south side of the bridge, the former corpse in the back of my car started kicking and yelling. The trunk popped open.

Factoid: look in the trunk of any car built in the past fifteen or twenty years, and you will find a little handle under the lid. That's for people who find themselves shut inside the trunk due to practical-joker friends or that long-lost Milli Vanilli CD spotted way in the back.

"Shit." I wheeled onto a side street at the mouth of the bridge and stomped the brake. I reached the trunk in time to mostly catch Kaylee Jerrel as she threw her screaming self out onto the asphalt. Her jacket and blouse were reduced to sleeves. She dragged herself away from me to some grass next to an apartment building. "It was so beautiful," she moaned.

"Tunnel of light? Harp music?"

"And such joy and bliss." She clutched her arms around her middle. "Now I hurt so much, in here. Oh, God." Her gaze skipped around. "I flew. I remember flying."

"I brought you back."

Her gaze settled on me. "What does that mean?"

"You were dead. I brought you back."

She flung herself at me without getting to her feet. "Can you send me back there?" Her hands clutched at my legs.

I tried peeling her fingers off my thighs. "No, not going to do that."

"Please."

"Look, you aren't wearing anything. What do you think the cops will do if they find you on your knees in front of me with a breeze blowing through your cleavage?"

Kaylee looked down, squealed, and laid her arms across her chest. I gave her my jacket, retrieving the gun from the pocket. Then I helped her to the car. Into a seat, this time. She sat quietly until I settled behind the wheel.

"So I was dead."

"That's right."

"How?"

"Someone blew up Tim's Diner."

"Oh."

Kaylee stared at the spot marked *Airbag* on the dashboard. In my experience, the formerly deceased were pains in the ass for half an hour after recovery. Graeme, the histrionic extreme, had spent hours rambling about how he hadn't believed there was anything on the other side. He'd been gone for less than a minute, and he'd come back yammering about this beautiful tunnel of light with music that sounded like what Mozart might compose if he'd stumbled onto cocaine. I could relate, what with swan-diving off Graeme's balcony after his body and going splat on the pavement. I'd had a taste of the tunnel too, but I didn't go on and on about it.

The GPS showed a large park to the south. I drove that way.

"Are you sure?" Kaylee said.

"About what?"

"Me. Being . . . you know."

"Worm food?"

"You don't have to be rude about it."

She sat in silence for ten or fifteen blocks, staring at her hands. Then with a glance at me, she opened the jacket and peered down at herself. "I'm sticky."

"That's blood. Yours."

"I donate at the Red Cross. If I don't eat, I feel groggy afterward."

"You got your supply topped up. And probably new lungs; I think pieces of those came out when I pulled Tim's front door out of you."

I found the turnoff into Galway Park and picked a spot sheltered enough to peel clothes off behind the car with the trunk lid open. I used my shirt to dry off my belly. Feeling somewhat better in fresh jeans, I picked a red T-shirt in case I'd missed some of Kaylee's blood.

Back in the car, I keyed in the motel's address.

Kaylee stared at me. "You meant it. That stuff about being the Messiah."

"Yup."

The Western Comfort Motel stood out. Someone had used black spray paint to change the first "o" in Comfort to a "u." I found parking well away from the doors.

"Stay put," I told Kaylee. She nodded, eyes glassy. I tucked the pistol into the back of my pants under my shirt, then headed into the lobby. A round young man with three chins sat behind the counter. The place smelled of pine cleanser and feet.

"Seth Brown," I said. "I have a room booked."

"Oh yeah." He pushed a pad to me.

I filled in the form. He moved like a hippo lounging in the sun, eventually digging a key card out of a drawer and meandering through the process of sliding it across the scanner and keying the room number in.

"Need your plate," he mumbled.

I filled out that part of the sheet.

He slid the card over. "Room two ten. Elevator's around there." He tilted his chins.

"Thanks."

"Oh yeah. Need your credit card."

I reached for my wallet.

"Oh yeah. Your friends find you?"

My neck turned to ice. "Friends?"

"Two guys an hour ago. Wondered if you were in yet."

"Guess I missed them." I made a show of patting my jacket down. "Must have left my card in the car." I nudged the door open with my shoe, then did my impression of Nathan across the parking lot. My still-empty Kimber jarred against my back.

I threw myself in the driver's seat, winced, extracted the gun, and got the car back onto the street. "Where are you staying?"

Kaylee looked up. "Staying?"

"Your hotel."

"I live here."

"I thought you flew in this morning."

Her voice had a slur, as though she weren't allocating much in the way of mental resources to it. "I did. But this is where I live. I just flew out to Cove for a couple of days."

"What's your address, then?"

"Pellier and Whitherwood."

I typed the names into the GPS.

"What's it all about?" Kaylee asked.

"Two guys showed up at the motel asking for me. I have no idea how they found out I'm here. I need somewhere else to crash."

"That's not what I meant. What's life all about? You're here for the Second Coming, right?"

"Life is about not dying 'til you have to. And the Second Coming isn't coming if I can help it."

"I really did die?"

"And I really brought you back. We're spinning our wheels here."

"That's not what I mean. I have a career. Had a career. I thought I had my last big score with this story, you know? I'm thirty-seven. There's Simone Pert coming up to replace me. And, Jesus Christ, the network is bringing in a petite redhead to do the weather because that's what some consultant told them they need. They want her to do her segment in a bikini."

"What channel is that again?"

Kaylee glared at me, then resumed staring at traffic. "My career is coming to an end. I just wanted one more great story. This thing looked national. Murders in seven different cities? All young men born within days of each other? But nobody will believe I got killed and resurrected. Or that I'm driving around with the next Messiah." She shrugged, eyes bleak. "So I could live another, oh, forty years with nothing to look forward to. Forty years before I die again. Shit."

I tried to cheer her up. "There are thousands of things that might kill you sooner."

We drove in glum silence broken by the tinny voice of the GPS. Our destination turned out to be a tower of steel and gold-tinted glass. The sign, perched in an oval lawn surrounded by asphalt, read, *Falcone Towers. Highrise living at its finest!*

Kaylee pointed at the underground parking and fished around in her purse. I swept her key fob past the sensor. The gate opened before us and, not much later, the elevator dumped us out on the sixth floor.

Kaylee led a busy life. Along one wall of her apartment were pictures and awards in frames. A photo of her with the fire chief, if the man's uniform was anything to go by. Another with a guy in an expensive suit.

She turned on the television. It seemed reflexive. Channel forty-eight, according to the blue globe logo in the lower left corner. She left it going, wandering into the kitchen and switching a black kettle on.

I had time to think now. I'd initially figured bad luck had almost got me blown up in Tim's diner with Nathan. Kaylee had saved our lives just by being a distraction. Five more minutes . . .

But no, someone knew my stops. So who'd talked? I'd told Mom which motel I'd booked; she thought I was on an impromptu vacation to visit my ol' buddy and half-brother Emile. I hadn't seen him since he and his mom left Cove City. I hadn't told Emile where I was staying.

Then there was Hilda Langella: police lieutenant and homicide investigator for Cove City PD. I'd known Hilda just two weeks now. She'd been on the spot when I raised Jamie. It's one thing to convince yourself you were mistaken about someone's injuries. But when a bullet goes through someone's eye, that's something else. Especially when the bullet falls out, rolls along the asphalt, and butts up against your shoe. And the eye folds out like a flower and rebuilds itself while you watch. And the dead person sits up and starts moaning about the tunnel of light.

I'd sat them down in a coffee shop, told Jamie to shut up about the tunnel of light, and gave Hilda the scoop about our family ties. Even did my water-into-coffee trick.

I popped my phone out of its holster on my belt, scrolled down, and hit the green *Call* button. She answered on the second ring.

"Langella here."

"Hilda, it's Seth."

"I know. Caller ID is a wonderful invention."

"How the hell did the bad guys know I was going to be here?"

"I have no idea. How?"

"Someone knew where I'd be staying."

"I see. Of course. I can understand why you would instantly suspect that a police detective used to keeping her mouth shut about investigations would blab to hired killers she has never met that you might be flying across the country to deliver a warning to their potential victims."

I shut my eyes. "Okay, I get your point. By the way, thanks for hooking me up with Sharkey. I'm –"

"Back up. How could I possibly know someone like Sharkey?"

"Huh? He's the gun dealer you –"

"There is no way you got his number from me since I don't move in those circles."

"Oh. Right. Wink-wink. Well, anyway, I'm fitted up with a couple of pistols, some used hand grenades –"

"How exactly does a 'used' grenade differ from a pile of rubble?"

"Sharkey says that just means they didn't come through official channels. Like, they weren't sold off by some supply officer eager to pay up his gambling debt by unloading some of the base's stock."

"That's an official channel, is it?"

"Yeah. An unofficial channel might be, say, some terrorist group in Clusterfuckistan moving gear onto the black market after they've stripped the fuses or replaced the powder with sand because they needed the parts for a bigger, nastier bomb."

"Ah. And you bought these?"

"Odds are they're perfectly good. I got them at a discount. Seventy bucks each."

"Of course this conversation is purely hypothetical. You didn't really buy illicit weapons in Summerton. Enjoy your vacation. I still have four unsolved murders on my files. Call me if you learn anything useful. Toodly-do." The phone clicked. Damn. So if Hilda hadn't talked, who did that leave? No one. I had to be missing something.

A hissing sound came from down the corridor. Kaylee, having a shower.

When she emerged she gave me an empty look. "I'm making tea."

"Just a cup of water for me. Got a spare towel?"

She opened a closet next to the bathroom door. "Here." An enormous beach towel with the Muppets on it. Great.

I showered, dried my chest on Kermit and my back on Miss Piggy, and put on fresh clothes. An alcove across the hall held a stacked washer and dryer.

"Mind if I use your washing machine?" I called.

A mutter came back that I took to mean, "Go ahead." I shoved my bloody jeans, shirt, and jacket into the washer and poured in some detergent. Then fiddled with the dial until the machine came to life.

Kaylee had dressed in jeans, and a T-shirt with Steven Tyler's face peering out under the Aerosmith logo. She sat on the couch, staring at the television. An attractive woman with a mountain of hair smiled from the screen. Kaylee caught my look. "Simone Pert. The consultant said she would make a better anchor than me."

I dug out my phone. Emile had given me several names and numbers; I picked the next one. Quentin Haze. His phone rang and rang and went to voice mail.

"Quentin, this is your brother Seth. You're in danger. Call me, please." I recited my number. Then I clicked off and scrolled to Emile's number. I got a shaky voice.

"Hello?"

"Hi. Who's this?"

"You phoned me, dude. You oughta know."

"Emile? This is Seth."

"I'm not Emile. And Seth? Nathan called us, freaking out. We're getting out of Dodge."

"Good. Listen. I need to know who you know. Others in the brotherhood."

"I'm busy. We've got a truck to load." The phone clicked. Asshole. Some people have no sense of family loyalty.

"I need to see Emile," I told Kaylee. "Why don't you go to bed or something? Rest. It's been a long day already." We were barely past noon.

Kaylee glared up at me. "I'm coming with you. This is still my story."

"You don't need to do that. I'll come back and tell you what I've learned. You can keep my clothes hostage."

"No way. I'm seeing this through. Maybe I can't put you and your brothers on television, but there's a story here. Someone is still murdering you."

3

I pulled over as the GPS chirped that we'd reached Emile's. We shared the street with an old cube van with BARC in big green letters across its side. Cardboard boxes for liquor brands ranging from Captain Morgan to Jack Daniels were scattered across the lawn of a two-story beige house.

Kaylee and I marched up to a door held open by a black plant pot with a dead rubber tree in it.

"Hello?" I called.

A face poked from a room to the right. "Seth?"

"That's me."

"Who's she?"

Kaylee stepped forward. "I'm Kaylee Jerrel."

The guy looked her up and down. "I'm Chase. I'm single. I mean, um, I'm busy." His head bobbed back.

We followed him. "Was it you I spoke to on the phone?" I asked.

"Yeah."

"You've talked to Nathan?"

Chase nodded. "He told us about Tim's Diner."

"Where are you going?"

Chase glanced at Kaylee. "You trust her?"

"I guess."

Kaylee gave me a look.

Chase shrugged. "Emile has another house ten minutes from here. We were planning to move there anyway next month. A lot of our stuff was already packed. We just stepped up the plan."

I blinked. "Emile owns two houses?"

"More than that. Runs his own company. Buys stocks, buys houses." Envy licked around Chase's words. "He's rolling in it. This house has gone up two hundred grand since he bought it. He's selling it off." Chase eyed me. "Do you think you can help us load the truck?"

"Who's 'us'?"

"Nathan called work and said he's throwing up, so his boss told him to stay home. He's upstairs packing."

Later I wondered how, after escaping getting blown up at Tim's Diner and ambushed at a cheap motel, I'd been roped into hauling furniture. Kaylee wandered past, carrying a lamp and a dazed look.

I peered dubiously into the back of the truck while Chase and I lifted a green couch into it. The stink of old dog surrounded us.

Chase caught the expression on my face. "It was all I could snag on short notice. I work for the Bureau of Animal Rescue and Care."

"Like the SPCA?"

"Yeah."

We loaded two more couches, a fifty-two-inch television, a coffee table, and three beds. "Just essentials," Chase said.

Nathan must have bolted here as soon as he got clear of Tim's Diner. "Made a hell of a noise when it went up, didn't it?" He grimaced, handing a box up to me. Maybe he figured I was to blame for him having to pack up his life in a hurry. Some people are like that: you tell them, "Run, someone's trying to kill you," and all they want to do is whine about the inconvenience you're putting them through. Like being dead wouldn't be inconvenient.

Chase watched Nathan mope his way past. "Emile figures this will all blow over in a couple of weeks." That sounded intended to appease Nathan.

"Based on what?" Nathan asked.

"He knows what he's doing. He drives an Audi."

I considered pointing out that the skill set required to drive an expensive car didn't actually match what you needed to keep from being blown up and shot by assassins. Only the awareness that I didn't have those skills either kept my mouth shut.

We had the "essentials" loaded by five.

"When does Emile get home?" I asked.

"Usually six-thirty. He couldn't take time from his schedule to help."

That sounded like Emile.

Chase drove the truck with Nathan beside him. Kaylee and I followed in my Camry. Kaylee looked at me. "Why are we doing this? I thought we were going to find out where more of your brothers live."

"We are. Emile is well connected. Right now this is doing us good. Don't you find you enjoy something physical after a stressful situation? It's like doing dishes after a crisis. It lets your brain turn things over and get mellow while your hands keep busy."

"If I wanted to do dishes, I wouldn't have bought a dishwasher."

The truck ahead of us slowed and pulled over. I parked a ways behind it.

They were moving into a mansion. Roman pillars held up two porches, and the house appeared freshly custom-built to look old and stately. The wood siding looked too clean and unblemished to be more than a couple of years old.

"Emile owns this?"

"Yup." Chase climbed out of the truck. "There's a garage around the side. It'll be easier taking things through there than through the front. I'll open it up from inside."

Kaylee's phone buzzed as she climbed from the car. She peered at it, yelped, and held it out to me.

I peered at the screen.

Quentin was killed ten seconds ago.
MTF

"Shit," I said. "Who is MTF?"

"My anonymous source."

"How do we know it isn't a setup?"

"We don't."

Chase peered over my shoulder. "Oh my God. What are you going to do?"

"I need to get to Quentin. I can bring him back."

Chase gasped. "You can do that?"

"Can't you?"

"Uh, no."

Nathan laughed. Not a pleasant sound. "His mom figured he'd be better off if he didn't know two fucks about what we are."

"Well, Seth brought me back." Kaylee glowered at me. "He can do the same for this Quentin."

I turned to Chase and Nathan. "I have weapons. But I could use some help."

They looked at each other.

"Well, you see . . ." Chase trailed off.

"Yeah, right," Nathan added.

"It'd help if I had someone there to raise me, in case I get hit in the back of the head or something. You know, shot?"

Chase scratched his nose. "It's, um, kind of sudden."

Nathan snorted. "You expect us to charge the guns with you? I almost got blown up. You can keep the hero complex to yourself."

So much for brotherly love. I headed for my car. Kaylee joined me, apparently unafraid to charge the guns. On the other hand, maybe she wanted another trip to heaven.

I drove past Quentin's house. A little cottage with a high peaked roof. I counted three houses past it to the side street. We took the corner and turned again into the alley.

I took the two Kimbers out and held one to Kaylee. She shook her head. "I'm not taking that."

"Come on. The killers have probably left, but it's better to have protection."

Kaylee eyed me sadly. "I can't take the chance. If I shoot someone, will that mean I won't get to go back where I was? I'll go to . . . ?"

She didn't finish.

"Hell?" I said. "I have it on really good authority there's no such place. But fine." I pocketed one of the Kimbers and shoved my door open. "Stay put."

"No way."

I popped the trunk and gathered up two grenades. Pondered the Sten, but decided against it. This time I made sure I loaded my pistols.

Kaylee walked beside me along the alley, counting houses until we reached Quentin's backyard. A decrepit little white wooden gate hung on hinges blackened with rust. I stopped, checked the Kimber, then sidled along the fence to the gate. I nudged it. Instant creaking. I lifted one leg over, then the other. Kaylee followed, moving like a blue-jeaned spider. I saw two small windows and a door in the middle, up four steps. No sign of movement.

I crept up to the steps and peered through a window. White cupboards and the edge of what might be a fridge. My eyes focused on the window itself and picked out the detail I'd missed: no glass.

Kaylee had stopped farther down the walkway. I glanced at her and motioned her to crouch low. The screen door beside me was shut, but the inner door hung open, the wood where it latched ripped apart. Someone had put a boot to it.

Thunder cracked around me. I saw a figure for a moment, then sound crashed again. My ears rang. I poked my pistol around and squeezed the trigger. Nothing happened. I swore and worked the pistol's slide and tried again. The pistol barked, louder than movies imply. I fired another couple of bullets into the house.

"Kaylee." I glanced back at her. "Get –"

She wasn't there. She lay farther back, belly oozing red. Froth formed on her lips.

Kaylee smiled, then coughed. "Is it fatal?"

"Don't worry. I can take care of it."

"No! Let me go."

"Don't talk crap. You don't have to die."

"I want to." She spat pink across her shirt. "I want to go back. Just let me go."

"Damn it, you've got info I need."

"My computer's password is Murrow. As in Edward R. Murrow. Capital *M*. Replace the *o* with a zero and use less-than signs for the two *r*s."

"Hold that thought." I squeezed another shot into the hallway and followed it in. The little alcove inside didn't give much cover.

A figure appeared to my left as a shot cracked into the wall. Quieter gun than mine. The man wore a dark jacket with a furry white collar.

I grabbed a grenade and threw it across. Then realized I'd forgotten to pull the pin. It still earned a squawk. The man bolted from the kitchen to a little corridor on the right. I fired and got a satisfying "Ergh!" for my efforts.

A patch of wall exploded next to me. I heard laughter and saw a familiar tall man in a black suit. He carried a short rifle. I squeezed a shot in his direction and he got out of the hallway.

"Antoine?" a voice called. "You okay?"

"I'll be fine," came a muffled reply. "Finish the bastard."

"Grenade!" I yelled, reaching for another. This time I popped the pin. The little egg started to hiss as I tossed it into the corridor. It bounced along the carpet. I dived for the kitchen.

And landed on the remains of Quentin.

Antoine yelled, "Max. The bomb's a dud. Take him out."

The one with the rifle cracked a shot in my direction.

Another clap of thunder sounded, much louder and meaner than his. It flung an instant wind through the corridor, as a body in a suit thumped down, head and one arm twisted strangely.

I stayed where I was on Quentin, pistol pointing at the doorway. Another figure loomed in the dust. I fired and it backed off.

Ears ringing for the second time today, I scrambled up. Max bled from a hundred rips, tears, and cuts. I recognized the little round glasses still hanging on his ears: the man coming out of Tim's Diner this morning.

Movement in the window caught my attention. The guy in the bomber jacket shuffled along the side of the house.

I raced through the house and found the front door in time to see the wounded man limping madly across the street. I squeezed the trigger.

Factoid: hitting something at a distance with a pistol is actually very hard to do. Forget what you see in movies and television.

My first shot hit nothing. He sped up and flung the driver-side door open. My second shot killed a mailbox. Tires squealed. One more shot thumped into pavement as he roared away.

I found Kaylee still aware. The pool around her had grown.

"I'm going to need your help," I said.

"Let me go. Beautiful . . . on the other side."

"You can die some other time. I still need those names."

"My computer. Desktop folder. Called Investigation."

"Can I have your phone?"

"It's yours."

"Thanks." I tugged it from her waist. "The guy who killed Quentin is calling in reinforcements. We need to get out of here."

"Then go."

"You've been hit in the belly. You could take hours to die." I crouched and slipped my arms under her.

"What are you doing? Don't fix me!"

"I'm not going to. But I don't want those guys to find you still alive. They might . . ."

"Shoot me?"

"No. They're serious. Might torture you to find out where I am."

Kaylee howled as I scooped her up. She weighed more this time, but I didn't have to walk as far.

I slid her onto the back seat. She lay gasping with each breath. I ran back to Quentin's kitchen. He was heavier, but I didn't need to be gentle. I tossed him over my shoulder firefighter style and hauled him to the car. He got the front seat. I buckled his corpse in.

"I'll probably need cash too," I said to Kaylee as I backed the car out of the alley. "I'm paying for this trip with my savings and vacation money. Black-market weaponry is a lot more expensive than I thought."

"Fine." She sucked in a breath. "Banking cards . . . Three . . . Same pin . . . Seven-three-two-three." She coughed.

"How about the key to your condo?"

"I won't need it." She laugh-gasped. Pink froth ran down her chin. "Hurts . . . How long?"

"I'm not sure. All the people I've seen die went really quick. Look, maybe you don't really want to go."

"Do!"

We reached the street and I cranked the car around, pointing the nose north. Then I glanced at Quentin and pushed the Resurrection Button.

Now I had time to think. The speedometer was too high. I eased off. No sense getting pulled over by cops. They might ask about the corpse. Depending on when they asked, the dead body might be either Quentin or Kaylee.

A bullet rolled down Quentin's chest and bounced off the armrest. My other passenger made hoarse sucking sounds. A good time was had by no one.

4

Some things just aren't done. Telling the woman dying behind you to hurry up and get it over with is one of them. I stayed silent as Kaylee made awkward and increasingly stomach-flipping noises.

We were a dozen blocks from Quentin's house and no one had followed. I pulled over and dug out my phone. Hilda answered. "What now?"

"Someone killed another brother."

"You can take care of that, right?"

"It's already done. He's in my car. I overheard one of the killers calling in friends. Can you phone it in, get the local uniforms to drop by? I don't want the cops here to have my number. Tell them you got an anonymous tip. About explosions. I used a hypothetical hand grenade."

"An anonymous tip made to a completely different city."

"Sure. Just get them to Quentin's house."

"Address?"

I recited it. "One more thing. I'm carrying a dying woman around. She's got a belly wound. The bad guys shot her."

An exasperated sigh. "I thought you could heal people. Or do you have to wait for her to die before you do anything?"

"It's not that simple. She's been dead before. She wants to die again. I promised I'd let her."

"She wants to die."

"Yes. What can I do with her? After she's gone, I mean."

"You're asking a homicide detective where you can drop a body?"

"Yes."

Beside me, Quentin moaned.

Hilda breathed in my ear. "Answer this honestly, Seth. Did you shoot her?"

"No, of course not. You can ask her if you like. The bad guys blasted her at Quentin's. Speaking of which, can you see if you have any records in your police database for someone named Max? And Antoine?"

"We typically need surnames."

"Max is dead back at Quentin's house. Antoine ran."

"Then Summerton Police will put this Max person's particulars into the system, like fingerprints. I'll be able to tell you who he is as soon as he is processed."

"How long will that take?"

"Depends on how fast the morgue works. Oh, there's an idea: take your girlfriend to the morgue."

"I can't just hand her over the front desk."

"Morgues always have somewhere out of the way for body delivery. They don't drag a corpse into a waiting room and perch it up next to a potted plant with a copy of *Reader's Digest* in its hand."

Quentin sucked in a long, slow breath. "So beautiful."

Kaylee coughed, sounding as though her throat were being wrung out. "Yes. Beautiful."

"Hilda, I have to go. Talk to you later."

"Sure. Anytime."

As I started driving again, I lurched the car. Kaylee wailed.

"Sorry," I said.

"First time didn't hurt this much."

Quentin straightened up and shook his head. "Wow. It was gorgeous. I've never felt . . . that was like the best tumble I've ever had."

"It was good for me too."

Quentin looked back between the seats. His eyes widened. "Damn, you're bleeding. I can fix –"

"No!" Kaylee and I said in unison.

"Why not? Geez, you're a mess." Quentin turned his gaze to me. "Seth?"

"That's me."

"I got your message. I was listening to voice mail one moment and flying up a gold and silver tunnel the next."

"And fuchsia? And green?" Kaylee asked.

"Green, yes. What's fuchsia?"

"Kind of a purply pink," I said.

"Oh." Quentin looked sidelong at me. "And screw you."

"Huh? What's that for?"

"I didn't want to come back." He rubbed his cheeks with his palms, fast, as if trying to rub dirt off them. "It even felt beautiful."

I did some math in my head. Kaylee's source had texted her more than half an hour ago. Quentin had been dead longer than Kaylee. That meant a lot of whinging to listen to.

"Quentin, I need you to focus."

"On what?"

"I need a list of names from you. You can't go home; the killers –"

"I heard you talking just now on the phone. You blew someone up in my house."

"That's right."

My phone chimed. Hilda.

"I reached a colleague at Summerton PD," she said in a brittle voice. "He's in homicide. He sent officers to the scene immediately."

"Did they catch them?"

"I told them my anonymous call said there'd been an explosion. There's no sign of one. And no body."

"What?"

"Nothing. No broken glass, no sign of damage."

"What about the back door? Someone kicked that in."

"The back door is locked. So is the front. The house is fine. This is not funny, Seth."

"Hilda –"

"That's Detective Langella to you." The phone clicked.

Quentin eyed me. "It's illegal to talk on your phone while driving in this town."

I swore. "Maybe I gave her the wrong address."

"You didn't. I heard. How much damage do you think you did?"

"I wasn't hallucinating."

"Heard the boom," came a wheezy voice from the back seat. "Back door blew. Saw a man go past. Oh . . . hurts."

I hadn't eaten since my morning flight. Breakfast had been blown up along with Tim, and Quentin's rescue had screwed the pizza plan. I was getting groggy and cranky, but I couldn't very well stop at a drive-through with Kaylee groaning in pain in the back seat. Quentin didn't seem the slightest bit peckish after his trip back from the afterlife. He just yammered on. Having Kaylee along for him to bounce ideas off of made it worse.

Heaven didn't sound like the stories. The two of them described a celestial circle-jerk. I figured it made a degree of sense, though; since we're wired up for pleasure, the Big Man might just use that same wiring to make heaven the eternally joyful place it's claimed to be. What's more joyful than a good banging?

I keyed *Morgue* into the car's navigation system. That sweet little GPS found it lickety-split. Downtown, eight blocks from Tim's Diner.

We were into evening. I couldn't drop a body off until nightfall. Besides, Kaylee wasn't exactly a body yet. Not enjoying the experience, but still alive. The hissing and choking from the back seat made that clear.

"Kaylee? Are you sure about this?" I asked.

"Yes." She coughed. "Let me go."

"I'm with her," Quentin said. "If someone whacks me again, don't raise me." He eyed me. "You've never been dead before, have you?"

"Actually I have." I remembered pitching myself off Graeme's balcony to the pavement seventeen floors below. I'd ruined sneakers, jeans, and an Eddie Bauer sweater. I hadn't even gotten out of the tunnel of light. I'd triggered my own resurrection while I jumped, so I had no time to cross all the way over before getting torn back.

The sucking sounds in the back seat began to subside. Quentin looked past the headrest. "I think she's unconscious. Her chest is still moving."

A police car passed us.

I looked over Kaylee's phone, then handed it to Quentin.

"See if you can find the number of the last person to text her."

He fiddled with it for a few minutes. "No number," he said finally. "Just initials. MTF."

"That's Kaylee's source. Maybe he's on her computer. Kaylee?"

Silence. Quentin started muttering to himself.

"What?"

"Just reflecting." He made a steeple with his fingers and stared at the dashboard. "Dying makes everything more real now. I mean, even going across for, what, an hour?"

"It's tougher the longer you're over. If you're gone for a few seconds or a couple of minutes, it's easy. But if you get to the end of the tunnel, into Dad's domain, you can get messed up." I glanced back at Kaylee. She looked asleep. Except her eyes were open.

We killed another hour until darkness fell. Then I fired up the GPS for the quickest route to the morgue. We followed its directions past a nondescript building with a little sign along the street marked, *Summerton Coroner*. Next to it stood a boarded-up restaurant.

I found an alley and wheeled into it. Starting out just wide enough for a single vehicle, it opened into a square alcove with a pair of garage doors and smaller door for human use. I glanced about. No sign of video cameras.

"Stay put," I told Quentin. I climbed out, scrambling around to open the passenger door. A quick check of Kaylee's pockets. She was still warm, but had no pulse. Have a wonderful afterlife, I told her in my thoughts. Then I gripped her wrists and dragged her out. It was an unceremonious funeral. I leaned her against the wall and bolted back to the car.

"Where to now?" Quentin asked.

"How about you stay with Chase and Nathan?"

"Okay. But Nathan is an asshole."

I took us down Center Street. Traffic crawled, even at this hour.

I slowed when we neared Tim's Diner.

"What are we doing here?" Quentin asked.

I tried answering. It came out like a canary being choked. Tim's Diner stood across the street from us. Not the remains. Tim's Diner, complete with faded sign, broad windows, and worn wooden front door. And parked next to us, Kaylee's blue Mustang. Not a mark on it.

We ordered enough food for five guys at the first drive-through we found. Then I drove Quentin to the house down south. I pulled in behind Chase's BARC van. "They're inside. Emile's probably home by now." I reached into the back seat for the bag of fast food, kept back a burger and fries, and gave him the rest.

He took it, looking confused. "You aren't coming in?"

"I have work to do."

Quentin eyed me. "You've been acting funny since we left downtown."

"You don't even know me. How do you know what 'acting funny' looks like?"

"Good point."

"Tell the others to call me when they have names and phone numbers."

"Sure."

I ate my burger on my way to Kaylee's condo, dropping half in my lap. She didn't need her underground parking spot anymore, so I left my Camry in it.

On my way up to the sixth floor, I pondered calling Mom on Kaylee's phone. No sense eating my own minutes. Then the idiot cog slipped out of gear: the cops would be checking phone records the instant they identified Kaylee's body. I used my own phone.

"Hello?"

"It's me."

"Oh, hi honey. How is your vacation?"

"I've only been here a day."

"Well, I'm glad you got away for a while. It will do you good. You need to relax."

"Yeah. Mom, I need to ask you something."

A sigh. "Do you need money already?"

"No. It's just . . . Have you heard from Locke lately?"

Silence. Then her voice came through like a growling bear. "What's going on, Seth? Are you still poking around in those murders? That's police business."

"That's our business."

"You can't count on Locke to help you whenever you call. Why do you think you haven't seen him since you were eleven or so? I told him I wanted you to learn to stand on your own feet."

"This is serious. There's stuff happening here that isn't normal."

"Maybe you should just get on a plane and come home."

"No. I'm here. I'm going to enjoy my vacation." And hope I live through it.

"Don't do anything rash. Don't do anything at all. Hang out with Emile. Find a girl."

"I kind of already did."

Mom laughed. "Oh, I love you."

I laughed too. It sounded sickly, as though my tongue were swelling up in my head.

"I have to go. If you hear from Locke –"

"I won't," Mom said.

"If you do, tell him to call me. Bye." I hung up.

"What do you want?" came a voice behind me.

I yelped and spun around, reaching for my pistol. Locke stood there in Kaylee's kitchen, arms crossed. Just as I remembered him. Purple shirt, black pants. He held out his hand. My pistol leaped into it.

He chuckled. "I have always wanted to do that."

I plowed ahead. "I need help. I'm trying to track down whoever is killing us."

"I know."

"I met this journalist, Kaylee Jerrel."

"I know."

"She's investigating –"

"I know."

"And she has a contact, an anonymous source who –"

"Me."

I stopped speaking, though my mouth needed a few more flaps to get properly slowed down. "You? You're MTF?"

"It stands for May The Force. I considered using the whole thing, MTFBWY, but I thought that too much of a giveaway."

"You got her killed, you know."

"She made her own choices. I merely presented a story to her. She wanted something to revitalize her flagging career. I needed someone to find your half-brothers."

"Why do you need help? You popped in here without a problem."

"I maintain a connection between you, your mother, and myself. It has existed since before you were born." Locke shook his head slowly. "I hold bindings with some of your siblings but I dare not create new ones. The Big Man is near to waking."

"My old man is waking up?"

"He is closer than he has been in centuries. If that happens . . . let us say we may or may not live to regret it, but those of us who do, will."

I had to think that through. He kept going. "Somebody is disposing of your brothers. This tugs at the Big Man's beard, as it were. If it continues, he may wake. In which case . . ." He let his words hang but punctuated them with a far-off thunderclap and a flash in the balcony windows.

"Locke, there is something else in play here. Whoever these guys are, they blew up Tim's Diner downtown and then Quentin's house. I drove by the diner an hour ago; it's fine. And the cops haven't found a lick of damage at Quentin's. What's so funny?"

"I have been making certain restorations to reality. It is necessary; it seems the Big Man is on some level aware at all times of where you and your brethren are and what you are up to. Chaos near any of you is like a bad smell while he is napping. Therefore it must be corrected before he notices."

"You did all that?"

"Affirmative, Captain."

"That's a Spockism; you're crossing your pop-culture references."

"I am branching out."

"If you can bend reality back into shape after some crazy bastard blows it to bits, why can't you find out who is killing us?"

"Think about the question. What makes you believe doing one necessarily means I can do the other?" Locke fluttered his fingers dismissively. "However, you are correct. A hundred years ago, yes, I could have done as you suggest. A decade ago? Certainly, with care. Now? With the Big Man restless enough to jump-start his very own brand of apocalypse? No." He motioned at the cupboard door beside him. It opened and a cup drifted out. "What you are seeing is merely a matter of shifting molecules. But digging into a soul or pursuing one? That is on a different plane altogether."

"Damn. It'd be nice if you could give me a clue here. The assassins seem to know who I am and where I'll be. They almost got me at the diner with Nathan; I literally bumped into the guy who planted the bomb. They knew which motel I'd booked. They were still at Quentin's when we arrived."

I'd never seen someone look so constipated so fast. Locke clicked his tongue. "I may have had something to do with some of that."

"Which part?"

"You understand, I cannot act directly. I mean, not too directly."

"What did you do?"

"Just a minor adjustment to local probabilities."

"What does that mean?"

"When you began to look into the deaths of your brothers, I came to suspect you could use a little aid. So I bent local probabilities in your favor. They will not be noticed by your father; they are far too diffuse."

I reached for a cup above the sink, filled it from the tap, and tweaked the water over to Sumatran with cream and sugar. "Locke, I'm not following. What's a local probability?"

"I trust you have noticed how at times you will meet a total stranger on the street, and then a day later you will see him again, and suddenly you cannot escape him? That is a localized probability at work. The odds of it happening are very small, but something has happened in his life or yours and suddenly you two are thrown together."

"I'm getting that, I think."

"Good. With probabilities shifted, the deck is now stacked, as it were, in favor of you encountering others who have previously been in the vicinity of your brothers. Since the people most likely to interact with you while having been near your brothers are the assassins, you are more likely to encounter them. Is this making sense?"

"You mean it was more likely for the killers to set off the bomb at the diner when I was there than at any other time?"

"I think that is accurate."

"Well, hell. I could have been blown to pieces."

"This is the best I can do to help. What would you prefer? That I make you bulletproof? Able to leap tall buildings?"

"Those are both great ideas. Throw in X-ray and heat vision, and I'll be able to turn in my guns and grenades."

"I cannot do any of that. If I change your physiology, the Big Man will notice."

"Fine, then. I don't see how your localized probabilities could magically tell the killers which motel I'd booked. The guy at the front desk said they asked for me by name."

"This I cannot account for."

"You're supposed to be borderline omniscient."

"If that were true, I would be borderline insane. Just look at the Man Upstairs. Not to mention Odin and Zeus and the rest. Certifiably bonkers, every last one. I preserve my sanity by not reaching too far beyond my grasp. And these days in particular, I must limit my powers.

"I am like the family cat creeping about the house in the middle of the night. If I yowl at an inopportune time, I may wake the master of the house and have a shoe flung at me. I am being very careful not to yowl, Seth. The universe as we know it depends on me not yowling. It also depends on you stopping whoever is orchestrating the deaths of your brothers. Such a structured attack on the Sons of Our Lord" – Locke said the last two words with a voice dripping mockery. – "only pushes your father closer to waking.

"However, someone is yowling in my place."

The white fox remembered metal jaws gripping her hind leg, gnawing into bone. Scarlet across snow, merciless pain, the waning throb of her heart. A passageway bright as snow under noon sun, a tunnel smelling of fresh-killed lemmings that led to a field of green where the sun never moved and no clouds crept the vivid blue sky.

The fox prowled about in this strange land, cornering a lemming at the base of a tree. The prey peered up with confused eyes. She felt no hunger; she had chased purely from instinct.

White bears sunned themselves on snow bordering an ice-covered lake surrounded by strangely lush greenery. The wrongness of the scene, of the clean edge of snow against green plains, sprouted a seed of curiosity in the fox's mind.

Other foxes greeted her with playful growls. Some wandered listlessly across the rolling fields, not responding to her. As time passed, many of the creatures she had met grew bored and did nothing at all. Their flesh thinned and became transparent. Soon they were barely shadows.

When new creatures came, the fox saw the opening and closing of the passage of light. Her mind swelled, encompassing new ways of thinking. She came to a revelation, which can be translated roughly from fox-think, a collection of smells, sounds, taste, and color, into: "Hey, I'm dead."

Soon another revelation followed: "Well, bear-crap. I'm bored."

The fox wandered. Forever the sun shone above, motionless and wrong.

Things move and change, *the fox thought*. They're supposed to. *Here, every blade of grass remained unaltered.*

The fox pulled out a stalk of grass with her teeth and dropped it on the earth. She peered at it, looking for anything that might suggest it was something other than a blade of grass. There was nothing to see but tiny ridges in the blade. She turned her attention to the area around it.

When she looked back, the blade she had torn free no longer lay there. It grew from the earth once more.

The fox uprooted the stalk again, spat it out, and stared and stared, touching her nose to it, which made her sneeze. She scratched her nose with a paw, never letting her eyes off the stalk.

The stalk grew.

Surprised, the fox reared back. The stalk shrank.

The fox trembled, leaning in. Once more, the stalk grew. The fox glanced about. The hills themselves had grown huge.

It's not growing, the fox thought. I'm shrinking.

She turned back to the stalk. It had rooted into the earth, blade waving in the gentle, unchanging breeze.

The fox leaned close to watch it swell. Leaned closer until it grew huge. The fox brought herself even nearer without moving. It felt as though she were pushing through a spiderweb. The stalk grew and grew.

She could see tiny shapes within the stalk dancing. The fox followed them as they spiraled about, immersing themselves amid others. This is what everything is made of, *the fox thought*. She snorted, entranced with discovery.

If I can shrink, *she thought,* can I also grow? *The world receded with this thought. For a moment there was simply grass and earth. Then she gazed at vast plains. A herd of* muskoxen moved. The creatures gave no sign that they were aware of the fox peering down on them.

I'm invisible, *the fox thought.* She gazed at her paw. The tiny shapes that made her were spread so thinly that they were like breath on a winter day.

As she grew, the bowl over the world became obvious. The fox could see the barrier, could set her nose to it. With hardly an effort, she slipped through.

Worlds blazed like stars. Something wounded and furious growled across the expanse. Terrible yet frightened eyes swept toward her. She recoiled, shrinking. The dire gaze swept past.

The fox looked at the world she had left, twinkling below her. That path led to monotony and fading into shadow. She saw a myriad of other worlds and chose one at random, scampering toward it. Even with the frightened monster at the edge of the multiverse, this was much more fun than endlessly chasing lemmings.

The Book of
Kaylee

5

Death rocks. It's utterly slutty. Gold and silver, fuchsia and green. Gold is warm raindrops on skin; silver is heat in my veins. Beneath it all, sensation drives through me like an unrelenting orgasm. I remember the body I once had: aches in joints after a run, the sway of breasts, the slide of cloth across my skin. Ecstasy arches an intangible back, coaxing sweat from the memory of skin and moans from a throat that no longer exists.

Amid this transcendent joy, I begin to sense others. A long cry drenched in delight. Another rising to join it, building a harmony. I hear my own wail, my intangible body thrumming in tune to a billion-strong orgy. I know those figures in gold and silver and green, all drifting like me. I imagine them, legs apart, arms outstretched, fingers splayed. No one is alone here.

I still remember back pain, cramps, a mouth full of early-morning moss and sand needing to be brushed away. None of it matters. I remember words that no longer hold meaning. Video. News director. Anchor. Mom. Dad. All that is real now is sensation.

A corner of my awareness muses that my body can cope with such relentless passion, even as bliss blossoms in every part of me. Human shapes erupt into the colored space around me. I wonder if I can speak with them, learn who they were before they came here. I wonder about their lives.

Then I forget what speak means, or what lives are. Ecstasy is all.

Something yanks at my middle and I fall. Solace is wrenched away, leaving me seared and wailing in anguish for the loss.

White circles glared from a gray ceiling.

A voice: "You're sure this is the one, Max?"

"Positive, Your Grace."

Figures moved above me, sharpening into focus. A young man and an older one. Both twisted their faces. The old man grew lines and curves. The young man grew a plumpness in his cheeks. They were smiling. *Smiling.* The word felt ancient, long forgotten. Pain stabbed my belly. Pain wasn't new. Simply forgotten, like smiles.

Cold hardness against my back. I felt a thump in me. Then again. A beating heart.

"There, there, young lady," the old man said.

A new face appeared, a hard face crowned with dark hair, the eyes empty behind little round eyeglass lenses. "What's your name?" it said, then lifted a familiar yellow and purple disposable coffee cup to its mouth.

The old man put a hand on this new shape's shoulder. "Maxemilian, let me ask the questions. Now, young lady, please tell us who you are."

"Don't know." My gaze took in rows of lights, a wall of metal at my head. Metal. The word tripped over something in my head and suddenly made sense. I shifted my neck and saw a square, black hole. Morgue.

Words came back to me, forming up like soldiers on a march. I understood them. My belly clenched and I turned onto my side, gasping for each breath. I heard myself wail.

I remembered a name. "Seth promised he wouldn't do it."

"What?" asked the old man with the kind face.

"He brought me back. He swore he wouldn't."

A glance passed between the old man and the young one.

"Actually," the young man began.

"Where is Seth?" the old man interrupted.

My body shivered. My guts burned. I struggled to lift myself with my elbows, and looked around. I lay on a steel table. At its head was a black square cavern, and across the wall were drawers with large handles.

I gasped, weeping. "The bastard."

"Seth is very bad," the old man said. "Can you take us to him?"

"He's not here?" Agony lurched through me. Already joy had slipped away, replaced with this fiery anguish. "Where is he?"

"We need your help to find him. Do you know where he will be?"

"My condo. He took my keys."

"And where is that?"

"Yes," said the man with the coffee cup. "The address, if you please."

"Pellier Street."

"Pellier and what?"

I imagined my building. Eight floors. Sign out front. "I need to see him."

The old man motioned at the others. "Then these men will take you there."

My Aerosmith T-shirt had a ragged hole in its middle. Dark stains lay across my jeans, the denim stiff against my legs. "I'm cold."

The old man stepped away for a moment and returned. "You may have my coat." He lifted it over my shoulders. "Go with these men. Tell them where to take you." He turned to the young man. "They may need you too."

The man in white nodded. He had Seth's eyes.

Seth must have brought me back, plunging me into this life again. The memory of pleasure was fading agonizingly quickly. How could he do this to me?

They led me along a corridor. A bearded man in a blue security-guard uniform looked on. He crossed himself repeatedly, whispering, "Hail Mary," as I passed. At the end of the hall were double doors, pushed open to a smell of car exhaust and rot.

"Come on," one of the men said, gripping my arm, dragging my coughing, wheezing self toward two white cars parked in the alley. The one in the black jacket climbed in behind the wheel, while the young man in white took the passenger seat. The one called Max and another pushed me into the back seat, putting me between them.

"Okay," the driver said, "where are we going?"

I shivered. "South. The bridge. Then east."

The car lurched, sending a spasm through my back. I huddled in the seat, gazing at cars creeping along. Dangerous, they were. Dozens of deaths a year from traffic accidents in the city. So easy to be killed. I tried crawling over the man next to me, a scruffy man in a blue hoodie. He swore and shoved me back.

"Calm down," Max said.

I hurled myself against him instead, my body yearning to be back in that beautiful place. He pounded my face with the back of his hand. Pain bloomed. I wiped my cheeks with my palm. My fingers came away pinkish red.

The men were silent. I wished for conversation, anything to distract me from the hollowness in me, the yawning hunger.

"Kindly stop that." Max's voice, full of menace. He drank from his purple and yellow cup.

"Hm?" I said.

"You were humming. Before it drives us all batty, please shut yourself up."

We drove in silence punctuated by the occasional, "Shut up." I fixed my gaze on the seats ahead of me, imagining Seth standing over me doing whatever he had done to bring me back. Chanting something, perhaps waving a smoking bag over me as part of some ritual, as they often do in zombie movies.

"We're across the bridge," the driver said. "Where to?"

"Pellier and Whitherwood."

"That's better."

Why hadn't Seth been in the morgue? The thought danced about and vanished, swept away by pain. My stomach hurt. My shoulders hurt. I came out of a fog of anguish to a dim memory of bashing my head against the back of the driver's seat. Someone had a hand across my face and a breast in the other. I bit his wrist.

"Ouch, Jesus H. Motherf – !" Something hit the back of my head, casting stars across my vision. I sank into my seat, pain throbbing across my vision like dancing bears.

"Can't we just shoot her and have Dev bring her back when we get there?"

I sobbed. "Don't bring me back."

"It's too late for that." Max gave me a nudge. "Is that it?"

I followed his finger. My building jutted upward ahead of us. I nodded.

The driver parked out front. The men climbed out, tugging my arm. Max tossed his coffee cup at the trash can by my building's door. "Antoine, be so kind as to open that for us."

"What about the security camera?"

"Theo?"

"It's wireless, boss. No worries; I've taken care of it."

"Just in case, everyone, try to look nonchalant."

The man in the bomber jacket crouched by the door and took something from his jacket pocket. I heard a scraping sound. He drew the door open.

"Excellent, Antoine," said their leader. "Stay down here. We'll call if we need you. Watch the emergency exits; they will be at either end of these hallways. Now, Miss, lead the way."

I took Max, the young man in white, and Theo – who had tugged his hood up and put on dark glasses – toward the elevators.

The men gathered around me. The elevator door slid open, and we stepped in. My head swam. I wanted to curl up in a fetus shape and cry.

"On your feet," said Theo, yanking my arms. I scrambled up from the floor. "Quit it, for Chrissake."

The man in white cleared his throat.

"Sorry, Dev."

The door slid open. I led them to the right. The corridor smelled of lemon-scented cleanser. When I reached the door to my condo, I realized Max and the jerk named Theo were with me.

Theo pushed me in front of the door. I kicked him in his shin, then yelped at the pain in my bare toes. He shoved me into the wall and reached past to pound his fist on the door. Meanwhile, Max crouched and began to fiddle with the lock.

This felt wrong. Maybe Seth hadn't brought me back, I thought; maybe someone else –

The door swung open, and Seth Brown stood there, his brow slightly cocked. "Hello?"

It all welled up in me then. I bolted at him. "You bastard!"

We went down together. I beat on his chest. A pistol appeared in Seth's hand, and a gunshot rang close to my ear. Then another and another.

Seth didn't look fit for it, but he threw me off and slammed his elbow into my middle. My breath whooshed out.

He shouted something, then leaped up and raced down the hall to my bedroom. Sounds of running and yelling. I cried, tucking my head into my arms. Seth came running back along the hallway.

"Please," I moaned. "Kill me again."

He stepped over me. A staccato sound of gunfire, followed by a shriek. Footsteps thumped along the hallway. More of the rattling sound of gunshots and a stench of burning.

"Oh, crap," someone moaned.

All grew quiet. I lay still, staring at the carpet, watching my tears turn the beige carpet dark.

Time must have passed. Voices came to me from the corridor.

"Oh, man, we are so screwed," came a whine, dragging out the last two words.

"Quit bitching, Theo. You'll live. Max got half his head blown away in the elevator."

"Couldn't someone have told us the punk had a machine gun? How the hell did he learn to use it working in a bookstore?"

Antoine stepped into view. "We need to carry Max while he recovers. Let's go before the neighbors call the law." A pistol caught the light from the hallway. The man smiled at me. "I'll take care of this one."

"Waste of a bullet," said Theo. "You know how expensive those are?"

"She can identify us."

"And say what? These guys brought me back from the dead and shot up my condo? The cops will just sign a form and ship her off to the white coats."

I looked up at them. "Do it."

"There, hear that?" Antoine turned smiling eyes to me. "Okay, then."

Theo caught his arm. "We need to go. The old man will be upset enough already."

Antoine glared at the other man. "How about I cap you instead?"

"It's unnatural to kill someone who wants you to. Let's get out of here."

The door slammed. Silence.

My condo smelled scorched, and bullet holes marked the wall along the hallway. I lay staring at them. When I struggled to my feet, the room gyrated. I laid my hand flat to the wall to steady myself. Gold and fuchsia sparks shot across my vision like fireflies. A memory of joy carved itself into my mind.

The phone jangled. Out of pure instinct, I picked it up.

"Hello. Perhaps you remember me," said a voice I knew but couldn't attach a name to. "News director to the stars. It would be nice to know you're doing your job instead of hanging around on a beach somewhere."

The name popped out of nowhere. "Tony."

"Could you please, pretty please, file a fucking report? What have you learned? Inquiring minds want to know."

"I can't talk. Not now."

"Kaylee, for Chrissake, what's going on? You sound drunk."

"I'm not."

"Come on in and let's talk."

"I'm hanging up now."

"This station pays your –"

I pushed the *end* button and dropped the phone. Tony wasn't important. The bullet holes in my wide-screen TV weren't important either. The hollowness in me sucked at my spirit. That memory of ecstasy held me in a fist's grip. I wandered to the bathroom and started the bath. My skin tingled as I retrieved Bob, my battery-operated boyfriend, from the compartment under the sink. I grabbed the showerhead on the end of its hose and twisted it to a pulsing spray. Lowering myself into the tub, I set my feet against the wall, took the showerhead in one hand and Bob in the other.

Uncharacteristically, it took a hell of a lot of work. When I finally came, it was a hollow and unenthusiastic sensation. I slid down into the bottom of the tub, crying in huge sobs. My hair caught under my shoulder and tugged painfully.

I jumped up, fumbling for the little scissors in the cabinet next to the mirror. Tugging at a mass of hair, I dug scissors into it. Blonde hair with dark streaks landed in the sink and on the floor. I hacked away, glaring at the face in the mirror. Sunken eyes. Ugly. I cut away a tangle and threw it to the floor. Another clump came free. In moments I had the whole perverse mass scattered around me. I looked at the mirror. An angular face with a bird's nest on top stared back.

Good, I told myself through a fog. I stumbled out of the bathroom and fell into my unmade bed. It smelled unfamiliar, musky. I pulled the purple blanket over myself and shut my eyes. Silver and gold filled my vision, with an echo of unrelenting pleasure. That was important. Only that.

Sleep refused to come. I staggered back to the living room. With a sense of revelation, I veered around to my dining room, kicked a chair over, and stumbled into the kitchen. I kept a brutally sharp paring knife with the utensils. I picked it up in shaking fingers and laid it against my wrist. My fingers twitched and spared my life; the blade fell, clattering across the floor, coming to rest under the cupboards. I sank to the floor, hunting for it.

Wasn't suicide a mortal sin? Where would I go if I opened my wrist?

I laughed, a bitter sound in my mouth. I'd never believed that stuff about sin and heaven and hell. Now I did. It's hard to hold on to atheism when you've been to the other side.

Seth had promised he wouldn't bring me back. Utter shock had filled his face when he opened my door. So maybe he hadn't. Maybe someone else did. That Dev.

He had Seth's eyes.

6

I cried until I felt ready to throw up. But even grief gets boring. I needed to get away from myself. Stumbling to the bedroom, I dragged out yoga pants and a pink shirt. My purse lay on the night table. I couldn't remember putting it there, but grabbed it, found a jacket, and wandered into the corridor. The apartment door was still open. I walked past bullet holes and dark stains on the carpet. They didn't matter. If the building burned down, that didn't matter either. The elevator groaned to a stop. I zipped my jacket partway up and wandered across the lobby to the double doors.

My feet ached on the cold pavement. A jogger ran past, sparing a glance. I felt his eyes digging into all the hurt. Traffic was a perpetual rumble growling at me.

The numbing cold on the soles of my feet became pain. Any discomfort became pain compared to what I remembered: rapture like I had never known.

I hobbled along, overbright sun spearing down upon me. A red bumper was beside me. The man behind the wheel held up his palms as if to say, "What the hell?" I had stepped right into traffic.

Scurrying back to the sidewalk, I wondered what it would feel like to fling myself before a car or bus. But that would be a mortal sin. The thought of not going back where I had been burst sweat from my skin and a drumbeat from my heart.

Across the intersection lay Ducky Mart. My late-night sanctuary. The rubber-ducky sign glowed invitingly even in bright morning sun. The chill of the handle made me flinch as I pulled the door open and stepped inside.

Welcome back, I thought. Peace settled upon me as I looked around. Every Ducky Mart I'd ever seen was laid out the same: convenience store shelves stocked with staples such as bread and cereal; a square alcove in the middle with two tills; and along the back, a row of tables in purple and yellow that matched the sign. Behind them, a counter for fresh coffees.

When insomnia drove me into the street, I came here with my laptop. Half my stories for Channel Forty-Eight had been written here at three a.m.

At the counter in back stood Braydon, the assistant manager. He sometimes read over material I was writing for a story. Beside him stood a shorter, stocky girl, also in yellow polo shirt and black pants.

The door had set the bell above to jangling. When Braydon glanced over, his gaze passed by and didn't register me. I tucked my hands in my pockets as I approached. The girl watched me warily, her gaze darting to the top of my head. Above her heart was a tag, purple lettering on yellow: *Hi! My name is Adele! Please be patient. I'm new!*

I came up to the counter as an old woman shuffled to her table, cane in one hand, double mocha in the other.

Recognition lit in Braydon's eyes and his mouth made a horrified circle. "Kaylee?"

"Good morning."

He stared at me, his gaze flickering to my hair. "How about an intravenous of espresso?"

"House coffee. Make it to go this time."

His brow pinched. He looked ready to say something but changed his mind. "Sure. What happened to your hair?"

"Salon accident."

I watched his back as he filled my cup. He was my height, perhaps twenty or twenty-three. He kept his hair trimmed short. I wondered if his head would be prickly or feel smooth beneath my fingers.

He turned with my coffee. I laid a five-dollar bill on the counter and said, "Are you seeing anyone?"

Braydon's face filled with scarlet. "Not currently." He held coins out for me, pouring them into my palm. I took them then switched them to my left hand and caught his wrist before he could draw back. My lips found his across the counter.

He blushed harder. "Kaylee, Jesus!" he murmured.

Adele stared.

That made me think of Seth. I pulled Braydon back to me, driving the thought away. This time he set his hands on my shoulders and held me back.

"Stop," he said softly, his voice full of command. He let me go and pushed the little gate beside him out so he could move next to me. His hand gripped my arm, steering me to the door at the back marked Staff Only. I had a vision of him laying my body over a sack of warm coffee beans, a heady smell of espresso and Italian blends mixing with sweat and sex.

When the door swung shut, he turned to me. "What are you on?"

"Nothing." I forced a smile, then caught sight of myself reflected in a shiny steel fridge. With too many teeth showing, I looked like a grinning corpse. I tried for sultry instead. "When do you get off?"

"Someone slipped you something."

"I'd like you to slip me something." Ouch, I thought. As a pickup line, that sounded pathetic even in *Thongs and Dongs Five: Hot Nights in the Dorm* – when Melody Melons decided to improve her university grades by screwing her professor.

His hands gripped my neck, cradling my head. He leaned close. I shut my eyes, expecting.

"Open your eyes," he whispered.

I did so. He peered at me closely. "They're clear. A little red. But not dilated."

I touched his chest. "Come home with me."

"Listen to me carefully. You're drugged. This isn't you talking. What you're doing right now, it kills careers. Do you really want that?"

"I want to feel good." My hands reached for him.

He pushed me away and stepped back. "Stay here."

"No. Just come home with me. I'll make it worth your while." More porn-video dialogue. I cringed.

"I'll be back for you in a moment." He fled, the door swinging shut behind him.

I followed, pushing it open a crack and peering out. Braydon leaned over Adele, having a hushed conversation. I caught his eye. He looked desperate. Good. He saw me and scrambled back to the Staff Only corridor. "Come." He didn't wait for an answer but took my hand and dragged me out the side door and into the glare of the sun.

"In," he said, tugging the handle of an ancient green hatchback. I flung myself into the seat, my heart thumping. At least his body would drive away the anguish for a while. I hoped.

"Where do you live?" he demanded in a dry, raw voice.

I wanted to laugh as I recited my address. He jerked the car ahead, glancing at me as he did so. Sizing me up. So I stripped my jacket off, letting my unbound breasts against my shirt do the talking. His car nosed into Pellier Street traffic. I loosened my shirt. His eyes widened and his throat moved.

Moments later he pointed ahead at my building. "Here?"

"That's it."

He pulled into one of the visitor spots and slammed the gearshift to park. He was out in an instant, holding my door for me, taking my arm, marching me to the door.

"Got a husband? Boyfriend?"

I laughed. "You."

He didn't smile back as I fumbled with my keys. We were inside in a moment.

"Did you drink something this morning?"

"Nothing." I hadn't touched food or drink since waking in the morgue. Staring up at faces I didn't know gathered around me. Dev. The old man whom the others called "Your Grace." Antoine. Theo. Max.

The elevator door slid open on my floor. Someone had replaced the glass, I noted dimly. That felt wrong; the repairs happened in the twenty minutes or so since I had left.

My mind veered to more urgent matters. Braydon smelled of maleness and coffee. Someone had shut my condo door. I shoved it open and clutched his shirt, pulling him inside. He drew back. "Now listen, Kaylee. You're on something. E, maybe – Ecstasy. Somebody probably put it in a drink. Where were you last night?"

"The morgue." I ran my hands over his chest. He caught my wrists and held them.

"Don't," he said. "What do you mean, the morgue? Is that some kind of club?"

"You're not my father. Look at me. I'm thirty-six. You're twenty?"

"Nineteen."

"There, see? I'm a . . . what's it called? If I had kids, I'd be a MILF."

"Yes, you would."

"Right. So I'm throwing myself at you." I lifted my shirt.

Braydon hastily shut the door. "No, let's not do that. This isn't like you."

"This is the new me. You can do whatever you want. It'll be your ultimate fantasy. I'll teach you. I – I've been told I do a great blow."

"I'm sure that would be educational." Braydon led me to the living room and forced me to the sofa. I lay back, staring at him with imploring eyes. He shook his head. "You don't really want this. This is the dope talking."

"You're a teenage boy. Why can't you think with your penis like you're supposed to?"

He smiled, brilliant and warm. "If the circumstances were different, maybe. But I'm not having you like this. Now lie still." Braydon picked up the blanket slung over the couch and laid it over me.

I stayed where I was. I heard him puttering about the condo. It sounded like he was looking for something. A moment later he returned.

"Your bath was running; it's a good thing the stopper wasn't in or you'd have flooded. And I found your hair . . . all over the bathroom." Braydon's face hardened. "How long have you been on it, Kaylee? I realize your job is tough, but this isn't the answer."

I began to cry. "I'm not on anything. I just need it. I can't stand this. It hurts so much."

"What do you need?"

"Yesterday I was killed by assholes. It felt so good being dead. It was so beautiful. Then I got pulled back at the morgue. My shirt was a mess. And now, oh, God, I need to feel that again."

Braydon's mouth screwed up in a knot. "Are you having a breakdown?"

I threw the blanket off and sat up. "No. I –" My gaze leaped past him to the wide-screen TV. I blinked, shut my eyes, opened them. Then with care, I struggled to calm my breathing.

"Braydon. Sorry. About all this. I've been through a lot lately." I didn't mention my two deaths. "Thanks for bringing me here. I appreciate it." I looked again at the TV screen, conspicuously missing three bullet holes.

"Don't even try it, Kaylee," the kid from Ducky Mart said. "I'm not leaving you alone."

"I'm fine now."

Braydon shook his head then rose and dug an iPhone from a pocket. He moved over by the balcony doors. "Hi, Adele," I heard him say. Then snatches of conversation. ". . . that reporter woman . . . don't know, some kind of dope. Maybe meth . . . don't think she knows how . . . got it . . . Just cover, okay? I'll call Steve to fill in."

He hung up and punched another number and wandered over near the windows. Finally he put his phone away. "I'm staying until you get over what you're on. This isn't up for debate."

"You can't stay; you have a job. You should get back there."

"I think it's more important that someone be here to keep an eye on you."

I glared at him. "Fine, then." I picked up the TV remote and clicked it on. The screen glowed. Channel Forty-Eight, of course. In high-definition and without bullet holes.

"Kaylee," Braydon said.

"What?"

"Why do you have a tag on your toe?"

7

Ducky Mart's assistant manager vacuumed my bathroom as I sprawled on the couch. I clutched the tag he had taken from my toe. It read, *Jane Doe*. I guess no one at the morgue recognized me from television. It's amazing how different you look when you're dead. The living need a sharp eye to pick you out of a lineup.

Braydon checked on me regularly. In the early afternoon, he made lunch, scrambled eggs with ham. I sat up, chewing away.

"Aren't you going to get fired?" I asked.

"We believe in looking after our customers."

"This is way beyond the call of duty. In fact, it's creepy."

He glanced at me. "Caring what happens to you is creepy?"

"Yes. I don't think your head office will agree that tending customers at home is part of the job description."

I spent a lot of my time staring in fascination at the lack of holes in my television. A dream? Maybe I hadn't really died and woken up in the morgue and been in a huge shoot-out between a son of God and the minions of . . . whatever Max and Theo and Antoine were minions of.

My phone sounded the jangle of notes that meant I had a text message. I found my purse beside me on the couch. I dug my phone out and read:

> Your car is downtown. A bylaw officer will notice it
> by noon tomorrow if you do not collect it.
>   MTF

No one else but my source texted in complete sentences.

"Braydon? It's from a friend. I left my car downtown. Can you give me a lift?"

He stared me down. "You're in no shape for driving."

"They're going to tow it by lunchtime tomorrow."

Braydon eyed me askance, picking up his iPhone. He stabbed buttons and put it to his ear then wandered over to the balcony for a whispered a conversation. Then he stepped back from the balcony. "I've talked to Adele. I was planning to drive her home after her shift. She'll come with us. I'll drive your car back here; she can bring mine."

"I'll get you my keys. You don't have to take me."

"I'm not leaving you alone. Look at yourself. You're a quivering mess. You're acting like a junkie."

"I'm not on anything."

"There are drugs you can get addicted to after just one hit."

"I did a story about that years ago. It's bullshit, urban legend."

"You aren't staying here on your own."

"I could call the police."

"And tell them what? How you hacked off all your hair and then wandered down to Ducky Mart for coffee and some nookie? Think about your job."

I tucked my knees against my chest. "Screw my job. I have no reason to go back to it. My boss is probably going to fire me anyway."

"That's the withdrawal talking. I'm staying here until six, when Adele gets off shift. Then we'll collect her and head downtown."

I bitched and moaned. It didn't help. Braydon ran a bath for me and told me if I locked the door, he would break it down.

I lay in the bath and cried. I didn't hear him come in. He lifted me gently out of the bath and stood me on my feet, then rubbed me down with a towel. He did his best not to look at me, though his pants had grown a tent. When I touched his chest, he pulled back and glared.

He brought me fresh clothing, including underwear and socks, and left me alone to dress in fresh yoga pants and a T-shirt. When I came out, he had raided my purse for my driver's license and car keys.

"Adele's waiting for us," he said.

I followed him meekly. Moments later we had Adele in the back seat and the nose of his rattling junk-heap pointed downtown.

"How was work?" Braydon asked.

"Fine," Adele said curtly. "Next time don't leave me stuck alone on the morning shift."

"Steve got there, didn't he?"

"At lunch time."

"Sorry."

I huddled in the front passenger seat and chewed my nails.

"I like the hair," Adele said.

I tried smiling. "Thanks."

"It kind of works that way, going everywhere at once. You could start a trend."

I looked back at her, expecting to see mockery in her eyes, but she looked at me with an air of innocence.

Adele and Braydon chatted about work. I tuned them out. By six-thirty we were creeping through downtown traffic. The sun had parked itself at the end of the street and was glaring down at us. The sunglasses I needed were, of course, in my car.

We neared Arthur Street, and Braydon looked around. "Where exactly is it?"

"Across from what's left of Tim's Diner," I said.

He gave me an odd look. "You mean that place?" Pointing.

I followed his finger and stared. Tim's Diner looked like what I remembered: old wooden door, a piece of which, Seth said, had killed me the first time. A green awning with *Tim's* in faded lettering shaded the windows. Four people, two adults and two young boys, were going in.

Braydon slowed. "There's your car."

"How do you know?"

"You've parked outside Ducky Mart a few times." He gave me an approving look. "Nice ride."

Braydon parked his junker several cars past mine. "Let's go. Adele, take my car."

I stared back at Tim's Diner. "Wait. I'm hungry. Can I buy you supper?"

Tim's Diner looked remarkable for a place that had recently been blown up. The tables were square with wooden chairs that looked worn down but had a certain character about them. The wooden door creaked shut behind me. The smell of fried chicken filled the air. Braydon gestured at a table and muttered, "I need the little boy's room."

Adele and I sat. Now that we were facing each other, I could assess her. She was one of those young women who aren't thin but aren't plump either. She carried herself with confidence.

"So," I said. "Do you enjoy working at Ducky Mart?"

Adele shrugged. "I've only been there a week. It's okay." She glanced at the hallway leading to the washrooms and leaned forward. "It's kind of cult-like. Whenever there's a shift change, the incoming staff gather in the back and say, 'Today will be a wonderful day. Today we offer sanctuary to our patrons who have had a hard day on the road.' If I were still taking anthropology, it'd be a great place to do a case study."

"You're going to college?"

"Part time. I don't want a mountain of debt in four years, so I'm spreading it over six or eight and working my way through." She smiled shyly. "I'm studying herpetology."

"Herpe-what?"

"Snakes and reptiles. I want to breed snakes."

"Can't they manage that without you?"

"My dad is a therapist. He thinks I have a phallic obsession. But then, he thinks everything indicates that. I've told him he should look into his obsession with phallic obsessions."

I looked around then said, "Isn't it strange that your coworker spent the day with me? Nothing happened between us, but he made me lunch and gave me a bath and . . ."

Adele stared at me blankly.

"Never mind." I looked away, embarrassed.

Tim's Diner seemed subdued. A shapely woman came to our table with menus. How did one ask whether the place had been blown up yesterday and magically restored today?

"Hmm," I said. She passed the menus to us and left before I could say more.

My reporter's sense had failed. Actually it had crashed, burned, fallen off a cliff, and tumbled through a fiery fall into a river.

Seth must have lied. The place hadn't blown up. Something else had killed me the first time, not a chunk of Tim's door. Maybe Seth had done it himself because he knew he could just wake me up in the trunk of his car.

I shook my head at that, remembering the missing holes in my walls and my television.

The woman came back to our table. I said, "Excuse me. I heard there was an accident here. Yesterday, I think."

"Accident?"

"Yeah. Some kind of explosion. Maybe nearby. Some people were hurt."

"No. No explosion. Not here." Her face fell. "Our boss, Tim, had a stroke and died yesterday morning. And two of our staff people died as well. All on the same day. Weird; a car accident and a heart attack. It makes you wonder. About life. And stuff." She shrugged, having emptied her profundity bucket for the day. "Ready to order?"

Braydon returned and joined us. "I am. I'll have a steak and fries."

We ordered. I asked for a glass of milk. A few years ago, I had been sitting in a dingy café on the south side, meeting my whistle-blower from City Hall while working on the story about the deputy mayor. I remembered seeing a man in a shabby coat. I had watched him fill a glass of milk half full of sugar. My source said, "It helps with withdrawal, until he can get his next fix."

The glass of milk, along with Adele's iced tea and Braydon's coffee, arrived. I poured a cup or two of sugar into it and stirred it with a teaspoon.

"Kaylee?" Braydon said.

"Wow," was Adele's contribution.

I lifted the glass, gestured a toast, and drained it in one go, choking down the last ghastly bit.

We ate. I listened to Braydon and Adele's conversation. For a while they argued about ethics and Ducky Mart. Was it proper to look after customers outside of work hours? Braydon said sure, but Adele thought it intrusive.

"What if the customer comes in looking distraught and messed up. What do we do then?" Braydon asked.

"We call for help. Police. Paramedics."

I wished I had brought my laptop or a notebook. I had thinking to do. I wished Braydon and Adele would leave and let me be alone. I tried alluding to that, but Braydon refused to fall for it, though Adele seemed eager enough.

The hole in me filled with agony. My thoughts refused to adhere to anything but the memory of bliss. A hand squeezed mine. I opened my eyes and gazed through tears. Braydon gripped my hand, smiling at me.

Adele leaned to Braydon, apparently thinking I couldn't hear her. "Are you sure we should be doing this? She's really screwed up."

"I'm not letting her wander about. We'll take her home soon. She'll be fine then."

I pushed my plate away. The philosopher came and laid a bill on the table, stereotypically placing it in front of the only man. I dropped my MasterCard on it.

The bill paid, we returned to the street as the sun set. Braydon led us to the intersection at the end of the block and we waited for the light to change at the crosswalk. I glanced to my right, across Arthur Street. Next to a pub, one man pushed another into an alley, kicking and shoving him into darkness.

"Wow," Adele said. "Feel like helping some more, Braydon?"

Braydon gave her a sour look.

When the light changed, we started across. My nerves jangled, thanks to a huge sugar hit.

Three years ago, while I covered a protest march in Stanhope Park, a couple of punks started beating up an older man. I stepped in, demanding to know why they were doing it. They looked into the camera, swore, and fled.

I had no camera man here. Interrupting a couple of guys in an alley pounding on each other could get me killed. The thought hopped up and down on one foot, waving frantically for half a block before I noticed it again. By then we were at my car. Braydon held the door for me. When I sat, he buckled me in then slammed the door and began to walk around the car's nose to the driver's side. I hit the seat-belt release and threw the door open.

A yell came from behind me. But ten years of running three days a week paid off. I reached the intersection as the light changed to green and raced across. On the other side, traffic filled up Center Street's lanes, blocking me from a race against the light. Braydon caught my arm. "What are you doing?" he asked, gasping.

I had barely worked up a sweat. "Helping that man."

"You can't do anything about that."

"Yes, I can. So can you." And getting killed doing something heroically stupid didn't actually count as suicide, did it?

"I won't let you get hurt."

"Then help. Call the police."

The light changed. I shrugged off his grip and ran. Behind me came a string of swearwords as Braydon huffed to keep up. In seconds I raced past the pub to the mouth of the alley.

A thin trail of red liquid moved across the sidewalk to the curb. My heart began to pound. It seemed my body resisted the concept of dying, though the rest of me yearned for it like a nine-year-old waiting for Christmas morning.

I peered into dimness. Partway along, past a dumpster and a mountain of trash pushed up against the side of a building, stood a small dog, the whitest I had ever seen. It had a narrow muzzle, eyes the color of dried blood, and a spectacularly thick tail. It licked busily at a puddle.

Footsteps pounded behind me and Braydon almost plowed me over. He caught himself and the dog looked up, blood soaking its muzzle. It growled, a low sound deep in its throat, which suggested, "This is my puddle; go find your own."

A sign from God, I thought. What was this animal a sign of?

Another set of footsteps, much more tentative. Adele moved in behind me. "Wow. Cute dog. What's it doing?"

It licked at the liquid trail, following it toward us.

Braydon's voice squeaked. "I think that's blood."

"Wow. Gross. Did they kill each other?"

Perhaps the dog isn't a sign from God, I thought. Maybe it's a test. But that led to essentially the same question: of what?

The dog came toward us. We moved backward out of the alley, giving it a wide path. The dog stopped and glared, then wandered out onto the sidewalk, following the trail of blood.

Perhaps an IQ test. Why would the creator of the universe muck about with sending little dogs to deliver information to a newly converted member of the faithful when He could talk directly in my head?

I rolled back the chain of thought to one phrase: "newly converted member of the faithful." I was, wasn't I? Atheism wasn't an option anymore.

"I want to go home," I said. My voice felt strong now. The void in me didn't feel so vast.

Braydon did his best with my car, grinding the gears only a bit and trying not to look like a gleeful child with a new toy. At home, he reluctantly parked it in the underground garage while Adele waited in the parking loop outside the lobby. He led me up to my condo and put me to bed.

"If you need anything, call me." Braydon found my phone next to the bed and tapped buttons. "There. My number is in your contacts. If you feel like going out and doing something crazy, like hitting on people in coffee shops or rescuing drunken brawlers from bar fights, the first thing you do is call me."

"Why are you doing this? I don't mean giving me your number. I mean all of it. This whole day. You don't even know me."

He didn't answer. The light went out. The door shut, its sound muffled by the bend in the hallway. I lay staring at the ceiling, the cup and a half of sugar in my veins ensuring sleep had no chance with me. I got out of bed, grabbed my phone, and moved slowly in the dark to the living room. Sprawling

on my couch, I clicked my television on. I stared at Channel
Forty-Eight for a few minutes. It showed Simone Pert's
"report" on the shooting of the next X-Men movie at Royal
Lanes College on the south side of town. I surfed the
channels, hesitating on CNN. Soon I came to the Vision
Channel.

Vision showed a documentary about Billy Morris, the
preacher who had built a huge church on the north side. His
son claimed to be a faith healer. I watched two minutes of
the young man helping an old woman out of a wheelchair.
He didn't look anything like Seth or Quentin. I shut off the
television. The chasm in me yawned open.

I had come by my atheism honestly; I'd read the Bible
cover to cover twice. All that carnage in the Old Testament
turned me off, and the inconsistencies in the Gospels didn't
make sense. I could see I wouldn't find answers in there.

No religion had ever presented me with a solid case for a
supreme being. But now I knew. The afterlife exists. I hadn't
seen God, but I had felt a Presence.

I lay on the couch beneath my thick, blue comforter,
feeling its weight, thinking it felt nothing like that sense of
floating surrounded by color, savoring ecstasy. I thought
about the pictures of Morris's megachurch. The place looked
huge, with ugly, angular architecture and white walls with
stark wooden crosses bolted to them. Stained glass had more
style.

Perhaps churchgoers needed that kind of place to
reinforce what they believed. They had nothing to support
their beliefs besides faith. But faith could crumble. So they
needed architecture and friends and family to hold it
together.

I knew heaven. Gold and silver, fuchsia and green and a
thousand colors else. And the sweetest, most melodic music
imaginable. I peeled my clothing off, vaguely aware that this
smacked more of a pagan rite than a Christian one. Goose

bumps rose on my skin. I didn't care. The chill battled the vacuum in me.

I pondered falling to my knees. That didn't seem a good idea after a decade of regular running.

"Oh, God," I said out loud, "I know you're there. I didn't believe before, but I do now. I'm your servant. Whatever you ask, I'll do. I won't look for a burning bush or a little white dog or any other sign. I'm yours in body, mind, and soul. I'm not asking you to take this pain away. I'm not asking for anything." The hollowness remained but over it lay a glaze of joy, as though the emptiness were a still black pool and ecstasy its gleaming surface. "Lord." I clasped my hands together and stared at the ceiling, feeling just a little ridiculous, "Do your sons need my help? I have nothing I will not sacrifice for you. Not even my life, though that doesn't really count as a sacrifice, does it? I ask nothing from you. I will try to be a good person. I think I have been, since you let me into a place of such pleasure and joy."

The phone rang. I ignored it, swept up in my own prayer.

My phone started ringing again. Then the buzzer on the microwave went off. I opened my eyes. A horn on the street below began to honk. The racket became a distraction. I stared at the phone on the coffee table. The caller ID read MTF.

I tapped the *Talk* button. "Hello?"

"Good evening, you silly twit," said a voice I had never heard before. "Please stop whatever it is you are doing before you destroy this world."

In that first world the fox entered, tentacled creatures sat in circles, slowly moving little blocks along lines on the ground. Most were rotund, reminding the fox of seals gossiping on rocks. Some were thin and wispy. One faded even as the fox watched.

The fox swelled until she could reach the fabric around this world. As she emerged into the expanse between worlds, she again felt something watching, something immense, powerful, and consumed by mind-numbing terror. She shrank out of its sight, making a path to another world.

The fox traveled many more worlds. They held creatures who never existed in the world she remembered living in.

Eventually she found a familiar world. Humans pursued her through broad tunnels with joyous yells. She fled past bundles of sticks on fire, which cast flickering light and created an appalling stench. The fox bolted into sunlight before a stone wall. Part of it appeared to be wood. Ignoring the clamor behind her, she slowed to study the cliff-face of wood. She remembered seeing things like this near human dens. She leaped at the wood, shrinking and passing through a tiny crack.

A broad field under a blazing yellow sun stretched out on the other side. Looking at her with surprised eyes, a human *kit and a mighty power in the guise of an grown female turned to face her.*

The kit gazed up at the white-maned human. "They let dogs into Valhalla?"

"Not usually," the power said.

The fox backed away, growling. The power smelled of that dangerously terrified vastness that sprawled across the borders of the multiverse. The fox could even see a cord spiraling away to bind it to the unseen monster.

"Go on without me," the power said. "Fólkvangr is right over there. I need to look into this." She gestured toward the fox.

"Wait," the kit said. "Fólkvangr? Isn't that just a big field?"

The power sighed in irritation. "The others will show you around."

"Wouldn't Valhalla be more fun? I've always wanted to learn how to use a sword."

"That's no place for a girl."

The kit wrinkled her nose. "I have to live with sexist bullshit even when I'm dead?"

"I don't make the rules."

"Is my brother here?"

Another expansive sigh. "Rachelle, your brother is alive, thanks to you catching the bullet that would have killed him. That's why you're here. I only bring heroes to this place."

"Can I text him?"

"That would get him landed in a mental institution. Now go on. Toodly-do." The power advanced on the fox, leaving the kit behind. The fox fled.

The woman blazed white and surged after. The fox glanced skyward and considered leaping clear of the world. But this place of fields and stones and yellow sun felt familiar after far too long in so many strange worlds. She dug her claws in and spun to face the woman.

"*Calm yourself, little one. I simply want to know what you are.*" *The power stopped and gazed at the fox. The fox stared back.*

"*I've seen many souls of animals. You're different. Where did you come from?*"

Something tugged at the fox's middle. She ignored it, keeping her gaze on the woman-power. The tugging became a wrenching pull and the world hurtled away beneath her, leaving the power staring in amazement. The fox watched a tunnel form, a passage of light with the delicious almost-forgotten scent of lemming.

The Book of
House Guests

8

SETH

Factoid: real coroners and police investigators aren't nearly as prompt and diligent as the guys you see on TV. A police detective told me this.

Hilda also said autopsies were typically done in the morning. If I left Kaylee's condo by nine, I'd be okay. Hell, I could probably stay here for days before anyone got around to looking through her place.

I spent half the night poring over Kaylee's computer and printing records. The jackpot was a spreadsheet with names and dates. It mentioned a ten-year-old boy murdered years ago, his birthday one day before mine. He would have been my age now. Whoever was killing us had been at it for a long time and had stepped up the pace lately.

Three more from down south last spring. Then Loren LeBron a month ago. Soon after, Graeme's apartment blew up with me in his bathroom. Kaylee's records had no mention of Graeme, since cops don't investigate the freshly resurrected.

There hadn't been anything in Cove's press about Graeme's apartment going to bits. Maybe Locke had adjusted reality there, too.

Kaylee had the computer equivalent of a whiteboard with scrawls in green and blue and red and orange, listing theories about who could be behind all this.

> Clones? A wealthy man had himself cloned for spare body parts. (Problem: they are not identical. Some are white, some black, some Asian.)
>
> Big Pharma? Someone tested a drug on the boys' mothers and is now getting rid of the offspring before they show signs of latent defects. Perhaps their noses fall off at twenty-five.
>
> Serial killer with a penchant for numerology? Someone takes issue with boys born in the same year between April 3 and 8.

I doubted Kaylee believed this stuff; she was just brainstorming. Why had Locke fed her information without answering her questions? Such as, who is behind all this?

My phone rang. In large text on its screen: *Locke*. No phone number.

"I cannot simply dip into people's minds anymore," Locke said. "The Big Man will assuredly notice. Kaylee's task was to find out who is behind this for me. Does that answer your question?"

"How can you pick through my brain if it's so easy to get caught now?"

"I established this connection twenty years ago. Breaking it now will get noticed; maintaining it involves doing nothing. Good day." The phone clicked off.

While the thought of being in Kaylee Jerrel's bed had crossed my mind, I'd hoped she'd be in there with me. Alive. Ah well. I slept from one until five, when I woke to a deaf vocalist, two drunk guitarists, and a drummer throwing an epileptic fit. I turned off her alarm radio without pounding it into rubble, then stumbled to the shower. Ten minutes later I had dried off and Kermit and the gang hung on the shower-curtain rail.

Breakfast was Raisin Bran and self-brewed coffee. I packed up and took my bag out to the hall, grenades and spare ammunition and all. My clothing was clean and dry, albeit with a brownish hue. I folded the pages I'd printed from Kaylee's computer and tucked them in the front pocket of my tote bag.

I heard a thump on the door. Checking my pistol was loaded, I put an eye to the peephole.

Someone who looked just like Kaylee stood there. A sister probably. She looked frantic. Well, hell. Maybe an early autopsy had already identified Kaylee? No, the cops would be here instead. Her sister must have expected her to call or something.

Damn. Okay, I thought, I'm an old friend from out of town, staying with her for a few days. Haven't heard from her. Like some coffee?

I opened the door. "Hi." Going for cheerful.

Two things registered at once. The woman wore a familiar blood-covered Aerosmith T-shirt under a long black coat. And Max, whom I'd played "bowling with grenades" with at Quentin's house yesterday, knelt in the corridor very much alive, a screwdriver and strip of wire in his fingers.

Kaylee Version 3.0 came at me swinging. "You bastard!"

I tugged my pistol free as Max rose, gun in hand. My arm wrapped around Kaylee, pinning her to me. The Kimber barked. Blood blossomed on Max's chest. He stumbled back. Another man, thinner, wearing dark glasses and a hoodie, poked his arm in and squeezed off a shot. I fired twice and missed.

Kaylee beat on me and put her hands around my throat. I flipped her onto her back. A hammering of footsteps in the corridor.

"Grenade!" I yelled. That earned a curse. I scrambled to my bag. When I bolted back with the Sten, Kaylee lay in a bawling, convulsing heap.

"Please," she moaned. "Kill me again."

I looked at her, sprawled and crying at my feet. "Sorry." Stepping over her to the door I poked the Sten out to the right.

It made a hell of a noise. It also had enough kick that in this precarious position, most of the bullets tore up the ceiling. I remembered my bag and stepped back into the room to grab it.

"Send me back," Kaylee moaned. "Please, do it."

For good measure, I held the Sten out in the corridor again and squeezed the trigger. The rapid bark echoed, punctuated by a shriek. I stuck my head into the corridor.

The man in the hoodie lay on his stomach, dragging himself along. Max had fled out of sight farther along, a trail of blood showing me he'd headed straight for the elevators.

I was the luckiest bastard on the planet. Maybe, maybe I had a chance of getting out alive. Not that dying had a bad rap. Kaylee must have spent half a day on the other side and sounded eager to continue the vacation.

I ducked into the corridor and backed toward the emergency exit at the end. A quick glance at the elevators. A head ducked out: Max. I fired and he disappeared. I ran. At the heavy steel door, I fumbled for the handle. With my heel, I shoved it open and sprayed bullets through the gap, just in case someone had come up the stairwell.

Hoo-hah! A healing hum throbbed, and it didn't come from me. I could almost see it, back in the direction of the elevators. That part of my morning excitement hadn't filtered brainward until now: someone had raised Kaylee and Max. Someone like me.

I swore and ran back that way, past Kaylee's open door. She wailed as I passed. I ran over the man in the hoodie, stepping on his ass, which earned a groan and a curse. At the elevator alcove a voice said, ". . . in the fire escape. Antoine, go."

In the elevator: Max, drooling blood, a phone to his ear, free hand holding the door. He saw me, opened his mouth, and took rounds in his throat and cheek, showering the wall of the elevator in a splatter of red. He died glaring at me as though I'd ruined his day.

Resurrection static filled the air.

I stepped into the elevator over the fresh corpse and found a man crouched in a corner. Blond. My age. My nose and eyes.

"Playing for the other team, bro?" I said. The elevator door slid against Max's leg. I tucked my foot under his knee and lifted it clear. The door closed. I hit the button for underground parking.

The guy in white looked up at me in awe. "The Antichrist."

"Enough of that. On your feet."

He rose. I put him between me and the door, and watched the numbers count down. I pointed the Sten at the doors when L for lobby appeared. But the elevator didn't even slow. The numbers shifted to P1 and the car trembled to a stop. The door whined open.

I stepped past the kid and peered at the garage. No sign of movement. Then my brother behind me: "Your Grace? The demon shot Max and it is kidnapping me. What should I do?"

I spun around. "Give me that." Snatching the kid's phone away from him. I pocketed it then motioned with the muzzle of the Sten. "Go. That red car."

I popped the trunk, threw my bag in, then hustled the kid to the passenger side. "Buckle in. No bitching."

The static buzz of resurrection rose to a keening shriek as it latched onto something. Probably Max. Well, hell.

Next hurdle: the parking garage exit. The nose of the car crossed the sensor beam, and the door began to grind upward, way too slowly. I rolled my window down and set the Sten's muzzle on the join between the car and the side mirror.

"You cannot fight us, demon," the kid intoned.

"I've done pretty well so far."

As soon as the door had cleared, I lurched the car into morning sun. On my right, Antoine came flying out the fire-escape door at the end of the building. Then he vanished as the car crested the hill and dropped down the other side.

"So this will be my forty days in the desert," my half-brother said.

"Nope. I've only got two weeks off." I laid the Sten on my lap. "I'm Seth."

The kid, was my age but looked fifteen. He stared at me like he was king of the island and I'd washed up on the beach. "I know your name, demon. I am Devan, the son of Our Lord, the Creator."

"Welcome to the club. We should get jackets and T-shirts."

I took us south. Devan sat with his hands in his crotch, looking sullen.

"So who is 'Your Grace'?" I asked.

"I do not speak to the spawn of hell."

"My mom isn't that bad."

Devan shut up and gazed straight ahead. He even pouted.

"Come on, we're half-brothers," I said. "We can at least chat."

His gaze swiveled to me like artillery guns. "We are not the same kind. I am the son of the creator of mankind. You are little more than the snake who tempted Eve."

"Is that what His Grace told you?"

Devan stuck his nose in the air and clamped his mouth shut. I picked a secluded spot beneath a fir tree and pulled over. I picked up Devan's phone and found the *Recent Calls* list. The name at the top read, *C. Moffat*.

"Moffat is 'His Grace.' Good to know."

Factoid: phones carry GPS chips. If you're kidnapping someone and carting him off to your lair, switch it off. Hell, take the battery out if you can.

As I pocketed the battery and headed the car south, I glanced at Devan. "Why don't you tell me about His Grace so I don't have to go to all the trouble of Googling him?"

Devan refused to look at me, but curiosity eventually prevailed. "What is 'Googling'?"

"Geez, where have you been?"

"I have lived in seclusion so as not to be corrupted by the sins of mankind. One day I shall be sacrificed to herald the end of this world."

"And you're okay with that? You realize the last time one of us got sacrificed, they nailed him to a post?"

A smile lurked at the corners of Devan's mouth. "On that day, mankind shall be judged. I shall stand at my father's side as the chosen ones walk the path to heaven."

Years ago Locke told Mom his biggest fear was that one of us boys might get sacrificed in a way that woke Daddy. Armageddon would kick off. Locke sounded pretty sure life would suck at that point.

"Do you know how many people your friends back there have killed?"

"The soldiers of the Lord must sometimes use the tools of violence. We must remove the Antichrists from this world and cast them back to hell."

"Did you happen to see Tim's Diner yesterday after your 'tools' tried casting Nathan Filman out of this world? At least eight other people were in there. You blew them to pieces. And that woman back there, Kaylee. She'd been dead for . . . well, a long time. Fifteen hours, minimum. Did you see her? You screwed her up hardcore by raising her."

"Our hearts must be strong, our wills must be unshakable – "

"Your horse-shit must be piled high. Yes, I get it. Does that list of hard things you do include visiting the families of the people you've killed?"

Devan shut up. Good timing. I brought the car to a gentle stop in front of Emile's house.

"No," Emile said. "Absolutely no." He hadn't changed much in three years. The gray suit was tailored to his bony physique, with a pinstriped white shirt and a narrow red tie hanging loosely.

Devan sat on the couch, arms crossed and nose high.

"Got anything to eat?" I asked, marching to the kitchen.

"You're not keeping him here," Emile said again. "You already dropped Quentin on us; we don't have another spare room."

I found the fridge and tugged it open. The smell made me gasp.

"Didn't you guys just move in here? Hell, I know you did. I helped haul your furniture."

The fridge was a lab experiment. Leftover pizza, apparently old enough for evolution to kick in, had responded to the chilly climate by growing green fur. An iceberg lettuce had morphed into a brown mass reminiscent of a serial killer's trophy head.

"That's Chase's collection," Emile said. "And don't change the subject. You'll have to take your friend somewhere else."

"He isn't my friend." I closed the fridge, my appetite having scooted off into the hills. I filled a cup with water and took coffee back to the living room. "He's our brother."

"Ugh." Emile shook his head in disgust. "This person needs to go."

"I can't do that, Emile. Please. Just for a few days. He knows who has been killing us."

Emile turned to Devan. "Tell us who has been killing our brothers."

"No," Devan said triumphantly.

"Well, that settles it. He goes."

My voice took on a whine I could have done without. "They've been using him. I can't just toss him out to go back to them. Besides, he knows where you live now."

Footsteps on the broad staircase. Chase and Nathan came wandering down. Chase wore flaming red pajama pants and a black tank top. Nathan wore a bathrobe which breezed open, fortunately revealing boxers. He scratched his neck. "Who's he?"

"Apparently," Emile said, "he works for the enemy. He knows who attempted to blow you up and murder Quentin."

"So what's the plan?" Nathan grinned. "Waterboard him?"

"He isn't staying," Emile said.

"He has to," I said. "Let's call Locke. He can explain this."

Emile's brow shot up. "No, leave him out of it."

"Who is Locke?" Chase asked. Nathan rolled his eyes.

I glared at Nathan, hoping he'd shut up. "My step-dad. Sort of."

Emile cleared his throat. "We don't need to involve him."

"I rather believe you do," an arrogant voice came from the corridor. Chase yipped like a puppy. Emile stiffened.

Locke came around the corner in his usual attire: purple shirt, black pants, black shoes. He really needed to work up a new wardrobe. "This is the one who has prostituted himself to the villains, is that correct?"

"Yup," I said.

"Who're you, exactly?" Chase asked.

"Locke," I said. "Also known as Loki. Coyote, the Trickster. Hermes. A couple of dozen other names. Maybe hundreds."

Chase crossed his arms. "Those are myths."

Locke gave him a condescending look, then eyed Devan. "You raised that poor woman after sixteen and a half hours? Have you no respect for the dead?"

Devan said nothing but stood his ground and stared at Locke. I hoped Locke would do that trick with his eyes; that'd take the piss out of Devan the Choir Boy.

Locke glanced at me. "You survived your encounter. Against three assassins. I am impressed."

"Me too." I gestured at Devan. "I think they brought him along to fix whoever might get hurt or killed. They didn't expect him to get snatched." They didn't expect me to be as well armed or lucky either.

"Yes, very lucky," Locke said. I wished he wouldn't do that.

"Now Emile doesn't want him to stay."

"Of course he should stay. We are attempting to prevent the end of the world. This young man is actively encouraging it."

Silence. Then Nathan laughed. "So we fill the bathtub and start dunking him 'til he blubbers a confession?"

I frowned and shook my head. "Torture doesn't work; he'll just tell us anything we want to hear."

"How about we do it for giggles?"

"We're the good guys."

"Drugs, then. Hop him up on something and question him."

"He could start casually flinging resurrections around while stoned. We could end up with dozens of rats popping out of the walls."

"You're kidding," Chase said.

"No, I'm not."

"How would he do that?"

I looked from Chase to Quentin to Nathan to Emile. Nathan spoke up. "Chase only found out what he is a few months ago."

"Then how did he find you guys?"

Locke coughed. "I had a hand in that. When the killings began, I decided it was time to introduce Chase to others in his family, in spite of his mother's wishes. By – ahem – coincidence, he was evicted from his apartment due to a noise complaint at just the moment when Emile posted an ad looking for a new tenant."

"I did wonder about that," Emile mused.

"Can we get back to what's important here?" I said. "Sit down, Devan." He glared his way to the chair I pointed at. "There's someone named Moffat involved in all these murders. Devan calls him 'His Grace.' That's all I have. If I had a computer, I'd Google him."

"Emile has a laptop," Chase said. "We're cribbing wireless from a neighbor. Maybe throw Summerton into your search to narrow the field."

Nathan snorted. "It can't be that simple." Quentin rolled his eyes and went back to setting up the TV.

Five minutes later, Emile, Nathan, Chase, and Locke were gathered around me at Emile's laptop. It's amazing how much you can find out with simple search terms.

Charles Moffat was the bishop of the diocese of Dunfriggin, which included Summerton, Cove, and everything in between. A local news report on the Web even had a picture: plump with graying hair, a doughy face, and a grandfatherly smile.

"Look here," Chase said, pointing over my shoulder at the screen. "He's talking at the Westin Ballroom. Tonight. To the Catholic Youth League. You don't suppose the whole Catholic Church is behind this, do you?"

Nathan chortled. "Yeah, maybe the Pope is running the show."

I gave him a dubious look.

He shrugged. "Why not? Think of the Crusades."

"That's a little before our time." I straightened up. "But it doesn't matter. This is going to be easy. We can show up, pop him, and bug out."

Nathan made a fart sound with his cheeks. "'We'?"

I had ten hours to kill before I went looking for Moffat –
on my own because my brothers, the Sons of the Almighty,
were almighty wimps. They had at least agreed to take turns
watching Devan. I pondered how to spend the rest of the
day. Wandering outside, I sat on the step and called Hilda.

"Hello, stranger and likely wrong number," she said on
the fourth ring.

"It's me. Seth."

"Since we don't know each other, that means nothing."

"I've cracked the case."

Silence descended, followed by, "You've only been there
two days."

"I've been busy." I filled her in.

"Well. That's all wonderful. Do you have anything that
will hold up in court? Keep in mind, you can't very well
testify about how this Devan fellow is ... you know. A
messiah."

"Can't you give me ideas? I'm going to Moffat's hotel
tonight. He's giving a speech for some kids. How about I just
blow him away?"

"In front of children."

"Okay, maybe I can get the evidence you need to lock him
up."

"Will your friend Devan testify?"

"Sure – against me, for kidnapping. He's in the 'hostile
witness' camp."

"I'm not surprised."

"Good-bye, Hilda."

"Wait. Seth, if you find out more about his cohorts, that
will help."

"Like what?"

"Names for starters."

"Right; I'll interview them in the hotel restaurant. I think blowing Moffat away will be easier. I'll try to do it when he's away from the kids. Bye."

"Seth, wait –"

I hit *Disconnect*. Hilda could be such a pain.

Emile stepped past me. Nathan followed with Chase.

"Where are you guys going?" I called after them.

"Work," Emile said. "You remember. Gainful employment."

"Who is watching Devan?"

"You are."

"You guys are all in danger, remember. Nathan, someone tried blowing your ass up."

He stopped at the sidewalk and shrugged. "I still have rent to pay. And the killers won't expect me to go back to work after they tried bombing me."

I went inside. Quentin was channel-surfing on the big-screen TV with Devan next to him. Our new brother's arms were crossed in a portrait of sullen bitchiness.

"Like something to read?" I asked. Then I turned to Quentin. "Got anything for him?"

"Nope. I need to pick up some stuff at my house. Can you help? Think it's safe to go over there and grab a few things?"

"Why not? Everyone else is screwing around. Odds are good the cold-blooded killers won't show up in the few minutes we're there."

"We'll have to take Devan with us," Quentin said.

"Lucky us."

After helping fill and carry boxes – again – I turned Devan over to Quentin's custody. Nathan had come home from work and keyed up a movie on Netflix for them. I headed out for my rumble with the Moffat Gang. I drove along Center Street, using the GPS to tell me where I was relative to the hotel. The Westin towered overhead on the left as I approached. I idled the engine in a "no parking" zone and stared at a row of glass doors lining the top of a set of wide steps. Kids, mostly in Catholic school uniforms, milled around in groups.

I watched for a few minutes, then realized someone might notice me staring at little girls in plaid skirts. Hilda was right; I couldn't plug a bishop in front of a bunch of Catholic kids. It just isn't done.

I nudged the gas and eased out into traffic. Farther down I came to Arthur Street not far from Tim's Diner. Moffat was going to give a speech just a couple of blocks away from where his men had set off a bomb and killed a bunch of innocent people. Then I remembered what Locke had said about tweaking local probabilities. Maybe it wasn't entirely coincidence.

I took the corner at the Arthur and Center intersection, and swung the Camry around. With the car parked, I sucked in a breath and checked my Kimber. Loaded and ready for business. Purely for defense, I told myself. Go in, look around, try not to get noticed. Simple. If the bad guys spot you, don't worry; they won't dare do anything in the hotel, where you might raise a stink and draw attention to them.

I pocketed the Kimber, zipped up my jacket, and stepped from the car. Lifting my collar I set off for the Westin. The door to Patrick's Pub squeaked as someone stepped into my path. A smell of beer hit me and I got a flash of black leather and white fur collar.

"'Scuse me," I mumbled and stepped to the side. I looked up.

Antoine.

9

We swore in two-part harmony. While I went for my pistol, Antoine went for my nuts with his foot, illustrating the fundamental difference between enthusiasm and experience. I turned sideways to save the lads, and he landed a swing to my jaw. When I stumbled back against the wall, he gut-punched me and snatched my gun away. My own pistol cracked the side of my head.

Antoine dragged me along for a dozen steps, then tossed me against an alley wall. My knees hit first, sending fire through my legs. I rolled and came up staring into the muzzles of two pistols. In a panic, I slammed the button. Resurrection static roiled around me. It had an air of impatience to it, as if it wanted Antoine to hurry up.

The killer grinned. "Little mouse. Where is Devan?"

He kicked me in my throat before I could get anything out. "There, patch yourself up. You can tell me where Dev is later. I'm sick of a little rat bastard like you interfering." His shoe slammed into my belly. "We've got a man who needs healing." Thump. Stars filled my head. "Can't take him to a hospital." Boot. Ouch. "You'll do a faster job anyway." Thud. I started to feel like a scene in the old *Batman* TV series. I could almost see the "Biff! Whack! Bang!" balloons around me.

As he came at me again, a surge of energy got me up on one knee. I swung at him with my left, going for his crotch.

He caught my fist in flight. With a pleasant grin, he took my fingers, the middle two, and wrenched them back. I squealed as pain lanced up my arm.

"Idiot," he muttered, letting me go. Through a haze, I saw him take something from his jacket pocket. A glove, empty fingers dangling. He rolled it into a ball and tugged my hair to pull me forward. Then he shoved the glove-ball into my mouth. It tasted as if he wore his gloves on his feet.

I gripped my fingers and yanked them straight again. Oooh, youch.

Antoine stopped and stared. "If I break your fingers, the least you can do is leave them broken for more than a minute or two." He kicked me again. By then I'd had so many boots to my stomach that one more didn't really contribute to the overall hurt. I started drifting a bit.

Your attitudes about injury change when you know it's temporary. If Antoine broke my arm, I could heal it so well, the break wouldn't show up on an X-ray. When I was a kid, I'd lost the end of my left thumb playing with a knife. It grew back. If Antoine cut pieces off me, I'd have replacements in a few hours.

I lost track of all the blows, and things got surreal for me. The agony reminded me of my ex-girlfriend Marisa. She'd invited me to meet her family. At their mosque. Mom thought I was going through a rebellious phase by going out with a Muslim. I didn't tell her my phase was fueled by Marisa's desire to rebel horizontally and often.

She wore a hijab when she picked me up, just her face showing. I had a head full of stereotypical visions of what the mosque would be like. I'd be stuck off somewhere with men wearing tea towels on their heads, and we'd sit on the floor to eat.

Nope. The mosque had a big hall with arches and a vaulted ceiling and huge glass chandeliers. The tables doomed the whole bigger-than-life effect. They were round and made of particleboard. The chairs had white plastic seats and metal legs.

The men wore suits. Most but not all of the women wore hijabs. Some wore skirts and dresses. Not what you expect from the evening news. First they knelt and prayed. The outsiders, a dozen of us, stood at the back to watch all the men bowing. The women were somewhere out of sight for that part. Then they led us to seats. I sat with Marisa, something else I didn't expect.

Her father gave me a disapproving look. I wasn't about to mention over dinner that I'd lost my virginity to his daughter.

We had steak, cut thick. We also had sharp knives. So while nervously fending off glares, I accidentally ran a blade across the back of my hand. This is how I received my one scar – the only injury I could never heal.

A beep distracted me from my memories and Antoine from his therapeutic beating session. Mr. Fists dug a phone out.

"Hey. Max. You'll never guess who I ran into just now." Pause. He took a moment to kick my shin again. "Seth Brown. I was coming out of Patrick's at the corner." Pause. "Just a few blocks from the hotel. If you get here –" Pause. "How long?"

Whatever Max had said upset him. He took it out on me.

"Look," he said, "get here as soon as you can. I'll keep myself amused until then."

Antoine put his phone away, a smile dancing on his lips. "Since you're going to fix yourself anyway, I may as well enjoy this." Thump. I moaned, barely able to discern that he had done something to my left arm. Resurrection static buzzed around me, flailing. Then came that whine that took it from white noise to a high note. I guessed it had latched on to a rat corpse in the dumpster.

I processed what I'd overheard in Antoine's phone call. The others were on their way but would take longer than he'd hoped. If I could just get to my feet, I could run for it into the street.

He kicked my belly again. A rib cracked inside me. I landed on my chest hard and found myself staring at that knife scar across my left hand.

In the mosque, my hand had bled furiously. I wrapped it in a napkin, burgundy cloth that kept the blood from getting noticed. Then I nudged my healing power.

It didn't work. I tried again, peering at my hand. Marisa and her father were in the middle of a chat next to me and didn't notice. Nothing worked. My hand kept right on bleeding.

I freaked. Gasped, moaned, and Marisa said later, passed out. This was a turning point in our relationship. In fact, it was the point where we stopped having one. I'd never got used to damage, or ongoing blood, while growing up. A wound, even a major one, just meant waking that part of myself that handled heals. The wound would close. I'd feel a bit tired, so I'd have a nap. End of problem.

Except this time nothing worked. I bawled like a kid when Marisa and her aunt took me into another room and bandaged my hand. The wound wasn't really all that bad. What was bad was that I couldn't do anything about it.

So I cried and whined, and Marisa got a look in her eyes that screamed, "Wuss." So ended my first real romance.

Locke explained it to me later: "You are part of one deity aspect; He gave you your power. If you step on ground consecrated by a different aspect, your power does not work."

"I thought Islam was part of the whole Abrahamic tradition," I said. We were having coffee at Mom's. Locke still came around, but only after she left.

"Muslims do not believe in the Christian Messiah. Neither do Jews. These aspects are distinct from one another. I suspect they were driven in that direction by their own followers."

"Their followers made them what they are?"

Locke looked embarrassed.

I changed the subject. "How would I know when I'm on consecrated ground? What if there is some old Indian burial mound under my feet?"

"Consecrated ground is not simply a patch of earth. It must have something on it to signify its aspect."

"Like a church. Or a mosque."

"Precisely."

Two days later I found a synagogue in Cove's south side, and wandered in with a safety pin. Inside the door I pricked my little finger. It bled. Couldn't do a damn thing about it. A week after that, I found the nerve to go into a Sikh temple and did the same thing.

Fortunately an alley didn't constitute holy ground. The sudden dissolution of the resurrection note brought my attention back to my aching flesh. My ears rang. I could barely see.

"I have a glorious sniper's rifle with a silencer," Antoine said, shoving me down and cracking my head against the pavement. "Remember the hit in Cove on Fifth Street? Right through the eye from 938 meters with a twenty-six-klick-per-hour gusting breeze. Then a little rat like you comes along and brings him back. True art, that, the Mona Lisa of urban hits. And you ruin it."

That was Jamie. I'd been coming up the street to his house when he dropped in front of me. A woman was bent over him by the time I got to him. I hit the Resurrection Button. She stared at the bullet dropping out of his eye socket. That was how I met Hilda.

It would have been nice if she were here now. But since I had no one else to help, it all fell to me. I nudged that invisible part of myself by the elbow. He came to life, looked around, and went to work. My floating rib on my right side hurt like hell as it moved back into place. A numbness settled into my fingers as the broken ones began to mend.

"Ah, wonderful," Antoine said. "Patching yourself. The fun can continue." He kicked me viciously in my belly. I groaned, spitting out his glove, and tumbled onto my side.

Antoine walked around me and kicked my side again, the kind of blow that could make you pee red for days.

"The other one," he said. "Graeme something. How did you two survive that? I went in with Theo when he planted the bomb under the coffee table. It took the side of the building out. We timed it knowing you'd be up there for a while." Antoine leaned down to slap my face. "Care to tell me? No?" He punched my jaw, snapping my head sideways.

He backed off, grinning. I got a look at him through my splayed fingers. The white fur collar on his jacket began to ripple. It reminded me of my cat, Zeus, sprawled next to the street, his fur pulsing and his body sucking his intestines back inside.

Antoine seemed oblivious. How much of anything, I wondered groggily, did a resurrection need to build a body? My hamster couldn't have been more than bones.

A white leg emerged from Antoine's collar. Antoine still didn't notice. He took a step toward me, cocking his leg for another shot. Then his collar grew a head, erupting like a pissed-off jack-in-the-box. A partially reborn arctic fox bit his cheek. This clearly wasn't on Antoine's list of expectations.

10

Antoine grabbed at the emerging animal. It didn't like that and raked teeth across his neck. Antoine sounded like a canary having its head unscrewed. He heaved the thrashing animal off. Blood soaked his jacket and shirt. The fox tumbled, twisting, still growing. Antoine gurgled. His pistol spoke twice. The fox flinched.

I pounced while Antoine was busy, ignoring my aching everything and hitting him in the gut with my head. He went down with an "Oof!" I punched him hard, gripping his weapon hand. When he kept his grip on the gun, I slammed my fist into his jaw again. He settled down. Blood oozed from his lacerated neck.

I tucked Antoine's pistol in my left pocket and my Kimber in my right. Then I hauled him to his feet. "Stay calm or I'll put a bullet in you."

"Ergh," Antoine said. His eyes were defiant but glassy.

"I'll happily kill you and put you in the trunk. But if you cooperate, I'll heal that gash."

A growl reached me. The white fox didn't seem especially bothered by taking two bullets in mid-resurrection. Its body had settled into a lean form with a bushy tail and a muzzle that came to a narrow point. Dark red eyes regarded me.

"Get lost," I said and dragged Antoine toward the mouth of the alley.

Antoine's eyes grew dull. My nuts ached and my arm throbbed. I let him lean against me, pulling him to my car. I tugged what was left of his jacket off, threw it across the passenger seat's headrest, and strapped him down.

While I climbed in, he fumbled with his seat belt. I punched him in the solar plexus to settle him down.

As I drove for the intersection, the light turned red. Hauling the wheel over, I cut off a Toyota pickup and made the corner. Across the street, at least two people were running flat out toward the crosswalk. Hoo-hah; if that was Max and gang, I was damn lucky. Again.

About twenty blocks later a phone rang. Antoine fumbled for it. I took it away and hit the green button.

"Hello?"

A smooth voice said, "Where are you? We're across from the alley."

"Back at the hotel," I said, slurring my voice. "He got away."

The voice on the phone didn't fall for it. "Who is this? Antoine?"

"Sure."

Silence. "Ah. Seth Brown. What have you done with Antoine?"

I dropped the pretense. "He's dead. And just in case you plan to raise him eventually, I'm driving his body as far as I can. You'll never find him."

Antoine made a choking sound next to me.

"You're Max, right?" I said.

"Perhaps. Perhaps not. Mr. Brown, you're only making things worse for yourself."

"Worse how? You're going to kill me harder? Anyhow, Antoine said you have a wounded man. Poor guy."

"You are a very lucky amateur, Mr. Brown."

"How are you making out without Devan? That must be tough."

"Why don't you return both to us? I see no reason for such animosity, Mr. Brown."

"Except for the fact that you've been killing my family."

"This is getting boring, Mr. Brown."

"Then we agree on something." I disconnected and shut off the phone.

Half an hour later we eased in behind Chase's BARC van. Antoine lay against the seat, hand on his throat, eyes closed. I left him like that and strode up the sidewalk to the house. Emile doing dishes with Chase. The TV blared upstairs.

"How did it go?" Emile asked, wiping his hands dry.

"Where's Devan?"

"Upstairs with Quentin and Nathan."

I laid a finger across my lips and said softly, "I have another one."

"Another what?"

"Guest. He tried to kill me. I was tougher and smarter and faster." That sounded pretty good.

"You're bringing more prisoners of war into my home?"

"Shh! Don't let Devan hear. Where else can I take them? The bishop has at least three men working for him. These guys are serious. I need information."

"Wasn't one prisoner enough?"

Nathan joined us. "Actually Devan is more of a hostage."

"Semantics."

I sniffed. "This guy killed at least one of our brothers. He told me so. He can tell us whether the bishop is the organ grinder or just one of the monkeys."

"Um, Seth?" Chase asked. "How are you going to make him talk?"

Nathan grunted. "Blowtorch pedicure."

I shook my head. "Truth serum."

The reactions to that suggestion were varied. Nathan: an eye-roll. Emile: a cocked eyebrow. Chase: a dangling jaw.

Chase spoke up first. "Where did you get truth serum?"

"I'll make some. I just need water."

"Wow."

Nathan laughed, his lip curled up like a knot.

"How," Emile cut in, "are you going to keep this man here? My home is hardly suited for holding either a hostage or a prisoner. If he makes a racket, the city's finest will come down on me. My budding but wildly successful career in financial speculation will come to a crashing halt, seeing me in prison with a herd of convicts inclined to take my last remaining piece of virginity, a maidenhead I have no desire to lose." He paused as if expecting us all to look impressed.

"We'll tie him up for tonight," I said.

"That's enough," Emile said sharply. "We can hold Devan – he at least keeps quiet – but we're not bringing a stone-cold murderer into the house."

"You could put him in the suite above the garage," Chase said. "Devan wouldn't have to know."

"He isn't staying," Emile said. "That's final. I'm not having a murderer in my house."

"Let's ask Locke about that," I said. "He can be here any moment."

Emile scowled.

"Is there a bathroom above the garage?"

"Yes."

"It'll do."

"I'm not giving him a bed."

"He's a prisoner; he isn't supposed to be comfy."

I went back to my car and found the passenger door open. Antoine was staggering along the street. I scrambled after him and grabbed his shoulder. He turned around, hand on his throat, looking hopeful. That changed when he saw me.

I led him to the house. Chase opened the garage. We pushed Antoine up the steps to the attic. Someone had left a rickety old wooden chair against the wall. I shoved Antoine into it. Chase looked on as I searched the suite. Bathroom, bedroom, living room with kitchenette. Two windows with

Venetian blinds let light into tiny living room. I lowered the blinds.

"We'll have to tie him up," I said. "Can you get some rope?"

"You can't keep him secure that way," Chase said, his voice breaking like a teenager's.

"I'll figure something out in the morning."

"I've got chains and dog collars in the truck. Lockable ones."

I stared at Chase in surprise. "Okay. Get anything you have."

Chase left and I leaned against the wall, eyeing the bleeding Antoine. He glared back as best he could through dull eyes.

My belly ached. Ribs were still moving back into position. I didn't look forward to the next hour or so. Sometimes when you have a serious injury and you start healing, your body shunts all the bits and pieces into your digestive system, including bone shards. At the end of the line, it feels like you lunched on barbed wire. That's really not fun. I have no idea why my old man set up our healing power that way.

Chase returned with a toolbox, a long chain, a handful of steel dog collars with padlocks, and a rusty iron panel with long screws in it. I took that from him and stared at it then looked at him quizzically.

"We can bolt that to the wall," Chase said. "Then we lock him to it, and he can't go anywhere."

So we spent half an hour setting up the room. We installed the panel on the wall away from the windows and the door. We made the chain long enough that he could use the bathroom without us having to let him completely free.

That didn't mean we were going to let an assassin wander the room. We locked him to the chair, steel loops around wrists and ankles.

"We need someone in here constantly," I said to Chase.

"We all work. Except Quentin; he's unemployed."

"Damn."

"Emile can get a webcam. We could stream this guy on the Net and watch him from our phones."

"And have someone hack into it? Not a good idea." I touched Antoine's neck and nudged a heal to life.

Chase jerked at the sensation pulsing through the air. "What did you just do?"

"Started fixing him. He'll be good as new in about an hour."

Nathan had wandered up the steps to look Antoine over. "Wouldn't it make more sense to leave him a mess? Let him hurt for a while?"

"Not if I'm drugging him."

"That hum," Chase said. "That's healing power?"

I looked at him. "Didn't you ever heal anything?" When he opened his mouth, I shook my head. "Never mind. I need to get some answers from butt-head here."

Antoine laughed. "I'm not telling you nothing."

My phone rang then. I glanced at the display. It was Locke. "I'm kind of busy right now."

"No, you are not," Locke said in a voice that shook around the edges. "I require you to be at the residence of Kaylee Jerrel immediately."

"Huh? I don't have time for that." My brain was stuck in Antoine-interrogation mode. "I'm dealing with –"

"The Big Man has not been this close to waking for five hundred years. Whatever Kaylee Jerrel is doing, you must stop her. Otherwise we shall witness the Apocalypse by dawn. Are you still too busy?"

Your priorities change when a demigod phones you in a peeing-his-knickers panic.

11

I found Locke shivering in my car. Climbing in, I slammed it into *Drive* and floored it.

"What the hell is happening?" I asked as we headed for Kaylee's.

He gave me a sour, scared look and dug out his phone. An instant later, a tiny "Yes?" came from it.

"Kaylee, you are still doing it. Stop right now."

"You again?"

"That is correct. Seth and I are on our way to you. Please do nothing until we arrive."

"You're coming here? With Seth? How do you know him? And . . . he didn't bring me back, did he?"

"You can meet the young fellow who did return you to this world, if you like. However, at this time stay calm and do nothing. Simply sit quietly and wait for us."

"I've been thinking," the tinny voice said. "I appreciate all you've done, but I'm not sure I'm going to pursue this story. I think I need some time away from work."

Locke shook himself – really shook himself. A wave thrummed up and down his body.

"What are you doing?" he screamed.

"To be honest, I've been praying. Maybe you think that's silly."

"Praying? Oh bugger."

"That's rude. I've come to realize there is more to my existence than I thought. You have no idea what I've been through."

"Stop it!" Locke bellowed.

I put my head down and stepped on the gas. Then I stomped the brake; the light ahead of us had turned red.

Locke covered the phone with his hand and said, "How long do you anticipate we need in order to reach her?"

"Twenty minutes."

He returned his attention to his phone. "Kaylee, do not do anything. Do not pray; do not even think. Let us speak of something else. How are your parents these days?"

"They're fine. What's so bad about me praying?"

"You are causing the end of the world. EOW for short. Just as it sounds."

"That's silly."

"You have been raised from among the dead twice. How do you define 'silly' now?"

"All right, point taken. What makes you think my praying will cause the end of the world?"

"You have a direct line to the Big Man. You have spent hours in his domain. Now you believe."

We got lucky. The lights were green for a ten-block stretch.

"Of course I believe," Kaylee said. "So do lots of other people."

"Other people hope. They are ardent hopers. They do not truly believe, not in their souls."

"What about terrorists? Suicide bombers? They believe."

"No, they simply gamble with high stakes. They hope their god is real, and they hope their deaths can show him their devotion. They are still simply hoping. You, on the other hand, know."

"What about other people who've had near-death experiences? They've been there."

"You did not have a near-death experience. You had two actual-death experiences, the most recent one for more than half a day. Note the difference."

Locke kept her talking while I tried to keep us on the road. Minutes later we were at her building. I wheeled into the loop out front of the lobby.

"Kaylee, ring us in," Locke said. "We are approaching your building."

"Why should I let two strange men in to my home?"

"Okay, I shall do it myself." Locke looked around guiltily then touched the door. It made a clicking sound. Again that wave traveled up and down his body. He tugged the door open.

"What do you mean?" Kaylee asked.

"We are approaching the elevators."

"I'll call the police."

"We would rather you did not. Now stay calm. And whatever you do, do not pray."

I looked around the elevator. No blood on the walls. And on floor six, no shattered glass, no bullet holes.

"You did this?" I asked.

Locke nodded. We strode down the corridor. Locke pounded on Kaylee's door with his fist.

It opened a crack, and Kaylee peered over the chain. "Why should I let you in? I can just call the cops."

"That would be unwise."

"Are you threatening me?"

"I am not."

"Hi, Kaylee," I said.

She glared at me. "You know who brought me back."

"That was Devan."

Kaylee looked as if a lawnmower had rolled over her head. "What happened to your hair?" I asked.

Her jaw trembled. "I didn't like it. I cut it off."

"Let us in."

Reluctantly she released the chain. We stepped inside. I looked around at the absence of blood on the carpet and bullet holes in the big-screen TV.

"You did a good job, Locke."

"Thank you. A little reality adjustment."

"You should reno Mom's house. She's talked about painting the bathroom for years."

"Alas, I cannot. This was simply a matter of restoring things to what they were before your influence. Your father will notice wholesale modifications to existing reality."

Kaylee glanced from me to Locke. Her gaze fixed on me. "Jesus, Seth. What happened to you?"

"Had a fight with one of the bishop's men."

"Bishop? Who –? Never mind. I thought you could heal yourself."

"I'm working on it. I looked worse an hour ago. You need to come with us."

"Why?"

"If we leave you alone, you'll cause Armageddon."

"That's garbage."

"I wish. Look. I can shoot you, Or hit you hard enough to break your jaw and knock you out. I don't need to worry about how much damage I do because I'll just heal you later. So fighting will only inconvenience us. How about we skip it?"

"How about you tell me why I shouldn't pray."

Locke wiped his face on his purple sleeve. "You are a true believer. The first one in . . . " He counted on his fingers. ". . . nine centuries."

"As I understand it, you have God on speed dial," I said. "Most people would be surprised as hell if someone actually answered their prayers. But my old man hears you. And if you keep talking, you will wake him up."

"God is napping?"

"And he is going to stay that way. Otherwise, the world ends."

Kaylee squinted at me, blinking like a strobe. "Isn't that why you're here? To launch the Second Coming?"

"Not that simple. The Christian god isn't alone. If He wakes up and triggers Armageddon, Odin will come to and kick off Ragnarok. Zeus and Shiva will come hopping back, along with Yahweh, Allah, and a whole bunch of aspects we don't even remember anymore. All hell will break loose. Heaven too."

"Wait. Odin and Zeus? Those are myths."

I made a buzzing sound. "Wrong. You lose the 'Jeopardy' round. God is wacko. Multiple personality disorder. Odin and Zeus and all the rest are part of him. Fortunately the most powerful aspects are comatose."

"But now," Locke said, "thanks to you, Jehovah is closer to consciousness than he has been for centuries."

"How do you two know all this?"

I shrugged and gestured to Locke. "Kaylee Jerrel, meet Loki. And Coyote, the Trickster. And a bunch of others."

Locke bowed.

"He also goes by the name Lucifer."

Locke glanced at me. "I prefer to keep that name to myself. It rather poisons the well, if you get my meaning."

Kaylee looked from me to him. "This is ridiculous. Seth, you believe all this? Who told you? This ... person? Why should you believe him? God is your own father."

"So what? Locke has been a friend of my mom since her old man threw her out for getting knocked up. He even paid for college when she turned eighteen. Should I believe my deadbeat dad knows what he's doing, thanks to a fawning biography written about his first bastard by some semi-literate fishermen? Did you read the part where he let his son get nailed to a post?"

"But heaven is real. I've seen it. Felt it."

"True," Locke said. "Heaven is a potent narcotic."

The Prince of Darkness and I drove Kaylee back to Emile's house.

"Absolutely not," Emile said in the kitchen.

Kaylee slumped into a chair. "I agree."

Emile looked her over again, disdainfully, then focused his attention on Locke and me. "We've got two of your guests already. This is getting out of hand. We don't have room for a third."

"Yes you do. And a fourth," Locke said with a glum look.

Emile stared at him. "No."

"I require a place to stay."

Emile scowled. "Locke, you don't need –"

"Imagine the doomsday clock. That started back in the days of the Cold War. Midnight represented when the U.S. and the Soviet Union were likely to be at open war with nuclear weapons."

"I want to be clear about something," Kaylee said. "My anonymous source is the Devil himself?"

"You are not the first journalist to make a deal with me," Locke said. When Kaylee's eyes grew wide, he added, "Oh, please. I am not after your soul. I really just wish to live out my own life as free of bother as possible."

"The Cold War," Emile said. "I wasn't actually born then."

Locke sighed. "The doomsday clock was a rather morbid countdown to total annihilation. We could have a similar clock now."

Emile's brow rose. "You're saying it's now ten minutes to midnight, and midnight is Armageddon?"

"No. Yesterday we were at ten minutes. Now we are at perhaps twenty-seven seconds. You understand?"

Emile swallowed. "We don't have beds for you all."

Locke bowed. "I shall borrow your couch tonight. I can access funds tomorrow and obtain something more comfortable then."

"Kaylee could use a bed right now. She's exhausted," I said.

"She can have the one in Emile's bedroom," Locke said.

Emile opened his mouth and shut it with a snap.

I took Kaylee upstairs. At the top of the steps, in the second living room, Devan, Quentin, and Nathan were sitting on the couches. I pointed out Kaylee to Devan. "This is what happens when you bring them back late. A few hours dead messes them up. Bad. Look at her hair."

Devan gave me a confused look. Quentin and Nathan rolled their eyes in unison.

"He needs to learn," I told them.

With Kaylee in Emile's bed, I headed back downstairs. At the doorway to the kitchen, I got a good look at Locke. Sweat had popped out along his hairline. I couldn't believe it. Nothing scared Locke. This was either an act or some kind of manifestation of his higher power. Maybe the larger version of himself was upset and this avatar responded in a way mortals could understand.

He caught me staring at him. "I need a drink."

"There's beer in the fridge."

Locke opened the door and winced. "Oh. New life and new civilizations." He grabbed a couple of Sierra bottles and slammed the door before Chase's pizza could flee. We sat at the round oak table. Locke chugged back half his beer, holding the bottle vertical. Gasping, he tore the bottle from his mouth and set it down. "The power has ebbed. However, Kaylee is still linked to the Man Upstairs." He slouched, eying me over the top of his bottle. "Henceforth I cannot make problems like bullet holes in Kaylee's walls or the carnage downtown go away." He shrugged sadly. "I have to be mortal or as close to it as possible. It shall be a comfortable mortality; I have maintained an estate on the West Coast and assorted landholdings and investments. Even so, mortality is not nearly as interesting or enjoyable as you believe." His gaze took on a wistful look.

I poured cold beer down my throat. "Focus, Locke. The other powers. What about them?"

"Odin is becoming aware. There are minor deities and spirits who have always been awake. They sense something amiss and are becoming agitated. You do not wish to see them agitated, trust me."

I drained my bottle. As if things hadn't been bad enough. "So don't count on you for help."

Locke looked ready to cry. "Oh, I can help. But only if you truly desire a front-row view of the Apocalypse."

She was trapped. Here the worldstuff was hard and solid and unmanageable and annoying. A silver strand of power joined the fox's spirit to that man-creature who had brought her here. The strand had already begun to grow thin, to dissolve.

More problematic was the throbbing cord of blue and green fire binding her soul to her body. That one grew thick and strong as she watched.

Destroying her body would break the binding. A memory of her hind leg in steel jaws thrummed into her awareness. She cringed. There had to be a less painful way of leaving this world.

The man-creature had formed the cord. Perhaps he could break it. The fox sent a burst of worldstuff along the strand that joined her to him, tracing its route to the man before it could dissolve. The strand firmed and thickened.

A ripple surged back from the man to her, a wave of alien thought pulsing into the fox's mind. The man called himself by the sound "Ssssethh." Seth Color-of-tree-bark-and-turds.

The fox trotted along the wide, stony path, following the strand linking her to the man. She walked among humans who paid her little attention, except for a small kit who waddled up and tried to fling arms around her, only to be dragged whimpering away by his mother. "Doggy!" he wailed.

The fox stared after the kit, then tried to get her bearings. As the sky darkened, she noticed the lights here were not the *flaring colors that had sometimes danced across her sky or the bright flickering fires humans had used near their dens. There were many, many lights here. They held steady but were much larger than stars.*

Stones with glowing eyes rumbled along the impossibly smooth rock paths. Twice a human stopped and tried to touch her back. She discouraged them with throaty growls. A human female passed, a small black dog on the end of a cord scampering before her. The dog barked, then yelped in fear as the fox stopped and stared at it.

What kind of dimwitted creature would allow itself to be tied onto a human? *she thought, then felt a wave of embarrassment as she noticed the cord joining her to the man called Seth.*

Soon she came to a part of the path with empty air beneath it. Humans walked along the sides while the stones-with-eyes roared along the center, farting an awful smell into the air. The fox joined the other walkers and made her way across.

What, *she wondered as she walked,* will I do if the man won't send me back?

The fox snarled at the thought. I'll chew his leg off.

The Book of
the Apostles

12

THE BISHOP

"Two missing persons?" the woman in a police officer uniform said.

"That's right." I had donned a cream suit with a black shirt and my white collar. The collar could be counted on to command respect – even awe.

"Names?"

"Devan Blueberry and Antoine Vermicelli."

Miss Bingham raised her brow and glanced with an odd smile at her shorter compatriot – *D. Rhodes* by her name tag.

Miss Rhodes said, "Vermicelli? As in the pasta?"

"Yes."

"As in the Vermicelli crime family?"

Beside me, Max smoothed his black trousers and smiled. "Our Antoine is the white sheep of his family."

"Devan disappeared this morning, and Antoine this evening," I said in an effort to keep the conversation on topic.

"Has Devan done prison time as well?" Miss Rhodes asked.

I blanched. "Of course not."

"So Antoine has," Miss Bingham said.

Max laughed. "Well played, ladies. Yes, Antoine did indeed spend several years in jail. However he has been entirely rehabilitated and is now a contributing member of society. He works for His Grace."

Miss Bingham's gaze narrowed. "What was he in for?"

Max licked his lips. "Is that truly important?"

"It may suggest a motive. Maybe whoever snatched them was after Vermicelli and got Mr. Blueberry as collateral."

"Devan vanished hours ago. Antoine disappeared this evening. They were both targeted and we know who took them."

Miss Bingham raised a sharp-tipped eyebrow.

Max told the story, much of it true, about how we had become aware of a Mr. Seth Brown in Cove City. Several young men had been murdered, and Mr. Brown appeared connected with them. He had sent threatening letters to the church (this part was false, but Max managed a convincing shudder of fright), and now seemed to have followed us to Summerton.

Miss Rhodes plucked a phone from her belt and tapped its screen. With a glance at Max she said, "And you are?"

"Max Cobber." Again his broad smile.

Miss Rhodes stepped back and turned away, leaving her partner facing us.

"So you didn't call after Mr. Blueberry vanished," Bingham said, "but you became worried about Mr. Vermicelli."

"We weren't certain Devan had vanished," I lied. "He grew up near this city. Perhaps he had encountered an old friend." We couldn't very well mention he had been taken during a furious gun battle with a demon this morning. "We became fearful when Antoine called to say he had seen Mr. Brown outside the pub at the corner. Soon after that, we couldn't reach him."

Miss Rhodes chose that moment to rejoin the conversation, stepping back beside her compatriot and giving Miss Bingham a nod. "Nothing on Devan Blueberry or Seth Brown. But Antoine Vermicelli went to prison for attempted murder and was suspected of a string of assassinations for the Danish mob going back a decade. Max Cobber spent eleven years in prison for strangling his client." Rhodes glanced up at Bingham. "Former lawyer, now disbarred."

Bingham's mouth quirked. "That's one way to get out of pro bono."

Max gripped the arms of his chair and squeezed until his knuckles turned white.

"Ladies," I said, "you're here to start police investigations of Mr. Brown and these disappearances, not to upset my employees. Antoine and Max did their time and have been fully rehabilitated. If this is how you treat people, perhaps I should have a word with the chief of police."

The two looked at each other. Miss Bingham cleared her throat. "Believe me, Mr. Moffat, we're on the case."

"Perhaps you should ask your chief to involve some of his detectives rather than you. This is a kidnapping, after all."

Miss Bingham blinked. Miss Rhodes smirked and said, "We'll certainly pass that along."

"Do that," I said. "And perhaps you could tell him we take umbrage at how his staff treat citizens in need of police services."

Again a look hopped between the officers. Miss Bingham smiled. "If you'd like to file a complaint, you can contact Internal Affairs. Or call the chief directly; I'm sure she would love to talk to you."

They departed, leaving me worried. What horrors might the demons visit upon Devan while these girls pretended to be police officers? The boy's soul was strong and his father, Our Lord, would protect him. Still I fretted. Demons are guileful and skilled at corruption.

We were so close to eliminating the last of the Antichrists. Forty there had been before I began the hunt, a number symbolizing tests and ordeals throughout holy texts –

mentioned over 130 times in the Bible alone. Now just nine demons remained. The nine most cunning, to test our righteousness and will.

Max turned to me, fingers twitching. "I am truly not sure about involving the police, Your Worship."

"If they find Devan, they will have served their part." I rose. "The demons likely know who and where we are now. We need to get out of here." I led him down the hotel's corridor of beige carpeting with dark wood wall trim. As we neared the door to Eugene's room, I heard a moan. Max gave a smirk.

I used my fist upon the door. "Eugene."

A mumbled curse greeted us, followed by abrupt cessation of television sounds. The door swung open to reveal my portly driver clad in white T-shirt and boxers.

"This must end, Eugene," I said. "The Lord took your manhood for a reason."

Eugene's gaze fell. "Yeah. Sorry. I'm trying."

"Did the film help with little Mr. Willie there?" Max asked, a wicked grin upon his face.

Eugene said nothing. His expression, however, spoke volumes.

"Never mind all that." I waved him aside to allow Max and me to enter. An old-socks odor lingered in the room.

"We must find new accommodations," I said to Eugene. "This will be your task. Something other than a hotel. Never mind the cost; we only need it for a month or two at most."

"You know, I saw a couple of houses for rent when we were driving up from the airport."

"Good. I want us relocated tomorrow. Theo has our credit card and even some checks. Talk to him in the morning."

I turned to Max. "Your job is to find us another of. . . those like Seth Brown."

Max leaned against the wall next to the closet and crossed his arms. "They've gone to ground. That won't be easy."

"I don't care how difficult it is. Theo needs to be healed. When you have one, call Eugene to find out our new location." I balled my fists. "We have been hurt by the temporary loss of Devan but will destroy these creatures yet. Have you seen the diner down the street?"

"Tim's? Not since I took the before and after photos." His breath became jagged and a sneer crossed his face. "There isn't much left of it."

Eugene shivered. "It's back."

Max gave us a confused look.

"Show us your pictures," I said.

Max lifted his phone and thumbed its screen. His face darkened. "Who has access to this?"

"They're gone?"

He scowled. "I will –"

I gripped his arm. "Relax. I heard the explosion from here. I even saw the fire engines and police racing to the scene. But earlier this afternoon, Eugene and I went out for a walk past it, expecting to find rubble and police tape.

"The diner is unharmed. We stopped in for a cinnamon roll. They are quite good."

Max straightened. "Your Grace, what are you suggesting? I set the charge myself. I heard the blast." There was enough anger in his words that Eugene cowered from him.

"I know you did your work, Max. But the Lord has brought it back. Intact. He appears to have cleared the minds of those who witnessed it – except us. We remember. And that is proof that our faith is strong." I carefully elevated my voice and raised my fist, just as I had read. Leaders needed drama, power.

"Gentlemen," I said, "angels walk with us."

13

I dreamed that night of Devan at age five, an innocent, bony little boy at the doors of the monastery in Dunfriggin, brought by grandparents at their wit's end. His mother died by her own hand in a hospital's psychiatric wing while being treated for raving about a voice in her bedroom.

The holy child Devan healed the bubbling flesh on my hand when I spilled a boiling kettle upon it. He drove away my doubts, healed my broken faith, and inspired me to more ambition within the Church than to be the bureaucratic equivalent of wallpaper, leading me to take the Bishopric of Dunfriggin. His existence showed me my life's purpose: protecting the Messiah as we prepared for the Second Coming.

I woke early, awakening the coffee maker. Then I switched on my tablet and looked at the list. I had placed asterisks beside the names of those we had dispatched to Hell – the majority. Two had question marks: Jamie Hick and Graeme Thunderbird, restored to life by the Seth demon. We would have to return to Cove for them when we finished with Summerton. I added a question mark to the name Quentin Haze and quietly damned the Seth Brown demon to the Hellfires that spawned it.

My apostles had grown cocky this past year. I should have known God would test any hubris. I needed to keep them focused, to curb overconfidence.

I closed the list and brought up Lionel Drumpf's biography of Pol Pot, *Wacko In The Wilderness*. Pol Pot knew how to sway his followers to his cause. He had a grace about him, even in the rough lands of Cambodia. Drumpf utterly failed to capture this side of him, focusing instead on atrocities.

Frustrated, I turned my attention to Warren Romanovsky's biography of Stalin, *Not The Life Of The Party*. Stalin had not been especially bright, but he had an intuitive understanding of how to steer the minds of his men. Unfortunately he typically employed fear, which didn't work on my apostles – Eugene being the exception.

The sound of a door thumping into its frame drew my attention. A glance at the clock radio beside the bed told me eight o'clock approached. I rose and stepped into the corridor. At that moment Eugene emerged from Theo's room farther along. He gave me a guilty look. "Your Grace. G'morning."

"Good morning, Eugene."

"I got the credit card from Theo. I'm getting breakfast. Then I'll look for a house."

"See that we have one today."

He rushed to pass me, eager to be off, but I stepped into his path. "Did you think over what I said last night?"

"Yeah. It's, you know, the cross I have to bear and that shit."

"Eugene!"

"Sorry. That stuff."

"The Lord took your manhood because you abused it. You need to put that life behind you. You aren't that man anymore. You understand?"

He blinked and nodded, eager to flee.

"Good." I stepped aside and watched him scramble to the elevators. Then I tapped on Theo's room.

Theo threw the oak door open. "Gene –" His eyes, hard and fierce, turned to surprise. He stepped back into the dimness of his room. "Your Worship. Come in."

I had already seen the red mark around his eye.

Theo had stacked his equipment neatly against the wall beyond the bed. Wooden boxes containing C4 were piled on top of each other, the top one threatening to tumble to the floor.

Perspiration beaded Theo's forehead as he limped to his desk and slumped into a chair, cradling his bullet-riddled arm.

"Did you sleep?" I asked.

He shrugged.

"Has anyone changed your bandages?"

A grunt.

"You have pain-killers?"

Another grunt. Theo turned off his desk lamp, leaving only the glow of the laptop computer's screen for illumination. It had been fortunate that the bullets had struck his left arm yesterday morning. A sling made from a shirt had grown pink spots as the day and night passed. I couldn't see the wounds in his leg through his green pajama pants.

"Did Eugene do that to your eye?"

Theo looked glum. "He figures we lost Antoine thanks to me. Because we were away from the hotel last night." His voice grew husky. "When the kids were here."

"I'll have words with him."

Theo sneered. "He's not one of us. Max has been inside, like Antoine and me. Eugene doesn't have anything on the line here."

"Yes, he does. Redemption."

"That's not what he talks about. He just wants his hard-on back."

"Enough of that. As for your injuries, Max will either find Devan or one of the demons," I said. "You'll be as good as new."

Yet another grunt, this with an echo of disbelief.

"Have faith, Theo. God will see you through this."

Theo looked up at me hopefully.

"Now, I need to know who Seth Brown has spoken to lately."

He shifted toward the laptop with a painful wince. "I downloaded phone records this morning. He called these numbers yesterday."

I peered over him at the screen, recognizing one: Brown's mother.

Theo pointed at another. "That one, second from the top, is unlisted. Should have a name soon; I've put out a search."

"Brown's phone will have GPS, won't it?"

Theo nodded. "The cops need a court order to get info like that. I can't pull that off."

"A pity."

Theo gestured at a blank line on the screen. "This is weird. He got a couple of phone calls like this."

"There is no number."

"Exactly. It's like he got a phone call from ... nothing." His cheek twitched. "You don't suppose he has connections with, you know, Homeland Security or something? Some badasses who can hide their phone numbers completely? Or find out who is cribbing their phone records ..." His eyes swelled.

I headed off that line of thought before he grew too afraid to do his work. "Is it possible to get records of his conversations?"

Theo shook his head. "We'd need someone in the NSA for that. Try bribing those guys and we'll all be back inside. You too."

14

I called the Eastglen Seminary and Church of Mary the Virgin to cancel my meetings for the day. Then I reviewed the book collection on my tablet.

Charisma, I had to admit, was not my strong suit. But it could be learnt by following the masters.

Idi Amin combined charisma with brutality. I wondered if I should show more brutality. Perhaps personal execution of a demon. The thought made me shudder. I really wasn't cut out for dealing with vermin directly.

Eugene phoned to say he had a house for us for two months. He used the fictional name and credit card Theo had contrived. Illegal, certainly, but we were at war with forces of darkness and must follow God's law rather than man's.

I knew far too many throughout the echelons of the Church whose faith could inspire them to impassioned sermons but could not carry them past words into deeds. Christ foresaw his death and stood his ground. Justin Martyr followed Christ's lead and faced bravely the prospect of his own beheading. Saint Justin must have considered throwing himself on Roman mercy or denying his faith to spare his own life. A long succession of saints faced the agony of death with heads high. Those men were guides and inspiration. Though frankly, with the exception of Christ himself they were terrible at being leaders.

My telephone rang again, Max's number crossing its screen.

"Your Worship, I located one. I haven't collected him yet, but can at any time."

"Which demon is it?"

"Daniel."

"The healer."

"The very one. Appropriate, don't you think?"

Daniel Morris, son of the Baptist minister Billy Morris, had appeared on his father's evangelical television show for several years. His mother, following her divorce in his youth, converted Daniel to the Catholic faith. That was enough for his name to find its way into Church records and so come to my attention.

His birthday fell between April 3 and April 8 as with all the demon creatures, clustered like shadows around Devan's holy birth on April 6.

Theo supervised while Eugene, grumbling and pale, carried equipment and toolboxes down to the car. Eugene drove carefully but Theo moaned with each bump and lurch, cradling his wounded arm.

The street widened to become Mole Boulevard. At the next intersection, Eugene performed a U-turn and carried us back up the block. He let the car roll to a stop outside a yellow bungalow.

"We're here," Eugene said, climbing from the car. He held my door. Theo followed me out, struggling to straighten his wounded leg. He surveyed the house with me, then made a choking sound, mouth wide and trembling. I followed his gaze across the street. Beyond a wooden railing stood a sign that read, *Shrieking Trees Park*. Legions of children climbed colorful arrays of pipes stylized to look like cars and helicopters.

"Theo," I said sharply. "Get inside."

He gazed at the children, unblinking. Eugene lifted bags from the trunk and carried two up the sidewalk to the entrance. A moment later he returned, walking jauntily, and said, "We got a terrific deal."

I motioned at the playground. "How do you explain this?"

He gazed at the park without comprehension. Then he looked from me to Theo. Realization dawned. "Oh. Shit."

"We will discuss this later." I gripped Theo's shoulder and turned him away from the children.

Eugene collected more bags. We followed him.

The living room had a hardwood floor and a little gas-fueled fireplace. Nothing on its walls, nothing to sit on.

I glared at Eugene.

"Your Grace, the furniture is coming this afternoon. I went to Ikea. They didn't want to deliver on short notice, but money talks. Even in Swedish."

15

Within the hour the other car arrived. Max was in the backseat while a young man drove.

Don't be fooled, I told myself. That was no frightened young man. It was Hellspawn: a creature of Satan bringing deceit and contamination. Max stepped from the vehicle, hand tucked into his suit jacket. The demon lurched awkwardly out.

I opened the front door to Max.

"Good day, Your Worship," he said.

"You?" the demon barked. "You're behind this? My pa is going to flay you alive."

"This is Daniel." Max gave the gangly creature a shove and closed the door.

"Pa always did say you can never trust a Catholic."

"That would be the Reverend Billy Morris?" I said.

"Yeah. We know who you are, Bishop Moffat. When he finds out what you did, he'll crucify you."

The demon, clad in black pants and a white short-sleeved button-up shirt, looked as though he had stepped off a college campus. He trembled, though his jaw jutted with bravado. A fine performance, considering his true father was Lucifer.

"Let's postpone the crucifixion." Max said dryly. "We require your services."

The demon turned to him, then flinched back from the look on his face.

Max gestured to where Theo stood near the windows, peering across the street. "Theo, join us."

Theo stumbled over, sling showing fresh red patches.

"This man," said Max, "has been shot."

"Shot?" echoed Daniel. "Crap! He needs a doctor. Who shot him?" His gaze locked onto Max's weapon.

Max gave the creature a smile. "That isn't important. Your talent is."

Daniel looked from Max to me to Theo, passing over Eugene as though he weren't in the room. "I'm not getting this."

Max raised his brow. "We need you to restore our compatriot here to health."

This suggestion led the demon to blink rapidly and moisten his lips. "I see." Color drained from his cheeks. "Well, you know, I can't do that, like, on demand. God has to call me, you know?"

"He is ringing right now."

The demon glanced about as though looking for an exit.

Max sighed, and his pistol's long suppressor moved beneath the demon's nose. "I don't think you truly appreciate the circumstances." The demon's eyes followed the pendulum-like movement of the weapon. "We want Theo restored to health. You have the power to do this but are hindering us. A very bad idea. It is in your best interest to work your magic on him."

Daniel swallowed. "Well, you know. Magic. That's like, a really good word. I mean, magicians, they make a coin disappear, but it's not really gone, you know? It's an illusion."

Dread crept like acid through my stomach.

Max pursed his lips thoughtfully. Then he laughed, a single sharp note. "Daniel, let me pose a question. Three weeks ago on your father's show in that monstrosity you call a church, he beckoned to a woman in a wheelchair in the front row. He called his only begotten – perhaps ill-begotten is the correct phrase – son forth. His son – that would be you, Daniel – approached the woman, holding out his arms. You made a ridiculous shuffling step toward her, your head back, your mouth open. You clasped the woman's hands, wailing. And lo! A miracle! The woman rose from her chair and walked! Now tell me, in truth how did you achieve this?"

Daniel shrank back. "Well, you know. This woman in the front row, you have to ask yourself how she got there. I mean, our church isn't exactly wheelchair accessible. You know? But maybe we keep some wheelchairs handy, inside, because when you're past the front steps, you can get anywhere you like on wheels. You know?"

Max smiled. His pistol focused on the middle of Daniel's chest. "Yes, Daniel, I think I do know. Tell me, have you ever healed someone? Anyone? Even yourself? Or, say, brought some manner of creature back to life? Turned water into wine? Anything of that ilk?"

"Uh, no. That sounds like superhero stuff."

Max glanced at me with a grin. "Superhero stuff. You don't read a great deal, do you?"

"Well, no."

"Daniel," I said, my voice dry. "You were born on April 6, is that right?"

"Yeah."

"And you're twenty-one."

"No, I'm twenty-four."

"Church records show you were baptized when you were eleven."

Daniel looked at me, then at Max. "I was fourteen."

"That is not possible."

"My ma split with my dad and filed for divorce when I was thirteen. She had custody so she figured I should be baptized Catholic like her. Dad went ballistic."

My stomach became a stone. "Then somebody wrote your age into the records incorrectly."

"I guess so."

Max laughed. "Thank you for your help, Daniel. Let's get you home."

A glimmer of relief surged across the demon's face. "Yeah. Cool." A glance found its way to Theo, who looked stricken.

Max made a dismissive gesture. "Don't mind him, he is an animatronic prop. We bought that second-hand from Universal Studios. Amazingly lifelike, isn't it?"

"Sure," Daniel said, dubious.

"And I do apologize for manhandling you into my car at gunpoint. I can be a trifle zealous about my work. Of course you understand."

A haunted look passed over Daniel's face. He rubbed a bruise on his jaw. "Sure."

After Max and the lad left, Theo slumped against the wall, weeping in pain.

"We will find another," I said.

My thoughts turned to my list. Forty names for forty demons; the number echoed through so many passages in the Bible. Forty days Jesus spent in the desert. Forty men banded together to murder the apostle Paul. My research had been meticulous. First I had believed there were seven Antichrists, then twelve. As the years passed, the numbers of those I found reached forty and rose no higher. We couldn't leave any to destroy humanity's chance of redemption through Devan. This sin-filled world needed the Apocalypse our Lord promised the faithful.

Forty demons. But now, if Daniel were not such a creature, we were missing one.

16

Theo and I sat against the wall with his computer on a box of equipment.

"Seth Brown must have telephoned one of his cohorts, someone we don't yet know about," I said.

"There are phone numbers I haven't been able to trace." Theo's face gleamed with sweat and he hunched his shoulders in pain. He had never once complained, taking the agony of his wounds as his lot.

"Find them. One must be the creature we're missing."

"Are we sure that one's even in this town? What if he's somewhere else?"

That discomfiting thought had come to me also.

A knock sent Eugene bolting past us. He threw the door open and raced outside. I rose, knees creaking, and peered after him. Two men in Ikea shirts carried boxes toward the house.

Theo remained huddled over his computer, trying to go unnoticed. Eugene carried a cardboard box past us, grinning.

Soon a large mattress wrapped in plastic and five smaller ones leaned against the wall next to the fireplace. One of the men, a grizzled fellow with a scraggly beard, nodded curtly at me. The other huffed as he carried yet another large box into the living room.

In minutes their white truck eased down the driveway and rumbled away.

"This is our furniture?" I asked, appalled.

Eugene beamed. "I saved us thousands of dollars."

Late in the afternoon, as Eugene tried to sort pieces of a wood-frame couch, Max returned pushing another young man before him. The demon limped, scowling. I had seen this one before in photos taken by Max and Antoine.

Theo made a surprised grunt.

The demon glared. "This asshole shot me." He flung something to the floor. It rattled and spun, coming to rest against my shoe: a flattened bullet.

"I merely ensured that you are what we believe you to be." Max grinned at us. "He successfully mended the wound in his leg."

"Not quite; it still aches."

"What is your name, demon?" I asked quietly.

Max laughed. "You will never guess, Your Grace."

"Jack Wackinoff the Third," the demon said.

Max cuffed the demon across the jaw with his pistol. "This is Nathan."

"You found him again? I expected him to go to ground after he survived the explosion."

"I drove to his place of work and looked around," Max said. "Then I merely waited until the end of his shift and got him before he set off to catch his bus."

Nathan Filman shrugged. "I still have to work. My phone costs me two hundred a month. Then there's rent."

Theo set his laptop aside and struggled up. "You're real? You can fix me?"

The Nathan demon looked at him. "What happened to you?"

"He was shot yesterday," Max said. "We require your talent. Heal him."

"Shot? Must have been Seth's doing."

"Seth Brown?" I said. "You know where he is?"

"Yeah, right, like he's crashing on my couch." The demon rolled his eyes. "No, he uses a special magic called 'phones' to tell us when he runs into you assholes. He shot you up and stole your pet, right? Devan?"

"Devan is the Messiah," I said quietly. "As you well know."

"Is that really what you think?" The Nathan demon grinned. "What makes you so sure?"

"God himself prophesied," said Theo, wincing as he struggled to stand. "Now fix me up."

Max turned to the creature. "Heal him."

"Or what?"

"Or I'll put another bullet in you."

Nathan glanced at me, then at Max once more. "My Dad won't like that."

"Your Dad is Lucifer himself," Theo said, his voice outraged.

Nathan laughed. "I've met Lucifer. He definitely isn't my dad. But let me get this straight. You figure Devan is here to bring on the Second Coming and the rest of us are. . . what?"

"Demons," Theo muttered.

"How do you know you don't have it the wrong way around? Maybe I'm the real thing. Or maybe it's one of those you already killed."

I opened my mouth to respond when Eugene said, "You know, he's got a point."

Max glared.

Eugene spoke again, his voice taking on a strangled quality. "Seriously. How do we know Devan's the right one?"

"We know," I said. "I have studied these demons. They are pretenders. Devan is the true Messiah. Now, creature, heal this man."

Nathan stepped back and leaned against the door frame near the basement steps. "If I don't, what then? Torture? Rip my fingernails out?"

"That sounds delightful." Max's pistol muzzle nodded in time with his head.

"Didn't Devan tell you anything about how we work? You already shot me. My leg isn't fully healed yet; that sucks energy out of me. I need time to recover."

"Liar." Theo reached behind himself with his good hand and dug out his little pistol. "Just do it. Heal me or I'll blow you to Hell."

"If I'm the spawn of Satan, what makes you think threatening to send me back to Daddy will make me sit up and beg?"

Max looked at me and shrugged. Then he swung the butt of his pistol at the creature. Nathan's head snapped sideways, and blood burst from his lips. He stumbled against the wall.

"You are here to heal our friend Theo," Max said cheerfully. "Do so. Or suffer the consequences. You know what consequences I mean, I'm sure."

The creature developed a tremor around his mouth, only to replace it with gritted teeth. "You haven't answered my question. What makes you think you have a goddamn clue which of us is the Messiah? Hell, I happen to know we're all it. There isn't any single one. The biggest screw-up in history."

"Ha!" Theo said. "You said 'goddamn.' No true son of God could take his father's name in vain."

Nathan snorted. "I went to Bible school. That commandment has nothing to do with saying 'Oh God' or "goddamn.' What it means is, don't do something in God's name that my old man wouldn't approve of. Kind of like what you morons have been doing already, blowing up Tim's Diner and such." He peered at me. "Do you even remember doing that?"

"The diner?" Max said. "Yes, of course. I sat near you in the café. I placed a backpack loaded with charges beneath my table."

"Screwed it up royally, didn't you?"

I reached for Max's arm too late. He surged forward with an inchoate bellow. Fists collided with the demon's chest, and the Nathan creature stumbled back. The demon's shoe caught on the lip of the top step. For a moment his arms flailed as though reaching for purchase. Then he pitched backward, hands closing on air.

His head made a crunching sound on the third step from the bottom. At an unlikely angle, his head led his body as it slid the rest of the way to the basement floor. The demon's legs shuddered and grew still.

Max gazed at the steps, sucking in a slow breath. Beside me, Theo moaned, "Oh God, oh God." Eugene held his arms at his sides, trembling, flexing his fingers.

Theo said, "My arm. My leg. They're not fixed." His throat made a burbling sound.

Max drew long, rough breaths. He straightened, buttoned his black jacket, and wiped his palms upon his pant legs. Then he turned, adjusted his glasses on his nose, and cleared his throat. "We'll get another." His voice sounded as though it had been shredded and taped back together.

A crunching sound from the basement drew our attention, and we turned as one. The creature's neck twisted, grinding bone against bone, shifting the head back into alignment. A long breath issued from the demon's body.

It opened its eyes and looked up at us. Its gaze settled on Max.

"Nice suit. Where did you get it, Prick's Tailors?"

The pigeon moved faster than the fox expected. Lemmings at least had the decency to burrow under snow where a quick pounce brought them up squirming for a pleasant meal.

A sensation of shifting jarred the fox, leaving her sick to an already unhappy belly. The cord linking her to the man had flailed about earlier, shifting from south to east. The fox had changed direction as well. Now the cord moved back south as the man returned to where he had been. She growled in frustration.

I won't chew one of his legs off, *she thought.* I'll chew two.

Images rolled into her mind. She shook her head in an effort to press them back, but they refused to leave – an unfortunate by-product of her attachment to the man.

The fox had become aware that her forced return to this world was accidental. The man had been defending himself from another human.

Seth's thoughts carried a captivating element – a sense of belonging she couldn't quite grasp. She had always been alone. Even after she died she had been on her own, though never lonely – the concept of loneliness was as alien as the wobbly seven-limbed orange creatures she had once chased across a hill. This sense of belonging the man felt was . . . compelling.

The fox attempted to imagine what it was the man believed he belonged to. It wasn't a sense of connection to the vastness at the edge of the world, but a binding to an idea. The man himself wasn't even aware of it. The fox dug through his mind for some means of understanding.

It was a sense of . . . mission.

Like a wolf, *the fox thought.* He believes he is protecting his pack. Even more than that, he believes he is protecting . . . everything.

The fox padded on. The man felt more alive than any other creature she had ever encountered. She was certain she had lived among the other worlds for many, many turns of the seasons. Nothing out there felt at all the way the man did.

She walked onward. Pigeons rested on the wires above. She eyed them mournfully.

Perhaps just a deep bite, *the fox thought.* He can keep his legs.

The Book of
Confession

17

SETH

When the Prince of Darkness tells you someone is launching the end of the world in Emile's bedroom, you do something about it. Fast.

My fist hammered the door. No answer. I threw it open. Kaylee was sprawled across Emile's bed, mumbling in half-sleep, lower half covered in blankets.

"Yo," I said.

Kaylee opened her eyes and started bawling.

Locke crowded in behind me.

"How's that?" I asked.

"A truly not-insignificant improvement upon matters."

When I knelt on the edge of the bed, Kaylee turned to the wall, sobbing. Now I got treated to a bloodshot-eyes-and-runny-nose view in Emile's wall mirror.

"You started praying in your sleep," I told her.

Tears ran down her cheeks. "Can't you just send me back?"

"Not going to happen."

"Bastard."

Emile appeared beside Locke in the doorway. He had worn a scowl all night, even while sleeping on the floor in the upstairs living room.

"Is anyone making breakfast around here?" I asked the world in general, tossing the words into a gap in Kaylee's racket. Emile glared at me and turned to Locke. I couldn't see Locke's face, but it must have been convincing. Emile fled.

I nudged Kaylee. "Come on out. Join the rest."

Reluctantly she slid out from under the covers, blowing her nose on the chest of the black T-shirt we'd borrowed from Emile's closet. I caught a flash of thigh clear up to her hip.

"How about some pants?" I hunted through an open box of clothes on the floor. A martial arts uniform in white with a red belt looped over it; sweaters; jeans; a collection of (ugh) paisley suspenders; track pants. I pulled out a blue set and gave them to Kaylee.

Quentin was Devan's de facto guard. He came down to collect breakfast for both of them, gave me a tired nod by way of greeting, and headed back up to the second living room.

Kaylee pushed cereal around her bowl halfheartedly.

"How come, if you have to be human now, you can still sense when Kaylee is talking to the Man Upstairs?" I asked Locke around a mouthful, hoping to dispel the gloom around me.

"Although I have had to strip my intelligence down to great-ape level, I still hold a connection to my chopra. That part of me sends new information periodically. And I can borrow his senses on occasion, as long as doing so will not draw the attention of the Man Upstairs."

"Your chopra?" Kaylee mumbled.

Locke coughed. "My higher self. There is this body, grown out of plasm and functioning as a mortal, and then there is my chopra, my part of the godhead's vast web of personae."

"Cool," I said. "Is Chop giving you anything else useful?"

Locke cast a glance at me with those disturbingly normal black eyes. "I shall keep you informed."

At that moment Chase came wandering in from the direction of the downstairs bathroom, wearing a black bathrobe. He filled a cup and set it next to me. "Coffee?"

I glanced at the cup and grinned at him. The water turned black and started steaming.

Emile snorted. "When will I have my room back?"

"I shall collect beds today," Locke said. "We will establish them in the downstairs living room."

"Can you get me one?" I asked.

Emile's brow shot up. "You're only temporary."

"Depends on Moffat. I need to interrogate you-know-who. Speaking of that." I jutted my thumb in the direction of Antoine, locked away above the garage. "Has anyone looked in on him?"

Locke started in on his cereal again. "This would be the man you captured downtown?"

I nodded, putting a finger to my lips while motioning upstairs in Devan's general direction.

Locke licked his spoon. "I see no reason to be concerned. If he had freed himself, he likely would have slit our throats in our sleep and departed with Devan."

Emile choked on his corn flakes.

"Where's Nathan?" I asked in a hurry to change the subject.

Emile glared at me. "He left early. Work."

"He went to work? Is he an idiot?"

Nobody answered. But no one disagreed.

"You're going to make truth serum?" Chase asked.

"Sure. I'll need to pick up syringes."

"You can buy them at any drugstore," Kaylee said, stirring her cereal again.

Emile set his spoon down. "That's ridiculous. Drugstores won't sell those to just anyone; junkies would be buying them by the bag."

"I have syringes," Chase said.

We all looked at him. He rubbed his dark hair with a green towel. "In the van. We keep a medical kit in case someone gets bitten – tetanus is no joke. So you can make truth serum out of water?"

"I need to see the chemical formula, but yeah."

Kaylee trembled and started sobbing.

"And she's off again," Emile grumped.

"I think," Locke said, "you need to find something for our Ms. Jerrel to do. To keep her busy."

I stared across the table at the live-in drama queen. "Like what? Oh, research. Kaylee, I need to know more about Moffat. Are you up for that?"

Emile huffed. "She's a wreck. Besides, what does she know about research?"

"How tough is it to use Google?" Chase offered.

Kaylee looked at him as if he were a bug. "You can get the basics off the Net if you know what you're doing. But to get the real goods, you have to lean on people."

Emile sniffed. "Of course you do."

I glared him down. "Kaylee is a top journalist. She knows a lot more about digging up dirt on people than all of us combined."

That got Emile's attention.

"You've probably seen her on Channel Forty-Five," I said.

"Forty-Eight," Kaylee said with a sniffle.

"Excellent." Locke clapped his hands together with a sound like a judge beating a gavel. "I recall seeing Emile with a laptop computer at this very table last night. Be so kind as to get it for our dear Ms. Jerrel."

"Wait, I need that for work. Isn't it enough that I've given her my bedroom and my clothes?"

"In point of fact, you did not," Locke said. "We confiscated them. Now you can supply Kaylee with a computer, which I am certain will get you into her good graces. You can collect your office machine for your own use."

Emile scowled. Then he studied Kaylee, a shrewd look filling his eyes.

Locke left on foot, grumbling about having to take a bus. I got Kaylee set up at the dinner table with Emile's laptop. Chase said he needed to get to work. I tried talking him out of it, which accomplished nothing.

"Then be careful," I said. "Don't take your usual route there or back here. And try to leave early, just in case the bad guys are anticipating when you go. And don't accept any deliveries like parcels."

His eyes bulged.

"Moffat and his crew tried blowing Nathan up and gunning Quentin down. You really think they'd have an issue with popping you at BARC? I doubt they're big animal lovers."

He gulped.

I rose and beckoned to him. "Before you go, give me a hand with you-know-who."

Chase followed me to the garage and up the steps. As we walked, I passed Antoine's pistol, silencer and all, over to him. He stared at it, speechless.

"This is the lethal end," I said. "If he tries anything, point it at him and squeeze the trigger. Repeat as necessary 'til he stops fussing." I shoved the door open.

Antoine sat where we'd left him. He lifted his head, groggy. "I need a piss."

I glanced at Chase. "Behind him. If he causes trouble, don't worry about hitting me. Just keep pushing lead into him."

Alert now, Antoine looked at me with cunning.

"Here's the plan," I said. "We're going to let you use the bathroom. Any trouble, and we'll blow you away, clean up the mess when your bladder lets go, and lock you back in the chair. Then I'll bring you back, so even having yourself killed isn't an escape. Get it?"

I stared him down.

"Got it," he said, pouting. A bit theatrical, I thought.

"Good." I unlocked his ankles first then his left arm. His breathing settled into a regular rhythm, not catching. Smooth. The breathing of someone going to lots of trouble to keep from giving away the fact that he was about to try something cute.

I slammed my palm into his nose.

Antoine's head snapped back. He hacked out a cough and slumped in the chair. "Fugg meeee."

I unlatched his arm and stepped back. "I'll fix your nose when we have you locked up again."

Antoine held his face, growling into bloody palms. He stumbled into the bathroom, rattling the chains on wrists and ankles. I watched him take a leak. Chase stood next to me, the pistol muzzle trembling. When Antoine finished, he staggered toward me, acting dazed.

"Quit playing games; you aren't that badly hurt. Lock up your ankles."

I waved Chase back behind the chair. Antoine sat and, of course, tried screwing around and faking the locks, setting them so the padlocks looked closed but weren't.

"Chase, shoot him through his head."

Fortunately Antoine didn't see the expression on Chase's face. "Wait." He latched the padlocks on his ankles, his mouth curling in a sneer. I locked his arms down.

"What now?" Chase squeaked.

"Get me a glass of water. And a syringe. And oh, yes; tell Kaylee to look up sodium amytal on Wikipedia."

I mended Antoine's wrecked nose while I waited for Chase. He still looked a mess, with all the drying blood.

"I've got some questions for you," I told him. "You're going to answer them. Not threatening you, you understand. Just keeping you up to date on how your morning is going to go."

He glowered at me. "I'm not telling you anything."

"We'll see."

Chase was back faster than expected. He held out a printed sheet. "This is all we could find."

$C_{11}H_{18}N_2O_3$ in block letters on a Wikipedia page, complete with molecular diagram. Sodium amytal. Also known as amobarbital.

"How do you do this?" Chase asked.

I shrugged. "It's easier if I can touch the liquid. That's how I learned to make my coffee. Burned my pinky getting the right temperature. But I can also do it by getting a sense of how the molecules are put together."

I studied the line sketch until I could picture it with my eyes closed. Then I gripped the glass of water he'd brought and visualized the molecules in it.

"Wow," Chase breathed. "Was that it? That buzz?"

"Yup. I hope. For all I know, maybe I've made liquid rat poison." Not likely, but I got a look from Antoine that was worth the price of admission.

Chase had more experience with needles than I did, so I filled the syringe and passed it to him, then held Antoine's arm. Chase found a vein and emptied the syringe.

"What now?" he asked.

"Never done this before. I guess we wait and see."

Antoine squirmed, then worked up a deep but hollow laugh. "Do your worst. I'm not talking."

18

KAYLEE

Sitting by myself at the kitchen table, I used Emile's laptop to browse salacious websites. I'd hoped a bit of arousal would stop the ache for what I had lost, but it didn't do much except remind me of the emptiness the afterlife had left behind.

The doorbell chimed, startling me out of Prissy Hardsuckle's debut in *Thongs and Dongs Nine: Flat Out*. Emile came bounding down the staircase, took a bag from the man at the door, and set up a sleek black laptop and portable printer on the table, humming all the while.

Chase raced in, excited and jittery, to ask me to look up truth serum. I shut down Prissy's introduction to Brad the Impaler and did a quick search.

"Can I print to that?" I asked Emile.

He nodded without looking away from his own screen. I printed Wikipedia's page, and Chase fled with it.

Depressed, I keyed "Charles Moffat" and "Bishop" into Google. It brought up the usual stuff: the diocese's website with a short bio about him and his "great works." Apparently he ministered to convicted felons. That explained what Seth had said about the crew he traveled with.

One of the top five links led to a YouTube video of an interview with Moffat. Curious, I clicked on it and found a clip from Ted Neumann's show. The right-wing nutbar interviewed Moffat about prison reform.

"Your Grace," Neumann said, "don't you think these people should spend more time in prison? They've done awful things."

Emile glared at me over his computer.

"If you have headphones, I'm happy to borrow them," I said.

He shook his head in snarky silence.

Stained-glass windows gleamed behind Bishop Moffat in his black robe and white collar. "I believe it is up to God to punish people. They are troubled souls, not monsters."

"Do you know what some of these 'souls' have done to kids?"

"These men had lost their way. I've spent a great deal of time showing them the path to God." A wistful sigh. "We have all suffered crises of faith. I see no reason to draw out their suffering when we can bring them to God and help them seek forgiveness."

I stopped the video and regarded the gray-haired man in the video window. *What was your crisis of faith?* I wondered.

Another search, back to Wikipedia, this time for anything about Bishop Moffat. Wikipedia had a brief description of Moffat's life. He had traveled the world, touring seminaries and churches, then returned to his home in Cranston outside of Summerton. At forty-nine – sixteen years ago – he started visiting prisons. He had ministered to inmates who were looking for God and not finding him in their cage. After a few years, he started dealing exclusively with Karl Rove Memorial Prison. He had also, for almost two decades, spent a great deal of time at the monastery of Dunfriggin outside the city.

I sat back and thought. Then I typed "Dunfriggin," "monastery," and "Moffat" into a search bar. I shunted links to a dozen browser windows and scrolled through them, trying to piece together Moffat's life.

"You really are a journalist."

I blinked at the sound of Emile's voice and looked at him over the top of my screen.

"Channel Forty-Eight's website has a picture of you." He grimaced. "Your hair looked better then. Have you ever done features? Or are you strictly hard news?"

"Nobody does just hard news anymore. You don't last that way. I did a documentary about the deputy mayor a couple of years ago." After I broke the corruption story that sent him back to his used car lot.

Emile nodded, apparently satisfied. The hollowness in me returned, sucking at my thoughts. I focused on Moffat, and the pain began to recede behind curiosity.

Charles Moffat had changed about seventeen years ago in some way that started him visiting prisons. All of this could have amounted to a friend saying, "Why don't you start ministering to inmates, Charlie?" But something niggled here.

A note in a web forum from someone mentioning Moffat's penchant for alcohol. A reference to an archbishop Sorenson, now a cardinal. A scandal involving the police looking the other way on a drunk-driving charge.

Bingo. Of course, I had nothing but a rumor. I needed confirmation. A phone call could do that.

"Like some coffee?" Emile asked as I rose.

"Yes, please."

Emile stood up also. "A suggestion, if I may."

I hesitated. He took that as an invitation to continue.

Emile held his hands out as though he were a conductor and I were the symphony. "I think you should turn your attention to a story about young entrepreneurs who have made it big in the financial speculation field."

"You mean like you?"

If he had a baton, he would have tapped it against an invisible podium. "Exactly."

"I don't think so."

"I think it will be brilliant. As you can see, I am extremely photogenic."

"Are you."

"Absolutely. Now, Seth knew me growing up. He can be one of your sources."

"I need my phone." I fled.

SETH

From the Antoine Vermicelli interrogation files:

Number of times "Not tellin' you nuffin'" was said: ~~4~~
~~5 7 10~~ 12

Skills: Trained in military reserve, great shot with a sniper rifle, makes a killer Denver omelette.

Hobbies: Reading, killing people, wearing lacy thongs. (Hoo-hah! There is such a thing as too much truth . . .)

"C'mon, focus, Antoine. Who is Moffat's boss?"
Antoine giggled. "Cardinal Thorenthon. Fat-tho."
I wrote, Cardinal Sorenson. "Is Sorenson involved?"
Antoine laughed in his dozy, half-asleep way. "He ith too dumb to live. Mackth ith in charghe. Theo handleth the money."
"Theo."
"Yeth."
I skimmed through my notes.

Eugene: Driver. Antoine likes him. Former actor?

Max Cobber (Cooper?): The brain. Tough, smart.

Theo Cussler, Kissler, Kessler? Handles the
money. Prison time for embezzlement. Pedo –
likes little girls. Antoine: "Happy to put a cap in him
for free." Also makes bombs. Antoine: "He learned
how in prison, ha-ha."

Antoine drooled. What a treat to watch.

"So it's just you four, Moffat's henchmen."

"He callth uth hith apothleth."

"His apostles?"

"Yesh. We're shaving our shouls. Doing God'sh work."

"Right." Antoine had shifted out of his lisp again, gravitating to his slur. Good; if he lisped too long, I started to talk like him. "Tell me more about you."

Antoine's face grew hard. "Phony."

Well, hell, I thought, here we go again. "Got it, you're a big phony. Let's move on." Last time I'd tried following this line of questioning, it had deteriorated into his babbling to himself. Who ever heard of an assassin with an inferiority complex?

"Phony," he mumbled. "Blood. Carnage. Watch 'em die. Phone us."

"Wow. You run a dial-a-hit call center?"

He turned his eyes back to me and blathered something that didn't sound like English.

"Forget about being a phony. Pay attention. Who else does Moffat plan to kill?"

"Cobber never tellsh. No namesh 'til a day or two before we shart watching 'em. Then we go hunting. Yee-haw. Hi-yo, Shilver."

I shook my head in frustration. "Shit."

"Okay."

"Don't! Just answer my questions."

"Okay."

"So Max Cobber doesn't tell you who the target is 'til you're heading out the door, is that right?"

"Shurre." Antoine rocked to one side like a wind-up tin soldier winding down.

"Tell me about Cobber."

"Uushhed to be lawyer. Hash an expenshive pen with a mountain on itsh top. Sharkey's pal."

"Sharkey?" I blinked in surprise. "That's who you get your hardware from?"

"Yerrrrghs."

"And Theo is hurt?"

"Yeersss."

I left him to chat with himself and took my notes to Kaylee. She was on the couch in the living room, laptop across her thighs. She looked up at me with a combination of bleakness and fire.

"Find anything useful?" I asked.

Kaylee looked at the screen as if trying to remember. Then she said, "Moffat avoided a drunk-driving charge with the help of his boss."

I handed her my steno pad. "See if you can match these names with Moffat."

She stared at the sheet, brows pinching together. "Okay."

"How are you doing?"

"Empty."

"I'll get you some food."

"I'm not that kind of empty." She turned her gaze back to the screen.

"If there's anything I can do –"

"Send me back."

"That I can't do."

"Won't, you mean."

"Yeah."

Emile sat at the kitchen table, a second laptop in front of him. I made myself a cup of coffee. He looked knives at me.

"What are you going to do with you-know-who when you're finished?"

I shrugged. "Not really sure." Then I made a pistol shape with my fingers. "Maybe that."

"That is cold-blooded murder."

"Only technically."

Around noon, Antoine started coming out of it. I made him a sandwich and coffee, and freed his left hand so he could eat and drink.

"Need the bathroom."

"You'll have to wait 'til Chase gets home."

He scowled at me and ate. When he finished, I told him to set his arm back in the locking band so I could secure the padlock.

Late in the afternoon Chase rolled up in his BARC van. Soon after, Locke arrived in a black SUV. Emile had Chinese food from Hung-Fu Noodles delivered, and we sat in the downstairs living room to eat. Kaylee picked at her noodle box with chopsticks and that disdainful air of *we who do not need cutlery*. Locke went after his noodles with a fork. It actually looked like an attack – noodle death by stabbing.

"We have work to do," I said around a mouthful.

That got the group's attention.

"Kaylee's dug up dirt on Moffat, but so far she hasn't found anything about his men."

She stared into her noodles box and clicked her chopsticks together.

I turned to Locke. "Can you and your chopra do anything?"

"Alas, I cannot. Terribly sorry. Any manifestation of my power in this world will push the Big Man that much closer to waking. I dare not."

"Okay, then," I said. "We need to talk to everyone we know. Everyone in the family, I mean. We put the word out, tell everybody to get hard to find."

"You can run but you cannot hide," came Devan's voice from upstairs.

Quentin followed closely with, "Shut up."

I looked at Kaylee. "You have a list, right?"

"On my computer back home."

"I printed it out; I've got it in my bag." I turned to Chase and Emile, lowering my voice. "Before we call anyone, we all need new phones – or at least new numbers. An – my man says Moffat has a guy who can trace phone calls. That's how they knew which motel I'd booked. So change your number. We need everyone to go to ground for a while."

"That will be difficult," Emile said. "People need to work."

"People need to stay alive. They can go on vacation. Or come here."

Emile glowered. "Excuse me?"

Then Chase decided to lob a bomb into the group; he made a high-pitched squeak in the back of his throat. "Shouldn't Nathan be back from work?"

20

KAYLEE

Emile made a great show of pacing back and forth in the kitchen, speaking loudly into his phone with someone at the Office Zone outlet where Nathan worked. No one had seen Nathan leave for the day.

Seth and the boys went back into moving mode, loading Chase's BARC van with beds and furniture. Emile had yet another house nearby.

I wandered in a mental haze, contemplating memories of heaven. Seth told me to help with the move, saying it would get my thoughts off my problems, but that just brought one of my problems on stronger. When I started carrying boxes out to the truck, Emile put his phone away and followed me like a puppy. When Chase reached for the other end of the mattress I wanted to move, Emile cut in and took over.

"You really ought to visit my office sometime," Emile said. "Then you can see where it all happens. As part of your story, you understand."

"Hmm."

We carried the box spring down the steps.

"My office has a spectacular view of the river and City Hall. I have always felt one should look down on City Hall." Emile chortled more than the line deserved. "That will make an excellent quote, don't you think?"

No, it won't. I kept that to myself.

We had the truck loaded by early evening. Chase and Seth climbed in to head over to the new place.

"9726 Mole Boulevard." Emile pointed up the street. "Just stick to this avenue. When you get to Mole, hang a right; it's three houses up."

"Can you fit one more in there?" I asked Seth desperately.

"Nope."

So they left, sticking me with Emile. Damn it.

I went upstairs to where Quentin watched a loud movie with Devan.

"Aren't you helping?" I asked.

"I'm on guard duty." A wave in Devan's direction. "Besides, none of this stuff is going." He looked longingly at the enormous television. "We're going to rough it."

Devan sat on the love seat, sipping from a water bottle, his knees up to his chest. Fascination and horror crisscrossed his face. Meanwhile, on the screen, one actor had started sawing off another actor's ear.

"*Reservoir Dogs,*" Quentin said. "My mom loves Tarantino's movies. She named me after him."

Devan glared at him with raw contempt. "Vile."

"Wait 'til you see Pulp Fiction."

I went through the rooms upstairs and picked out things to take. Emile followed me and provided unnecessary help.

An hour later the front door flew open.

"Shit shit shit!" came from Seth downstairs.

I headed that way, glad for the distraction.

"What is it?" Emile called from the top of the steps.

Seth made a slitting gesture across his throat. Then he whispered, just loud enough to carry over the racket from the upstairs television, "Cops!"

Emile sucked a breath through his teeth. "Oh no."

I stepped past him to the staircase as Chase and Seth scrambled past us. Emile followed me, his face a mask of fright.

"Act natural," I said.

"I am. This is how I act when the cops have come to take me away to prison for kidnapping."

"Then try acting like someone who isn't guilty. We don't even know if they're looking for us."

I opened the door. Two women officers were walking along the sidewalk. They turned at the path to our house and marched toward us like soldiers.

Emile's face turned ashen.

"Quiet," I whispered. "Nothing to worry about."

From upstairs someone yelled, "Hell!" and cut off.

The officers stopped at the open door, ignored me, and faced down the man beside me.

"Hello," the taller of the two said, "Are you Emile Chantal?"

"No. Yes. I mean, yes, I am. What can I do for you, officer?"

"You can tell us where Seth Brown is," the shorter officer said. Mirror shades hid her eyes.

Emile chewed air.

I tried on a sweet smile, which probably looked ghastly. "Who are you looking for, Flora?"

The woman's gaze swiveled to me. "And you are?"

"Kaylee Jerrel, Channel Forty-Eight News."

Both officers rocked back as though I had swung at them. Recognition dawned on their faces, followed by a wariness that came out in a throbbing vein on the taller woman's temple. Their gazes flickered to the bird's nest on my head.

"A salon accident," I said. "I'm doing an exposé. You'll see it next month on the six o'clock show."

Officer Flora Bingham's brow creased. "We're looking for a young man. Seth Brown. I believe you know him." She looked at Emile.

"I knew him out west. Before I came here."

"And you spoke to him recently. Is that correct?"

Emile choked. I intercepted the question, slipping my hand into his. "Sweetie, there haven't been any calls from anyone called Seth Brown." I smiled at the officers. "Emile is my boyfriend. This Seth person is in some kind of trouble?"

The shorter woman, Dorothy, took off her glasses. "We aren't at liberty to say."

A thump came from upstairs.

"Well, then," I said, "we're in the middle of moving."

"It would help if you answer our questions."

"We have. We haven't heard from anyone named Seth Brown. What did he do? Kill someone?"

Flora's brow shot up. "Oh, no, nothing like that. I mean, we aren't at liberty to discuss our interest in Mr. Brown. Mr. Chantal, you have roommates. Is that correct?"

"Tenants."

I squeezed Emile's hand. "I'll get them; I'd love to hear what you ask them."

"That won't be necessary." Dorothy cleared her throat and drew a business card from her flak jacket's pocket. "If you do hear from Mr. Brown, please contact us immediately. This is part of an ongoing investigation." I could picture the projection on the inside of her skull, a vision of herself featured in slow motion on Channel Forty-Eight with my voiceover intoning, "Next on NewsNite: Did city police cross the line?"

SETH

The fuzz. Damn.

Chase and I ran up the steps as Kaylee and Emile moved to cover the door. Quentin came toward me, opening his mouth. I drew a finger-line across my throat.

Chase stood like a statue beside me. Quentin had turned white. I shifted my gaze to Devan.

Once in a rare while, the patron saint of dumb luck steps into your life. Things have gone totally wrong, and now a mean ball of shit is heading straight for a fan. But the patron saint takes pity on you and does two things: she puts you near the flight path, and she calls your attention to a beautiful black leather catcher's mitt that happens to be lying at your feet.

I saw the change in his eyes as he launched from the couch.

"Hel-ffff!" My hand caught his mouth. He flailed and kicked. Quentin pounced on his legs. I flung Devan against the couch and tried sitting on him. He elbowed my ribs. We knocked over a stool, sending a plastic water bottle shooting toward the stairs. I got Devan into a headlock, but his dance moves made it impossible to hold on.

Chase scooped up the bottle as if it were somehow important. Then he tugged his left sleeve over his hand and soaked it with water, all the while that Quentin and I wrestled with Sir Devan of Grand Mal. Chase held his sleeve over Devan's face. A mix of sweet and rot filled my nose. Devan became dead weight in my arms. My hearing receded to a dull throb.

Chase had a dumb grin on his face. My hearing rolled back in, and I heard him giggling. ". . . practicing that all day."

"What did you do?" I meant to say. It came out, "Wmgogly?"

Apparently he could translate that. He answered around his idiot smile. "Chloroform. We use it to put down small animals."

"Gurgle," I said. Then the room leaned over and slapped my face with the couch.

The stupidest animal in this world plodded away from a large French Country style house. The fox struggled with the revelation that she now recognized "French Country" as a kind of human den. When the huge white dog reached the mouth of the cul-de-sac (another concept invading her mind), she watched just long enough to see it wander off drooling along the sidewalk, nose to the ground, wheezing.

The fox raced onto the porch, pawed and whined at the door, then slipped away to the cover of a shrub. The door opened with a creak as she burrowed beneath the bush, leaving only her white back showing.

"Bonzer?" a female human said.

The fox whined softly.

"Okay, boy. Just a sec."

The fox panted in expectation. The sound of lumps landing in the metal bowl made her mouth water. Food had been hard to find, with the exception of a squirrel she had cornered last night.

"There you go, Bonzey. Come and get it."

The fox crawled through the shrub to the other side, out of sight.

"Silly dog," came the amused voice. The door thumped shut.

The fox scampered back to the porch, wolfing down the nuggets of food. They tasted nothing at all like fresh lemming, or anything else she knew, but they filled her belly.

A thunderous roar. Bonzer charged along the sidewalk, looking a little like a polar bear the fox had once fled from after stealing a seal flipper.

The fox leaped over the short fence into the neighbor's yard. Bonzer followed at a dead run. The fox cleared the next fence and the next. Bonzer gained with each jump.

Wait, she thought, why am I fleeing? She dug her claws in and turned. Bonzer barreled toward her, jaws wide.

The fox flicked a tiny burst of worldstuff over the dog's soul. Bonzer stopped his front legs before his back ones, creating an end-over-end pile-up of stinking dog.

The idiotic thing shook drool from his lips and took a tentative step forward. The fox pondered sending another jolt of power. Then bared her teeth and pounced – landing nose to nose with poor Bonzer. He yelped and scrambled to an urgent appointment elsewhere.

The fox continued her trek, glad of a fuller belly. She knew where Seth Color-of-bark lay asleep. That other mind still seeped into hers. She had abandoned the thought of biting even a small piece of the man's meat out of him. Someone trying to save the multiverse likely needed all his parts.

Seth trusted the power called Locke that lurked in his den.

He didn't seem to know about the other one, bound to the man above the garage where the stone-with-eyes was parked.

The fox scratched her chin with a hind paw and mulled this over. The creature over the garage smelled of blood and death. A cord of worldstuff – plasm, according to Seth's thoughts – joined it to the mind of the captive human. It clearly could influence the man. A new thought followed: Can I control Seth Color-of-bark through our bond?

To her astonishment, the idea made her feel like she had eaten a month-dead lemming.

The Book of
Exorcism

21

SETH

The grandmother of all headaches sat knitting away on top of my neck.

I woke sprawled on a couch with loud music from another room urging the pain along. Locke sat across from me on the floor, his back against the wall, legs crossed at the ankles.

"Welcome back," he said.

I rubbed my fingers through bristly hair. "What . . . ?" The room did a pirouette. I shut up and shut my eyes.

"You were dosed with chloroform. Our man Chase spent much of his workday practicing making it from tap water. A fortunate thing, really."

My mouth tasted like I'd eaten something raw that had spent a week dead near a sewage outlet. "He didn't need to get me as well. Where's Devan?"

"Chase and Quentin took Devan's unconscious self to the new house. Chase chained him to a wall in a spare room. Devan is not likely to be pleased when he wakes."

I rose slowly and rolled my neck. "I don't suppose they took Antoine as well."

"The assassin? They did not."

"Can you help with him, then? We need to get out of here."

He gave me a doubtful look. "I suppose. It is unlikely I shall draw the attention of your father through this course of action."

"Any word on the cops?"

"Kaylee dealt with them. Having a journalist present while they performed a warrantless search apparently did not appeal."

Locke joined me for a walk downstairs. I stopped in the kitchen for a glass of water, and discovered there weren't any glasses. Kaylee knelt next to a box, setting the last of the bowls into it.

"Any cups?" I said over her music.

Kaylee shook her head. "Packed," she mouthed.

"Can I have that bowl?" I pointed to it.

I filled it from the tap. "How are you?" I yelled.

She gestured me closer. "Emile wants me to interview him for some documentary that would shorten my career to the day after it aired." A pleading look filled her face. "Can you tell him I'm not interested?"

"Why don't you tell him that?"

"I have."

"Try again. Good luck. Me, I have a killer to drug up so we can move him to the new house."

"Have Emile talk to him; that'll put him under in no time."

I gave her a grin and handed the bowl back.

Locke and I ducked outside and took the staircase up to Antoine's makeshift cell. The suite smelled musty. Venetian blinds cut the afternoon light down to movie-theater levels.

Antoine's head snapped up when we entered. I drew my gun and made a show of checking its magazine so he'd get the message. He looked contemptuously at me, then moved his gaze to Locke.

Locke gave him a cheery smile. "Good evening. I am the Devil himself."

Antoine looked him over and grinned back. "I'm the Devil's nastier brother."

"No, you are not. I would recall if I had a brother. I am part of the godhead. You are merely a mortal, possibly with a psychosis."

Antoine tugged on the iron loops around his wrists. "I could kick you to death with one foot free, even chained in this chair."

I cleared my throat. "Here ends the pissing contest. Antoine, old buddy, old bean, the plan is as usual: you cooperate or we shoot you."

He grimaced. "I need the bathroom."

"You can have it after we drug you."

I passed my pistol to Locke and motioned him to stand behind Antoine. It occurred to me Locke might not be capable of shooting the killer. Well, hell. Antoine didn't need to know that.

I grabbed the syringe and glass of amytal from the shelf. He glared but didn't flinch as I gave him a smaller dose than usual. Hopefully enough to sauté his brain but leave his body able to walk as far as the garage.

I rubbed my aching temples then unlocked the loops that held him to the chair. Chains between his ankles and between his wrists limited his movements. He got up gingerly, stretched his legs, touched his toes. I stepped well back.

He motioned sullenly at the bathroom. "I need more than a whiz this time."

"I'll watch. No privacy here."

That bought me a sour look.

I shrugged. "Trust me; this is going to traumatize me more than it will you."

Antoine strode into the bathroom and took care of business.

"Pretty thong," I said by way of conversation. That earned me another murderous look. Antoine got his revenge a moment later when the fragrance wafted my way. I got us both out of the bathroom as fast as I could.

Amytal works quickly. In a few minutes he began whistling his baked-idiot rendition of "Jingle Bells," adding a festiveness to the proceedings. I gave him a couple more minutes, then took the dog collar and chain off his neck and motioned toward the door.

The killer's eyes swelled. His lip quivered. "What are you doing with me?"

"We're just moving you."

Antoine stumbled to his chair and slumped. "Ergh. Look. My family hazh money. Lotsh of it. My uncle. He'll pay."

"If we were getting rid of you, we'd just do it here and carry your dead ass out and dump you in a ditch somewhere. We have to move house, so we're taking you with us."

His gaze darted back and forth. Locke stood, arms crossed and looking bored.

Antoine giggled. "Going for a walk." He rose on wobbling legs.

"Good." I gestured at the door. He wove toward it, stopped as though he had forgotten something, and pulled the door open. Then he stepped forward into empty space, the chain between his ankles catching.

Locke caught him by his shirt collar. "I suspect if we leave him to negotiate the stairs with his legs chained together, we shall have a broken heap at the bottom."

I pondered that. If it happened, I'd have to heal him. That just might purge the amytal from his system, which would leave me with a fully functional trained killer in chains. I had a feeling the chains would be less of an issue for a drug-free Antoine than they were for Antoine on truth serum.

"Hold still." I knelt and unlocked the padlocks holding the ends of the chain to Antoine's ankle irons. Then I stepped past him out onto the first stair.

"Antoine, take the steps one at a time and go slow. Understand?"

"Shhhurrre."

"Good."

Antoine hummed a jaunty tune I didn't know. Locke followed, scratching an itch on his neck with the pistol muzzle. The killer started tapping the tips of his shoes on the steps as he made his way down. By the bottom he was swaying and murmuring, "Daisy, Daisy . . ." I held the door into the house for him. He stepped in, grinning and muttering.

I caught Antoine's shoulder and turned him toward the garage door. Antoine kept turning until he faced us. Drool made its way down his chin.

His gaze fell on Locke. "Old friend."

"He's not your friend. And you're wasted." I pointed at the garage door. "Go that way."

The chains on his wrists rattled as he walked. I looked at the chain I carried for his ankles and told myself I should just lock his legs together again.

At the door to the garage, he turned again. His mouth widened in a clownish grin. "Herm . . . Herm . . ." A long whistle came from him. "Hermes."

I blinked and looked at Locke.

The Prince of Darkness shrugged. "A lucky guess."

"How does someone just happen to guess you used to be a Greek god?" I asked.

It must have been residual effects of chloroform. My head throbbed, which distracted me and slowed me down. Should have paid more attention to Antoine than to Locke. The killer's wrist chains were in flight when I looked back at him. They took the side of my head. Down I went, the ankle chain unwinding from my wrist. Through a haze I saw Antoine swing his chain to catch Locke's gun, flinging it against the wall. It bounced along the floor, coming to stop a few paces beyond my reach.

Locke's eyes flashed, literally flashed, shifting from human-like black irises in white to his usual whirling galaxies.

"Oh, bugger," he said. Antoine fired a kick at his belly. The Prince of Darkness dropped like a sack of stones. Not something you see often.

"Pain," Locke wheezed. "Yuck."

I dived for the pistol. Antoine stepped over me and booted it into the corner next to the garage door. I rolled onto my back and kicked him in the balls. He screwed up his face as if he'd swallowed a mouthful of hot peppers then he laughed. "That works better when you haven't drugged up this body, little mouse." The slur had vanished.

One hand closed on my shoulder. Strong. Inhumanly strong. And his eyes . . .

Like Locke's now. Galaxies spinning in darkness. As Locke would say: Oh, bugger.

"Locke," I gasped. "The gun."

"Ow," he moaned, massaging his belly with his hand. "Terribly sorry, old chum. I really cannot get involved."

Antoine giggled and muttered something in a language I didn't know. He grabbed the ankle chain and slammed it against my head, knocking me on my stomach. Then the links were around my neck pulling me to my knees. I struggled to work my fingers between the chain and my throat, but that didn't help much. Through all this, I wondered how long a resurrection would take. Hit the button, I'd be back in a few minutes. Assuming I died quickly and the rez latched on to me instead of a dead mouse in the house's crawl space.

Then I discovered I couldn't visualize the button, couldn't hold on to it through the throbbing in my head. The world faded to black.

22

KAYLEE

I had even more reason to die now that Emile had lodged the idea in his head that I would be making a documentary about him. Out of sheer desperation, I turned on someone's tablet and speakers to drown him out. The music was two parts techno to one part country, guaranteeing mental indigestion. It was still better than listening to Emile.

I finished packing the dishes and stacked the box in the living room. Emile set down two open boxes of books.

"Just need my business books," he shouted, trying to be heard over the music. "Managing my companies is paramount." He gave me the thoughtful look I'd learned to dread. "My cousin Laura will be a great source. I manage her investments. Set up a plan that combines assorted no-load mutual funds to get her a much higher rate than market return."

I pondered pounding my head against a wall.

A thump made me wonder whether someone else was listening to Emile too. It came again, followed by a scrabbling sound at the front door.

Emile yelled on about investing early and how a professional such as himself could get you fourteen percent compound interest steadily over thirty-five years if you were prepared for a little risk. I ran for the door to get away from him and threw it open.

Something brushed past. My gaze swiveled down to see that little white dog race across the room. I wondered how it had followed me all the way from downtown. Was it a sign from God, after all?

The fluffy tail vanished into the corridor to the garage.

"Wha –" Emile began. I ran after it.

I stopped dead around the corner. Emile plowed into me, catching us both before we hit the floor. Together we gawked.

A stranger had a chain around Seth's neck and was choking him purple. This could only be one man: Antoine. The dog's teeth were in his shin. The killer growled and hammered a fist down at the animal. It leapt deftly out of reach, Seth's eyes popping as the chain wrenched his neck. A white blur hurtled back in. Antoine pulled the chain free and swung it, catching the animal's belly. The dog yelped, staggering back as Antoine flung himself at the garage door. I only noticed the pistol when the killer scooped it up.

We were going to die. Marvelous.

The animal leapt up, jaws closing on Antoine's pistol arm.

"Aarrarraggharharrrrrrrrrrgggggg!" Emile roared, running at the killer. His feet left the floor as though gravity had simply turned off. His right leg jutted out ahead of him while his left tucked under his butt.

The killer stood glued in place by Emile's bowel-loosening bellow. Even the dog stared as Emile's foot collided with the killer's chest. The pistol skittered across the floor. The dog let go and scrambled back to watch the fun.

Emile launched a blizzard of punches and kicks. Antoine blocked with equal speed.

The dog attacked. Antoine saw it coming and kicked it in mid flight with a stomach-turning crunch.

Seth was crawling toward the gun, moving as though his left arm didn't work. The white body landed on him, bowling him over. The dog didn't get up.

How best, I wondered, to get myself killed in all this? Terror made my heart race and my knees wobble, but that was just the physiological part of me, the living body insisting on staying that way. The thoughtful side recognized that if Antoine got the gun and I fought him for it, I could probably take a bullet. On the other hand, maybe that would count as an indirect form of suicide.

Indecision is a bitch. She and I were not supposed to be on speaking terms.

23

THE FOX

The fox enjoyed death by snapped neck about as much as she had enjoyed death by bleeding into snow. At least it finished faster. With a shake of her soul, she rose from her body.

The power bound to Antoine hovered behind him, shaped of blue crystals or sharp-edged stone. Claws lashed. The creature turned a piercing glare upon her. The fox growled back and prepared to pounce.

Then whiteness blazed, that distinctive glare of impossible light that only shone through a gateway between worlds. A heady smell of fresh lemming filled her nose.

The fox snarled. Only dead things lay through there. She pulled back. The portal advanced, reaching for her.

The frightened vastness ruled this portal. Another trap, *the fox thought, remembering metal teeth sinking into her leg. Her soul barked. A burst of plasm shot into the coruscating lemming-flavored maw. The portal closed on its prey. Plasm rippled as it snapped shut.*

Good, *the fox thought, turning her attention back to the chiseled blue monster. She wasn't about to leave the protector of the multiverse to a petty brute like this.*

SETH

When Emile came screaming into the room, it looked like he really had earned that red belt. He laid into Antoine like a madman. But Antoine, even on amytal, did a little better.

The gun lay near Locke, but he was about as useful right now as my nipples. I went for it and got a shattered kneecap for my trouble. That hurt worse than being strangled. I couldn't even heal myself since I might need to do something else any second now. A heal would suck away my strength.

For some bizarre reason, the arctic fox from Antoine's collar had appeared and sunk its teeth into Antoine. Had it hunted him down for wearing its fur? Maybe I was just hallucinating from oxygen deprivation.

Antoine kicked the figment of my imagination hard. The fox's body tumbled into me. It didn't move, tongue danging from its mouth.

The drug seemed to make Antoine see double now. He kept making wild swings at air while Emile pummeled him. Then he got lucky and sank a punch and a kick. When Emile went down, Antoine stumbled past Locke, snatched up the pistol, and turned back to Emile. Emile came up off the floor fast, his face crimson, contorting in a mix of rage, pain, and fear.

Point blank. The gun barked; even a pistol with a silencer makes a loud noise. The back of Emile's head sprayed red across the floor.

The drug must still be messing Antoine up. He moved as though attempting a Michael Jackson moonwalk with a ferret swinging from his testicles. Kaylee stood like a statue, I had a cracked knee, and Locke treated the whole thing like a spectator sport. His eyes were in Milky Way mode, which usually meant he and his higher self had tuned in to each other. He did nothing.

I hit the Resurrection Button. Maybe Emile and I could trade resurrections enough to suck all the bullets out of the pistol. A lame chance, but what the hell. The rez whined to a high note with no hesitation.

Then Locke said, "Oh, bugger. You really should not have done that."

"What?"

"The resurrection."

"But Emile –"

"It has gone to that animal, not Emile."

I stared at the bundle of white fur. "That?"

"It is dead, Seth," Locke intoned. He reached to clasp my arm. I tugged free of Mr. Useless.

"Please, old chum." Locke grabbed my arm again, digging fingers into bare flesh.

Wowza. A new scene overlapped my vision. Locke now had a glowing white shape filling him, too bright to look at, with a narrow silvery wire uncoiling into the distance. If I moved my eyes, the coil of wire seemed to vanish into the point farthest away from wherever I happened to look at that moment.

Two coils of the silver grew from me, one attaching to Locke, the second vanishing into the distance.

Antoine waved the gun around while doing the funky chicken. A yellowish glow pulsed within his body. A towering blue shape with jagged edges overlapped him, a head and a half taller. Even the blue creature had a winding cord that emerged from its neck and spiraled away.

A blazing white thing had the crystal monster's left arm in its jaws. Fox-shaped, but bigger. A silver wire uncoiled from the corpse beside me and advanced on it. The fox turned burning blood red eyes to it and bared translucent teeth. Then it spit. A ripple of something thrummed in the air and nailed the wire in flight. The wire from its body and the rippling pulse of something-or-other wound around each other like mating snakes. The wire grew straighter, like a cord being pulled tight.

"What the hell?" I said.

Locke pointed at the blue crystal creature. "That is a phoni, or phonus. A murder spirit. It appears to be inhabiting Antoine's body."

"What's the fox doing?"

"Attempting to extract the creature from Antoine. Impressive, that. The phonus is part of the godhead like me. In ancient Greece the phonoi would drive people to kill each other for the sport of it."

"So why don't you get off your ass and do something?"

"I am aligned with the mythos of Christendom these days. If I challenge one from Zeus's pantheon, I threaten to wake Zeus himself. If that occurs, Jehovah will also certainly wake. It is best they never meet."

"Hey, wait a minute. The fox is a ghost now?"

"Apparently."

The phonus kicked at the white spirit. The fox backed off, teeth gleaming like knives, then leaped at it. This time it caught the phonus by the throat. The phonus separated from Antoine.

"Oh, now that is interesting," Locke murmured.

The phonus, flaring like burning alcohol, sprawled out on an invisible surface above the floor. As the fox ripped at the creature's throat, something showered up, thick and dark.

"Locke? Is that blood?"

"Not precisely. But you have the correct idea."

The wire from the fox spirit to its body grew taut.

"That's the resurrection taking over, isn't it?" I swore. "If the fox goes back to its body, there won't be anything to fight that thing."

"Alas, that is correct. I rather suspect we are screwed."

Remembering Emile, I slammed the Resurrection Button. Static buzzed around us.

Locke uttered a groan. "Oh, it is much too late for that. Emile will not be here in time."

The fox's strand tightened and pulled it back toward its body. Claws scrabbled at air, and the phonus was dragged partway before the fox's jaws lost hold. The phonus clutched at the wound in its throat, catching the shower of darkness from within itself. It lay not quite on the floor, more like two or three inches above, but appeared to lift itself up, struggling to stand.

"If we were in, say, a church, it wouldn't be able to do anything, right?"

Locke glanced at me with those blazing eyes. "We are not on consecrated ground."

The phonus staggered toward Antoine's prone body. His crotch, arms, and legs had flickering dark shapes in them. Injuries.

"Maybe we don't need to be." I flung myself over Locke. My shattered knee lodged a complaint in triplicate as I caught hold of Antoine's wrist. Heal, I thought, and felt familiar warmth surge through my hand.

Even without me touching Locke, the video-game view lingered. Whiteness surged down my arm into Antoine's body.

Locke's voice rang with astonishment. "Oh!"

The phonus didn't look happy. Its crystalline claws descended on Antoine, but a spark arced out of him and slammed against it. Mr. Crystal reared back.

I tightened my grip on Antoine. "Mine, asshole."

The phonus turned and lunged at me. Behind it leaped a blazing white fox-shape, the cord binding it to its body drawn out like a guitar string. Jaws closed on the wire that wound away from the crystal monster. The cord snapped.

The phonus screamed, diving sideways at the garage door. Its severed cord danced like a high-voltage wire spitting current. The cord melted away, shrinking into the monster's body. The creature passed through solid wood and vanished.

KAYLEE

"That," Locke said, "was brilliant." Seth held Antoine's arm.

I stared, still shaking, at the two of them. "What just happened?"

Seth grimaced. "Give me a moment. Right now – ouch – I need to do something about my knee." He rolled, wincing, onto his back and straightened his leg.

"You can heal yourself, right?" I immediately felt stupid saying it.

"Yeah. But it's no fun. Get that chain. I've started healing Antoine. The truth serum we shot into him will get purged. Lock his ankles together."

I stepped over him to the assassin. Seth tossed a keyring to me, and I locked the padlocks into place.

Beside Locke, the white dog hopped to its feet. Eyes like dry blood stared at me, unblinking, then turned to Seth. The animal barked in disgust and started licking blood off itself.

"I don't understand what happened," I said.

Seth gritted his teeth and struggled to sit up. "Antoine was possessed by a demon from ancient Greece. The fox's ghost dragged it out of him, but the creature got free when I resurrected it – the fox, I mean. The demon tried to go back into Antoine, but I triggered a heal. That protected him. I think."

"It did," Locke said. "You funneled power from your own aspect into him. The phonus could not cross that barrier. A brilliant play."

Seth gave him a sour look. "Someone had to do something."

"Can we back up a bit?" I said. "That is a fox? Where did you get a fox from?"

"I resurrected it from the collar of Antoine's jacket."

I blinked.

Seth grinned. "Antoine is here because I ran into him outside a pub downtown. When he pulled his gun, I punched him so hard, I thought I'd killed him." Locke gave him an odd look. "Turned out I hadn't. But anyway, I started a resurrection and his fur collar turned into a full-grown arctic fox." He scratched the stubble on his chin. "I'm glad the rez latched on to his collar instead of the leather on his jacket. Otherwise I'd have had to pull Antoine out of a cow."

That shot down the sign-from-God theory. "So it followed Antoine here just because he used to wear it as his collar?"

Locke grunted. "I believe it had other reasons."

"How could it have found Antoine? We're miles from downtown."

"The animal appears to have returned to this world with a much-improved résumé," Locke said with a wary look.

"How could it hurt something that's part of the godhead?" Seth asked.

"A phonus is the merest sliver of the godhead's totality. Battling it requires little strength or intelligence." Locke raised his brow. "Of course, this animal would have fared much better had you not forcibly returned it to its body after Antoine killed it."

Seth gazed at the floor, embarrassed. "Damn, I know. It was winning too." He shrugged. "That cord coming out of the phonus. A connection to the godhead, right?"

"Correct."

"And the fox chewed through it."

Locke shifted, looking uncomfortable. "If the phonus is a free power now, I may have to track it down eventually. It cannot be allowed to wander about on its own."

The fox gave him a sideways look.

At that moment a gasp drew our attention. Emile's back arched. His eyes flew open, and his jaw fell. Then he turned over and dipped one cheek in his own blood. He flung himself up, wiping his face on his sleeve. "It's real. The tunnel of light, everything. It's fucking real."

Locke snorted.

Emile gazed at him for a long moment. Then he began to cry. Huge convulsions and sobs. Seth reached out, almost involuntarily, but Emile didn't see. He stumbled away toward the living room, head in his hands.

I gulped as sweat popped out on my forehead. Mr. Interview-me-about-my-idiotic-career was a pain in the ass. But Mr. Flying-drop-kicking-martial-arts-master had a lovely firm butt.

THE FOX

What, *the fox wondered,* do I have to do to get a meal around here?

The Book of the Committee

24

SETH

I rested on the floor while my mangled knee fixed itself. It still felt aflame as I straightened up and tried not to snark at my stepdad. Despite all I owed Locke, watching him sit around doing nothing during Antoine's rampage gnawed.

I motioned with my chin at the napping assassin. "Shouldn't he be awake by now?"

"One would think so."

"We'd better get him to the other house."

Locke propped the door to the garage open. Limping, I took Antoine's legs while Locke hoisted him up by his arms. Kaylee opened the door to the backseat and we heaved him in.

"What are we doing with your pet?" Kaylee asked.

The fox bolted at her, snapping at her ankles. She hopped back with a shriek.

"I believe it dislikes being referred to as a 'pet,'" Locke said. The fox barked, its tail in the air.

"Is it coming to the new house?"

The fox's ears straightened at that. It hopped over Antoine, slipped between the front seats, and sprawled on the passenger side.

"I guess that's a yes," I said. "Where's Emile?"

Kaylee turned an intriguing shade of pink, which made no sense. "Showering, I think."

"Can you bring him along when he gets out? He probably shouldn't be driving."

"Me? Why can't Locke?"

Locke cocked a Spock-like eyebrow. "Somebody has filled my vehicle to its very roof, leaving no room for passengers."

Kaylee's voice mixed desperation with giddiness. "He wants me to interview him for his moronic documentary." I began to wonder if she had another meltdown coming on. She didn't have enough hair left for a second round.

"You just need to drive him to the new house," I said. "It's not a tough job."

In the awkward silence I expected Kaylee to bitch some more about Emile. Didn't happen. I considered worrying about it, then decided driving a formerly possessed assassin forty blocks with a wild animal riding shotgun gave me enough to fret over.

Antoine spent the trip comatose. The fox licked itself and watched me drive. Locke followed in his SUV.

At the new house, the fox jumped out of the car with me. It looked around, settled its ears back, and trotted away toward the asphalt. At Mole Boulevard, the fox looked each way and bolted across.

"Hey, don't get yourself killed. Again."

Cars passed. The animal pounced on something, then rolled around in a frenzy. A moment later it came trotting back across the street. When it got closer, I made out the pigeon in its mouth.

"Ugh. Eat that out here."

The fox growled a response around its mouthful. I left it alone and went inside to open the garage. The living room had the smaller pair of couches; we'd left the big one upstairs in the old house. The dining table and chairs were tucked into a kitchen considerably smaller than what we had before.

Locke and I backed our vehicles into the garage and carried Antoine into the house. I went downstairs to look for the others and found Chase in the closet, bolting an iron panel to the wall. It had a thick loop jutting out of its rusty plate.

I cleared my throat to get his attention. His eyes grew wide when he saw me, and his gaze traveled up and down.

"Geez," he said. "What happened to you?"

I looked down at myself. A gruesome reddish stain covered my left knee. "Our hired killer got loose."

Chase gasped.

"Everyone's fine," I said.

Chase eyed me. "Are you upset? I mean, about the chloroforming?"

"You'll have to show me that stuff; it could be handy knowing how to make it."

That earned me a grin.

"Are you ready for our guest? He's unconscious."

Chase picked up a length of chain and padlocked it to the panel. "I think he'll be fine here."

Locke and I carried Sleeping Beauty into the basement, trying not to bounce his head off anything. He snoozed even as we put the dog collar on him.

"Awgh." Chase's nose wrinkled. "He needs a bath."

"You're welcome to give him one. Where's Quentin?"

Chase pointed.

I found Q in the room at the far end of the basement corridor. Devan sat with his back to the wall, a chain binding him to an iron panel above. He gave me a snooty look.

I beckoned to Quentin. "We need a meeting."

We went upstairs. Something scratched at the door. I opened it and found the fox licking bloody fur around its mouth.

"Order us some pizza?" I asked Chase. "When Kaylee and Emile get here, we'll have a council of war."

"What about the dog?" Quentin said. The fox bit at his ankle. He jumped back with a "Hey!"

"Don't call it that if you want to keep all your body parts."

KAYLEE

I quickly shoved stuff I'd stacked on the passenger seat of Emile's car into the trunk, then crouched to peer in the side mirror. My hair looked dreadful, hacked to shreds. I bit my lip and pondered what I could do with it in time for Emile to get out of the shower. Then I came to my senses and glared at the moron in the mirror.

The horizon began to take on a hint of red. The action movie of Emile beating on the assassin played across my thoughts, clashing with the dreadful sitcom of Emile telling me how brilliant his "documentary" would be. Who would want to watch twenty-somethings troll the stock market when they ought to be out there getting some?

Ahem. My mental voice cleared its throat in embarrassment.

When I returned to the house, the hiss of water from the bathroom was gone, replaced with a slurping sound coming from the corridor to the garage. I rounded the corner. Emile had put on black jeans and a red T-shirt. He had a bucket and a mop, and the hallway smelled of lemon cleanser and vinegar. He was mopping up his own blood.

I stood watching him in silence until he noticed. He shook his head slowly. "It's going to ruin the hardwood."

"Yes."

He stopped pushing the mop and squinted. "That gray streak. Brain matter?"

"Maybe."

"And those." He nudged a set of small fragments in the puddle. "Pieces of skull?" His hand crept to the back of his own head. He pushed the fragments to one side and ran the mop through the puddle, swirled it about, and dunked it in the bucket.

"Coffee?" I asked. My voice climbed to a shrill note.

"The coffee maker has been packed."

"Oh. Right."

The mop had turned dark red. Emile swished it about in the bucket and held it above to drip pinkish water then he mopped up more. Finally he peered at the bucket then at the spot where his head had landed after Antoine killed him. He shrugged and carried the bucket past me to the bathroom. He did have a fine butt. I followed and watched him pour the bucket out, admiring his long, lean fingers, the ripple of muscles in his arms. He rinsed and filled again, and went back to the mess in the corridor.

"So," I said, fishing for a conversation starter. "You've never died before."

"No."

"And you didn't think any of it was real. The afterlife stuff."

He stopped pushing the mop. "I thought it was just a silly story. The tunnel. The music. The river."

"River."

"The wide one. With the sand."

"You went to a river when you died?"

"Didn't you?"

"No, I went to . . . somewhere else. But how could you not know about the afterlife?"

He blinked in astonishment.

"What I mean is," I said, "you're one of . . . you. Didn't your mother tell you about your conception?"

Emile choked on something that began as a laugh and turned into the bastard child of a snort and a sob. "Isn't there something you need to put in the car?"

"No. It's packed."

He mopped in silence, then returned to the bathroom to empty the bucket into the tub again, making it look like a gruesome murder scene. Scarlet streaks stained white enamel. I looked on as he used the showerhead to rinse the bath.

Emile followed me to his car. He didn't seem to notice I would be driving his Audi. A minute later, as I drove, he dug something out of his shirt pocket. Small gray stones rattled together in the cup of his hand.

I hazarded a guess of what they could be and wished I hadn't. Then I had to ask.

"Bone fragments," he said tersely.

"Right."

"Look, they fit together like a puzzle."

"That . . ." Makes me want to barf. I finished with, "Is neat."

"Yes."

Treating pieces of one's own occipital plate as keepsakes was weird. Well, actually it was interesting. I looked at him sidelong. His right hand ran through his hair. "It grows back to the same length it was before."

"So did mine," I said eagerly. "I mean, before I hacked it off. And actually I didn't get shot in the head. I got blasted in my chest." I arched my back and pushed out my breasts. "They did grow back to the same size."

An aghast part of my brain played back my mouth's record. My cheeks burned.

Emile scrutinized his bone fragments. "Why did you do that to your hair?"

I swallowed. "I don't know. I felt it tugging on my head and that hurt. Not much. But after . . . the afterlife, I couldn't stand that little bit of pain."

"I used to cut my cousin Laura's hair."

I looked at him, expecting to see mockery in his eyes. "You do hair?"

"No. Just hers. She wanted it cut for school one morning. So I did it. It looked good. She asked me to style it for her high-school graduation. I looked up hairstyling online. We put four dozen pins in it."

"Wow."

"What?"

"You don't seem like the hairdresser type."

"What does that mean?"

"I just mean, you don't..." I shut my mouth, which seemed the best option.

"You passed the Mole Boulevard intersection five blocks ago," he said.

I turned us around at a gas station and got us to the house, parking the car out front. We climbed out. A little bungalow greeted us. Across from it lay a park called Shrieking Trees. The remains of the sun cast long shadows among the playground equipment in its middle.

Inside, the boys had gathered at the oak dining table in the tiny kitchen. The fox had its own chair. Quentin seemed bored but Chase had an eager air to him. Seth looked irritated for some reason, while Locke, in his purple shirt, hands clasped and resting on the table, looked like a judge presiding over a courtroom.

"We're talking about our next moves," Seth said.

"I ordered pizza," said Chase.

Quentin gestured around the table. "We don't have enough chairs."

Emile shrugged. "I'll sit on the couch." He turned and wandered, shoulders slumping, into the living room, his gaze on the little pieces of skull in his hand.

Quentin watched him. "He's awfully quiet."

"He's coming to terms with having been killed," I said.

"We heard. Gone for what, thirty seconds?" Quentin rolled his eyes. "Get over it."

Men. They can even turn dying into an ego issue.

25

SETH

"It's not the right color for an arctic fox at this time of year," Chase said. "I wonder if it'll change."

The fox barked.

"I wouldn't know," I said. The fox stared back at us with its tongue hanging out of the side of its mouth. Having it up at the table felt creepy. The fox acted like being part of the discussion was a given.

"What now?" Quentin asked. "Is your pet kind of like – "

The fox pounced, landing squarely on the table and knocking my beer bottle off. I caught that before it hit the floor and came up to see the fox with its nose an inch from Quentin's and a low snarl in its throat.

Locke grunted. "Loosely translated, I believe that means, 'For the last time, I am not a pet.'"

Chase watched its tail, which jutted straight out behind it. "It understands us? It came back to life smart?"

"I suspect it left this world decades ago," Locke said. "Its spirit is substantially larger than one would expect."

The fox hopped off the table and sat back in its spot between Locke and Chase.

"If it's smart, maybe it can communicate," Chase said. "Hey, Fox, do you understand what I'm saying?"

"Gr."

"That sounds like a yes. Wow."

Quentin snorted. "You looked at it; it made a throaty noise. That doesn't mean it's talking."

"Okay. Fox, growl once for 'yes' and twice for 'no.' Understand?"

"Gr."

"Were you, um, dead up 'til a few days ago?"

"Gr."

"This is stupid," Quentin said. "Ask it something it would say no to. Fox, are you really a monkey in a fox outfit?"

"Gr. Gr."

Silence. Chase spoke up first, his voice drenched in awe. "Maybe we can teach it Morse code."

Quentin leaned his elbows on the table, his eyes narrow. "A short growl for a dot, a long one for a dash?"

"Gr," the fox said. "Grrrrrr."

Quentin's throat quivered. "Holy shit."

"We don't have time for this," I said, thumping my fists on the table. "People are dying and Nathan is missing. Can we focus?"

Kaylee and Emile arrived then. We had one free chair at the table, but Kaylee went over to the couch when Emile did and sat with him. I couldn't figure out what had gotten into Kaylee. She sat on the couch next to him, crossed her legs, uncrossed them, fidgeted with her fingers. She reminded me of a girl I went to high school with, who always acted that way around the jock-of-the-week.

"We need to figure out what we're doing next," I said. "All the brothers need to know they are in danger. Kaylee, you have how many names? Ten?"

"Something like that. But let me see if I understand what Moffat is up to. He wants to reduce your numbers to one. Just Devan. Is that right?"

I nodded.

"How many are there? How long is that going to take?"

Locke drummed his fingers on the table. "There are a lot. That is enough to know for the moment."

I rolled my eyes. "According to Antoine, Moffat figures there were forty of us born. Apparently that number is all over the Bible."

"Is he right?" Kaylee asked.

Quentin laughed out loud.

Locke fluttered his fingers in that annoying way he had when he wanted to change the subject. "It really does not matter. As we have seen, his men could trigger Armageddon just by what they have done thus far. The Man Upstairs may wake at any time." The Prince of Darkness wiped his forehead with his palm. "I did not anticipate this. I believed I could disrupt the mythos enough with all of you to ensure there could be no chance of a Second Coming, at least not in the way the Big Man wishes."

Kaylee made a great show of clearing her throat. "Look, I just want a straight answer about how many of you there are. Or don't you know? And Locke, what did you have to do with all of them being born at once?"

We were quiet. Locke actually blushed. Chase looked at us in confusion. "You know, I've wondered about that myself. I thought there was only supposed to be one Messiah. How many of us are there?"

I sighed and looked at Locke. He gave me a pained glance and shrugged.

"Six hundred and sixty-six," I said.

"Six hun –" Kaylee had a coughing fit and pounded her chest with her fist. "That's ridiculous. Why would God sire that many of you?"

"I'd like to know too," Chase said petulantly.

Locke rose and spread his arms. The quintessential performer. "Very well. Twenty-two years ago, the Man Upstairs came near to waking. Believe me, you have no wish for a power such as he to wake. In that state near to consciousness, his feverish mind decided to conclude the prophesy he had put in motion when he sired the first of you."

Chase sniffed. "Jesus Christ."

"Precisely. Now, He found himself a virgin of childbearing age – no mean feat, these days – performed a miracle, and informed the young thing that she was special and now carried the Messiah. The girl was thirteen."

"Statutory rape," Kaylee said.

Locke coughed. "In any event, she had no wish to be special. And so with the help of her brother who had saved money for a car and who has never let her live it down to this day, she caught a bus to the nearest abortion clinic where medical intervention proved more than a match for the miracle."

"Oh," Kaylee said.

"I had hoped the Man Upstairs would return to deep sleep. He did so before in recent times."

"Recent?" Chase echoed.

"Yes. There was an incident about nine hundred years ago, in Rome during the Crusades. Miracles. Weeping statues. That was due to a true believer." Locke cast a glance at Kaylee. "I dealt with the matter."

"So He tried again," Quentin said. When Locke raised an eyebrow, he added hastily, "That's what Mom told me. He tried again and again and again."

"Precisely. Please do not interrupt. The next one pilfered her older sister's morning-after pills. The third had an aunt familiar with a folk remedy involving certain plants. The Man Upstairs would come near to awareness and collapse back into dream. But each time he began to wake again.

"This brings us to a fateful night. It was on this night, July sixth, that he came closest to waking fully, and in mere minutes, he cast about in frustration and found a thousand Christian virgins across the world, particularly in parts of

North America where the fundamentalists are at their most insane.

"And lo, it came to pass that I, Locke, sometimes called Loki and Lucifer, and a hundred other names you need not know, decided direct intervention was necessary. I returned to this world and visited these young mothers-to-be and didst inform them they should keep you little brats and that, yea, the voice they heard going on about the Messiah was correct."

Locke sat down. Silence prevailed. Looks were passed around the room like a collection plate in church.

"Hmm," Kaylee said. Emile played with some little rocks. Chase chewed on his lower lip, making him look buck-toothed. Quentin nodded knowingly as though he had helped reveal a great secret. The fox yawned and spat out a feather.

"Now that we've cleared that up," I said, "let's make some notes on all the brothers we know. We need them to become hard to find."

"How many are you connected with?" Emile asked Locke. "Seth and me and who else?"

"Adam. Frank. Mark. Hiro. Torin." Locke ticked off names on his fingers. "Others who are not local."

"What about Nathan?" Kaylee asked.

A patronizing glance from Locke. "If I had a connection with Nathan, I could inform you of his location and what they have done with him. Alas, I met Nathan too recently."

"What do you think they've done with him? And why haven't you reported his disappearance to the police?"

"That'll prompt embarrassing questions," I said.

"They could be torturing and murdering him, and you don't want to be embarrassed?"

"I don't want to be in jail while Moffat's crew are out here hunting down the rest of us. We need to work phones and e-mail; the brothers near Summerton need to know about Moffat and his crew."

"E-mail won't work." Emile rattled his rocks together and stared at them. "No Internet service here. Unless we use our phones."

"Expensive," Chase said.

I glared at him. "Then we need to get that installed. Call the cable company or whoever does it here."

"That will take a few days," Emile said.

"Someplace has to have Internet nearby. A coffee joint."

Quentin cleared his throat. "I don't know this neighborhood. If we were on the north side –"

I cut him off. "We aren't. Enough said."

"If Locke is part god, why can't he find out where Moffat is?" Chase asked.

Locke shrugged, sighing. "I cannot – dare not – use my chopra at this time. The Man Upstairs remains close to waking, and that has pushed other aspects of the godhead near to consciousness. Each manifestation of otherworldly power draws them closer to alertness. I used my sensory powers earlier only because the phonus had emerged."

"Speaking of which," Quentin piped up, "what exactly is a phonus?"

"Ancient murder spirit," I said. "From Greece."

"And the guy in the basement had it," Quentin said.

Locke and I nodded.

"Does that mean Antoine is going to be saintly now that it's gone?"

We looked at Locke.

"I have no idea," he said. "The phonus may simply have used what it found. Perhaps it did nothing, preferring to enjoy observing the mayhem Antoine caused."

"It wasn't weak," I said. "When it realized who you were, it fought off the effects of the amytal well enough to beat us all up."

"Gr." The fox followed that with a plaintive whine.

"If ancient gods and spirits are real," Chase said, "what about unicorns? Vampires? Leprechauns?"

Locke clicked his tongue. "How much time do we have? Unicorns were a result of a drunken Sumerian spying a gazelle with a broken horn. Alcohol fueled the birth of an astonishing number of myths. Scientology is an exception; Hubbard was cold sober when he dreamed up those space aliens. But the gods are part of the godhead, encompassing differing aspects of it. When the godhead suffered its mental breakdown, it fragmented into thousands. Vishnu, the old Aztec deities, Jehovah, all of them are unaware of the others."

"You're aware of them," Kaylee said.

Locke smiled. "I am unique."

The fox barked and looked toward the door. Then the doorbell rang.

Chase shoved his chair back. "That will be the pizza."

"I really need a bath," Quentin said, smelling his own armpit. Not a treat to see just before dining.

Emile got up from the couch and wandered away to the back door. Kaylee watched him with a troubled expression.

I sat looking at Locke as the masses dispersed. So much for resolving anything.

26

KAYLEE

Seth and Locke sat glumly at the table while Chase laid out pizza boxes. I put two meat lovers' and two Hawaiian on a plate for Emile. He sat on the back step. I saw a tremble sweep through his shoulders as he let out a gentle, controlled sob. I held back a moment. Then I stepped out to join him.

Emile hastily wiped his nose with the back of his hand. "Good evening."

I sat. "So what's up?"

"What do you mean?"

"Do you need to talk?"

He looked away at the low fence that bordered this little patch of land around the house. "No."

"Okay."

"Yes."

"That's okay too."

He said nothing.

"How could you not know you were one of the new Messiahs, saviors, whatever you are?" I asked. "Seth's mother told him. Yours must have said something."

"My mom told me I was the son of God. But my mom has Tootsie Rolls for brains."

"Come on, you can turn water into anything. Heal anyone. Raise the dead. Where have you heard of that before?"

I offered him the plate of pizza. He didn't seem to notice. "I believed she was trying to keep my father's identity a secret. I suspected he was a mutant with superpowers. Like in comics."

"You're kidding."

Emile gave me a sideways look. "If your mother said your absentee father is the creator of the universe, what would you think?"

I looked at the grainy sidewalk at the foot of the steps. "I suppose I'd probably think she was . . . getting odd. So you thought your real father had superpowers."

Emile nodded, a pink sheen nudging into his cheeks. "I thought someday I'd put together a costume."

"A costume?"

"Maybe a black cape. And a pair of high-grade water pistols on my hips."

"Water pistols."

"I'd turn the water into something like pepper spray. Or chloroform, like Chase did."

I sat with the aspiring crime fighter and tucked my hands between my legs.

Emile frowned. "Don't tell the others. Please."

"I won't." A beat of silence. "What would you call yourself?"

"I hadn't figured that out. I thought the press would come up with something." He gave me a hopeful glance. "If you'd heard about a masked man kicking the hell out of criminals while spritzing them with pepper spray, what would you have called him? Hopefully not something pathetic like The Waterboy."

"Is that why you took up martial arts?"

Emile nodded.

"You're good."

"Thanks."

We shared a silence, the kind only two people recently killed and raised can share.

SETH

Sitting with the Prince of Darkness. Eating my fifth slice of Portly's Pizza. Feeling shitty.

Quentin wandered around the house in a red robe after his shower. When he sprawled on the couch and stared at the wall, I realized he was missing television. Being raised from the dead should leave you messed up like Kaylee or radically changed like the fox. Quentin apparently didn't have sufficient imagination for either option.

"Do not think badly of them," Locke said. "They do not know how to cope with all that has happened. It is surreal. Terrifying. The mind shuts down."

"They can be surreal and terrified all they want, so long as we get Moffat out of the way." I bit into pepperoni and Italian sausage and ripped the slice apart. "Bastard had the nerve to sic the cops on me. After what he's done."

"Nobody suspects one in his position. For your part, I imagine it will be easier to push him out of this world than to involve the police."

The fox whined. I reached to scratch its head. It snarled and backed off, then trotted to the front door and stood there, gaze fixed on me.

"You want out?"

"Gr."

I opened the door. The animal fled across the street, its white fur gleaming in the lights illuminating the Shrieking Trees Park sign. After watching it scamper, I put my jacket on, hitching the collar up to head outside for fresh air. Our neighbors in the house at the north end of the block were in a hurry. Two white cars lurched out of the driveway and thundered past. I tucked my hands into my pockets. Nightfall suited my mood.

Sitting with Locke left an acidic taste in my mouth. Of course, since he held a connection with me, he probably knew what went through my mind. In that case, I might as well use it.

Locke, we had a serious "toss your legs over your shoulders and kiss your ass good-bye" moment with Antoine and the phonus. The best you could do was to tweak your eyes so you could watch the full show. For an all-powerful being, you were pretty useless.

When I started going after the killers, I'd figured I'd be dealing with crazies you could put down with a well-placed bullet. Or even lots of not-so-well-placed ones. Ancient demons were never supposed to be part of the mix. My luck tank had to be down to fumes.

I missed my apartment back in Cove. It had a view of the ocean if you squinted between the towers to the west. Wordwings paid my bills and gave me access to all the books I could possibly want to read. Thanks to Locke, I'd met half a dozen of my brothers. We got together at Macy's Grill most Fridays for hot wings. We didn't exactly have a black cloud of destiny hovering over us. We worked or went to college. Dwayne had a skiing accident that left him paralyzed for fifteen minutes. He told us that story over beer while giggling at the rescue people who bundled him up and took him down the hill then banned him for life from Gray Mountain Resort for faking his injury.

We didn't think much of it when Loren stopped showing up. It's a restless age. But everything changed when somebody blew up Graeme's twelfth-floor apartment with me in his bathroom. I had to toss his body off the balcony and jump after him. And after I watched Jamie drop from a bullet through his head, I figured life was turning into a James Bond film.

"Gr?"

I looked down and found the fox strolling along beside me. "Hello."

"Gr."

We walked on, its claws ticking on concrete.

"I raised you, you know."

"Gr."

"I've been dead before too, did you know that?"

"Gr. Gr."

"Yes. I had to trigger a rez on myself on my way to the pavement." I made a plummeting motion with my hand.

The fox chuffed.

"My brothers have all these talents. What do they do with them? Nothing. Okay, creating my own coffee is pretty trivial. But at least I'm out here doing something about the killings."

I stopped walking. The fox took a few steps ahead, then turned and peered up at me.

"Just a thought," I said, reaching for my phone. I had a choice now: my old one, or the Samsung that Locke had bought. He'd outfitted us all with new phones; feeling guilty, I figured.

I picked my old Motorola. The bad guys already knew I talked to Hilda. They wouldn't learn anything else if I called her once more from this number.

She answered on the fifth ring. "Hello, Seth." In the background came muffled voices. "Since I haven't heard of a Catholic bishop being gunned down in Summerton, I presume you came to your senses."

"I snatched one of his henchmen instead."

"Did you."

"We drugged him with amobarbital –"

"Truth serum. Not admissible in court. And who is 'we'? No, wait; never mind. What have you got that I can use?"

"Moffat has four men working for him. He's been doing this for more than ten years. I may be able to get names and dates."

"Send them to me anonymously. Create a Gmail account in an Internet café on one of their computers, e-mail your information to me, and never touch the account again."

"How about I send you everything I have, even the questionable stuff, and you can figure out what you want to use?"

"Good enough for me."

"I need your help. Moffat has the police looking for me. He sang a song about me stalking him."

"Don't get caught. And send me your stuff sooner rather than later."

"Come on, you can talk to the Summerton cops."

"And tell them a bird told me they shouldn't chase down a guy whom a priest claims is stalking him?"

"You could put it more delicately. Tell them I'm helping you with an investigation."

"That works on television. In the real world, it nukes careers."

"Bull. Just tell them you have an informant."

"An informant who is stalking Bishop Moffat."

"Okay, how about this? I have the informant's phone. I can probably get you Moffat's number. You can get his phone's location, I'll drop in and take care of family business, and you won't have to worry."

"GPS his phone? If he was a missing person, I could do that. Or a judge might sign a warrant if I had evidence Moffat had done something. You're not giving me anything to go on. And by the way, if you saw it on a TV show, odds are good it can't be done in Real-Life-Land. Besides, if you finish this guy, I won't have anything to clear four murders off my case files. Speaking of television, I'm watching season four of *Lost* on Blu-ray, or was before this phone call. I spent a whack of cash on it, and I really want to know who is going to die next. Toodly-do."

"Thanks, Hilda," I said to the empty line. "You've been a huge help." I closed my phone and pondered tossing it into traffic.

27

KAYLEE

Emile went inside, leaving me alone on the back steps. I followed moments later and found Locke sitting alone at the table, two empty bottles of Kraftebrew in front of him and a third in his trembling hand.

"Seth has departed for an evening stroll," he informed me. I hadn't asked. "The animal is with him. He is currently pondering destroying his cellular phone."

The door to Emile's bedroom at the end of the hall closed with a wooden thump. I went to mine, leaving Locke to talk to himself. The bed was already set up with a wine-colored comforter and two enormous pillows. Somebody had set a black laptop bag next to it. I wondered if that had been Emile. I'd have to ask him. Which gave me a reason to knock on his door.

I re-thought that thought and winced. I couldn't stand Emile, couldn't bear to be in the same room with him when he started droning on about his investments and his companies and why you needed both an operating company and a holding company and why you should set up the holding company so it owned the operating company.

His death had changed him. He hadn't mentioned money-making since his resurrection.

A vision coursed through my thoughts: Emile, in a dance of kicks and karate chops and fists, pummeling a professional assassin. My belly tingled.

The front door slammed. Footsteps pounded through the house and down to the basement. They had a "Seth" kind of rhythm. A yip accompanied them.

Moments later the footsteps came up the stairs. This time they included a bellow: "Get your asses in here." A growl joined in.

I found Seth standing in the kitchen next to the table. He held a pistol. It had a long muzzle, unlike his usual automatic. An assassin's weapon, complete with silencer. Emile raced out of his room and stopped next to me. Quentin and Chase joined us in staring at Seth with a mix of foreboding, anticipation, and curiosity. Locke just sipped his beer.

Seth had a glint in his eye, lurking somewhere between madness and climax. "We're going to do things differently this time. Sit down."

"There aren't enough chairs," Quentin whined.

Seth pointed the pistol at him. "We aren't using Robert's Rules of Order for this meeting. We're using Seth's Rules. First rule: get stuff done. No bitching and no endless questions about our friend the fox. I'll stand. The rest of you, park it."

The fox stood next to Seth, wagging its fluffy tail. This detracted considerably from Seth's tough-guy stance.

Quentin smirked and said, "You watch too many movies."

The gun made a loud burping sound.

Quentin stumbled, shrieking, "What the hell?" A bloom of crimson erupted on his chest. "Oh, crap, that hurts." With that, he slumped into a chair.

Chase looked apoplectic. "Holy – ! Are you crazy?"

"It isn't permanent," Seth said.

"You shot him."

"Like some too?"

Chase went silent and white.

"Now let's talk." Seth motioned at the table with the pistol. "We have work to do. I need everyone you know. Names, phone numbers. Assemble a list so we can warn everyone at risk. Then we're going to brainstorm about how to track down Moffat. I want answers or I'll start shooting. Again."

Emile peered at Quentin, who had stopped bleeding and gasping. "Seth, this is insane."

"He'll get over it."

"You know you can't kill us."

"Not planning on killing anyone. Ask Q how it feels to be shot."

"Hurts like hell," Quentin wheezed. He plucked something from his chest and set it on the table – a bloody lump of bullet.

"How much ammunition do you have?" Emile said, glaring. He cracked his knuckles. "What do you think will happen when you run out?"

The pistol muzzle waved in his direction. "When I run out of ammo, my sidekick takes over." He gestured at the fox. "I recommend a good ball-chewing."

"Gr."

"This is interesting," Locke said.

"Quiet. We aren't having a repeat of earlier. We're actually going to get something accomplished here."

The whole crabby group sat. Seth pushed a blue clipboard across the table. "There. Names. If you have them handy, put down phone numbers too. Chase, you start and pass it to your right."

"Make it left," Quentin said, glowering up at Seth. "My arm is numb."

"Can you show me how to do a heal?" Chase asked.

Seth pointed the gun at him. "You'll get firsthand practise if you don't stay focused. Once we have that list, I want ideas. How do we find Moffat?"

"You expect us to be creative at gunpoint?" Emile asked.

"Sergei Korolev designed the rocket that put Sputnik into orbit while stewing in a gulag. He found motivation; so can you."

Chase pushed the pad over to Emile, who glared at Seth. "What if we refuse?"

"Forget for a moment that I'm pointing a gun at you; don't you think it's a good idea to contact our brothers and tell them psychos are hunting them?"

"Can I change my shirt?" Quentin asked. "It's sticky."

"Live with it."

Quentin scowled and shut up. The pad made its way around the table. There were stains on the page, as though someone had been crying. I glanced around the table and got as far as Chase. His brow oozed sweat that ran down his face and dripped onto the tabletop.

"Seth, ease off," I said. "Chase looks like he might pee himself. He's the only one who hasn't died yet." Chase blushed like a virgin.

"I can fix that," Seth said.

"Just let him be."

Locke set his beer bottle down; it wobbled and he caught it before it fell over. "Kaylee is correct. You are getting what you desire here. Be mellow."

One didn't often hear Locke lay down the law with Seth. But then Seth still looked ready to shoot someone on principle. With a grunt, he plunked the clipboard on the middle of the table. "If you think of any more names, jot them down. In the meantime, we'll carry on with part two: how do we get our hands on Moffat?"

Silence. We looked at each other.

Chase put up his hand. "Um. You can get Moffat's phone number, isn't that right? From Devan or Antoine's phone."

Seth nodded. The pistol, now pointing at Chase, nodded in agreement too.

"So why not, um, call him and say you want to meet somewhere and, um, exchange Devan for Nathan?"

Seth shook his head. "These guys are trained killers. We'll be at a disadvantage."

"Emile can fight," I said. "So can that." Pointing at the fox.

"If we turn up with Devan, he will be able to heal them or bring them back. I want to wipe them out in one sweep, full stop. No resurrections. We need the element of surprise."

Quentin wiped bloody hands on his shirt. "How about this: we call Moffat and tell him we're a radio show and he's won free tickets to a basketball game. We just need his address so we can deliver them right to his door. Then we show up and blast the hell out of him. If we lob grenades through the windows, it won't matter if we finish off Nathan as well. We can just bring him back."

Seth raised his brow. "That's got potential."

I laughed out loud. "You really think Bishop Moffat and his cronies will fall for that? Don't be stupid."

The pistol drifted my way. I felt a momentary thrill, wondering if Seth's trigger finger would twitch. But he would just bring me back. The bastard.

"What's your suggestion?" he said.

"I haven't got one yet."

"Better hurry."

"Is that the best threat you can come up with? You'll kill me?"

"Not going to kill you. Just inflict excruciating pain."

"Look, if you want to get to the bishop, I'll call the local diocese and tell them Channel Forty-Eight wants an interview. I could have Moffat in a studio tomorrow."

"You can do that?" Emile asked.

"Hmm. Probably not." I rested my head on my palms, elbows on the table. "I haven't talked to my news director in a few days. He thinks I've gone crazy."

"Can you still pull strings?" Seth asked. "Maybe set it up somewhere else?"

"Moffat may recognize me. You can bet his people will check me out. If they go to the channel's website, they'll know who I am from when they brought me back in the morgue."

"Then tell them someone else is going to interview him. That Pert woman."

"No way. I'm not giving anything to Simone Pert. That –" I snapped my mouth shut and changed tacks. "She's a lightweight."

"I'm not talking about her actually interviewing Moffat. Use her name to get Moffat to show up. Then we blow him away."

"Then what about the rest of his men?" I said. "It sounds like Moffat is the boss but the others do the wet work. You have to get them too, in case they keep on killing your brothers."

Seth tapped the pistol's silencer on the tabletop. "Not necessarily. Antoine says Moffat's lieutenant tells them who the target is, just a day or so before they go out. So we need to dispose of Charles Moffat and Max Cobber. We'll have to be careful with Cobber. From what Antoine said, it's a safe bet that his tricycle wheels are missing a few spokes."

"Maybe you can cure him," Chase said.

We all exchanged looks. Quentin said, "Huh?"

"What happens if you heal someone who is mentally ill? Does that make him normal?"

"Seth's dropped heals on himself and it hasn't done a damn thing," Quentin said.

Seth glared. "Ha ha."

Chase eagerly pressed the point. "Maybe Cobber is crazy on account of a brain tumor or something. A heal should take care of that. Right?"

"Probably," Seth said. "My mom had a lump in her breast. I ran a heal on her."

"Wow." Chase coughed. "Did you have to, you know, lay on hands?"

Quentin barked a laugh. "In other words, did you grope up your mother?"

"No, I didn't. Like another slug?"

Quentin shut up.

I shoved my chair back. "Listen to yourselves. You sound like a bunch of teenage boys."

"I must concur," Locke said. "This is extremely inappropriate, to discuss Seth's mother this way. Kaylee is correct to be offended."

"Thank you so much for your support," I said, glowering at him.

Seth tapped the gun on the table. "And no, you don't have to touch someone to do a heal. You just have to point the heal at them. Mom was scared when she found the lump. I tried a heal, and it disappeared. End of story. Let's get back on point. Seth's Rules of Order, remember?"

The fox growled, a low rumble in the back of its throat that cut through Quentin's smirk.

At that moment Locke said, "Oh, bugger," and rubbed his temples.

"What's up with you now?" Quentin said, rolling his eyes.

Locke winced. "There has been –"

"Another disturbance in the Force?" Seth finished.

"Alas, that is correct. Frank. Jerome. Mark. Their links broke, all of them together." His eyes crossed and uncrossed. "Adam went also, just now."

A stunned silence claimed the room. I spoke up first. "Four? What could have happened?"

The fox growled. Seth growled at the same time, a sharp, impressive eruption from deep in his chest. He pounded his fist on the table. "That's obvious enough. Moffat and his crew happened. They've come out of their corner swinging."

THE FOX

The fox had the unsettling feeling that she had been as stupid as a dog before her first death. Obsessed with the next lemming or mating or a chin-scratch with a hind paw.

She enjoyed her present company. These creatures raced around like lemmings, but had more purpose than an endless need to fuck or feed.

Something in the plasm had begun to reek. It stank like a polar bear emerging from its den after months burrowed beneath the snow. The stench made her soul gag. Powers moved, formidable beings that could rend the heavens apart and destroy the paths between worlds – even the worlds themselves.

She was hunting hares now, hares the size of the multiverse with ears as long as galaxies and teeth that could rend a soul into chaos.

Should I be so happy about this? *the fox asked herself. Then she thought,* Of course!

The Book of
the Excitable Dead

28

THE BISHOP

Max needed some time to calm his nerves after his bout in the basement with the demon. The creature appeared to suffer pain and certainly made hideous noises, but continued to provoke Max until he finally wearied and came upstairs. He glanced at me, breath ragged, and turned his gaze to Eugene who huddled near the fireplace with his back to the mattresses.

"Get down there." Max stabbed a finger at the staircase, his voice full of danger. "Watch him." Eugene scrambled to his feet and fled to the basement staircase.

"We shall need another," Max said. He straightened his collar and glasses, muscles jumping in his neck. "I will be back soon." With that, he strode out the front door to the cars.

Theo watched the door long after it slammed shut. I crouched beside him. "We have our work to do, Theo."

I pored over telephone records with him. Poor fellow, he'd grown groggy as the day wound on. I pressed him to hold focus. Theo found lists of numbers gleaned from Seth Brown's cellular phone records. He cross-referenced them with an online phone book, matching those that were listed and following other means for those that were not.

"Plenty of people post phone numbers on their websites." Theo's jaw bounced against his chest. He lifted his head and blinked. "Morons. Companies put 'em up too. Loads of stuff. It's so easy to find people's filthy little secrets." A laugh burst from him. "The judge at my trial. You won't believe what I found on him. Dare to send me to the cage."

"Theo, concentrate, please."

"Right, Your Worship. How about this one?" He scratched a fingernail on the screen. The name in the online phone book, black text against a slightly yellowed background, read, *Chantal, Emile.* "Look, Brown called that number four times in the past week."

I straightened, my knees crackling. "Good. It's a beginning."

Theo's voice had taken on an increasingly pronounced slur. "Are you sure that's one of them?"

"I'll find out right now."

I walked down the steps to the basement. I took care to step around the pools of blood and the teeth into the large rec room where Eugene leaned against the wall. The creature, tied with cloth torn from one of Eugene's shirts (donated under protest), sat opposite him. Glowering at me, the demon opened his mouth and showed a full set of teeth.

"Everything grows back. Kinda makes the whole torture thing moot. How is Max doing?"

"Max is not your concern. I have questions for you."

"If the top of the list says, 'Will you suck the bullets out of my chump Theo,' the answer is still no."

"Which of the others have left the city?"

Nathan rolled his eyes. "How would I know?"

"Quentin, is he still here?"

A snort.

"What about Adam?"

"You're asking the wrong guy. I'm not my brother's keeper." He laughed.

"Emile?"

"Right. He couldn't fit all his money into a suitcase."

I picked a name out of the air. "Thomas?"

He hesitated. A veil of confusion passed across his face. "Sure." A transparent lie.

At that moment Max returned. I climbed the steps when the door slammed. He came alone.

"The four who share a house near the university appear to have remained," he said gravely. "Their home is in a gated community. They work together in a convenience store that has an assortment of video cameras inside and out." He shook his head in frustration.

"We've found the missing one," I said, describing my ploy with the Nathan creature.

"Impressive, Your Grace," Max said, though his gaze wandered to the basement staircase and his chin twitched.

Theo leaned against the wall, his head resting on his chest. How far we have fallen, I thought, gazing at the boxes of disassembled furniture stacked against the wall. We had left a luxury hotel for this.

"What about . . . ?" Max motioned at Theo. His breath grew harsh. "Shall I do a bit of additional arm-twisting?"

"It's pointless. What can you do that he can't recover from?"

"That just means we can prolong his agony." Max appeared giddy at the thought.

"We must find another way."

"We could extract the bullets ourselves."

The thought made me recoil. "Do you know a physician? Someone with a past, like our friend Hadley at the morgue?"

"Everybody has a past, Your Worship."

"Think on it. In the meantime, we need furniture assembled."

Max cleared his throat and glanced at the heaps of boxes. "It would have been better to buy furniture ready-made."

"Eugene thought he was saving us money."

"If we get Theo healed, that will free him, myself, and Eugene for the task. Three armed men assembling Ikea furniture. Truly a recipe for carnage and bloodshed."

"Be that as it may, order us food. We need it, especially Theo."

Max reached for his phone.

What to do? I wondered. My thoughts were scattered. Before we met, Theo faced eternity in Hellfire for what he had done, but he might find redemption in our work. This was a true test of spirit. Reduced to this empty house with a creature from Hell in our keeping and Devan out there amidst its kind. God wouldn't permit His son to be slain; that would surely enrage Him and bring His wrath down upon the Hellspawn. But Antoine? He could have been shuffled out of this world and into . . . what? The arms of the Lord for all his service? Or Hellfire for his years of murder before I put him to God's work?

I stepped into the bathroom and knelt, door locked. Prayers refused to come. I wanted to weep. Perhaps the glory of driving these creatures from the world, of witnessing the return of our Lord, would fall to someone else. The thought opened a chasm in me and I ached to fill it with tears.

It was here, in the belly of despair, that the sensation came upon me. My cheeks grew flushed and my heart began to pound. A wave of power thrummed through my veins. Images filled my mind: Antoine, injured with a demon hovering near him. The Seth creature grasping his arm. A little white dog, teeth bared and snarling.

I opened my eyes. *Oh Lord, what have you given unto me?*

All my doubts washed themselves away and I rose to fulfill my destiny.

"Max is out," Theo said. "Went to get food."

I read more of Stalin's biography while I waited for dinner. The carnage he inflicted on his own people made my heart race.

Max entered through the door to the garage, setting brown paper bags on the floor while balancing a tray of drinks in the crook of his arm. I took the tray from him. He nodded in appreciation, then retrieved coffee in a purple and yellow disposable cup.

"Theo, my friend," he said, passing a cup down, "this will cure you."

"I hate Ducky Mart coffee," Theo said in a dull voice.

Eugene shouted from the basement, "I'll have some!"

Max cast a withering look at Theo. He opened a bag. "Hung-Fu Noodles."

Theo struggled to eat noodles and beef with Max beside him sipping coffee. I took coffee and chicken teriyaki downstairs for Eugene.

"Any chance I can get some of that?" the Nathan creature asked as Eugene took his box.

I ignored the demon and returned to eat with Max and Theo. The vision from earlier held my thoughts. I had seen a creature – I felt certain it was Seth Brown – sending healing power into an injured Antoine.

A plan, born of that vision, began to unfold. The creature in the basement would save Theo after all.

Once we had all finished eating, I knelt with Theo and explained what I needed him to do.

Max looked curious. "You believe it's as simple as that?"

I nodded. "Your gun please."

He hesitated, then reached into his jacket and drew it free.

"You must control yourself, Max. Whatever the demon says, ignore it."

My lieutenant's face grew hard. "If . . ." He thought better of his remark and shrugged. He helped Theo to his feet.

"Theo?" I said gently. "Are you ready for this?"

He winced and nodded.

I called to the basement. "Eugene, bring the demon upstairs."

The creature appeared, clothing covered in dried blood, arms lashed behind.

He looked around at us. "How was dinner, boys?" His gaze took me in as I held Max's pistol. "What now? Torture again?"

Max cleared his throat.

The creature turned to him. "Feel any better after kicking my ass around the basement?"

"As a matter of fact I do," Max growled.

"Max," I said. "Step back."

"Yes, Max," the Nathan creature said. "Go stand in the corner and think about what you've done."

Max leapt toward the creature, reaching for his throat.

"Stop!" I barked. "Stand back, Max."

He froze, teeth grinding, and moved to the wall.

"Well done, Max," the creature said. "We'll have a biscuit for you when –"

I shot it in the shoulder.

Eugene yelped at the thump of the suppressed pistol shot but Max grinned. Theo grew quiet. The creature cursed, then stared at me, brow raised.

"What's that supposed to accomplish?" The demon peered at the wound. "Wow. That smarts."

Then I felt a kind of pressure in the back of my mind, a foulness emanating from the creature as it launched the healing process.

"Theo," I said.

My man stumbled to the demon and gripped its bare arm.

"What the Hell?" the creature said and shook him free. Theo caught the arm again, this time at the wrist behind its back. The creature tugged away but Theo held tight.

"Stand still," I said and gestured with the pistol.

The creature laughed.

Flesh around the bullet hole in its shoulder rippled and a tremor pulsed down Theo's injured arm. He began to cry in jagged little sobs. The creature stared in confusion, looking at its own wound. Then back at Theo.

"Shit."

A bullet from the creature's shoulder fell onto the floor. Another bullet emerged from Theo's arm.

Max sniffed. "That is impressive."

The Nathan demon pulled hard but Theo clung in spite of the great sobs bursting from him. I could almost see the healing power flowing from the demon's body to his. It faded away into nothingness.

"Theo," I said, "you can let go now."

He reluctantly released the creature and flexed his arm.

"Well," Nathan said in a voice that quivered. "I guess I should be going."

"To Hell," I said and shot it in the temple. Then I sent another bullet into the heart. It sank to the floor, eyes gazing at nothing.

The weapon had grown warm and comfortable in my hand.

"Theo, clean yourself up," I said. "You smell of pain and blood. Have a long, hot bath. It will do you good. When you get out, we plan." I handed the gun back to Max with some reluctance.

I thought about all the great speeches I had read. Hitler was particularly good at motivating followers with just a gesture.

"Gentlemen, we will strike a decisive blow against these creatures." I lifted my gaze to the ceiling and raised my fist. "Tonight."

29

I went out for a while to absorb this sensation coursing within. The power rolling through me as I hurled the demon back to Hell had come near to overwhelming me. I savored it, murmuring a prayer as I walked. The Lord had seen fit to give me strength during my darkest hour of fighting these monsters. I was His chosen soldier.

Returning in the twilight, I saw an all-too-recognizable figure on the grass of the park. The families from earlier had trickled away, leaving just a mother and two daughters. The children played in the sand near a pair of swings. Beyond stood Theo. Clean now, and clearly recovered from his ordeal, he had put on a white track suit and was pretending, with little balance or skill, to be performing Tai Chi. I circled the playground and approached him. In spite of his show of movement and the twists of his arms, I could see that his gaze remained fixed on the two young girls.

"Theo," I said when I neared. He jumped, startled. Guilt descended across his face.

"We have planning to do."

"Yes, Your Grace."

In the barren living room, we sat on boxes that might someday yield furniture.

"I want these four dead, all together. A single powerful strike."

Max looked up from the list of names on my tablet. "Well. It's an intriguing approach."

Theo performed push-ups nearby, savoring the use of his arm and leg. Eugene was against the wall near the fireplace, gazing at the patch of floor where he'd mopped up the creature's blood with Theo's ruined shirt. The demon corpse lay over beneath the windows.

"Your Grace," Max said, "All four live together in a gated community east of the university. The place has cameras. We cannot strike them while they sleep. And they work together in a Ducky Mart littered with even more security cameras. Several will be at work right now, but we can't just storm the place. And our sniper is rather unavailable at the moment."

"I don't care about the risk," I said. "I want them dead tonight." The mere thought of the slaughter of these demons affected me in ways that would make Eugene envious. I had to lean forward to conceal my excitement.

"While I applaud your desire to rid us of them swiftly," Max said, "I would really and truly rather not go back inside. They don't let you argue your way out of mass murder."

"I have a way." Theo shifted his feet beneath him, panting. "Gideon."

"Gideon?" I echoed.

Max shook his head. "We cannot bring someone else in. Certainly not a stranger."

Theo smiled. It was drenched in a canny madness. I had learned to appreciate this part of him. "Gideon is downstairs."

We followed him into the basement. Assorted equipment had been stored unopened while we waited for his recovery. He set to unpacking in a frenzy, unfolding his collapsible workbench, tearing electronics and long pipes from cardboard boxes, and thumping packages marked C4 on the bench – earning an "Eep!" noise from Eugene each time one struck.

Theo joined two pieces of stovepipe together and screwed some kind of contraption onto a bracket in the middle. Then with a gleam in his eyes, he picked up a plastic box and lovingly opened it, sliding a blue panel free.

"This," he said with a husky voice, "is Gideon."

We peered down at it.

Eugene was the first to speak. "You made a little rocket out of a dildo?"

Theo glared. "Gideon isn't just a little rocket. Or a. . . one of those." He touched its shaft. "It's loaded with C4. The tip has an impact trigger. When it hits something, *boom*." He gave me a beseeching look. "Your Grace, this can destroy a convenience store. Flatten it. Blow it to smithereens."

Max cleared his throat. "We get the picture. How far will it fly?"

"Set up properly, we can fire it half a dozen city blocks away."

"I see. How do we launch it?"

"It's on a timer. We can mount it on a tripod and walk away without anyone noticing. Or, if you want hands on, you can rest it on your shoulder and fire by pressing the button here." He pointed at the stovepipe. "Safer to have it fire itself since I haven't been able to test it. I can't say for sure if it'll fire properly or just blow itself to Hell. Begging your pardon, Your Grace."

My hands had become clammy with excitement. "If it works, it will flatten the Ducky Mart?"

"Absolutely."

"Pack it up."

Eugene gave a strangled sound. "I guess I should stay here with His Worship and put together the beds, huh? It'll be a long night for you guys. You'll want to tuck in as soon as you're back."

Max gave him a contemptuous look. "Your Grace, I think Flaccid here should drive."

Eugene's eyes widened. "Sir, I think –"

"Don't do that." Max patted his pistol in its shoulder holster.

"Quiet, all of you. I want us on our way in five minutes."

"Us?" Max echoed.

I nodded. A general's place should be at the front of the charge.

30

The store lay fifteen minutes away. Max drove the first car, parking beneath a street lamp whose bulb had failed. Our Max rarely lacked for a cup of Ducky Mart coffee in his hand. He eyed the colorfully lit convenience store with wistfulness.

My heart raced at the thought of the Hellfire soon to rain down upon the creatures within.

This Ducky Mart stood across from a multiplex theater called the Silver Star. To my left lay a park where Theo tended to Gideon.

After a few minutes he walked toward us nonchalantly.

"Time?" Max said.

"Ten minutes." Theo glanced at his watch. "More like eight."

"You should learn remote detonation, my friend. Terrorists have refined the use of cell phones."

Theo's face turned a shade of white. "What if someone calls a wrong number while I'm setting up? What if my mom calls?"

"Ah."

My thoughts thrummed, eager for the kill. We were taking the battle to the demons, driving them back to Hell. They couldn't harm Devan – I grew certain of this with each passing moment – but they felt loyalty to their own kind. Perhaps they would parley with us. They had Devan and

Antoine's phones. We'd tried to call them for two days, to no avail. Maybe, after this, they would be prepared to discuss returning the one true son of God to God's chosen soldier.

Max lifted his binoculars once more. He had identified three demons within. I could barely make out their figures with the naked eye, two at the kiosk in the center of the room and one in the back where the coffee makers were.

Eugene drummed his thumbs on the steering wheel while Max joined Theo and myself in the dimness under the failed streetlamp.

"I wish I'd picked up a coffee," Eugene said, leaning out the window. "I hate hitting this place."

"I understand," Max responded with uncharacteristic softness in his voice. "It is a shame."

"All those beans. Finely roasted."

"To perfection," Max said.

"With a sprinkling of chocolate on whipped cream. They make the best lattes."

"It's true." Max added a long, drawn-out sigh.

A man and woman in middle age, clasping hands as they walked, crossed from the theater and entered the convenience store. I had hoped to avoid the loss of innocent life but steeled my spirit. Strangely, part of me thrilled at the thought of even more death.

"What have we here?" Max pointed. A slender young man strode toward Ducky Mart.

"Another customer," I said.

Max sniffed. "Adam."

"One of the creatures?"

"Exactly."

"We can take them all, then."

"Perhaps. It's too late for this one to be coming on shift; they typically begin work at nine."

We watched. Theo beside me took Max's binoculars and stared at the building. "I think he's buying stuff."

"How long for Gideon?" Max asked.

Theo consulted his watch. "Four minutes. Give or take."

I touched Theo's shoulder and motioned at the binoculars. He passed them to me. The demon who had entered – I had to be careful not to think of them as young men – now stood at the counter. He had two bottles of soda before him and leaned over to speak with the creature at the register. A grin erupted on his face as they shared a laugh.

"Theo?" I said. "How long?"

"Two minutes."

"Do we have Antoine's rifle in one of the cars?"

Max's brow rose. "Your Grace, none of us has Antoine's proficiency."

"Get it."

Max and Theo glanced at each other. Theo opened the trunk of Max's car, lifting out a familiar black case.

Max said, "Your Grace, I believe Theo is more familiar with rifles. I prefer pistols."

I released the clasps holding the case shut. "I'll do it."

That brought looks of shock. Then Max gave me a condescending smile. "Your Worship, I really think. . . "

I gripped the rifle and felt an odd familiarity. My fingers found the safety. I let the magazine slide out, checked it, and worked the breech to load a round into the chamber. Then I laid the weapon across the roof of the car and put my eye to the telescopic sight.

"If this creature leaves that appalling shop," I said, "I don't see any reason not to take him as well as the others."

Max laughed. "You are full of surprises this evening, sir."

"Theo," I said. "How long?"

"Less than a minute."

"Wait for the rocket to fire," Max said. "It may be sufficient to finish our friend. If he succeeds in crossing the street, leave him."

I looked at him sharply. "Leave him?"

"We do not want to draw attention. You will have a small, magical window. If he departs but remains within the parking area, he is yours. If he moves beyond that, you can have a crack at him later."

Anticipation and ecstasy jostled for space in my mind. The figure in the convenience store pushed the door open and stepped out. He scratched the side of his neck, glanced each way, and stepped toward the street. Then a roar erupted from the park. A stream of smoke shot across the street. Ducky Mart burst like a balloon full of fire, the concussion hurling its windows out. The roar died away in an instant, leaving a crackling sound.

Eugene murmured a curse full of wonder.

I peered down the scope. The figure who had left Ducky Mart had been flung to the ground. He now picked himself up, turning to stare at the flames, arm above his head to shield eyes from the glare.

My finger caressed the cool trigger and I squeezed delicately. The rifle thumped against my shoulder. The creature dropped and didn't move again.

"Impressive," Max murmured. He reached out and took the weapon, returning it to its case with a flourish. "It's time we departed."

"No."

His eyes swung to me, as did Theo and Eugene's.

"We stay and observe," I said.

"Your Grace. Remaining here could lead to embarrassing questions from the police."

"Have faith. No one will suspect us. The police expect the perpetrators to be gone before they arrive."

"They assume that only because it's the wise thing to do. Your Grace."

"Max, we stay. Let's ensure the creatures are truly gone. Theo, go get your tripod."

"Sir, may I call your attention to the sheer scale of the explosion? No one survived that. And your shot was... remarkably accurate for someone who has never fired that weapon."

A crowd had gathered from the movie theater and we blended in easily with the mass of people staring at the rubble littering the sidewalk and street. The Nathan creature lay dead in our home. I had led my apostles in this charge. I gloried in the fact that these demons were cast back into Hell on my orders. I should have taken a more active role in our service to the Lord before this.

"We can't be certain they're gone until we see the bodies removed," I said. "These creatures can heal themselves and each other. If there is a spark of life left in any of them, they may all return. Be brave. We shall stay and be certain God's will is done."

31

KAYLEE

Seth was really too thin to pull off the warrior-full-of-righteous-rage look. He just looked shell-shocked. Emile managed an appearance of coiled, serene power. Poor Chase looked ready to burst a blood vessel. Quentin fled the room, muttering about his shirt.

"Where are they?" Seth asked. "Kaylee, your records have Adam's address, right?" He didn't wait for an answer, bolting to where his tote bag lay beside Emile's. He tore a sheaf of pages from its pocket and flipped through them. "West Edmond Street. I've got Adam's number on my phone." He plucked his phone from his belt and stabbed buttons.

"Adam was at their place of work," Locke said, his voice grim. "The convenience store that employs the four of them exploded. I saw it through his eyes before his soul departed."

Emile turned to him, brow raised. "You can do that?"

"Only with those I am bound to."

"Such as me. And Seth."

"Yes."

"On point, people," Seth said. "They work at a Ducky Mart, right? Where?"

"Near the university," Locke said. "On Broughton."

"Fifteen minutes away," I added.

Seth grinned. "We may beat the cops."

"You want to go down there?" Emile said. "Moffat's crew will kill us too."

"They're not going to stick around. If I get there soon, I can rez the boys. Who is with me?"

The fox jumped up with a throaty sound.

Quentin reappeared, wiping a towel that was now a shade of pink across his chest. "I'm watching Devan."

"He's chained to the wall," said Seth. He turned to Locke. "You?"

"Perhaps so. Yes, I shall join you."

"Good." Seth scooped up a tote bag near the door.

Locke raised his thick brows. "You need weapons?"

"It pays to play safe."

I rose. "I can get the press there. All I need is a cameraman. I just need to make a phone call."

Seth gave me a patronizing look. "You plan to go on the air with your hair like that?"

I faced the kitchen window, peering at myself. It looked like birds could nest on my head. "Oh, God." Desperate, I turned to Emile. "You can do hair?"

"I can certainly improve that."

"What about me?" Chase asked.

Seth looked distracted. "Stay with Quentin. Check Antoine often. Chloroform him if you have to."

I reached for my phone on the table and keyed up Channel Forty-Eight. Urma in reception answered.

"Hi, it's Kaylee. Don't say anything; you aren't really talking to me."

A gasp. "Tony is on the warpath. He says you haven't called in ages."

"And I'm not talking to him now. Put me through to . . . who is on cameras today?"

"Bobby is in the editing room, I think."

"Put me through."

A moment later Bobby Hale picked up the phone. "Hello?"

"Bobby. It's Kaylee."

Silence. Then: "Tony wants your head on a pike."

"He can't have it. But he is going to feel a lot better when I'm done. I need you tonight."

"I'm flattered."

"Bring your gear. Write down this address." I recited it to him.

"Tony has announced he is firing you."

"He'll change his mind. Get going. Right now."

"What are we shooting?"

"Keep this to yourself, Bobby. Someone bombed a Ducky Mart."

"Christ!"

"It happened just a few minutes ago. Get moving. We'll have this story before anyone. I'll meet you on the spot. Just get yourself there and start shooting. Hell, take the satellite van; Tony will probably want to break in on regular programming." I clicked the phone off.

Across the table from me stood Emile. He gripped kitchen scissors, clicking the blades together. "With a nip here and there, we can turn that into a professional mullet in ten minutes."

"No mullet tail."

"Then we'll thin out the edges and gel your bangs."

"You better know what you're doing."

"Do you really believe I can make it any worse?"

SETH

Mole Boulevard's tract homes flew past the Camry's windows. Then Locke said, "Seth, a radar trap lies beyond this hill."

I stomped on the brake to bring the needle back to the speed limit. A cop had parked on the edge of the street, radar gun on a tripod in front of the car. We rolled calmly past and up the next hill. As soon as we were over the crest, I trounced the gas pedal again.

"How come you can tell there's a radar trap when you can't rummage through someone's head or find out where Nathan is?"

"It is a mystery."

I glared at him while trying to keep at least some of my attention on the road.

A sigh. "I funnel away some of the photons which have bounced off the documents detailing where the speed traps should be located. Photons are massless, so the Man Upstairs notices nothing when some go missing. I can do the same with radio waves, which is how I know the police and a fire engine have arrived. An ambulance is on its way."

The terrain changed from tract homes to strip malls to residential high-rises.

I drove toward flashing blues and reds, pulling over some distance from a pair of white sedans. Locke and I climbed out and headed toward the lights. The fox loped along at an easy run.

What used to be a convenience store looked worse than Tim's Diner had. An audience gathered across from it. The store's windows lay in fragments on the sidewalk. The only signs of fire were wisps of smoke curling up from one corner. Two cop cars and a fire truck were positioned so their headlights illuminated the building. A crew of firefighters poked around the rubble outside. Nearer the store, police stood over a body. It lay uncovered. I always figured as soon as you got to a scene such as that, you covered the dead people up. Not these guys. I could make out two more cops inside, stepping over wreckage. Another ran yellow tape around the building, using a trash can, a newspaper box, and a couple of streetlight poles at the corners.

"The rest must be inside. How about we go over and wake up that one?" I headed in that direction.

"What will the police think?"

"They'll think, 'Gee, maybe we better not say in our report that this guy came back to life.'"

The two cops with the corpse started toward us, hands on their gun belts. I glanced around. Any chance of something else nearby that could be dead?

Too much. The cops intercepted us. One raised his hand. "That's far enough, gentlemen."

Then Locke opened up. "What happened here? Is that – ? That cannot be Adam!" He wailed long and loud. "No! Not my son, please, no!"

An Oscar-worthy performance, if they gave Oscars for Lamest Performance by a Slumming Deity.

The cops took their hands off their belts. "Sir, please stay calm," the plumper of the two said.

Locke fell to his knees and plunged his face into his hands, just in case they didn't get the message. "What happened to him? Oh my stars, it cannot be!"

Even the fox looked askance at that line.

"Er, Dad, please," I said gently. "These nice men will let us see him. Won't you?"

"We can't do that, son," Tubby the Cop said. "The investigators are on their way."

More sirens approached. Damn. I wondered if I could pull off a resurrection at this distance. There might be a dead rat in those dumpsters to my right. Or a hunk of beef. It could be problematic if a steer started tearing the dumpster all to hell.

On the other hand, it'd distract the cops.

The sirens drew closer. Three more cop cars wheeled up, tires screeching. Behind them came an ambulance.

I knelt next to Locke and peered up at the cops. "I'll look after Dad."

One of them gave me a glance that said thanks.

I led the weeping Locke away. He leaned on me and whispered, "I am certain these officers are feeling an element of sympathy for this poor man and his recently slain son. We can shift ourselves closer."

"Too many witnesses. Look around you." Cars were stopped and the crowd along the street had grown.

At that moment a van with Channel 48 in huge letters along its side rolled in. No room for miracles here. Damn.

"The cops will clear the bodies away and send them to the morgue," I said. "We'll get them there."

A large man had climbed out of the Channel Forty-Eight van and now opened its rear doors. A woman with mile-high hair, wearing a blue dress and little black jacket, had joined him.

Two men and a woman arrived in a blue sedan. They all had "We are professionals" in their strides and manners. Homicide detectives. I recognized the style: Hilda Langella out on the coast moved the same way, as though they had all taken a course in Intimidation: Beginner to Intermediate. Guys like Antoine had stumped up for Advanced.

"We wait," I said. "Stay here."

"Gr," the fox responded, its ears pricking up. Locke stayed put also as I wandered toward the remains of Ducky Mart. One of the cops took notice and came toward me again.

"I'm sorry. This is a murder investigation," he said officiously. "You'd best be keeping back."

"Yeah. My poor dad . . . that one there is his son."

The cop's face softened. "Your brother."

"Oh. Yes. That's right. We just wanted to know when you'll be sending the bodies to the morgue."

"When the coroner is done. She should be here any minute."

"It's important that they get there really soon. It's part of our religion, see."

"Your religion says bodies should go to the morgue quickly?"

"Yes."

The cop eyed me. Then someone behind him yelled, "We've got survivors!"

The cop waved me back.

I wandered back to Locke. Paramedics helped two people out. The survivors looked remarkably intact considering the rest of Ducky Mart. The medics put them into the back of the ambulance and drove away.

Damn. When were they going to do something about the bodies?

"How long can they be on the other side before they get all messed up like Kaylee?" I asked Locke.

He plucked at his chin and considered that. "The rules are different for you. It makes no difference if your kind are true believers; you already have your binding to your father. However, emotionally it would be best if we left them no more than an hour. Two, I would suggest, at most."

Two hours. What would Adam and the others be like after two hours of endless orgasms?

32

KAYLEE

I didn't recognize the woman in the mirror. Emile had thinned my hair on the sides, but on top it still stood out in all directions. Ten minutes ago it looked like a crazy person had tried hacking herself bald. Now it shone with roguish elegance. This is a woman with attitude, it said. A woman who knew she ran the show. A woman who didn't need a Leaning Tower of Hair like Simone Pert.

"Good," I said. "Let's go."

"Like that?"

I looked down at myself and choked. I still wore Emile's green T-shirt and blue track pants, a combination guaranteed to cause some kind of seizure in my viewers.

Emile snickered. "Come with me."

He led me to his room at the end of the hallway. It oozed chaos. Cardboard boxes and a pair of matching lamps made from bullhorns lay on the bed. At its foot was a heavy blue trunk. Emile lifted its lid, extracting a white turtleneck sweater and sharp black pants, which he draped across the boxes.

"My ex-girlfriend Maureen," he said. "She was about your size."

I had no bra. When I muttered that aloud, Emile blushed and went to his closet. He avoided my eyes as he handed me a white bra and panties.

"Emile, how long ago did you split up?"

"Three months."

"And you've kept her clothes."

He gave me a blank look. "She may want them back. Eventually."

I dressed fast but carefully. Emile drove as I tried and failed to reach Bobby on his cell. Emile handled the car like a maniac, blowing by police wrapping up a speed trap. A cop stared wide-eyed at us as we shot past. Emile cranked the steering wheel in a turn that screeched the tires. Ahead lay a smoking ruin beneath the familiar sign of a Ducky Mart convenience store.

Bobby Hale had parked the Channel Forty-Eight van near the police cordon, his usual in-your-face approach to catching the story on video. Emile ground the car to a stop. I bolted out.

And stopped short. Bobby, had his back to me, camera on his shoulder. Before him, towering hair making her look like Bart Simpson's mother, stood Simone Pert with a microphone in her hand.

My stomach sank into my shoes. My legs carried me in long strides toward the van, and my nails dug into my palms. Then I heard Simone's voice: ". . . no idea yet who did this, but police have suggested it may be a terrorist act." Her gaze flickered to me, caught my eye, and shifted back to the camera. "Back to you, Deanna."

Then she melted. "Oh, God." Finger to her earbud. "Skip? Can't you send the script to the truck's printer? Come on."

Script? For live news? What the hell?

Her gaze found me. "Kaylee, what a wonderful surprise. I thought you were fired."

Bobby, who hadn't seen me until now, whirled about. Then he admired his shoes.

"A surprise?" I said. "I called this in."

Simone's mouth formed a heavily lipsticked O. "Tony told me to cover it." Her gaze danced to my hair. Bobby stared at it too before looking at his Nikes again.

"How did Tony find out?"

Bobby looked everywhere but at me, which answered the question.

Simone's eyes unfocused. "Deanna? Yes? The police chief. Okay. Yeah. We'll be on again right now." She gave me a desperate look and glanced to the cameraman. "Bobby?"

The turncoat lifted his camera onto his shoulder and turned his back on me. I dug out my phone. Urma answered.

"This is Kaylee. Put me through to the asshole."

"Just a moment."

A click, followed by country music, didn't improve my mood.

Another click. "Good evening, Jerrel. Busy? No, of course not because you're fired."

"This was my story. I called it in."

"Journalists do stories. They call for camera people and they report to their news directors. They don't pull prima donna bullshit."

"When have I ever defaulted on a story?"

"This time."

"I have a story about a band of killers who have been busy for more than a decade and you think I should hack it together in a weekend?"

"If you have a story, show me some footage. Who is your camera?"

"I'm working with my own guy," I lied.

"Games bore me, Jerrel. You're off the company clock."

"Because Simone is such a qualified, hard-hitting journalist, is that right?"

"Simone delivers."

"I've heard."

"Now you're just being catty."

I glared at my phone, then spotted Seth and Locke across the street near Seth's car.

Willpower brought my attention back to the conversation. "Tony, this story is mine. The people I've been tracking did this, blew up Ducky Mart."

"Why don't you write up the story, and we'll have Simone do the interviews? She's now front and center on it."

"I am not handing my story over to Simone or anyone else. Do you happen to recall the highest-rated documentary in Channel Forty-Eight's history? That little story about the deputy mayor taking kickbacks from half the gangs between here and the West Coast, not to mention embezzling from the city? The journalist who put it together, who spent months losing sleep to research and doing real investigative reporting, took three national prizes. Remember that? I got those ratings, Tony."

"You were thirty-one then and still a size four."

There are moments when the universe grinds to a halt, stops dead, and ever so slowly begins to move again. "Tony, did you really say that?"

A tiny voice said, "No, of course not."

"To a journalist?"

"You misunderstood me."

"To a real journalist? Who records her phone calls?" Damn it, I wished I'd thought to turn on my phone's recorder app.

At that moment I looked past Seth at two white cars parked beneath a streetlight that had burned out. My heart almost shot out of my throat.

"Tony, am I really fired? Because if so, I may as well shop this story to CNN or Fox. That smell, Tony? That's a Peabody ripening on the vine. It will look good on my shelf next to the National Award for Broadcast Excellence. And when I'm done with this story, I have an idea for my next one."

The phone made a sputtering sound before I turned it off.

Emile stared at me. "You're fired?"

"That isn't important. I think Moffat is here."

Emile started turning to follow my gaze. So I grabbed him and tugged him into my arms. His eyes widened as I kissed him. A wave of . . . distraction rippled through me.

"Oh, hell," I whispered, looping one arm around his neck while fumbling with my phone.

"Oh, hell?" he echoed, confused.

"I need to call Seth."

He held me close. "What's happening, Kaylee?"

"Shut up. I mean, quiet. I mean . . . I'm sorry." I tapped buttons on my phone, trying not to notice the smell of maleness boiling from his skin, the warmth of his chest, and the firmness of his arms.

33

THE BISHOP

Theo snuck in behind the cars, attempting to vanish in the shrubs nearby. Eugene huddled behind his steering wheel. I remained in the open, leaning against my car. Max joined me there. I suspected he didn't want to look weak in front of the men.

The fire crew doused the few flames left in the remains of Ducky Mart. We watched the police intercept a pair of men racing toward the devastation. One wailed, throwing himself to his knees, grief-stricken over the death of the creature sprawled in the rubble in front of the store.

Max cursed in a voice that rang with merriment. "Your Holiness, I believe you made the correct choice in keeping us here. Would you have a guess as to who that is?"

I followed his gaze to one of the civilians talking to the police.

"That," Max said in a hush, "is Seth Brown."

"You're joking."

Darkness tinted Max's features. "I never joke."

"How could he have reached here so quickly?" I asked.

"A miracle?" Max suggested with a sardonic glance.

"We've flushed him out," I whispered.

Theo emerged from the shrubbery and laughed. "Easy shot. You could drop him from here."

"Ahem," Max said. "Please note the extreme police presence."

"We don't want him dead yet," I added. "He knows where Devan is."

A press van roared in, tires screeching. From it emerged a small woman with tall hair and a big man. They took up station in front of the destroyed store, a camera on the man's shoulder.

A green car rolled to a stop partway down the street. Another woman and a young man bolted from the vehicle. The woman got into a brief argument with the news team. Soon she was shouting into her phone. The young man gave me an odd sense of burning rage. I sensed a familiarity about him, realizing he had the same scrawny build as Seth Brown. A name leaped into my thoughts: Emile Chantal.

Emile before me, crouching, clutching his belly. As I fire the pistol in my hand, he tumbles back from the shot to his head. A little white dog leaps at me.

I shook my head to clear my thoughts after the holy vision, then nudged Max. "Look at that one. Our missing demon."

Max raised his brow. "You may be correct, Your Grace."

"I know I am."

We waited. The woman stopped shrieking into her phone and flung herself into an embrace with the Emile demon, making me wonder if these creatures held power over the minds of women.

SETH

Locke stood next to my car, tap-tapping his foot. The sound began to twist my brain cells into knots. Out came another corpse. I checked my phone for the time. We'd been there almost forty minutes. Damn it. How long would the drive to the morgue take?

"Note the performance by Kaylee and Emile," Locke said. Well, hell. They were necking just a few paces from the Channel Forty-Eight van.

"Gr." The fox bared its teeth.

My phone rang. I glanced at it and saw Kaylee Jerrel across it. I looked from her and Emile to my phone, confused, then tapped the green button. "Hello."

"Hi, it's me."

"You and Emile look busy."

"That's not important. Keep looking at us. Can you be casual and not give anything away? No sudden shock?"

"Like the shock of watching you and Emile having a tongue-suck session? Sure."

"That's just crass. And Moffat and his men are in those cars behind you."

I almost bit my own tongue. "Really?"

"I'm not absolutely sure, but those cars are damn familiar, and I think I recognize a couple of the faces, even at this distance."

I turned, pointing my face at the ground, and flicked my eyes up to glance back along the curving asphalt. Two cars in the one unlit spot along University Avenue.

A third body came out of the skeleton of Ducky Mart.

"If they've recognized us, they'll be following," I told Kaylee. "Get behind them." I tucked my phone into my jacket. I'd left my pistol in the car door's pocket. A glance into the car told me the tote bag with the rest of my weapons lay nestled behind the driver's seat.

A fourth body came out on a gurney.

Good, I thought; that had to be the last.

Except Moffat and his cronies hadn't cared about the customers in the place. We stood around pretending to be gawkers while three more corpses were loaded into the van.

"We have to go," I said.

Locke turned to me with his brow arched. Then his chopra must have downloaded a fresh update into his human brain; his eyes swelled. "I cannot involve myself in this. Not directly."

"Yeah, I know. You're just here for sightseeing. Get in."

The morgue crew climbed aboard the van, and it began to roll.

KAYLEE

Seth's rental car started pulling out.

"What now?" Emile asked.

"We go to work." I scrambled to Bobby's vehicle. He had left the doors open. I spotted a camera bag marked Canon and unzipped it: the camera, two batteries in side pockets, a box of Mini DV tapes.

Simone stood before Bobby Hale, who had a satellite camera on his shoulder. I picked up the Canon bag and marched toward Emile's car. Moffat's two vehicles had pulled out. They cruised after Seth and Locke, who'd followed the morgue van.

I flung myself into the passenger seat, shoving the camera bag between my legs. "Drive."

"Where are we going?"

"Wherever Seth goes. Probably the morgue." I punched redial on Seth's number.

SETH

My phone chimed. I fumbled with it while keeping one hand on the wheel. Kaylee. "They're following us, right?" I said.

"Yes."

Locke was talking to himself, shaking his head.

"Kaylee, I'm hanging up. We'll take care of Moffat's people." I stabbed the phone's red button. "Locke, don't worry. They want us alive. They want Devan back." I grinned shrewdly.

"I cannot use firearms. In fact, I dare not participate at all."

"I'll take care of business." The thought of Lucifer as a pacifist made me snort. "You don't have to use 'em; just pass 'em to me. As soon as we reach the morgue. Right now, get them out. The Sten, a couple of grenades."

"Gr," the fox said. I got the point: it had no problem joining in on carnage.

Locke reached into the backseat. "This bag is rather heavy. I do believe a strap is caught on something. Ah. I see the door is closed upon it."

"Damn it, Locke."

"Please, I am attempting to retrieve your rather lethal hardware." Then came the sound of a clasp unlatching.

My tote bag didn't have clasps. It had zippers.

Locke cleared his throat. "This is rather awkward."

"What?"

"I do believe you gathered up the wrong bag. We have Emile's laptop computer."

34

I could not. Fucking. Believe it.

"I left my hardware behind," I said. Aloud. Just to ensure the concept of my own mind-boggling stupidity sank in.

"This was hardly deliberate," Locke said.

"We have armed assassins following us. We have this" – holding up my pistol – "to fight them off with. What's wrong with this picture?"

"Seth, old chum –"

"Nine rounds. That's all I have." Okay, I told myself, move on from your own dumbassedness. Wallowing will get you killed. I thought fast, my gaze on the tail end of the van. I scooped up my phone and thumbed Quentin's new number. The phone rang and rang.

Finally a peevish voice answered. "Yeah?"

"We have a problem. The killers were still at the place where Adam and the others got blown up. Now they're following us."

"Geez."

"No kidding. We couldn't get to Adam and Jerome and the rest, so we're following a van to the morgue. I need you to meet us there. Bring my bag of weapons; it's near the door."

A brief, thick silence. "That's a problem."

"There's no time to waste. Get moving. Have Chase drive you –"

"I'm on a city bus heading for the terminal. I'm catching a night train east. My stepdad's girlfriend has a hobby farm."

I squeezed the steering wheel. "You're doing a runner? We don't have time for this."

"You don't but I do. Ciao."

"Wait. You can't just leave."

"Sure I can. You're the big hero."

"You wanted to go back to the afterlife. This is your chance."

A moment of thoughtful hesitation. "A blaze of glory, huh? When I got killed at my house, it was quick. But you know when you shot me? That hurt. I mean, that really hurt. I'd rather go peacefully. And frankly I'm not so eager now; I'll get back there someday. I'll wait. And you know, Seth, you're losing it. Coming unglued. Going bat-shit. This whole hero complex is sending you into the land of white coats and rubber walls."

I ground my teeth. "Someone has to stop Armageddon."

"What makes you think Armageddon is coming? Locke? He's as crazy as you are. Go home; that bookstore needs you more than the world as we know it. I'm going really far away, and I'm going to pick blueberries with my stepdad's girlfriend, and if I hear that a wacko called Seth Brown died in a shoot-out at the morgue, I'll laugh out loud at the irony."

"Fuck you very much, Q." I disconnected.

I called Chase and filled him in.

"I don't have the BARC van today. Why not call the cops?"

"The cops are looking for me, remember? Get a cab. Tell the driver there's an extra hundred bucks in it if he can get you to the morgue in fifteen minutes or less."

"Where is the morgue?"

I punched it up on the Camry's GPS and zeroed in on it, reading off the address.

"Okay. Hey, I found your sack full of – holy cow. Grenades?"

"We don't have much time. We'll be there in twenty or twenty-five minutes. Call a cab." I slammed my phone into the center console. It rattled against the parking brake. A questioning growl came from the backseat.

THE BISHOP

"Your Grace," Eugene said in a strangled voice, "we're being followed."

"We are?"

"The couple in the green Audi."

I almost cursed. "You have your pistol?"

Eugene's voice rose several notes. "Yes, sir."

"Let me think. Take us to the Church of Saint Mary the Virgin. These demons cannot set foot on holy ground."

"Are you sure, sir? Didn't we find them because they were baptized and christened in churches?"

That had not occurred to me. "Even so, we shall face them on our Lord's ground. Take us there."

"What if they follow Max?"

"Then we follow them in return."

Eugene veered onto a side street. The green car turned in pursuit.

SETH

Locke chewed on his fingernails. I couldn't see the fox in the backseat, but it was the only part of this crew that seemed relaxed. I imagined it having a contented lick at its flank. I tried to concentrate on driving, but my thoughts kept turning to mental images of my own bullet-ridden corpse. Cheerful, that.

My phone rang: Kaylee. "The car with Moffat in it just pulled off. They aren't behind you anymore."

I dared to hope. "What about the other car?"

"It's still following."

"How about you have Emile rear-end it when I give the signal?"

"We followed Moffat."

"Come on, we're in danger here."

"You're heading for the morgue, right?"

"Yes. I think."

"If they kill you all, we should be able to get there in time to raise you."

"That's not the point. I'd rather skip the dying part entirely."

"Seth, I'm after a story here. I have a camera. Wherever Moffat is headed, we're going to stick it in his face and ask him tough questions."

"Okay, we'll just drive off to the morgue and be slaughtered. Thanks."

"Passive-aggressive much?"

"How many are there, anyway?"

"In the car behind you? Just two. I think."

"Well, hell."

"I'll call in a bit. Don't get killed. If we don't hear from you in half an hour, we'll try getting in and bringing you back."

"Great." I disconnected. We crossed over the High Street Bridge and into downtown.

Locke moaned and shuddered. "Oh, this is a nightmare."

"How can the Prince of Darkness, Loki, Hermes, and Raven all rolled into one be such a wimp?"

"I shall survive this, whatever happens. However, I am discovering an aversion to the concept of this body dying, especially dying horribly. Bits shot off, holes in me. Ugh. All that blood. Do you know how long it can take to die from a belly wound?"

"They don't want us dead. We know where Devan is."

"Suggesting we have torture to look forward to," Locke said. "I suspect I shall be yearning for a belly wound."

"You're not helping here."

"Dreadfully sorry."

The van began to slow down. Its right-turn signal came on, blinking yellow-orange. Maybe we could at least pull up alongside and raise Adam and the others before Moffat's men gunned us down. It'd be something. Of course, if the van pulled away, the resurrection would hop around until it found something else dead, and who knew what that might be? A rat in the sewer system? A bird? Someone's leftover fast-food burger, made of who knew what?

My phone rang again. I hit the button. "Hello."

"It's me. Chase." Out of breath and gasping. "I got a crazy cab driver. I'm outside the morgue."

"Cool. They deliver the bodies around back. Watch for a gray van."

Ahead, the van signaled another turn.

Locke motioned at a figure walking fast along the sidewalk. "That appears to be Chase."

The van slowed to a crawl and crept into the alley. I cruised past. "Chase, we passed the alley where the van pulled in. Get in there. Hide somewhere where you can see us when we pull in."

In the rear-view, the car following us hung back behind a red pickup. Likely they wondered why I hadn't followed the van.

"Chase, get out my Sten gun and get yourself hidden. We'll be coming down there and going right by you. Hose the car behind us. Don't worry about who gets hurt; we'll fix any bystanders."

Locke, talking to himself in three languages I didn't know, hunkered down as we approached the alley. I cranked the wheel, taking us into the narrow passage. We passed two dumpsters. I couldn't see Chase. That meant the bad guys couldn't either. The alley widened but the van, parked sideways, left barely enough room for a vehicle to pass. I took us just beyond the van and hit the brake.

The rearview showed headlights creeping up behind us. I scooped up my phone, dug out my pistol, and threw my door open. "Come on!"

Locke looked confused before shoving his own door open and bolting, the fox leaping out behind him.

Come on, Chase, anytime now. Lay it on them.

I turned as soon as I was out of the Camry and squeezed a couple of shots into the windshield of the approaching car. Brakes wailed. Doors flew open. I dropped behind my car's nose as bullets thumped the side of the van. Moffat's men fired high and wide.

I put my phone to my ear. "Quick, Chase, take them out."

It was still on hands-free. His voice blasted my ear, even though he tried to whisper. "How do you work this thing?"

35

KAYLEE

Emile drove past Moffat's car near Summerton's Church of Mary the Virgin and tucked us into a free parking slot. Moffat stepped from the car, smoothed his pants, glanced in our direction, and promptly fled up the steps to the church. His portly driver followed.

Moffat leaned back, tugging on a massive dark wood door. He didn't bother waiting for his driver to catch it behind him; the other man struggled to pry it open also.

I eyed Emile, who gave me a guilty look. "Well?" I said.

He grimaced. "I feel rough leaving Seth behind like this. It seems disloyal to the team, if you get my meaning."

"Seth is armed; we aren't. He can take care of himself. He even has the devil incarnate with him. What we're doing is important. I need you to handle my camera."

"I've never used a professional camera. Just my little digital point-and-shoot."

"Same idea. Except you point and leave it running. Stick to filming Moffat over my shoulder. If you start from my right, stay there. If you shift from one side to the other, the footage will look wonky on the eleven o'-clock news." This assumed, of course, that Tony would even let the station broadcast my work. Which meant I needed to bring in a story that just killed.

I reached into the backseat for the camera as Emile got out of the car. "Okay, here is the *on* button. We're rolling. I'll leave it on autofocus. I want you to get a shot from the side, so that I'm partly in the frame but Moffat is all there. Understand?"

"Absolutely."

I eyed him sharply, certain for a moment that he mocked me. But the camera's controls had his attention.

I hung on to the mic with its long cord. As we strode along the sidewalk, I had a chance to absorb the forbidding towers of the church. It was a stone castle with huge spires roofed in turquoise that looked able to pierce heaven. Arched windows, of course, and three stories up, pillars with ornate carvings of saints looked out at the city. Surrounded by steel high-rises, the place was an anachronism, but a beautiful one.

We marched up the steps. At the top I pulled on the door. It creaked open with a sound straight out of a Dracula movie.

Within was a kind of lobby, larger than my condo's living room. The walls gleamed, light dancing on wood that bordered on black.

The inner door creaked the same way the outer had. Beyond sprawled the church's main hall. I caught a gasp in my throat. The ceiling rose and rose. Along the sides were statues in bronze, each easily ten feet tall, all male, all looking beatific or heartbroken. One figure on my left had his arms bound behind him. A cloth, made of stone, encircled his middle, and half a dozen bronze arrows protruded from his torso. His face was turned to the ceiling. Another had his hands raised, palms open, fingers grasping air.

Chandeliers hung on chains from the ceiling. They were made of brass in long, S-shaped curves, arcing down and up, ending with an enormous candle bulb.

From straight ahead came angelic voices. The blue-robed choir was made up mostly of boys, though one or two girls were in among them.

"Feel free to film," I told Emile. "But when we get to the bishop, keep your mind on the job."

"Yes, ma'am."

I glanced at him, expecting to see a taunting look. He wore a serious expression, camera held firm and steady.

"One more thing," I said. "Don't speak. Period." We set off between two rows of pews.

Ahead stood three men. I recognized Moffat and his driver. With them was a tall priest in a black robe.

"Excuse me, Bishop Moffat," I called, keeping the mic cord looped over my shoulder to ensure Emile wouldn't trip on it.

The men turned as the choir grew quiet.

Moffat glanced warily at his driver. The plump man had his hand inside his tweed coat. His eyes were like saucers.

I stared at him, discomfited. I knew this man from somewhere. The jowly face didn't look right, but I knew I had seen him before.

I had no time for that right now, so I threw on my most disarming smile. "Welcome to our fine city, Bishop Moffat. I am from Channel Forty-Eight News. Can I have a few minutes of your time?"

His eyes narrowed with surprise, gaze flickering to Emile. "What would this be about?"

"We only just learned you were here. We wanted to learn your feelings on prison reform. You have worked with prisoners. Isn't that right? Our viewers will benefit from your experience."

The priest beside him gestured at the members of the choir. They began to step down.

"Does this suit as a backdrop?" the priest said. "I am Father Hamblin. And you, young lady?"

"My name is Kaylee Jerrel."

Moffat's desperate eyes grew wide, as though he were anticipating a bomb-drop at any moment. So I dropped one.

"You may have seen me at the convenience store that exploded earlier this evening, Bishop Moffat. I was with the press van. Before that, we met at the morgue. On the day you lost Devan."

His expression was priceless. I love this work.

SETH

"Listen, Chase. Is the magazine in place?"

"The magazine?"

"The clip. That long thing sticking in the side."

"Oh. It's there."

"Good. Pull the bolt back."

"The what?"

A bullet interrupted my in-fight tech support, slamming against the van.

"Mr. Brown," a voice called.

"What?"

"I would like to discuss a matter with you. You have something we want."

"Not interested."

A door slammed. "Hey, what –?" came a voice followed by two quick gunshots.

Locke dropped flat. I thought he'd taken a slug. Nope; he peeked under the van. "I do believe one of the morgue attendants came out. They dispatched him rather appallingly."

"Damn." I went back to my phone. "Chase? Still there?"

"Yes," he whispered. "Those guys are practically beside me. I can read 'Levi's' on the back pocket of –"

"Not important. Pull the bolt back."

"What is that?"

"The thing that slides back, on the right. You'll see a big spring inside."

"Uh-oh. A bullet fell out."

"Don't worry. It just means there's a fresh one in the chamber."

"It still isn't working."

"Damn it. Check the safety."

"Where's that?"

"Just above the trigger."

"Did you not have bombs in that bag also?" Locke asked.

I brightened. "Hey, Chase. Plan B. Get –"

Plan A interrupted. Staccato gunfire filled the world. Bullets rattled along the walls, pummeled the side of the van, chewed metal. A shriek. I couldn't resist a look. Max, pump-action shotgun in his hands, ran to the doorway near where the van had pulled in. A man in gray coveralls sprawled there, his body holding the door open.

Here came Chase, head canted at a weird angle to cradle his phone, Sten flashing and barking. "I think I've figured it out," he said in my ear. "I got one of them. He's . . . Ugh." Then he treated me to the sound of his dinner returning. I quickly disconnected.

"We need to get in there," I said to Locke and the fox.

Locke shrugged. "Alas, I can do nothing more."

"You can drive the getaway car."

"That I can."

"Be ready to lay rubber."

Chase finished burping in 3-D and came tearing up along the side of my rental.

"Gimme the bag," I said. "And don't point that at me."

He unslung my tote bag and tossed it at my feet. I opened it and dug out a fresh magazine. "This should keep you going."

"Oh, man."

I pointed at the doorway. "We'll have to go in. Are you up for this?"

"The one I didn't shoot will be right inside the door."

"We can raise each other."

Chase groaned. "No. I can't."

I scowled at him. "Damn."

"Besides, why not go through the van?" Chase tugged the door open and pointed. The back of the van opened into the morgue.

I gave him an appreciative nod, then climbed in and dug out the second Kimber, holding the two pistols Hollywood action-movie style. Gurneys had been wheeled back into the van. I stopped where the van's tail end encountered the open garage door. When I peered around the edge, a gunshot bit into the opposite wall of the van.

Something poked my back as I recoiled.

"Chase?" I said. "Is that the Sten?"

"Oops."

"You don't know how to do a heal either, do you?"

"No."

"Shit."

A metal table sat in the center of the room. I poked both pistols out and squeezed off shots, then took a glance. Double doors swung gently back and forth. I tumbled across the floor and knocked the table over. It clanged as it landed. I caught one steel leg to keep it from rolling onto its top, which was good because the sound of it hitting the floor earned a thunderous shotgun blast that made the whole table ring.

On the wall next to me were two rows of drawers. Big metal drawers with rubber-coated handles.

"What now?" Chase asked. His voice wobbled.

I pointed at the drawers. "The boys are in there. We bring 'em back. You can cover me, can't you?"

"Sure." To show me he meant it, he stuck the Sten out and squeezed off a line of bullets that took out the little windows at the tops of the double doors.

I dropped one of my pistols, stood up, and tugged open the first pair of drawers. The bottom one had nothing. The upper one: Adam. I hit the Resurrection Button and tried another. A familiar face, though not one I knew; I had only the shape of his cheeks and nose to go by. Also, he had a yellow shirt with a shredded Ducky Mart logo.

Chase sensed the resurrections. He flinched and looked around.

"Mr. Brown," Max called. Chase hosed gunfire at the doors. Max ignored that. "You may be aware we are all on a bit of a clock here. The police will have been notified. We can expect them in mere minutes."

The fox wandered through the van and trotted around the interior of the morgue, sniffing along the wall. It didn't seem particularly perturbed by gunfire around it.

"Mr. Brown, would it not be easier for all concerned if we negotiated a settlement to this impasse?"

"Impasse? We have Devan; you guys have nothing."

"We have a list of your brothers, and we shall keep hunting you down until we have destroyed you utterly."

"Good luck."

"In fact, we destroyed one earlier this evening. Mr. Filman. Would you like to know how?"

"No." I pulled another drawer open. A short, plump woman in her fifties, naked. I tried another drawer lower down. Another sliced and diced corpse in a Ducky Mart uniform. I hit the Button again. The chill of the room raised hairs on my arms. The bank of drawers made up a wall-sized fridge.

One of the bodies moved. Adam. He rubbed his eyes.

"Welcome back," I said.

He struggled to sit up, asking the old standbys. "What happened? Where am I?"

"Gimme some time; I'm busy here."

Adam looked around. "This looks like a mortuary."

"You win the 'Jeopardy' round." I dragged a drawer out and found an old man. I tried another. Sure enough, Brother Number Four. I hit the Button again. Meanwhile, the previous rez whined up into a high note, coming to an abrupt stop.

Adam gasped. "What was that?"

"Later. Just follow Chase over there." It always amazed me that so many of my half-brothers were clueless about our talents.

"Mr. Brown." Max again. "I understand your position. You very much want your siblings back. Please, let us discuss this like civilized men."

"Friend of yours?" Adam asked.

"He's one of the people who killed you." I jutted my chin at the others. "And them."

"Is that Jerome? And Mark?"

"Sorry. Yes. The clown on the other side of that door blew up Ducky Mart with you in it."

"No; I'd left." Adam shook his head. "I remember this terrible hot wind against my back. Then I was looking at all that fire, and something hit me hard." His eyes kind of glazed. "Then I went flying through this tunnel. Then . . ." His face turned bright red.

"A never-ending orgasm?"

"So they actually killed us, huh?"

I didn't respond, distracted just then by the naked fat woman who sat up and started screaming.

36

THE BISHOP

Here on my own holy ground I found myself twitching like a wounded bird. The woman Devan had brought back from the dead stood before me with a microphone. Beside her, the demon who called himself Emile Chantal pointed a camera.

Worse, the moment I had entered the church a wave of exhaustion had come over me. I no longer felt the resolve I had experienced earlier this evening.

The woman flipped her notebook open with a flourish. "It's so good to see you again, Bishop Moffat. Please tell our viewers what brings you to our fair city."

I straightened. So far this evening I had shot two creatures of Hell and watched my men destroy three others. I had no time for weakness. "Well. As you know, Summerton is part of my diocese. I come here regularly. Not often. Regularly."

"Why didn't you remain at the Ducky Mart to talk to the police? You and your apostles were witnesses to the explosion."

"We were busy, we had – Wait, what do you mean, my apostles?"

"The men who work for you. Max, Theo, Antoine." She then turned to my driver. "You must be Eugene, another apostle. Is that right?"

Eugene blinked into the camera lens. "Yeah, no, well, no."

The woman's eyes narrowed. "Have we met before?"

"No."

"Have you ever been on television? I'm sure I've seen you."

Eugene looked like a rabbit staring at a wolf.

"Excuse me," I said. "We really don't have time for this."

"Your men are all released criminals, aren't they? Theo was locked up for embezzlement, which he pleaded guilty to because he thought further investigation might reveal his inappropriate fixation on children. Max and Antoine were incarcerated for murder and attempted murder, right?" She cast a look at Eugene. "What did you do?"

"Uh –"

I quickly cut him off. "These men are simply my assistants."

"And you call them your apostles."

"No. Of course not. Only Christ our Lord had apostles."

"I thought those were disciples."

"The same thing."

"What about Devan? Do you call him an apostle or a disciple?"

"Um. Who?"

"Devan Blueberry." The woman motioned with her notebook. "Never mind. Now that he has gone missing it doesn't matter, does it? Devan had no family, right? You cared for him in the monastery outside Dunfriggin."

"How. . . Uh, that's correct."

"I thought you didn't know him."

"I remember him now. A fine lad."

"It must have been fascinating, having such a special child."

"Well. Every child is special."

"Why didn't you turn him over to the authorities?"

"His mother had requested that we take him in, so we did."

"How did she manage that? Wasn't she dead by suicide? Or did Devan bring her back to life?"

"We had a God-given duty –"

"And an illegal one."

" – to care for the child."

"Do you believe in miracles, Bishop Moffat?"

The question thundered through my thoughts. "Each morning's sunrise is a miracle. The changing of the seasons. The leaves turning color."

"I meant have you ever witnessed something that most people would call a miracle. Someone being healed. Or raised from the dead."

"Only a son of God can perform such tasks."

"*A* son of God?"

"*The* son of God."

"Of course." The woman smiled. "Let's move on. According to Antoine –"

My voice sounded, even to me, as though I were being choked. "I don't know anyone called Antoine."

"Oh? A moment ago you called him one of your assistants. I have photos of you at Karl Rove Memorial Prison talking to a Mr. Antoine Vermicelli. You're on record as helping to arrange his release, even though the police believe he murdered people for the Danish mob. Are you having Antoine and the rest of your crew kill these men because you believe they're agents of Lucifer?"

"I don't have a crew. I have no idea what you're talking about."

Next to me, Father Hamblin hung on every word. This would circulate through the diocese in no time. Such talk had a way of crippling one's calling.

The reporter followed my glance at the priest. "Is the Church as a whole involved or are you doing this alone? Perhaps we should ask this gentleman." She turned to Hamblin, her eyes like searchlights. "Are you aware the bishop has had eleven young men murdered in the past three months alone? Do you know he started his rampage with a seven-year-old boy more than a decade ago?"

"You can't prove anything." My own words sounded like an admission. "Seth Brown, a known psychopath, kidnapped Devan. We have the police on the case, and if there is anything you know, I advise you to call them. Things will go much better for you if you cooperate. In fact, I'm calling the police right now." I plucked my phone from my belt.

"That's a great idea," the woman said. She watched me with a serene look painted across her face.

SETH

The freshly resurrected woman sat up and wailed, "Brian! Brian!"

Then she rolled to her feet and stumbled to the corridor, arms outstretched. She shoved the doors open. Thunder echoed and she dropped flat to the floor as the door swung shut again.

Chase stared after her. "Why did you bring her back?"

"I didn't mean to." I bolted to the doors and saw a figure dart from one of the offices, so I fired in that direction. A shot quieter than Max's shotgun slammed into the door.

A wail behind me. A couple of former corpses were stumbling to their feet, shambling around in a daze.

"This way," I yelled. "Get out. You're free."

"It felt so good," the old man wheezed, shuffling toward the doors.

"Hang a left," I said.

The other one, a small man just a few years older than us, staggered along with him. They shoved the doors open.

I caught a glimpse of a bearded man in a blue uniform, revolver in his hand. He cracked off a shot, and the smaller of the formerly dead men dropped. I threw myself against the wall. "Hey, you. Guard. We're the good guys. Shoot the guy in the suit."

In response, a bullet thumped into the wall near me. Aw hell. I squeezed off three rounds.

Adam hadn't moved off his slab. "What are you guys doing? This is disgusting. Can't you leave those people in peace?"

I glowered at him. "We'll explain later." I ran back to the bodies of our comrades, and this time I hunkered close and touched one as I hit the Resurrection Button. "Adam, can you shoot? I don't dare leave him, or the rez will latch on to someone else."

"Yeah. Okay." He took one of the Kimbers from me and tentatively stepped toward the door. Chase crouched, peering out.

"That guard in uniform is on Max's side," I said. "Shoot him too if you get the chance."

"Right," Adam said. Then a shot cracked the air and he stumbled. "Oh, geez." Blood ran down the side of his head. He put his hand to his temple, swearing.

A shadow fell across the floor. I raised my pistol. Then the fox bolted through the opening. A scrabbling of claws. A burst of gunshots. A shriek – a human shriek. The fox came tearing back through the gap between the doors, just as a crash of gunfire hit the back wall. It tumbled aside, out of reach of the bullets, and came to its feet licking red fur around its mouth.

"Thanks," I said.

"Gr."

"Mr. Brown," came Max's voice. Chase blazed the Sten in his direction.

A gunshot, quieter than mine thanks to Max's silencer. Chase flinched. Blood appeared on his left shoulder.

He stared at it. "Crap, I'm hit."

"Gimme a moment," I said. "I can patch you both up."

Chase shut his eyes and clenched his fists. The pain must have been excruciating.

Then I realized it wasn't the pain causing him to do that. It was initiative. A blast of static filled the air. It had a different flavor to it, kind of thinner, as though the volume on his radio were turned low.

"How's that?" His eyes popped open. "That should take care of it, right?"

The buzz of static wound up into a shriek. He looked around in surprise. He looked like a kid learning to use a fork for the first time: he stabbed at everything. Three more bursts of static thrummed in the air.

"Chase, stop. Those aren't heals you're firing off; they're resurrections."

More dead people interrupted us, sucking air. This time a young woman and another man farther down on the slabs jutting out of the refrigerator wall.

The three bodies of my brothers hadn't moved. Resurrections flew right past them as if they didn't exist. This reminded me of not being able to heal because I cut myself in Marisa's mosque. But that had been consecrated ground – Allah's ground.

I looked down at my brothers in their shredded Ducky Mart T-shirts. "Oh, shit."

KAYLEE

I thoroughly enjoyed my ambush interview with Charles Moffat.

"I serve the will of God," Moffat said, his voice much higher than it had been earlier. "And the police will want to talk to you, young lady." He thumbed a button on his phone.

I smiled. "Of course they will want to talk to the others who serve you, as well. Max Cobber, for example. How many has he killed for you?"

"We have never –"

"Did Nathan have any luck healing your men? Is he a good replacement for Devan?"

"Devan is the true son of God!"

Beside Moffat, the priest stopped breathing.

Moffat grunted. "I mean, I don't know anyone named Nathan."

"Thank you for your time. I'm sure you'll be seeing yourself on the six o'clock news."

"Wait. You can't do this."

"Of course we can. We're the press." I looped the mic cord around my arm. "Have a wonderful evening." I waved vigorously at the choir; some of them waved back.

Moffat turned the full bore of his glare on his driver. The driver who looked so familiar.

"You know what to do," Moffat said, grinding his teeth.

"I do?" the man said.

Emile and I ran for the church doors, Emile taking the lead and heaving the doors open. We raced to his car, Emile puffing with the camera on his shoulder and fumbling with his car's remote.

Behind us came Moffat's driver, panting also, his hand inside his coat.

The trunk popped open. Emile slung the seven-thousand-dollar camera into it. I cringed and tossed the mic in with it.

Too late. We turned and found Moffat's driver right behind us, a quivering pistol in his hand.

"All right," he began.

"Aarrrgggghhhaarrararagggggggg!"

Emile did a spin worthy of a figure skater. His foot struck the other man's shoulder, throwing off the pistol's aim and driving the man toward the back of the car. His head struck the open lid of the trunk with a horrible crunching sound. The gun fell. The man hovered a moment, then melted to the sidewalk.

Emile stared. Then yelled, "Get in!"

"Right." I glanced once more at the unconscious man, and an image rolled through my memory. More than an image: a particular scene. The face ran toward double chins, but those dimples stood out. And the shape of his jaw, the curve of his neck. I'd seen that neck arch more than once, the muscles standing out like ropes.

"Oh, my God. Emile, I do know him."

"What?"

"He played the prison guard who took Mona Ridingcrop to her cell in *Naughty Girls Twelve*."

37

SETH

Bodies sprawled everywhere. Those killed for the second or third time lay in weird contortions. The newly raised stood around like they expected someone to call the meeting to order.

"We have to go," I said. "I need to talk to Locke. Something big is happening. We can't afford to dick around here."

Gunshots in the corridor punctuated my words. Two of the freshly raised fell again.

My brothers stared at me. Adam spoke up. "That guy out there killed me."

"Adam, I can't bring back the three who were inside Ducky Mart. That means the place must be consecrated ground."

That got me another disbelieving look. "That's crazy."

"What's crazy is, maybe it's the whole chain. We need to get out and find out what's going on."

A bullet hit the wall above me, inspiring Adam to fire out the door.

"Chase, Adam, get back here." I waved them over and pointed at the van. They scrambled into it.

One of the morgue's tenants pushed against the door and came scurrying back into the fridge room. For a moment, through the gap in the swinging doors, I saw a gleeful Max fire into the woman's back. Behind Max limped the guard, cradling the arm the fox had mauled.

I reached into my tote bag and brought out a grenade. Adam swore. I tugged the pin and wound up in a bowling swing. The grenade rolled under the double doors and out into the hallway. Max's footsteps pounded away down the corridor. I ducked down, my back against the overturned table, and shoved my fingers in my ears. The room shook. Something big and heavy slammed against the table I hid behind.

I staggered to my feet amidst the dust the blast had stirred up. Bullets thumped into the back wall of the morgue. I scrambled for the van.

Chase was in the driver's seat, grabbing at the keys dangling from the ignition. The engine rumbled and the van lurched forward, swaying as he veered right. The fox came scrabbling out of the morgue, leaped off the ledge where the vehicle had been backed up, and landed next to me. We drove thirty feet before brakes screamed, flinging us forward. Locke sat in my Camry, parked in the mouth of the alley.

"Out," I said. Adam shoved the passenger door open. "Take the keys," I yelled at Chase. We ran for the car. Chase, Adam, and the fox piled into the back as I leapt in next to Locke.

"Who brought the dog?" Adam asked.

"Gr!"

"It tried to bite me!"

"Drive," I said.

Locke floored it and we were away.

Chase trembled. "What a rush! I'm amazed the cops aren't all over us."

Locke humphed. "Summerton Police would have received twenty-seven calls reporting gunfire had I not intercepted them." He tapped his temple.

"Hey, I'm still shot," Chase said.

"Me too," Adam chimed in.

I fired up a couple of heals.

"Oooh," Chase moaned. "Thanks."

I wiped my brow. I hadn't noticed all the sweat until now. "Locke, we have a real problem."

"I am certain blowing up the morgue is a problem."

"It's bigger than that. Notice who's missing?"

THE FOX

The explosion in the place-of-the-dead had given the fox a headache throbbing in behind her ears. She curled up on the soft padding of the stone-with-eyes, shut her eyes, and tried napping. This achieved nothing, so she sat up and peered at the passing traffic. She understood that mortals had built this stone-with-eyes – this car – by shaping plasm, changing it in useful ways. Much as the fox did in building passages between worlds where the plasm wasn't as dense as it was here.

Her thoughts turned to Seth. In the battle with the blue creature, Seth had touched the Locke power and saw the bindings between himself and the vastness, and himself and Locke. But he could not see the winding thread that joined him to the fox.

The fox noted how some buildings had winding strands of chaotic plasm piercing their walls from somewhere beyond the world. Parts of the vastness reached out to these buildings. The buildings were marked distinctively. A steeple. A cross shape. A dome.

There were other places also, like those caverns with the yellow and purple glyph above their doors. But those strands were dark, thin. Concealed.

The fox studied how the cords curved up and looped down to touch mortals. Legions of mortals were bound to these places.

The fox probed Seth Color-of-bark's mind. A pack, perhaps?

Or an army?

Seth feared the places called Ducky Mart.

This needs to be sniffed out, *the fox thought as she scratched her cheek with a paw.*

The Book of
Nathan's Ear

38

THE BISHOP

I emerged from the Church foyer barely in time to see the journalist's car speed away. There was no sign of Eugene. I called Max and paced, fuming, as I waited.

When Max screeched up I outlined what had happened.

"Eugene taken too?"

"Yes."

"Your Grace, he is hardly a strong-willed fellow. If they took him, we have to assume he will talk."

"Surely he is stronger than that," I said, but the words felt bitter and empty on my tongue.

"If he gives the location of the house, there is incriminating evidence... Theo's laptop has all our financial information and the target list. If that were to fall into the hands of the law, I think you would learn firsthand what prison is like." He opened the passenger door. "And then there is the corpse in the living room. Time is of the essence, Your Grace."

"Where is Theo?"

Max's lip curled. "In the trunk. Mr. Brown got lucky again."

Once we reached our bungalow, I gazed in frustration at the mass of unopened furniture boxes Eugene had spent a great deal of money on. I ignored the body of the demon as we loaded everyone's suitcases into the car. Max used a towel to wipe faucets and any wall switch or doorknob we may have touched.

Finally Max returned from the basement carrying a small set of devices and three of Theo's C4 boxes. He donned black gloves and pulled the body of the demon onto its back. Then he set the devices on the floor where it had lain, clipped something to its collar and ankle, and turned the body back over, concealing the devices.

I looked at him quizzically, and Max glowered. "If Eugene reveals this house, they will come looking for this fellow. When they shift the body, the results should be amusing."

A thrill shot through me as I envisioned the scene. "Well done."

We drove downtown. Max parked outside the Marriott's glass doors. He grabbed the laptop bag and his suitcase while I took mine, leaving the all the rest filling the back seat. We strode in and up to the counter.

"Two rooms," Max said. "For three nights." He handed over our Visa card.

A young, well-dressed man tapped keys on his computer and slid the card through a slot.

"Mr. Heronymus, I'm afraid your card is declined."

Max glared. "That card has a limit of ten thousand dollars!"

"Perhaps you should call Visa," the man said, struggling to smile. "Maybe you're a victim of identity theft."

"Run it through again."

The young man did so. "I'm terribly sorry. Do you have another card?"

We returned our bags to the car, both flushed with embarrassment.

Max settled behind the steering wheel. "Eugene," he said as he drove. "He spent huge amounts on a house full of Ikea boxes, which are probably already scattered across the street.

If we see him again, remind me to shoot him somewhere painful."

"How much money do we have?"

He shrugged. "I have no idea. But we do have Theo's computer."

We parked outside one of those Ducky Mart stores. I saw *Free Wifi* on the window as we went inside.

Max collected two yellow and purple cups and set them on a vivid purple table for us. He sipped his, cradling it lovingly. "One of the true pleasures in life. Ducky Mart does an amazing Ethiopian blend, smoky but refined." His gaze drifted to the ceiling, filling with a dreamy look. "Ah."

My head began to ache, perhaps due to the color scheme. I massaged my temples with my fingertips. I felt disoriented.

He set his cup down reluctantly, unzipped Theo's bag, and brought the flat black computer out. I left him to it and tried to drink my coffee, which tasted like burnt socks to me.

Max cursed. "I hope Theo is roasting well right now."

"What?"

"He password-locked our accounts and the records of our investments. And our Visa account. I can see e-mail. Apparently he registered for assorted child pornography services using our card, but I cannot access anything else." He thrust the computer back. "There is only one thing to do."

I nodded. "We'll need one of them. The last few demons."

"To bring him back. Yes."

The moment we stepped outside Ducky Mart, my confidence returned in a surge. With it came a yearning for savagery fiercer than I had ever known.

As we drove, Max said, "We need a landing pad. I preferred using the Visa of our fictional Mr. Heronymus, but if we must use ID directly associated with us, then so be it."

I touched his arm. "Max, God would not have brought us this close to destroying these creatures only to steal the opportunity from us. He is testing us. We must be subtle and smart."

Max glanced at me thoughtfully. "There is one thing I haven't mentioned. It sounded insane at the time, but I'm certain I heard correctly."

Irritated, I said, "Heard what?"

"At the morgue, I overheard a hushed conversation where Mr. Brown said he couldn't bring back those who died within Ducky Mart itself. However, the man you shot in the parking lot was alive and well when they departed."

I turned in my seat and stared at him. "He couldn't raise those blown up in Ducky Mart?"

"I heard the words 'consecrated ground.'"

I searched Max's face for some sign of a lie and found none. "Those stores are ubiquitous these days. There is another." We passed a Ducky Mart in a little strip mall.

"They raised at least half a dozen people at the morgue," Max said. "I wish they had launched just one more resurrection. That would likely have brought Theo back to us."

I laughed, feeling a weight lift from my spirit. "Max. God truly works in mysterious ways." I laced my fingers together, setting my chin against my knuckles, and sank into thought. "God has given us a sign. We just have to destroy these creatures on consecrated ground, which the Lord has seen fit to conceal beneath something as banal as a chain of convenience stores."

Conviction stormed the ramparts of my mind. *I am the sword of God,* I told myself. *I shall destroy them all.*

<<Wow, cool.>>

The alien words pulsed through my head. *Ridiculous,* I thought and pushed them away.

39

SETH

The only sound in the car was the snoring of the fox. I spotted Adam in the rearview using his shirt to wipe blood from his temples and hair. Chase had a giddy look, as though he hadn't purged all the adrenalin yet. As if he wished the excitement hadn't ended so quickly. Locke ate his fingernails to the roots as he drove.

Adam tossed the question at last. "What about Jerome and Mark and Frank?" It had been drifting around inside the car like a fart on a cold day.

"Locke?" I said.

"I believe we will know more when we return to the remains of the convenience store."

"Ducky Mart is on consecrated ground?" Adam asked.

"Something other than the Man Upstairs has claimed the earth it rests upon," Locke said. "Some other aspect of the godhead."

"Like Allah." I held up my scar for Adam to see.

"What's that got to do with your hand?"

I filled them in on the episode with Marisa in the mosque, leaving out the part where I bawled and fainted.

Chase turned as pale as Adam. "Wow. So we don't dare have a serious accident in a church or –"

"Churches are not an issue, as your father is their landlord," Locke said. "However, any place claimed by a different aspect is problematic. Mosques, synagogues, temples. Apparently Ducky Mart is in that fold."

"What kind of god would turn a convenience store into holy ground?" Chase asked.

Locke shrugged. "Countless legends denote spirits and deities which have claimed dominion over locales where they focus their power or offer sanctuary."

"Sanctuary twenty-four/seven with a cup of coffee and a doughnut?" Adam said.

"Perhaps." Vague and cryptic answers were part of Locke's job description. Bombast and obfuscation are well-known traits of deities. Of course, so are mindless destruction, random rape, and petulance. Hanging out with gods isn't all it's made out to be. Especially when they refuse to be any help in a fight.

Kaylee phoned to find out whether we were still alive.

"We made it out. No help from you guys."

"But you retrieved your brothers, right?"

I groaned. "Long story."

"Oh. Tell us later. Do you have any truth serum left?"

"On the shelf in the room where we have Antoine chained up. Why?"

"Later." The phone clicked.

We reached the university district and rolled up outside the Silver Star. Across the street lay what had been a Ducky Mart. A crew in yellow Public Works jackets swept the shattered glass off the street, a couple of bored cops looking on. DO NOT CROSS tape encircled the store itself. The crowd had left now that the dead bodies had been hauled away.

"You were outside," I told Adam. "They shot you down. Everyone else died in the blast." I turned to Locke. "Can you see anything?"

His eyes flashed into galaxies for a moment. "Alas, naught. Perhaps after its destruction, it was abandoned by the aspect that had claimed it."

"Any chance we can get inside?" Adam asked, leaning toward the window to get a better look. That meant hovering over the fox, who growled and discouraged him. "I left my iPhone in my locker in the back."

"The cops will ask questions if you wander over and say, 'Excuse me. I died here about an hour ago and I've dropped in to pick up my stuff.'"

"I just want my iPhone. I didn't plan to chat them up." Adam shrugged. "So you figure all of them are consecrated to something?"

We found another Ducky Mart thirty blocks away. The rubber ducky logo shone like a beacon.

Locke's eyes kicked into galaxy mode again.

"Anything?" I asked.

"I sense nothing amiss."

We climbed from the car. The fox joined us. Together we marched toward Ducky Mart's double doors. When we reached them, I turned to the fox. "You'll have to stay out here."

It growled ascent.

"That thing is smart, isn't it?" Adam said.

"Very."

I held the door. Adam, Chase, and Locke stepped in.

Then Locke made a high-pitched squealing sound. He windmilled backward through the doorway. Staggering across the sidewalk, he stumbled off the edge of the curb. I stared after him.

The Prince of Darkness looked pale as a bedsheet.

He returned to the sidewalk in time for a delivery truck to rumble past.

"That place." His voice trembled. "So empty."

"What do you mean?" I was pretty sure he didn't mean the snack shelves had run low.

Locke, as near to all powerful as any aspect could be, shook like a willow in a howling storm. "At any given moment, I can feel my higher self, my part in the godhead – until I cross the threshold into this place. It is as though I get abruptly severed."

The fox looked on with interest.

"What about us?" I asked. "Are we okay in there?" I jutted my thumb at where Chase and Adam were wandering among the aisles.

Locke shivered. "I have no idea whatsoever."

"Okay, then. I'm going in."

I drew a breath at the door and tugged it open. Then I stepped through onto the linoleum. I didn't feel any change. I'd figured maybe there'd be something like a feeling of coldness. Instead I felt revulsion, but I'm pretty sure that had to do with the color scheme. I turned my attention to the little pinky-purple tables. At one sat an old man playing a scratch-n-whinge lottery ticket. A couple of Asian teenagers stood at the tills in the center of the store, eying me warily. Another fellow, short and stocky, lurked behind the counter at the back, a wall of coffee makers and glass bottles of dark beans standing like Roman sentries behind him. The lids to the jugs did look like Roman helmets. I strode to the back and found the fridges full of bottled water. I took one to the counter and dropped money into the Asian girl's hand. She made change while I unscrewed the top and took a sip.

Chase and Adam came up to me. "What's up with Locke?" Chase asked.

I led them to the tables. "The link in his brain can't get reception in here. That creeps him out."

Locke paced outside. His arms didn't swing properly. He had a stride that made you think he'd read *Walking for Dummies* and skipped the hard parts.

"How about cranberry juice?" I said. Chase shrugged. I sent a sliver of my power into the water, nudging it over into juice.

Correction: I tried to nudge it over.

We fled outside to Locke, who stopped lurching back and forth.

"Nothing." I held the bottle to him. He took it as though he thought it might be full of acid or poison or both. His eyes flashed into galaxies.

"Emptiness. Damn. I have seen this before, lads. Not for many years." He tapped his fingernails against the plastic of the bottle. "Holy water."

Adam paled. "You're kidding. Is it safe?"

"It will not harm you. However, it has been marked by . . ." He gestured at the store. "It has been marked by that. Whatever that is. An aspect of the godhead with which I have never had dealings. Or which is beyond my perception." His shoulders stiffened. "This is not acceptable. I am free of the others. I can cross among their worlds. This is not supposed to happen. Oh, this is a nightmare. There may be more around me of whom I am unaware. This aspect is awake." He gestured at Ducky Mart. "It must be, to manifest such power as to block me from my own chopra." His chin quivered. "Whatever aspect we have here has claimed territory."

It seemed best if I took over the driving. The Ducky Mart tour continued, more somber now. Locke refused to set foot in any, insisting on wandering around outside with the fox. I bought a couple of hotdogs for it. The fox sniffed at them, pawed the overcooked meat out and nibbled on it. All I got was a dirty look for my thoughtfulness.

"My roommates . . ." Adam said. "Where did they get sent?"

Locke shrugged. "I do not know this. The aspect that rules Ducky Mart almost certainly has a place for them."

Chase shuddered. "What would Ducky Mart heaven look like?"

"If that's the almost certain possibility," Adam asked, "what's the less certain thing? What else could this Ducky Mart god have done?"

Locke coughed into his fist. "Obliteration."

"You mean torn apart? Permanently dead, no returns or exchanges?"

Silence.

"Are we absolutely sure it's just Ducky Mart?" I asked. "What if it's every convenience store on the planet."

We stopped at a gas station and bought a water bottle. I had the water turned into Pepsi before we stepped out of the place. We wandered out to Ramsey Street and gazed at four lanes of traffic roaring past amid the smell of motor oil and pending electrical fire.

"We must discover more about this," Locke said.

"We have Emile's laptop," I said. "If we find a late-night coffee shop with wireless, we can find out more about Ducky Mart."

"Ducky Mart has wifi," Adam pointed out. We glared at him.

Chase gestured across the street. "How about Starbucks?"

We gathered around the computer. The fox lurked outside, treating us to the view of it peeing on the lawn.

Chase said, "The chain started as Ducmont and Sons thirty-one years ago. They changed the name when they franchised. A Japanese company called Kiseiiki bought them out twenty-six years back. At that point they started taking over the convenience-store industry. Seven-Eleven has over forty thousand outlets. Ducky Mart now has – wow – one hundred ten thousand." He looked at the rest of us gathered at the table. "Doesn't that seem wrong? That's a Ducky Mart on every corner. Even small towns have them now."

"How come no one noticed?" Adam said.

"Lots of people noticed." Chase gestured at the screen. "The Wall Street Journal said Ducky Mart is the retail success story of the decade. According to Forbes, Kiseiiki's stock has gone from seven bucks a share to ninety-four in less than two decades."

"Are there any reports of odd activity surrounding Ducky Mart shops?" Locke asked, rubbing his cheeks. His knees shook – actually shook.

Chase drummed the edges of the keyboard. "Define 'odd.'"

"Miracles."

"Like someone finding a cookie with Elvis's face on it? That stuff happens all the time. You can buy the cookies on eBay."

"This is not a useful topic," Locke said.

"No kidding." I got up. The woman at the counter eyed me suspiciously. I gave her a sickly grin and lowered my voice. "Look, we need more to go on. Locke, what is this thing at Ducky Mart? Are we talking ancient god?"

Locke peered up at me with huge, round eyes. "I do not know this. I can always sense other aspects of the godhead. If a Valkyrie walked in right now, I could see her for what she is. However, the entity that has claimed Ducky Mart as consecrated earth is not merely beyond my ken but also beyond my Barbie, G.I. Joe, and Elmo."

A short Hispanic man came out from behind the counter, moved to the table next to us, and began wiping it down. He gave me a glare.

I forced a smile. "We play an online game. Gods and demons and weird shit. It's all in good fun."

He straightened. "Like World of Warcraft?"

"Yeah."

"Cool."

"So," I said brightly to Locke. "Your character can't detect this entity, right? DM is off limits?"

Locke glanced at the man. "I believe if it were ancient, I would be capable of seeing it. Most likely it is new. If it came about in the past thirty years, it is very, very new." He rubbed his cheeks with his palms. His hands shook. "It is not supposed to be possible anymore: a new aspect fracturing off from the godhead. Or so I believed."

"When was the last time that happened?"

Locke scratched his chin thoughtfully. Like so many of his mannerisms, it looked as if he'd seen the gesture in a movie. "There was one, let us see, in South America. It appeared in a Mayan city during their Pre-Classic period, approximately two thousand years ago." He caught my narrowing look. "Oh."

I nodded. "This one has come up because our births threw everything into flux, right?"

Locke avoided the question. "A number of ancient powers are nearing the point of awareness. It may be that tension between them caused a new entity to emerge in the cracks."

"So what can we do about it?"

"Wait," Chase said. "Is it really a threat? Do we know that?"

Locke grimaced. "Of course it is a threat. It is a god aspect of which I know precisely nothing."

"We know virtually nothing about you, but you seem okay."

"I am unique."

"Locke," I said, "what if you went into a DM and manifested some power. Let it know what you are."

"I cannot do such a thing. If this being is old, it could damage me significantly. If it is young, it might injure me by accident. If it is entirely unaware of any others, introducing me could cause it to lash out in fear. That could prove catastrophic."

"For who?"

The small man at the counter wandered over to us. "Hey. This sounds cool. What's this game called?"

We looked at each other.

"Sky –" Chase began.

"Ever –" Adam started.

"Panth –" Locke said.

"It doesn't have a name," I blurted out, glaring at the others. "We're beta testers. It hasn't been released. It isn't due out for another six months."

"And they don't have a name for it yet?" he said, looking suspicious.

"No, they don't. That's up to the marketing department in Seattle, and you know how those bastards can be."

"Oh, yeah. Right." The coffee jockey, who clearly didn't know how "those bastards" could be but thought he'd look like an idiot if he said so, shrugged knowingly and wandered away.

"Let's get out of here," I said. "I've seen more of Ducky Mart in the last two hours than I needed to in my life. Let's go home and get some sleep."

"That doesn't sound any better," Adam said. "I'll have to talk to Laci." At my quizzical expression, he added, "Jerome's girlfriend."

"Does she know what Jerome was?"

"Not likely. His last girlfriend dumped him after he told her; she wanted him to see a counselor about his 'delusions.'"

We dropped Adam off around midnight outside the gate to his subdivision. A pair of cameras watched from the gateposts as he gave us a glum wave.

We drove home in silence. I tried to get my head around what Locke had told us. Distracted, I didn't register the flashing blue lights until we reached the intersection where Dicker crossed Mole.

"Gr?" came from the backseat.

I leaned on the brake pedal. Four cop cars and a black van with *Police* in huge letters along its side. Farther up, Channel Forty-Eight, Fox News, and CNN trucks parked on the grass of the median.

A cop ahead of us held up her hand and approached.

"Oh, bugger," came from you-know-who.

"We are so screwed," Chase moaned.

"Grrrrrrr."

40

KAYLEE

"Emile," I said, "pull over. Somewhere out of sight. We need to move our friend in the trunk into the backseat."

"Why?"

"Trust me; we just do."

Emile eased the car over. We were passing through a seedy industrial stretch. He picked a dark spot between streetlights.

We manhandled Eugene out of the trunk. His breathing was shallow, much like his dialogue during most of his acting career. We tumbled him into the back, laying him out on the seat.

Emile scratched his chin. "Kaylee, this is a bad idea. If he comes to he could try grabbing me. That could get us killed." He glanced sideways at me. "I know you're kind of looking forward to that, but –"

"I'm not. Well, not as much. I have a story to file. As for keeping him under control, I have a solution." I pointed across Trevor Street at the shining lights of the Fun'n'Frolic Adult Emporium. In spite of the hour – past ten o'clock – the place was still open.

"See?" I said when I got back to the car and flung myself into the passenger seat. I held out the DVD I'd bought: *Full Thrust*. "That's him. They painted him green; this is another *Star Trek* rip-off. Look at the shape of his face."

Emile nodded at the figure in his blue shirt, tucked between two women whose red tunics and skirts looked ready to fall off. "Eugene Longfellow."

"They never use their real names."

Emile looked at me as if I were dimwitted. Then he picked up our prisoner's wallet from the coffee tray near the gearshift and tugged the man's driver's license out. He laid it on the DVD case next to the image and compared the faces. "Eugene Hocksley, meet your alter ego." He turned the DVD over; his eyes widened. "I see why he chose 'Longfellow.'"

"Would you do the honors?" I held out one of the sets of pink, furry handcuffs I'd bought.

Emile rolled his eyes and opened his door. In seconds he had the unconscious man cuffed. "Why would Bishop Moffat have a porn star on his team?"

"We'll ask our friend back there when we get him home."

Emile eyed me askance. "You plan to interrogate him?"

"Seth can make truth serum; so can you."

Emile was silent.

"You can, can't you?"

"If I have a sample. I don't see how he can do that just by reading a Wikipedia page."

Then I remembered where we had left Seth. I plucked my phone from my pocket and keyed his number. "Are you people okay?"

"We made it out. No help from you guys."

"But you retrieved your brothers, right?"

"Long story."

I asked about his truth serum, then disconnected and opened a browser on my phone.

Emile said, in a voice full of wonder, "They survived. Seth and Chase actually survived. Against assassins."

Streetlights passed. I thumb-typed on my smartphone's little keyboard. In seconds I had Eugene Longfellow's Wikipedia page up, which featured a long list of his movies

(*Thongs and Dongs Three, Four, Six*, and *Nine; Frat Boyz;* and a bunch of others I hadn't seen) but very little substance. I dug deeper. Chat forums dealing with our prisoner. Pages of black text on a pale gray background in tiny print. I skimmed them, eyes aching.

"He dropped out of the business a year and a half ago," I said. "No reason given."

Except... I found a reference to drug use. Viagra, of course. It had been a boon to the business, porn directors being the only people who saw four-hour-long erections as a good thing.

"Do you know pilots can't take Viagra for twelve hours before a flight? It affects vision, throws off your perception of green and blue."

Emile snorted. "Mistaking a golf course for the sky would be a pathetic way to end a flight."

"Put the DVD down while driving."

A blog by porn actress Amy Splits had a note about our man Eugene:

> Poor Gene, Viagra dependency is one thing, but
> when even that stops working, you know someone
> is punishing you.

"Oh," I said. "I think I've found it."

"What?"

"Eugene back there can't get it up anymore. Not even with drugs. That's our bargaining chip."

A wail erupted from the back seat. Eugene Hocksley/Longfellow lay on his side, hands cuffed behind him and eyes shut. The blood from his temple had congealed after oozing down to his nose. He appeared to be unconscious. Except that he made a dreadful mewling sound.

"He's crying," I said. "He's unconscious but he's crying."

After a minute of that sonata, Emile turned on the radio. Eugene moaned along to Lady Gaga.

Emile backed into the garage and we hauled the semiconscious Eugene into the house. We set him down in the living room, still handcuffed. He peered up at us through bloodshot eyes. "Bastards."

"You may want to be more polite than that," Emile said. "We could break your arms."

"Please." I clutched Emile's arm to quiet him down and turned my attention to the other man. "Listen, Eugene. We want to make a deal."

Eugene turned his attention to the hardwood floor, pouting like a child refusing to go to bed.

"We can give you your erections back."

That got his attention. His gaze flashed to me. He looked downright hungry.

"Didn't Devan ever heal you?" Emile asked.

Eugene shook his head. "Never got hurt. I drive for the bishop. Never even had to pull my gun out 'til today."

"Didn't it occur to you to ask Devan for some help?"

"God is punishing me for my sins. That's why he took away . . ." Eugene looked down his body. His lips trembled.

I smiled. "Maybe we can do something about that."

"What do you want?"

"Moffat's location."

Eugene laughed. "The Church of the Virgin."

"I mean where he is living." I knelt next to Eugene, who flinched back. "I'm a reporter. You are now my anonymous source. We're going to set you free. I want a simple trade. We fix your little – well, not so little – affliction, and you tell us where Moffat is hiding. We need answers soon. If we don't get them, we'll turn you over to the cops."

"Right. And I'll tell 'em about this little kidnapping, and off you go to the slammer."

Emile crouched next to me. "So perhaps we'll off you after all."

Oh, God. Men and their pissing contests. "Look, Eugene, as a show of good faith, we'll give you back your woody. Just because you were great in *Thongs and Dongs Four*. You and Allie Katte were amazing together."

"She is tiny. Almost couldn't –"

"More than I need to know. Anyway, as a show of good faith, my friend here will take care of your problem."

Emile's gaze bounced around the room, skipping from wall to wall to floor to coffee table. "I've never actually done this. Seth knows more about it than I do."

"Haven't you ever healed yourself?"

"That's different."

"No, it isn't. Just project it or something."

Emile watched me, his mouth screwed up in a pinched O shape. Finally he rolled his eyes. "Okay, I'll see what I can do." He knelt and glared at Eugene. "Now you, don't try anything, or you'll be stuck in limp-land the rest of your days."

Eugene licked his lips, his brown eyes wide with anticipation. Emile moved next to him and put his hand on Eugene's stomach. "This is as close as I'm going to the guest of honor here." He shut his eyes.

After a moment Emile opened them. "There. I think."

I nudged Eugene's leg with my toe. "What do you feel? Any change?"

He shrugged, crestfallen. "Not a thing. Not –"

Eugene concluded his remarks with a scream to rival Emile's tae kwon do yell. He kicked at the floor. His back arched. He wailed in agony and thumped with his heels. Then he threw himself side to side, shrieking.

"What did you do?" I yelled at Emile.

"Nothing! Just a heal!"

Then the right knee of Eugene's beige trousers exploded into crimson, as though his kneecap had gone off like a bomb.

"Kaylee?" Emile said, looking at me for guidance while Eugene kicked the coffee table to pieces.

"Don't just stand there; get his pants off!" I screamed.

"I'd rather not." But he complied, crouching next to Eugene's flailing form and loosening the poor man's belt and fly. He grabbed a pant leg and tugged. Eugene's pants gave way at the blood-drenched knee. While Emile tumbled back, Eugene landed a kick on his shin.

Eugene's knee jutted from the ragged remains of his pant leg, looking like a slab of meat doubling as a pincushion. Tiny nails worked their way out. As they fell free, the man's thrashing flung them away.

I crouched and peered at them. "Surgical pins."

Emile leaned over me and wolf-whistled. "We're fortunate he didn't have a plate in his head."

Eugene sprawled on his side, looking as if he'd been through a war. Blood stained the hardwood laminate. He moved his leg gingerly. The panting and choking slowed. He pushed a wheezy string of words out. "Wow. Hasn't felt that good in ten years. Messed it up in college." He sucked huge breaths. "Playing rugby."

I waited for my heart to wind back to a more sensible pace. "You're welcome. Now tell us where we can find Moffat and the rest."

A suspicious look flickered across Eugene's face. He struggled to sit up and stared at his knee. "What a mess." He flexed his leg. "That feels amazing. It actually moves all the way. And my God, it doesn't ache."

"Moffat," I prompted.

Eugene added a few more mutterings about his knee, though he stopped sounding so full of gratitude. His gaze flickered to my chest. "I need to know if . . . the rest of me works properly."

"I'm most emphatically not helping with that." I beckoned to Emile. "Grab one of the laptops."

"We don't have Internet here."

"Oh. Of course." I reached for my phone and held it up for Eugene. "We can bring up something on this to get you excited. The screen is a bit small."

He shrugged. "It'll do."

"Okay, what do you want me to look for?"

"How about Prissy Hardsuckle and Catrina Cupps?"

"Sure." I typed in the names. A list of sites popped up in Google. "You want them together?"

"Sure."

"Video or pics?"

"Photos are fine." Eugene looked as though his cup ranneth over with giddiness and fright. I clicked a link. Pictures filled the little screen. Prissy and Catrina were entwined around each other in ways you won't see on network TV. "How about that?"

"Yeah. Sweet."

I looked back at Emile. "Why don't you hold this for him? I'll leave you guys alone. It may help if he doesn't have me peering over his shoulder." Or at his crotch. That thought I kept to myself.

"Could I get a glass of water?" Eugene asked.

"I'll give you five minutes. Hmm, maybe I'll make it ten."

I left the boys alone to bond over pornography and found a glass in the kitchen. I paced. I drained the glass myself then washed it at the sink and refilled it.

A wail erupted from the living room. I raced back. Eugene tossed back and forth on the floor, moaning. His one exposed leg kicked at the floor.

"Didn't work," Emile said mildly. "No effect. I think his problem is psychological."

"You bastards," Eugene moaned. "You filthy bastards. You promised."

"Oh damn." I sighed. "Okay, then. Plan B."

Antoine snored in the basement closet, his arms and legs bound together with chain leading to a steel plate on the wall. He'd managed to nap through Eugene's knee explosion and the accompanying yelling. I collected the syringes and bottle from the upper shelf. Back upstairs I showed it all to Emile. "I don't know how much to use."

"Then try half a needle-full. If we kill him, I can bring him back."

I filled the syringe. "Here, can you do it?"

Eugene uncurled himself and glared at us dangerously. "You're not coming near me, you bastards."

Emile sighed. "Sorry." He booted Eugene in the groin. Eugene doubled up, knees to chest, and Emile bent down to stab the syringe into the porn star's arm.

"How's that?" Emile asked as he capped the needle.

"Fine. I wonder how long it takes to act."

We sat on the couch. Eugene glared at us. "I'm bleeding from that pig-sticker. I could get infected."

"I'll heal you," Emile said.

"Moffat's right, you people are evil."

"We gave you your knee back," I pointed out.

Eugene didn't have a comeback. He giggled instead. "You bashtards. If my hands weren't locked I'd . . . birdies."

Emile grinned. "Apparently it doesn't take long at all."

The interrogation took ages. Eugene drooled and talked to himself about "the business." I bent forward to tap my knuckles on the hardwood. Eugene's darting gaze settled on them. "We need answers, Eugene. Where will we find Moffat?"

His words slurred into one long, "Gotohelllllllll."

"Just give us an address."

"Address. Addy. Addy Wood. She could suck golf balls through a garden hozzzhhhhe."

"Let's start over. Tell me your real name."

"Eugene . . ." He looked confused a moment. His eyes glazed. "Eugene Hocks . . . Hocksley."

"Good. And your favorite color."

"Blue. Green. Bluey green."

"How old are you?"

"Thirty-one. Thirty-two in Augusht. Happy birthday to you, happy birthday to you –"

"That's great, Eugene. Now where is Bishop Moffat staying? Another hotel?"

"Nooooooo. Nodda a ho . . . ho . . . ho . . . Santa."

"Where, then?"

"House." Eugene drooled. "Like this one. Weird. Weirrrrd. Freaky. Strange. Ugggh. Even shmellsh the shame."

"A house. Where?"

"Go to hell. Hello. Hello Kitty. Kitty Prince gave me crabs on our first shoot." Eugene guffawed. "Shcratched myshelf raw. Next time, Kitty, shave your . . . kitty."

"Stay with me, Eugene. What's the house address?"

"Mollllllle."

"Mole Boulevard?" I asked.

His tongue lolled around in his mouth.

"Yesh."

"Wow," Emile said.

"Now the number, Eugene. Come on."

"Nine. Sheven."

"Nine seven what?"

"Ninety-theven bottles of beer on the wall, ninety-theven bottles of beer. If –"

"Eugene, the address. On Mole Boulevard."

"Nine. Theven."

"Yeth – I mean, yes, we know that."

"Who told you?"

"You did, Eugene."

"My jeans?"

"Tell us the address of the house where Moffat is staying."

"Ninety-theven-ninety-four. Mollle."

Emile touched my arm. His eyes were like saucers.

"What's wrong?" I asked.

"That's at the north end of this block. My holding company owns it. We've been living practically next door."

I choked. "Fuck me!"

Eugene giggled. And giggled.

Emile stood up. "What are the odds? And what do we do now? Check the place out?"

"God, no. That's for the police. I want these assholes in jail. But first I need to make some calls."

Eugene's laugh climbed in pitch, turning into a twanging cackle. We both turned back to him. His trousers had sprouted a tent – not a pup tent. Definitely a teepee.

"I think you cured him," said Emile, staring.

Eugene howled with glee. "Freddy came home!"

41

"Tony. It's Kaylee."

"You're still fired."

"Then you don't want the story about the crazy bishop and his hired killers?"

"What have you got?"

"We know where they have been hiding out. The police are on their way."

"Where?"

"Last time I called something in, Simone scooped me. So I'm not giving anything away."

"Don't screw with me, Jerrel."

"That will never happen. What will happen, if this doesn't go down exactly according to my specs, is CNN will get my footage. Send one of the satellite vans to the south side. Have the driver call me when he crosses the bridge. I'll tell him where he's going. And the driver better not be named Bobby Hale."

"I run the news department around here, not you."

"Is that because I'm not a size four anymore?"

Silence.

"Tony, send me a satellite van. Or I'll send you a lawsuit."

42

SETH

Weapons in the backseat. A wild animal beside them. A cop at the window. We were so screwed, we'd be walking funny for weeks. Except the cop leaned down, smiled, and said, "You can't come through this way, sir."

"But we live right there." I pointed, trying to keep my hand from shaking.

"Okay. Pull in over here. The rest of the street is cordoned off."

I eased the car to the side of the street. There were more cop cars and vans farther up, clustered at the north end of the block. A crowd of gawkers were gawking.

The fox climbed over the seat to hop out with me, sweeping her tail back and forth.

Locke and Chase joined us as we headed toward the people gathered on the street. A Channel Forty-Eight van idled on the other side, across the median that began at the midpoint of the block. Farther on: four police cars and a van in front of a house.

Kaylee, mic in hand, stood in front of a stocky man with a large black camera on his shoulder. "Police have raided this house and retrieved a quantity of weapons."

A glance in my direction. She kept talking without acknowledging me.

Another cop in uniform stood nearby. I looked past her and did a double take. Emile, in a long black trench coat, panned this way and that with a camera. I nudged Locke and pointed. We came up beside Emile.

"What's going on?" I asked.

His face split into a grin. "We've cracked the case. This was Moffat's hideout."

"This is where Moffat was staying?"

"Kaylee isn't going to mention him until we're sure the police have him." He chuckled and leaned close. "We ambushed him at the church and got excellent footage. He looked ready to pee himself." Then my brother lifted the camera back onto his shoulder. "I'm busy. You should pack us up again. The police will be all over this block for days to come."

I backed off. Emile turned his camera back toward the police, then paused. "Don't worry about the fellow in the living room. We'll explain when we're finished."

We stood around for five minutes, gawking at the scene with the rest of the herd.

"How could these guys move in up the block from us without us knowing about it?" Chase asked.

I turned to Locke with a glare. He had the grace to look embarrassed. "Dreadfully sorry."

"Can you turn off that probability trick now?"

"Alas, no. It must remain until the crisis has past."

"By 'crisis' you don't just mean this stuff going down right here, do you? You're talking about everything. Armageddon, the works."

"Precisely."

We headed back home. A blue-black unmarked car cruised past with blue lights flashing in it grill. Beside me, the fox whined.

We wandered into our house. A heavyset man wore overly snug track pants that looked like Emile's. He pushed a mop back and forth in the living room. He had a roundish face with bloodshot eyes.

"Hi," I said. "Who are you?"

"I'm Gene."

"You're a friend of Emile? He said he'd explain when he got back."

The man blinked rapidly. "Sure. I'm just doing some cleaning up."

"You're with Channel Forty-Eight?"

"No. Not really. I'm . . . a friend. I guess."

"You hungry? We could use some grub."

"There's a Chinese place near here," Gene said. "They deliver in half an hour."

"Hung-Fu Noodles."

"That's it."

"Great." I looked over at Chase and Locke. "Food, everybody? We can all toss twenty bucks into the pot."

The fox said, "Gr. Gr."

"Does that mean you aren't hungry or you don't have money?"

The fox said nothing, which made sense. From her point of view, this was like being in a dentist's chair with your mouth clamped open and having the dentist ask, "What is your view of the current unrest in Libya as it pertains to maintaining Middle East stability?"

"Hungry?" I asked the fox for clarification.

"Gr."

Gene looked on, impressed. "That's a smart dog."

"Gr!"

"Don't call her a dog if you want to keep your 'nads," I said. Then I turned to the fox. "I'll bring you some water and we'll figure something out."

Chase remembered the beer supply in the fridge and soon we each had a bottle of Kraftebrew open in front of us. I looked at the faces around me, avoiding Gene's. I wanted to talk, but couldn't with him here.

After a few sips from my bottle, I figured we all needed to unwind. Locke up-ended his bottle and wandered to the fridge for another. I was glad I could just crawl into bed now and forget everything for a while. Then the whole house shook. With it came the kind of thumping bass note that goes right through your belly at a rock concert.

We looked at each other. Then bolted for the door.

KAYLEE

My camera operator, Deco, smelled of cigarette smoke. He looked bored as he filmed my spot in front of Moffat's rental house. But Deco always looked ready for a nap, even during the most dramatic moments.

I spotted Flora nearby. If I talked to her directly, she'd be in trouble – but I still had her business card tucked in my purse.

I picked up my phone.

"Hello?"

"Hi, it's Kaylee. What have they found in the house?"

She stared directly at me, then reconsidered and turned to gaze at the street. "I can't talk to you. This is police business."

"That's very sad. I think we could help relations between the police and the press by opening up here. After all, I was open to the police when I called in this situation."

"You called this in? If there are things you aren't telling us –"

"Of course there are. But you can't do anything with them anyway. If I tell you everything I know and you go off and try busting the people involved, your case will get thrown out because my information is sketchy at best and probably not legal anyway. I gave your people enough to justify a search warrant, and I even checked to make sure

Judge Wiley was up to signing it. So let's chat. What have they found?"

"If you want a real story, check out the morgue. Someone vandalized it and dragged the bodies all over the place. It's a travesty. They doped the morgue crew with something, and now those poor guys are moaning about a tunnel of light and the walking dead."

At that moment a car drove up, one of those big four-door boats that may as well have "I am an unmarked police car" stenciled along the side. I recognized Jack from Homicide.

"Flora," I said, "have they found a body in there?"

"Okay, yes. They have. Now I need to get back to work."

A huge officer bellowed, "Back. Get back." His fellows joined him. Flora and Dorothy and the other uniformed officers set up a front line and drove us all back.

Then came a burst of light and a wave of thunder which picked me up and flung me. Dust walloped out of the house in a hot wave that swept through the police officers, tossing them around like dolls.

I rolled onto my side, unable to tell how much time had passed. Dust grew thick in the air. Nearby, a caped figure rose, casting a long shadow across the scene. The figure shook dust free, fabric fluttering in the shifting air.

I rubbed my eyes with my fingertips and stared. The scene twisted in my head, then righted itself, and I realized what I was seeing: Emile, trench coat billowing around him as he strode with purpose toward the house. I scrambled up and staggered after him.

He slowed at the steps to the house and I caught up. The two officers lay on their bellies. One made horrible gasping sounds. His shredded back ejected gouts of scarlet. My belly heaved as his life drained into the earth.

Emile knelt and touched the man's shoulder. His voice reached me, seeming far away. "Stay calm. You've just had the wind knocked out of you."

The flesh had already begun to close when he stepped over the man. He touched the other cop, then strode up the steps into the house. I followed.

Jack Lear leaned against a wall, head open. Another police officer had lost several parts, with the rest pressed into a cavity in the wall. Drywall and paint had cracked in the blast. Emile went to each of the bodies, then rose and looked around grimly. He glanced at me, barely registering my presence, then he removed his iPhone from his belt. Light blazed from its camera flash. He swept this around the room.

On the floor was an orphaned foot. Against the far wall, near a gas fireplace, was something that looked like a deflated and deformed basketball.

"Ah," Emile whispered. He knelt. "Ugh."

A ripping sound, like heavy cardboard being torn. Emile pocketed something.

"What are you doing?" I whispered.

"Nathan was in here."

I nodded. "They booby-trapped his corpse."

He blinked at me. "How do you know that?"

"I don't. I'm guessing." I looked around. "You want to raise him? That's going to be a problem."

He grabbed my hand and led me toward the door. "We need to go."

Outside, Flora Bingham stumbled toward us. She stopped at the steps, all professional now, wiping grime from her face with her sleeve. "What are you two doing? Isn't it tragic enough? You really need to go inside and film it up close?"

"Do we look like we brought a camera?" I retorted.

Emile cut off her response. "Your men got lucky. None of them died in there. You'd better check them out."

Flora looked ready to burst into tears.

Emile strode ahead of me. I caught up with him. "Nothing we can do about Nathan?"

"We can do plenty." He tapped his coat pocket. "I have his ear."

I remembered the tearing sound. Now I really wanted to be sick.

"You need to be on the air," Emile said. He smiled at me. "I have work to do myself."

He stepped back. His coat fluttered. It really did look like a cape. I flung myself at him and kissed him. Then I went back to work.

SETH

Gene stood beside me at the back of the crowd, staring at the remains of the house. He muttered something. When I looked at him, he whispered, "They booby-trapped it."

A moment later Emile came toward us, his coat catching air behind him. He stomped up. "What the hell are you people doing? Why did you let him go?"

Gene gave a sickly grin. "Hi."

"Let him go?" I echoed.

"We had him handcuffed. In the living room. I told you that!"

"He wasn't cuffed. And all you said was don't worry about him."

"He's one of the bad guys. You know? They kill us. They murdered Nathan and bombed my other house."

Gene backed away, hands out. "I didn't know they were going to do that."

Chase's voice squeaked. "We've been sitting here drinking with one of Moffat's men?"

"Yes," Emile said. "This is Eugene Hocksley. He drove Moffat's car." He glared. "How did you get free?"

"Those handcuffs you buy at sex shops aren't police grade." Gene tried to look ingratiating. "I've used plenty. They have a tiny lever; click it, and they pop open." He held up his hands. "Hey, if I was a problem for you, I'd have let Antoine and Devan go. Or I'd have just taken off. I never hurt anyone; I just drove for the bishop. Besides, I owe you guys." His face took on a pleading look.

I looked at him. "For what?"

"That isn't important," Emile said quickly. "But okay, you've got a point."

A look of hope. "I can stay?"

"No. But neither can the rest of this coffee klatch. The police will be here for days. You need to find another place to go. Consider yourselves evicted. Now, I have work to do." With that, he raced on to our house.

We wandered back to our beers at the kitchen table. I eyed Gene. He looked like someone's pudgy, not very bright brother.

I rose and went to the fridge. The stench of Chase's traveling life forms hit me like a slap. I stopped breathing long enough to find some deli meat that hadn't turned green yet and slammed the door shut. I put the meat in a casserole dish and took it to the fox. Her nose twitched.

Chase drummed his fingers on the tabletop in a weird rhythm. Locke wobbled like a pendulum. Suddenly everyone talked at once.

Eugene: "Look, just so you know, I'm not gonna turn you in or –"

Chase: "I've never held a gun before, never mind a machine gun –"

Me: "Well, hell."

Then a buzz of muffled static throbbed in the air. Chase and I looked at each other.

"Resurrection," I said. "Downstairs."

We ran to the steps. Locke gathered himself up to follow and Eugene just looked confused.

Emile knelt in the center of the basement rec room. On the floor before him lay something fetus shaped and bloody. With two silver studs in it.

"What the hell?" I said.

The resurrection buzz wound up and vanished. The thing on the floor began to bubble.

Emile looked up at us. "They killed Nathan in that house. I took this from what was left. I'm bringing him back."

I gazed at him. "From just his ear?"

He shrugged. "You brought your fox back from a fur collar. At least Nathan is fresh." He headed back up the stairs.

The ear twisted and stretched. Eugene and Locke came up behind us. Locke grunted. "Ah. Intriguing." He wandered away to the steps.

A clunk came from upstairs. Locke appeared, lugging a chair down the steps, beer in hand. We looked at each other. Then, wordlessly, trooped upstairs to collect chairs and booze.

In the basement we formed a circle and drank as we watched Nathan's ear turn into Nathan. It was that kind of night.

43

KAYLEE

I barely noticed when Emile returned. He appeared behind Deco, holding the Canon camera he'd gathered up from where he'd dropped it after the explosion.

I wrapped up the broadcast and told Deco to head back to the station. He agreed with a tired smile. I called Tony.

"We have some good footage of the scene," the news director said. "We'll edit it but we need you here in the morning to put a soundtrack to it."

"I've got loads of footage of my own."

"You better not disappear on me again, Jerrel."

"Never, Tony. And just to show there are no hard feelings, here's a free tip: someone vandalized the morgue earlier this evening."

"Vandalized the morgue?"

"Apparently they dragged the bodies around. Shot them up too."

"Jesus. This town is going to hell."

"You have no idea. I'm going to edit my own footage. I'll show you a sampler in the morning."

I clicked off my phone and beckoned to Emile. "Let's go home. We have more to do."

"More?"

"I want to edit our Moffat footage and get this story assembled. Are you up for an early-morning drive to Channel Forty-Eight?"

Emile nodded, his expression all business.

"We don't have Internet at the house, do we?"

He shook his head.

"Then do you have anything that can edit video on either of the laptops?"

"OpenShot."

"That will do."

In the house, muffled conversation came from the basement. Emile and I walked to his room at the end of the corridor, discovered stacks of boxes that didn't leave room for anything else, and retreated to my room next door. Someone, probably Locke, had picked up a small desk on wheels. Its surface tilted for convenient laptop use. The laptop I had used was in its case beside the desk.

Emile set the camera down. "I've never done video editing."

I sat on the bed and smiled up at him. "I have."

"Then let's get to it." His face split into a grin, sweet and boyish. With the prettiest dimples I had ever seen.

SETH

Nathan's ear had morphed into a doughy little human-shaped lump. Arms and legs emerged, along with a round head and bulging eyes.

Something rippled through the air. I looked at Locke.

He belched. "That, I believe, is the return of Nathan's spirit to his body."

It was. Baby Nathan sucked his first breath. "What the hairy fuck?" came out of him in a high-pitched voice.

"Relax, old chum," Locke said. "Your body will need time to rebuild itself."

Chase pushed his chair back. "Need the bathroom." He stumbled away to the staircase.

We sat in silence, drinking. I had two empties on the floor next to me. Locke had a half-circle of six in front of him. The fox did a walking tour of Nathan, sticking her nose into his armpits and his crotch. Nathan was still too uncoordinated to bat her away.

Chase scrambled down the steps. "Seth, you have to come. Kaylee is praying in her room!"

"Aw, hell." I scrambled to my feet. Locke did a kind of weaving thing and slumped back into his chair.

I followed Chase in a mad race up the steps, the fox yipping along behind me. "You're sure?"

"Yes!"

I shoved past him at the top of the steps and flew at the door to Kaylee's bedroom. The door banged open. "Stop! Right now!"

The first part of the scene to register was Emile on the bed naked, back to us. The second: shapely female legs looped around his hips. Third: Emile's glare as he turned around. And the fourth, impossible to miss: Kaylee's bark, "Shutthegoddamndoor!"

"Gr," the fox said.

The return to the basement was more subdued. Locke hadn't moved. Eugene looked at us curiously. Nathan was self-absorbed, as usual.

Chase's voice took on a slight whine. "I heard her say, 'Oh, God, oh God.'"

"No doubt." I dropped myself into my chair and took another tug on my beer.

Silence.

"It *sounded* like praying."

"I'm sure it did."

THE FOX

Much scrabbling at the door had persuaded Seth to open it. The fox waited for a car to pass, then scampered across the wide flat path to sprawl at the base of a maple tree.

Since the battle with the phonus she'd had no opportunity to examine the cord that regrew when Seth resurrected her. Pulses coursing through her brain and nerves fed the cord and kept it strong. In the moment before the cord attached to her spirit, she had spat plasm at it in annoyance. It responded by flaring brilliantly, undulating like a tree branch in a howling storm. And the cord lengthened. Not much, but enough to let her fight the phonus.

The fox tugged at the cord. It grew taut and firm. She pulled again, blowing raw, chaotic plasm over it. The strand allowed itself to stretch for a moment before snapping back. The fox grunted. When she had stretched it before, the cord was fresher. She leaned into it gently, drawing the tendril taut without jerks or tugs, and sending more plasm through it.

The strand grew, narrowing as it stretched and thickening again when it soaked up the plasm. The fox's soul moved a little farther away from her body. She glanced about in embarrassment, but nothing could see that her soul seemed to wear a dog's leash. She moved farther still. With each burst of plasm washing over it, the cord stretched.

This is lovely, *the fox thought. Her soul-gaze took in the ripples in the plasm of the world. Tendrils of power crisscrossed the sky.*

A familiar dark strand pierced the wall of the house where Seth and his pack were. The fox's spirit followed it and stopped outside to ponder the situation. The being called Locke prowled within. The strand binding his human body to its power was a thin threadlike thing. It seemed his body could detect little beyond its own senses.

Emboldened, the fox passed through the wall – and found herself in the room where the female Kaylee lay with the male called Emile. The strand she had seen wound in coils above them before touching the woman's temple.

The fox growled. She tugged hard on the cord binding herself to her body. The cord snapped tight, dragging her back.

A human voice: "It doesn't look like a car hit it."

Another: "Of course it got hit. It isn't just having a nap."

The fox raised her head and snarled. A hand jerked back as its owner yelped.

"Bart! You said it wasn't breathing!"

"It wasn't!"

The two humans raced off, rocking in that odd way creatures on two legs moved. The fox peered skyward, noting the path of the strand from Kaylee. One of the humans who had almost touched her carried a similar strand. Both cords wound through the air toward the west. The fox followed them.

She passed other humans. More strands wound up from their bodies to cross the sky.

Following the dark cords, the fox reached a cavern with a bird shape over its entrance. She chose a spot in an alley to lie down and ease her spirit from her body. The cord drew taut. She eased forward, stretching the cord until her spirit reached the walls of the cavern.

The Ducky Mart looked like the others she had seen with Seth this evening. Without the distraction of her mortal senses she could study the cavern in greater detail. The plasm that formed the building's walls had been altered in a way the fox had never seen. The shifting particles lacked chaos. Cords other than dark ones like Kaylee's would be suppressed and weakened the instant they crossed the barrier.

How many mortals were bound to these places? How many of these Ducky Marts were joined together by faint passageways nearly impossible to sense? The fox whined in surprise. Having noticed the passages, she couldn't understand how she had missed them before. They reminded her of the tunnels of light that led from this world to others. But the passages were dark, concealed like the cords.

A figure came to the glass from within. The fox peered up at a young female human. Of course, she wouldn't be able to see the fox's spirit. Then the woman's eyes fixed on the fox and smoldered with yellow fire. She bared her teeth and lifted a paw. The fox recoiled and fled. Slamming into her body, she leapt to her paws and scrabbled down the alley and across the street.

Halfway back to Seth's den, panting, she finally filtered her encounter with the woman at Ducky Mart through Seth's mind. The baring of teeth was what Seth called a smile. And the gesture with her paw? Beckoning.

Shaken, the fox continued home.

The Book of
the Phonus

44

SETH

We settled into a south-side mansion owned by Chase's uncle. Locke forked out for the rent. Emile loaned his furniture since he and Kaylee were hotel-hopping. We'd told them we would always knock, but Kaylee remained skittish. It was like she didn't trust us to respect privacy. The house was gorgeous and huge and tucked into a cul-de-sac called Matchbox Place with only three other houses. The greenery of Galway Park surrounded it and the back patio looked down on Galway Lake.

Feeling glum, I went for a stroll on the park's loop through the woods. The fox joined my pity party. Along Galway's west edge, the path paralleled the street. A strip mall sprawled on the other side of six lanes, with a Ducky Mart taking up the corner lot. The fox growled at it. Not in an angry kind of way. More as though she wanted to ask something. Being limited to gr/gr-gr must be frustrating.

I brooded along, letting her lead. The fox bolted after a pigeon once but didn't catch it. She rejoined me, tail lowered. She'd eaten the Doggy Yumyums I'd put out for her this morning under protest.

Emile and Kaylee had confronted Moffat. On camera, no less. Then they found Moffat's hideout. I should have done that. I felt like a fifth wheel. Moffat and Max were still out there somewhere but, with the killers down to just the two of them, nobody else was especially worried anymore and didn't want to be careful. That pissed me off. Max was dangerous and Moffat apparently more so than he used to be. At least the fox seemed to understand my mood. The others acted like everything would be fine.

My phone rang. Nathan said, "Better get back here. Antoine's awake."

"Shit, don't go near him. He could be out of his mind after all those years with the phonus in him."

"He's your problem, not mine. Just get here."

"What's he doing?"

"Performing Shakespeare." Nathan snickered. "He's pretty good."

I ran the trails to the house, up the marble back steps, through the enormous kitchen, past the laundry room where Eugene was folding towels, and then down the steps past Devan's cell.

Nathan leaned nonchalantly against the doorway to the walk-in closet where we'd locked Antoine. The killer was against the far wall, chains rattling.

"You!" he bellowed when he saw me. "You did this to me." A fist raised. "I'm mad, 'tis true, 'tis true 'tis pity, and pity 'tis 'tis true."

Nathan grinned. "*Hamlet.* He's done that one a lot."

The fox brushed against my leg to peer in. Antoine's eyes widened. "Shoo! Out, damned Spot!"

Nathan roared with laughter at that. "She'll chew your nuts off if you call her that again. Spot's a dog's name."

"Grrrr."

"If I had a blade, I would carve you as a dish fit for the gods," Antoine moaned. He didn't sound particularly scary.

"*Julius Caesar,*" Nathan offered.

Antoine surged at us, chains stopping him halfway across. "What did you do to me?"

"What's with all the Shakespeare?"

"Huh?"

"'Let's kill him boldly, but not wrathfully; let's carve him as a dish fit for the gods, not hew him as a carcass fit for hounds.' That's the bit where Brutus and Caius are planning to kill Caesar."

Nathan looked at me in surprise. I shrugged. "I read a lot."

"I haven't read that since high school." Antoine's face cracked into a quivery smile. "I had a wonderful English teacher. Mrs. Luoma. She liked to quote Shakespeare. And Christopher Marlowe."

"'Hell is a frame of mind,'" I said.

"She used that one too. Marlowe was . . ." Antoine's voice wound down like an old tape player. It came back faster and higher. "You did something to my head!"

"You were kind of possessed. By a Greek murder spirit. When it was torn out of you, it jumped to Moffat."

Antoine's brow pinched in confusion.

Nathan scowled at him. "Your precious bishop killed me with your phonus inside him. Sent me to the most boring afterlife imaginable."

Locke had figured that out when Nathan described his five hours of tedious death. Nathan had wandered the sand along a wide river. He could make out hills and mountains on the other side. The River Styx, Locke told us. Death by phonus apparently meant you got sucked into the Greek afterlife and had to wait around for Charon to come along in his little ferry and haul your corpsesome ass across to Hades.

Antoine yanked at the chain, shoulders bunching. "You unholy monster, what did you do? When I get out of here, I'm going to hunt you down like a frog."

"A frog?"

"You can't hold me. I'll escape and make bad things happen. Blood will have blood."

"You're borrowing from Shakespeare again."

Antoine slumped against the wall, wrapping his arms around his knees. "Now hast thou but one bare hour to live, and then thou must be damned perpetually."

I sighed and picked myself up. "I'm getting Locke down here. He'll want to join us in this ride to Crazyville."

45

KAYLEE

My documentary took two days to pull into shape. Hours in the editing room with Deco, hours out on the road getting shots of me discussing the case against Bishop Moffat with the Church of Mary the Virgin as the backdrop.

Then Tony called me into his office. "Kaylee, we can't run it."

Tony Serban had pasty skin and a permanent slouch, as though his brown toupee weighed him down. His desk was a fire hazard. Tony kept five huge stacks of papers on it and two laptops. The computers were always on, always hot, always sitting on papers turning yellow from the heat.

"Why not?" I demanded.

"Evidence. The police need evidence to lay charges. We need evidence to stave off a lawsuit. They have nothing to tie this bishop to the explosions at Ducky Mart or that house. Or to any of these murders. As long as the police won't press this, you don't have a story."

"We don't depend on the cops to approve our stories," I said. "Besides, the police aren't saying anything; that's a clear sign they're digging deeper into this."

"You think we should take a lawsuit – from the Vatican, no less? We're not running anything that says a Catholic bishop has spent more than a decade killing kids when you have no hard evidence. Your footage makes it clear Moffat's a lunatic, but that isn't a crime, and you asked plenty of nutty questions that your viewers might wonder about."

"I have a source from the inside circle of these killers," I said. "Possibly two. Will that do?"

"Give me something I can verify."

I got up. "Fine. Someone will talk. I'll tell them we'll make them famous; they can get a book deal out of it. True crime."

As I strode across the newsroom, three of my fellow reporters were at their desks, carefully avoiding eye contact. The rumor mill had ground along while I was away. Probably Tony had laid a foundation for firing me by spreading the word that I had taken a fast train to the funny farm. Despite claims of pursuing the unvarnished truth, journalists clamp onto rumor like a baby to a breast. I eyed Simone's immaculate desk as we passed. Even her computer keyboard looked scrubbed. The only thing out of place was a half-full coffee cup. An evil voice in my brain suggested I nudge it over onto her neat stack of papers.

I called Emile as I hit the door. "How is your day?"

"The insurance company is trying to make a case for the explosion at the house being an act of God. My lawyer has pointed out that while Al-Qaeda may view terrorist actions as acts of God, the law does not. I'm going to win and the insurance company is going to pay. How are things going for you?"

I told him.

"With all due respect to your boss, he's an idiot."

"I know. Are you free? I need ..." I need you. I caught the words before they could spill out. "I need some company. How about we get some food?"

THE BISHOP

"Here she comes," Max said.

I peered over the dashboard as Kaylee Jerrel descended the steps of Channel Forty-Eight's office building. A corner of my mind imagined her pleading eyes as I squeezed my pistol's trigger.

I put a hand on Theo's gun, the metal warming beneath my fingers.

After two days of watching Chantal Investments' office, we started tracking Kaylee Jerrel instead. We followed her across half the city as she visited various locations with a camera operator, spending far too much time outside the Church of Mary the Virgin.

Max sipped his Ducky Mart coffee. I had joined him in this habit. If the Lord saw fit to consecrate the earth beneath a convenience store chain, partaking of their appalling coffee was my duty.

When Kaylee Jerrel steered into traffic, we set off in pursuit. Max kept two or three cars between us and the woman's blue Mustang.

"Be careful, we can't lose her this time." I imagined the Emile Chantal demon on its knees, doubled over, my weapon barking at it, the demon's body flinching and flopping back.

<<That's it, Charlie, kill them all,>> came a gleeful thought. I winced. One shouldn't relish destruction.

<<Why not?>>

I massaged my eyes, attempting to push the thought back into the depths of my psyche.

46

SETH

Locke looked both pissed and pissed off as he opened his bedroom door. "What is it? I am saving this world you appear to value so highly."

"Antoine is awake."

He scowled at me. "Does he remember anything about the phonus?"

"He hasn't said anything. Wait, can't you tell that just from rummaging through my brain?"

Locke pursed his lips. "I am far too busy at the moment. My connection with my chopra has grown thin. It is consulting the powers in the higher realms, attempting to determine precisely what this Ducky Mart aspect is."

"Take a break. Maybe you'll get some fresh ideas. Come on; Antoine offered up the lamest threat in history."

Locke followed me into the basement. Nathan stood grinning in the doorway. Antoine huddled in a corner.

"Thou mayest torment me as his wretched son hath done in murdering my Horatio; but never shalt thou force me to reveal the thing which I have vowed inviolate."

"*Hamlet* again," Nathan said.

Locke shook his head. "More correctly, Thomas Kyd's *The Spanish Tragedy*. It is not nearly as well known, but

Shakespeare borrowed vast swaths of his own play from it. Impressive." He gave a nod to Antoine. "You have read it?"

"Pleased with their deaths, and eased with their revenge, first take my tongue, and afterwards my heart."

Locke looked at me then back at the prisoner. "Well?"

"Well what?" Antoine said.

"Are you going to finish it?" Locke grinned unpleasantly. "In Kyd's play, this is the point where Hieronimo bites out his own tongue."

"If you do that, I'll just grow you a new one," I said.

The killer cringed. "That's disgusting."

Locke sighed. "Your assassin is apparently well read. Or at least has read one play. It was popular in its day, full of torture and violence. Like a modern R-rated film. I, however, am attempting to prevent Armageddon and must attend to that."

"I thought you might be interested –"

"I am not." Locke's nose twitched. "This man is appallingly smelly. Can you do something about that? Perhaps a bath."

"That isn't going to happen," I said. "Though I can bring him a damp cloth."

Antoine's mouth quivered. "I'm a Vermicelli. You have no clue what I'm capable of. I've killed dozens of men. I can do that to you too."

"See?" I said to Locke. "He doesn't sound as tough as he used to."

Locke slowly nodded. "His speech suggests his heart is out of it. I suspect the phonus was the root of his desire to kill. Note also the undercurrent of stark terror in the inflections of his words."

"Yup." I crouched across from Antoine, rocking on the balls of my feet. "Okay, listen carefully. Up 'til a couple of days ago, you were possessed by a kind of evil spirit. We got it out of you."

Antoine stared a moment and laughed half-heartedly.

"I'd find it ridiculous too if I hadn't seen it leave you. But it's true. A murder spirit. Do you really feel like you want to kill people now?"

The ex-killer grimaced. "It's what I do. I'm good at it."

"And you read Shakespeare, or Kyd, or whoever. And Marlowe."

"Well, yeah. *The Spanish Tragedy* . . ." Antoine took on a faraway look. "Rather bloody. I've never liked horror or violence in my stories. I'd rather have plot and characterization."

Nathan decided Antoine wasn't an interesting spectacle anymore and left. Telling Locke to watch over Antoine earned me a glare from the Prince of Darkness. I brought fresh clothes, warm water, a washcloth, and a towel. Antoine toweled himself down. The whole exercise gave me the shakes, thanks to flashbacks of the last time Antoine had his legs free. But he did all of this meekly, not a peep or even a suggestion of trying to end my life.

Locke's phone buzzed. He took the call while he was supposed to be watching Antoine.

"Bes, what do you have? Tell me the news is good." A pause. "Oh, bugger. Bugger. There must be more than one in Cairo." Another pause. "Well, damn it all. Thank you."

He clicked off. Meanwhile Antoine stripped down to his red thong.

"That too," I said.

The killer looked bloody knives at me.

"Come on, it's been riding up your butt for days. It's not exactly fresh as a summer day."

With a dispirited shrug, Antoine popped the clips on its sides and tossed it onto the heap of laundry. He dressed in the clothes I'd brought.

"Feel better?" I asked.

"Yeah." Antoine ran his hands over his legs. "Can I get something to read? And a glass of water? And food?"

We left him there, taking the stinking clothes with us. I tossed them in the laundry hamper in the basement, and we went upstairs.

"I cannot attend further interruptions," Locke said crisply.

"If there is anything I can –"

"This is a matter for the powers. Please remain out of it. And do not bother me with matters such as our friend here."

"What do I do with him? Let him go? What if he's still a killer? I could send him to the afterlife, but if he isn't really responsible for what he did..." I shrugged. "This is complicated."

"The afterlife hardly qualifies as punishment," Locke pointed out. He headed for the staircase.

"I know that," I called after him. "But, even so, I don't want to kill people indiscriminately."

Locke just walked away. I went looking for lunch and a book to give Antoine, wondering why I was surprised. I knew the Devil could be a real asshole.

47

THE BISHOP

Miss Jerrel drove into a turnabout outside the Rover's Inn. I touched Max's arm and gestured at a sporty green car parked ahead of her. A lanky figure climbed from the Audi.

"Success!" Max beat a jaunty rhythm on the steering wheel.

I reached for my pistol.

Max caught my hand. "Let's observe first."

Miss Jerrel and the demon embraced and walked down the street together.

"Stay here," Max said. He flung his door open and smoothed his trousers, giving me a gleaming smile. "Perhaps they're simply off for a walk. I'll call you as they return." He tucked his hands in his trouser pockets and set off nonchalantly.

I pondered pointing my pistol and watching him drop in the street, then shook my head and drove that thought away. Gazing up at the cream-colored building, I saw a man in a white bathrobe at a table near a third-floor window. A fleeting thought suggested I sight my pistol on him, but I resisted.

A tapping on my window had me looking up into the face of a dark-skinned woman. I concealed my weapon and slid the window down. "Yes?"

"There's water leaking out the back of your car."

"Oh. Thank you. I'll have that looked at."

She nodded and wandered away.

Max returned, breathless. "Those two went to a restaurant. They will be there awhile. I believe we have some time to take care of poor Theo."

We drove two blocks to a filling station with a large white freezer marked *Ice*.

I went in to stretch my legs as Max purchased four bags. Glancing about outside to ensure there was no one nearby, I opened the trunk. Theo's corpse lay with knees tucked against chest. We had packed ice around him this morning at our motel, a sordid place with an appalling smell in the bathroom. Max lifted out old bags that were now chiefly water, and flung them against the gas station's wall. One had already leaked out, soaking the trunk. He cursed as he laid new bags against Theo's body.

"Hopefully," he said, wiping his damp hands on his pants, "we won't need to do this again." He slammed the trunk shut and looked about. "Ah." A gesture across the street at a Ducky Mart. "I'll supply us with coffee and snacks."

We ate chicken wraps in silence, watching Miss Jerrel's car. I let my thoughts wander. Jesus survived forty days in the desert, enduring an onslaught of temptations from Satan. Surely Devan could sustain his soul for five days amongst Satan's creatures.

<<Well, this is monotonous.>>

I turned my gaze to Max. "Yes it is."

"It is what?"

"Monotonous."

<<Wow.>>

Max glanced at me. "I didn't say a word, Your Worship."

I pursed my lips and turned back to the view of the street. My mind must be playing tricks on me.

<<Now that was creepily creepy.>>

"What's creepily creepy?"

Max turned to me, brow up, as a voice murmured, <<Zeus's gray beard.>> Max's mouth didn't move.

"I could have sworn . . ." I let my voice trail off and shrugged. A feeling of elation swept through me, curling my toes in my shoes.

<<That's remarkable.>>

Max looked again at the street, biting into his remaining wrap. I opened my door.

<<Wait. I want to see these mortals.>>

"I need a stroll," I said.

<<Oh, Zeus, he's off to pee again. If only his bladder weren't so bloody old . . .>>

As I walked past a little café up the street, I said out loud, "Hello? Is someone there?"

Silence reigned. Then a meek voice said, <<You really can hear me?>>

"Yes. What are you?"

I had the oddest sensation of something peering over my shoulder from behind me.

<<Bloody Hades.>>

"Are you an angel?"

<<Okay, let's be sure of this. If you really can hear me, say this number out loud: one million two hundred thousand seven-hundred and eighty.>>

"One million two hundred thousand seven –"

<<Ares' burnished blade!>>

"Ares' burnished blade."

<<This isn't supposed to be possible.>>

My heart began to thump. "You must be an angel. Oh my Lord, You have blessed me with one of Your own. Angel, are you to be my guide?"

<<I suppose. I am carnage and death. I drive mortals to push their fellow men from this world onto Charon's boat, to sail thence to Hades.>>

"Hades? That's a myth. You must be an angel sent by the one true God."

<<I grew from the heart of Cronus himself before the days of Zeus. This is refreshing. I haven't had anyone to talk to since . . .>>

"How long have you been here?"

<<In you? A day or so. I used to ride your man Antoine, but then . . . I really don't want to talk about it.>>

"You were in Antoine? Can you find him again?"

<<No.>>

"How is it that I can hear you now, angel?"

<<I'm not sure. When we were in that purple and yellow place the other day, I felt a kind of tugging sensation. Not painful like when that dog-thing dragged me out of Antoine. This felt like something pulling gently on me. When you left the store, I snapped back into you. Maybe it bound me more tightly to your mind.>>

My phone rang.

"I see them," Max said. "Best return to the car, Your Grace."

48

SETH

Tap-ta-tap-tap-ta-tap came from the front door.

The last time I'd heard that knock, it was Hilda Langella at my apartment door back in Cove. But she was probably watching another episode of *Lost* on Blu-Ray and wondering why her case list hadn't shrunk. The knock came again, insistent. I opened the door.

"Hello, Seth," Hilda said, fist poised to rap again. Hilda. Police detective. Here. Where we kept two prisoners. And a "person of interest," who was currently folding our laundry in the kitchen.

My voice came out all scratchy. "What are you doing here?"

She glanced past me then around us as though someone might be spying. "Work."

"This isn't a good time."

The cop grinned. Not a pretty grin. Kind of lopsided. "You have prisoners. I could bust your ass for kidnapping and forcible confinement. But I won't. I have more important concerns." With that, she settled her hand on the door and pushed. Hard. I backed up.

Gene stopped folding and watched with curiosity.

"This is Lieutenant Langella," I said hurriedly. "She's a police detective from Cove."

Gene's eyes popped wide.

"She's on our side," I said, hoping that was still true.

Hilda looked Gene over. "Eugene Longfellow. I saw you in *Prissy on Top*." Her gaze tracked his body, hovering over his paunch. "What the hell happened?"

Gene rubbed his stomach. "Long story. Personal. You don't want to know."

"You're probably right." Hilda gave a dismissive shrug. "You have someone here I need to see."

"Antoine?"

"Loki."

Huh? I thought. Her eyes swung back to me, blue flames burning in them, stabbing at air two inches in front of her face.

My mouth moved. I wanted to ask why she'd never mentioned being a power before and how that could have slipped her mind, but the best I could manage was, "Locke's drunk."

A door scraped behind me. You could smell the booze on Locke from ten paces. He hadn't shaved for days. His normally immaculate purple shirt hung loose and wrinkled over his belt.

"Brrrynnhilda," he slurred. "That bashtrrrd is lying. I am fine. I have got plenty dumb. Done. Mucky Dart. Mucky – Ducky Dar – The shtore god is undetectable."

"I got your messages," Hilda said. "Your chopra is in touch with my chopra. We have matters to discuss."

"You have a chopra?" I squeaked.

Hilda ignored me, her gaze on Locke. "You're playing at being human, and it's starting to show."

"I hashe to pee and poo. Morality. Mort. Mortality ish dishgushting."

"Try thirteen hundred years of PMS and Aunt Flo." She shook her head quickly. "Let's talk."

He nodded, holding himself upright by gripping the edge of the table. A belch, long and hideous. "I shall pour you a glassh."

"Not here." Hilda made a gesture around us. I had a feeling she meant all around us, not just this room. She stabbed a finger at Gene. "This one. He worked for the bishop?"

I nodded fast.

"And the one that was inhabited by the phonus. He is downstairs?"

"I can get him."

"That won't be necessary."

The world went away.

A field. A sky mottled with gray clouds. Before me, a wall of stone and wooden gate that towered to the sky.

"Holy crapoly." Beside me stood Eugene, his gaze at the massive gate. Next to him –

I drew my pistol, throat constricting, and pointed it at the killer. Antoine had his back to me, peering about, head darting this way and that. Eugene stepped back, out of the path of my pistol. Antoine swiveled around and blinked.

"Don't hurt yourself with that," he said.

"How did you get free?"

He shrugged. "I have no idea. I was reading that book you gave me – not really a Harry Potter fan, you know – and suddenly I was here." He rubbed his neck. "This is incredible."

Above us came a howling roar. We gazed at a huge bat-wing shape, like the Bat Signal in gray. Then came a ululating cry, and hurtling across the cloudy sky burst a horse shape in blazing white, following a path that wound around the bat shape.

"Where are we?" Eugene mumbled.

Then I got sucked into the sky. Like Superman but with a lot less control, hurtling up with wind buffeting me around.

I came to a halt between the Bat Signal and flying horse. There was an instant to make out the shape of Hilda on the back of the animal, her silver-white hair blowing about in the gale.

Then the interrogation began. It felt like having my skin peeled off while a thousand eyes looked at every cell in me. All through it I heard conversation in a language I couldn't understand. The words went right into my mind and twisted things around and stretched things out, and in between crying at the pain and gasping at the appalling pressure on my skull, I gathered that if I was smarter, it all would have made sense to me.

Then I fell. I hit the ground on my feet and stopped dead.

Antoine and Eugene were standing nearby. Antoine turned toward me and I stared into the muzzle of my own pistol.

"You dropped this," Antoine said, "when you did your flying act."

I stood, gasping for air – or whatever the substance around us was. That pistol muzzle looked huge. In a panic I tried thumping the Resurrection Button. Nothing happened, no buzz of static, nothing.

"You should get some firearms training." Antoine held the gun out at arm's length. "Don't hold it sideways like you see in the movies; that's moronic. It's inaccurate, and the shell casing gets kicked up into the air. I had a job taking care of a car dealer once who cheated my uncle on a Rolls Royce. When I showed up in his house to blow him away, he got freaky and pulled a gun. He chased me out onto his lawn and fired off a round, holding his gun that way, gangsta style. The shell casing went straight up and straight back down onto his arm. Those things are hot when they fly out of your gun, so it burned off a strip of skin. He dropped his gun." Antoine shrugged, embarrassed. "So I did my job and went home to collect my pay."

Then he tossed the pistol to me. I scrambled to catch it. A moment later he threw the magazine to me.

Shit. I couldn't think straight. Wanted to cry. Imagining flying around in a maelstrom, getting pieces of my soul torn out and looked at. "Thanks a lot, thong-boy."

Antoine flushed bright red. "Asshole," he said and turned away.

I stared after him.

"Thong-boy?" Eugene echoed. "What did that mean?"

"Never mind."

"Is that about the red thong?"

I gazed at him, trying to figure out what to say next.

"I found it in the laundry. I thought it was yours."

I choked on whatever I might have been about to say. At that moment a scream carried across the field. Antoine went hurtling up, arms and legs flailing.

Eugene and I stared up for long minutes. When nothing new or interesting happened, he looked at me, somehow looking down his nose even though the top of his head only came up to my chin. "You know, he's right."

"About what?"

"You are an asshole."

"I'm not the one with the kink."

"So what if he likes wearing it? Everybody has something."

Eugene wandered away by himself and sprawled on the grass.

I shook my head and started walking in the other direction. I wished I was back home in my own apartment, or emptying a box of books onto the shelves at Wordwings. Day-to-day stuff. Mundane stuff. Stuff where I could kind of think about how I was the son of a deadbeat deity without having to look the concept in the eye.

Some distance away, I could make out a small, lithe figure striding toward me. Long, dark hair. When she got closer and I could make out her features, she looked almost plastic.

"Hello," she said shyly.

"Hi."

"Are you dead too?"

"No. I was brought here alive. I think. Wherever 'here' is."

"Fólkvangr." The girl gestured at the stone wall with its gate. "That's Valhalla."

I stared, surprised, at the wall. "Wow. That means . . ." I gazed skyward. Things suddenly made sense. "Hilda. She's a Valkyrie."

"You know her?"

I shrugged. "I thought I did. She never told me about this."

An uncomfortable silence. Then the girl said, "I'm Rachelle."

"Hi, I'm Seth."

"That's her up there, isn't it?"

"Yes."

"What's the other thing? With the big wings?"

"Locke is his name. Or Loki."

"Wow. I never knew all this stuff was real. Mythology. You know?"

"I know. I'm still getting my head wrapped around it myself. What are you doing here?"

The girl sat on the grass. "I got killed. There was a gang shootout downtown. I'm from Cove City. I protected my friend Shirlie and my brother." A flush of embarrassment filled her plastic cheeks. "Hilda says I'm some kind of hero. That's why she brought me here."

I flipped through the channels of my brain for anything I could remember about Norse mythology. Valkyries were Choosers of the Slain; they picked out the heroes worthy of Valhalla.

"Shouldn't you be inside there?" I pointed at the gates as I sat.

"I wanted that." She sighed. "Hilda figured I'd be better off out here. Which is kind of sexist when you think about it. I told her I'd rather go in there and learn how to use a sword and really have fun. But we got interrupted when this little white dog showed up and she went flying after it." She gestured skyward. "Like that. I didn't see her again until now."

"I'm from Cove too," I said. "So you've been dead how long?"

"I'm not sure. There's no way to tell time here. The sun never moves." She rolled her eyes. "It's boring. I thought there'd be more people here. Hilda said she and her sisters bring heroic people here all the time. But there are very few kicking around. You'd think we'd at least find lots of Vikings, but maybe they're all inside the gates."

I hadn't heard of any shooting back home. But then, I'd flown to Summerton less than a week ago.

A shrieking sound. I looked over in the direction of Eugene. Antoine hurtled out of the sky, hitting the ground on his feet. You'd think he'd be turned into a pancake.

Physics didn't work the way it did back on Earth. That felt funny to think. This place wasn't Earth but didn't look much different from what I was used to. Just kind of artificial.

"Your friend is back," Rachelle said, pointing down toward where Antoine and Eugene were. The pair of them sat together on the grass, leaning toward each other, deep in conversation.

I sighed. "They aren't my friends. We got dragged up here together, that's all. I think we'll be sent back soon. I hope so, at least."

"You don't suppose I could go back?" Rachelle looked at me hopefully. "This place bores the hell out of me."

"I could bring you back, if I had something of yours."

"You can do that?" She brightened. "You mean like, something special to me? My hairbrush?"

"No. More like a body part."

Her face fell. "Oh."

"You know, my brother Nathan got raised from just his ear. I bet if we got some of your hair, that'd be enough."

Antoine and Eugene looked our way.

"Come on, I'll introduce you."

As we neared them, I made out the first snippet of conversation from Eugene.

". . . if you're prepared to go gay for pay, you can make a killing."

"What about residuals?"

"Forget it. In this business, you get paid by the scene."

Antoine hushed him, looking warily at Rachelle and me.

"What are you guys on about?" I asked, trying to figure out how to apologize for my thong-boy remark.

"Antoine's career," Eugene said.

"His career?"

He glanced at the girl beside me. "In my business. I'm thinking of going into management."

I stared at Antoine. "You want to go into porn?"

Rachelle cleared her throat. "Should I be listening to this? I'm only seventeen."

"Maybe you should go for a walk."

She stayed put.

"Who is she?" Antoine asked.

"This is Rachelle. She died heroically. That's why she's here." I explained where "here" was.

"Wow," Eugene said. "I thought that stuff was just a lot of hooey."

Antoine shrugged. "Back to what we were talking about. It sounds like it pays well."

I'd expected some awe from them. We were outside the gates to Valhalla, after all. Doesn't happen every damn day.

I chortled derisively. "You're going into the porn business with a name like Vermicelli? You know what that means? 'Worm noodle.'"

Eugene gave me a contemptuous look. "We'll come up with a stage name."

Antoine actually looked giddy. "I was thinking Antoine Maverick."

"Hey, that's pretty good. Aaaaaah!" Eugene hurtled up toward where Locke and Hilda's chopras hovered. Antoine and I stared after him.

An uncomfortable silence. Finally I broke it by saying, "Where did you get a name like Vermicelli anyway?"

"My grandfather. He came from Denmark." Antoine looked glum. "When he got into the mob business, he figured since all the gangsters he knew of were Italian – he'd seen *The Godfather* a dozen times – he should have an Italian name. He didn't know what it meant, and he figured Vermicelli sounded great. We've been stuck with it ever since."

Antoine looked around, discomfited. "You don't suppose someone I sent across is here, do you?"

"I doubt it. Nathan ended up next to the Styx instead of here, and it sounds like he was killed by the phonus that used to be in you. So your victims probably went there too."

"It was messy, killing all those people." He glanced at me. "You know what that's like."

"You kill people?" Rachelle said.

I pictured Max, blown up in Quentin's house. And Max, his brains all over the elevator in Kaylee's building. "Yeah, I know –"

Eugene plummeted back, looking shaken. Then our living room rolled into reality, leaving Rachelle behind. Hilda stood next to Locke. She turned and looked us over, her nose in the air. "I have work to do. Loki, stay off the booze. Toodly-do."

With that, she was out the door.

Locke rubbed his neck and went into the kitchen, where he poured himself three fingers of scotch.

Eugene stared at me. "Uh, Seth?"

I nodded. "It happened."

"Valhalla?"

"Yes. You, me, and Antoine. And Rachelle." Damn, I thought; she must feel abandoned. Again. I needed to talk to Hilda about that. Being stuck in a boring eternity had to be worse than oblivion.

Eugene looked around. "Where's Antoine?"

I went downstairs and found him in his chains. He had his back to the wall, book in his lap.

"Hey," I said.

He looked up warily. "Hey. Can I get my own clothes back?"

"Tell me, do you feel like you just woke up from this weird-ass dream about you, me, and Gene outside the gates of Valhalla with a teenage girl?"

While his eyes popped out, I knelt and unlocked his chains.

49

THE BISHOP

Angel, I thought. *Can you hear me?*

<<No. Ha-ha, that was a joke.>>

It wasn't funny, Angel.

<<I'm really not an angel.>>

You must be. I could see the obvious alternative, but that didn't bear consideration.

<<I'm not a demon either. You spend a lot of time thinking about God. Myth. Zeus and Athena now, those are gods. Serious gods with attitude and thunder. I bring death. You are my vessel. You're better than Antoine. It took more than a year before I could work him up into killing. Charlie, you have a solid murderous streak, real fanatical bloodthirstiness. That's the only reason I haven't prodded you into sticking that gun in your own mouth. I've thought about it. If you blow your brains out, your soul can sail away on Charon's boat while I hop over to Max. He strikes me as having loose wires in his skull. Very promising. Hey, check this out.>>

A wave of strength surged through me. Ecstasy combined with confidence. I could do anything. That journalist was powerless against me.

The sensation vanished, leaving me gasping.

<<Isn't that amazing? I can dial your feelings up and down. It's as though I'm sitting before a huge panel of gauges, and I just need to twist these little black knobs. Like this one.>>

Mind-numbing terror.

"Stop that," I moaned.

Max glanced at me. "What?"

The sensation vanished. "Never mind."

At that moment our prey returned, striding hand in hand toward their car. Max flung his door open with a grim smile. "It's time for business."

KAYLEE

Emile and I had a spectacular dinner at Ariadne's down the street from our hotel and walked back hand in hand. It felt as though he had always been part of my life.

When we reached the turnabout he said, "Kaylee I need to say something."

Oh, no, I thought. The Talk. He'll say it's been fun, and I really like you, but I want us to just be friends. His toothbrush will disappear from next to the bathroom sink and my bed will feel cold and empty again.

"It's about my documentary."

Oh, no, I thought. It's worse.

He stopped and turned me toward him. "I've been thinking about it a great deal." His fingertips touched my temples. "I have to say, you're amazing at what you do. But you're happier doing news. Hard, gritty, dig-deep-and-get-dirty news." He kissed me gently. "Do you think you could talk to your colleague, Simone? I think this is more up her alley."

I had to clench my throat muscles to keep from gasping with relief. "That's fine. I'll talk to her."

"I'm sorry," he said.

"It's okay."

Then a voice behind me spoke up. "Ms. Jerrel?"

Emile looked up and his eyes widened. I turned. There stood Max Cobber and Bishop Moffat. They both had right hands tucked into their jackets. They both wore black trousers and black jackets and shoes. Behind them a familiar white Chrysler idled, door open.

"Ms. Jerrel, Mr. Chantal, would you please come with us?"

I caught Emile's arm.

Cobber held open his jacket, revealing the grip of a pistol. "If you don't come, I'll be forced to shoot you."

I laughed. "How long do you think that will last this time?"

Moffat tapped the side of his head as though he had water in his ear. "You have no idea what we're capable of."

"Aside from incompetence," Emile said, "you may be right."

"You," Moffat's gaze sharpened. "You were with the beast. And Hermes. I slew you myself."

Max glanced at him in surprise. "Your Grace?"

Emile's brow shot up. He glanced at me. "The phonus, I do believe. And the beast would be Seth's fox."

Cobber cleared his throat. "Excuse me. We really don't have time to chitchat. Let me be clear. If you force us, we will wound you both, and then we will don these." He held up a balaclava, its eye holes lifeless. "We will drag you to our car, counting on you, Mr. Chantal, to heal you both. Alternatively, if you come with us now, you can plot your daring escape."

"How do we know you aren't going to just kill us?" I said. "The bishop here is carrying a murder spirit. It wants us dead, if I don't miss my guess."

Moffat drew a small ugly pistol and motioned with it. "The car. Now."

I turned to Emile. "How about we just run in opposite directions?"

Cobber's pistol almost leaped into his hand. "I am an excellent shot, Ms. Jerrel. I can shoot you both in the leg, and we'll take you with us regardless."

"In front of passing traffic?"

A shrug. "You'll both be healed good as new. It will be difficult for witnesses to claim you were shot down in public if you have no sign of wounds. Now please. Get in the car. We really don't have all evening."

Moffat took our phones. Cobber made Emile drive, directing him north. Moffat sat in back with me, his pistol trained on my side. He had a creepy smile on his face every time I glanced his way.

Locke would know where we were, thanks to his connection with Emile. He could find us and bring Seth. Seth would probably kill us all by accident, but he could fix that later. Perhaps he would finally leave me to the afterlife. So, I thought, I may as well enjoy the drive.

On the other hand, if I lived, an attempted kidnapping would wrap up my story nicely. And it put me right smack into the story. A hell of a way to conclude my journalistic career. Come to think of it, it didn't have to be a conclusion. After this, I could trot my résumé to CNN and go national. Maybe I could have my own show. Write a true-crime book about the psychopathic bishop.

I spent the twenty or thirty minutes of the drive mulling over career options until Cobber's voice brought me back to the present.

"Turn here."

I looked around as Emile made the corner. A small sign for Galway Park passed us. We were on a service road from the look of it: gravel with dense woods on either side.

Minutes later we stopped. Dusk had fallen. Cobber got out first, taking the keys from Emile. Moffat pointed with his pistol. I sighed and climbed out. He gestured us around the back of the car. Cobber hit the button to open the trunk.

A body lay nestled among bags of ice.

"Wake him," Moffat said.

"How long has he been dead?" Emile asked, bemused.

"A few days. That shouldn't make a difference to you." Cobber's grin stretched across his face, turning his cheeks a cheerful rosy red. "We are on a clock. We would like Theo alive in the next few minutes." He stepped over to me, his pistol's long, black muzzle – wider than the rest of it – shifting from sighting on my left breast to my right.

"You don't understand," Emile said. "You can't bring this man back. He has been dead for too long. We don't dare."

"Ms. Jerrel here spent half a day as a corpse," Max said with an oh-so-reasonable smile.

"We can kill her again," Moffat rumbled. His own pistol currently pointed at his right foot. I got the feeling he hadn't had Cobber's training. Cobber kept his trigger finger along the side of his weapon. Moffat's finger caressed his trigger, eager to blow off a toe.

"You could, yes." Emile set his hands on his hips. I pictured him in a superhero costume. Something black and red, with high-impact plastic armor across his chest to make him look muscular. "You can also try shooting me in the shoulder, but that won't work the way it did with Nathan; that was a heal, but here you need a resurrection."

"Interesting. You know about Mr. Filman's death."

"I brought Nathan back."

Max scowled. "A transparent lie. We heard about the explosion on the news. It must have reduced his body to pieces."

"Did you also hear about how miraculous it was that none of the police officers on the scene died? I healed them and brought out part of Nathan. You guys can't destroy enough of us to prevent that. You can kill us, but Seth can bring us back with one fragment."

"That's fascinating," Cobber said. Then he stomped on my left foot. I howled in agony, stumbled, and sank to the stony ground. He then thumped his pistol against the side of my head. Stars flew.

"What are you doing?" Emile roared. He surged toward me. Moffat's gun came up to halt his movement.

"You can heal her," Cobber said in a voice that suggested he was just making conversation. "You may do so at any time. Meanwhile, if you prefer not to have poor Ms. Jerrel in pain, return Theo to us."

"You don't get it," Emile said, his voice dry with desperation. "If someone's dead that long –"

I cleared my throat to cut him off. he shook his head at me. "There isn't any point in holding back. If someone is dead that long, they come back messed up. That happened to Kaylee. They're heaven junkies. Death is addictive. Handling Theo will be a nightmare."

Cobber smiled. "I'm familiar with nightmares. I've caused more than a few." He held his hand out and helped me up. I stood unsteadily on my foot, which I couldn't help but notice Emile hadn't healed. Then Cobber twisted my arm. It gave a liquid snapping sound, and pain shot up into my shoulder. I screamed.

"Oh, my," Cobber said. "That's dreadful."

Emile took a step. Moffat made a clicking sound in his throat. Emile's fist clenched. Warmth spread through my arm and foot. I moaned. The arm straightened itself out without any help from me. Bones lurched back into place.

"Ah, I see you're mending Ms. Jerrel." Cobber twisted my fingers back. "What else can we do? Perhaps the wrist?" He gave my arm a sharp twist. I shrieked.

"There is no way Theodore made his way to the home of the Lord," Moffat said quietly. "He was a twisted excuse for a human being. He believed he could find redemption, but hadn't yet paid for his sins. He will be thankful you tore him from the Devil's chains."

"There's no such thing as hell." Emile swallowed. "Kaylee?"

"Don't," I said. "Just don't. They can keep torturing me."

Cobber pistol-whipped me across my head. I fell, catching myself with my palms, which sent agony up my arms. The broken one continued to twist itself back into shape, which hurt like mad.

"Whatever you do to her, I can heal her." Emile's voice trembled. "Besides, you don't have a chance. They're coming for us right now."

"You expect the creature watching us through your eyes to rescue you?" Moffat said.

Emile drew an abrupt breath.

Moffat smiled, all teeth. "Yes, I am aware of this, little one. I can see this joining. It is Hermes to whom you are bound. He is nigh unable to hold his liquor, even now."

Emile's throat wobbled. His gaze flickered to me.

Cobber laughed. He sounded like a machine simulating laughter. "That's remarkably good, Your Worship. Now, Mr. Chantal. You have only to bring Theo back to us and then we can all depart. If you do not, Ms. Jerrel must suffer the consequences. Note the emphasis on the word suffer." With that, he reached down and twisted my right breast. Hard.

"All right." Emile's voice was soft, but I heard it despite my own screams.

I glared at him. "Don't, Emile." Even as a part of me muttered a prayer of thanks.

He sighed, face white. "It's done."

"Excellent," Cobber said.

The heal moved up into my temple, then across my chest. I felt warmth through my scalp and wiped away blood. The wound closed beneath my touch. Cobber shoved me with his foot, sending me sprawling toward Emile.

Emile helped me up. "I had to."

"You do realize that if you are lying," Cobber said, "I will do much worse to the lady."

Bullets emerged from Theo's back and rolled down into the trunk. He drew a shallow breath.

Cobber grinned and motioned us to get back. "Thank you for your cooperation."

Then Theo burst into wracking sobs. "Oh, God. It was so beautiful." He stretched his arms out. "And holy shee-it, I'm effing cold!"

"My," said Cobber.

Revulsion spread across Moffat's face. "No, that cannot be right."

Theo flung himself up and out of the trunk, wailing, "Let me go back. Oh, please, send me back."

Cobber gave a posh little titter. "Perhaps the fundamentalists are correct. A bit of belief in the Almighty is all that is required for passage to paradise, regardless of behavior. Gives us all hope, does it not?"

50

THE BISHOP

Theo sat on the grass, whimpering like a small child as full night came on.

<<Can you shut up your man? He is giving us a headache.>>

Be quiet, I said in my thoughts.

<<When can I take them?>> A surge of bloodlust accompanied the words.

You'll have your chance soon, Angel.

Elation filled me, a vast pool of joy rising through my body, filling my mind and soul. The angel's work, of course, but that didn't diminish the sensation in the slightest.

The Emile creature glanced about, head jerking like a bird. Kaylee Jerrel wore a pleasant expression, as though she looked forward to being cast into Hell.

<<You mean Hades.>>

No, I don't.

Large trees littered the terrain. No sign of human life marked the land here.

"Well, then," Max said.

The Emile creature looked us over, contempt upon his face. "You're just going to whack us after we brought back your friend?"

"Of course."

"Allow me." I lifted my pistol.

"The woman first," Max said.

"No, me," Theo moaned.

Max raised his eyebrows. "Theo, we require your help. Perhaps after you have given it, we shall send you to your reward."

"Promise?"

"We'll see. Now please shut up so we can kill these people."

"I want *you* to do it," said Miss Jerrel, glaring at Max.

He blinked in surprise. "You prefer that I shoot you dead rather than leaving it to His Worship? This is a new one. Typically people beg pitifully for their lives, offer money or sexual favors, weep appallingly, pee themselves. None have ever expressed a preference for who does them in." He spread his arms wide and gave a long, happy sigh. "I do appreciate it when somebody brings something fresh to the table. When you've done this a lot, the events run together. It becomes factory work. 'Oh, please don't kill me. I'll do anything.' Bang. Or, 'How about a blow job?' Boom. After a while you yearn for something to make that particular death memorable. A desperate flashing of the breasts –"

"Forget it." The woman rolled her eyes.

"Oh, I had no intention of suggesting you do that. It's already happened. Twice. It gets old quickly."

"Just get on with it," the Emile demon said.

A red fringe enveloped my vision. My pistol trembled. "Let's finish them, Max."

"Max, I want *you* to shoot me, not him, damn it!" Desperation drew lines around the woman's eyes, clear even in the descending darkness.

I lifted my pistol. "This is not your decision."

Max caught at my arm. He looked as though he were enjoying this spectacle. "Please, Your Grace. The creature. Take him."

"I want both."

"I think we can honor Ms. Jerrel's last request. It is such a refreshing one. Please, take Mr. Chantal. I recommend once through the skull. We have no reason to make them suffer now."

I lifted my pistol. Ecstasy filled my soul.

The creature grasped the hand of the woman as if it could feel love. I squeezed the trigger and the weapon jerked. A hole appeared above the demon's right eye.

The woman held on as the body slumped to the ground. Kneeling, she extricated her fingers from his grip and looked up at us, glaring.

I aimed for her head.

"Don't you dare," she said.

Max laughed. "Good day, Ms. Jerrel." His pistol thudded twice. Two dark spots appeared above her eyes. She slumped in a heap, as though her body had merely been switched off.

Rage filled my mind. Max crouched beside the body of the demon and began to dig through its pockets.

I sighted my pistol on the back of his head.

<<There now, that's great,>> the angel said. <<Do it, Charles.>>

But I need Max. We have more demons to get rid of.

<<You can do it without him.>>

No I can't.

<<Charles, do you really think he or Theo or the rest have any respect for you? I know Antoine didn't. They're in it for the chance to kill and create mayhem. All those ridiculous books you read? 'How To Be A Charismatic Leader.' They make fun of you.>>

Shut up.

Max still rummaged through the clothes of the corpses.

"What are you doing?" I asked in a strangled voice.

"I don't want them identified readily if they are found soon. Would you be kind enough, Your Grace, to gather up some leaves and cover them?"

I stared down the muzzle of my weapon at the back of his head.

"Your Grace?" he said, his back to me as he reached over to empty the woman's pockets.

My finger caressed the warm metal of the trigger.

<<That's it, Charles. Just a little squeeze.>>

Leaves rustled.

"Grrrrr." A small white dog stepped out, teeth bared.

<<Oh, no.>>

Max rose, hand on his gun. "Isn't it cute? We may have to dispatch the owner, of course."

My gnawing need to kill dissolved, replaced with overwhelming fear. The angel's silent voice shook: <<Run! >>

What is it, Angel?

<<That is the monster that tore me out of Antoine. It made me bleed! Flee!>>

That's what you fear? Someone's little dog?

<<It's not a dog! Run run run run!>>

"Max. We go now."

I reached down and tugged Theo's arm. He stumbled up, weeping and praying.

Max followed reluctantly, glancing back at the animal and the exposed bodies. "Hell."

We stuffed a clumsy crying Theo into the car. One of the phones on the dashboard chimed. Max looked at it, snorted, and held it out to me. "Mr. Chantal is receiving a call. You should take it."

Across the face of the phone glowed a single word:
Seth.

KAYLEE

I remember this tunnel of light. The music carries me as I spread my arms and rise toward a glare of whiteness and silver. I bask in the feeling of warmth. There is no heartbeat here, no breath.

"Beautiful, isn't it?"

A perfect rendition of Emile appears beside me, skin flawless, eyes an aquamarine blue. He is transparent at first, but his features harden into reality.

"It is," I say. "Aren't you supposed to be going to the river?"

"Probably. Wherever we go, we won't be there long," he says.

I turn to him, aghast. "No. You didn't!"

A shrug. "Just before they shot us. Two resurrections."

"That isn't possible. You can't raise yourself."

Emile smiles. "Of course I can. Seth did it back in Cove City. He told us all about it."

"Shit!"

THE FOX

The fox went for a walk by herself because she didn't want to hurt the man's feelings. The Yumyums he had bought had given her a dire case of the Fiery Yellow Splatters and an excruciating desire to be dead.

The fox could exit her body at will, if only for short periods. She was glumly certain that when she returned, the Yumyums would still lurk within, as eager to get out as they were now.

She wandered until her digestive system stopped snarking, then found a flock of Canada geese in a clearing. A sprint and leap brought one down. Soul-sight revealed the indignant spirit of the bird as it rose. A passage of light opened and swallowed it.

The death of the goose brought unwelcome attention from the rest of the flock. They moved toward the fox, wings half-spread, hisses filling the air. The fox snarled, flicking a wave of plasm that rolled across their spirits. The geese stumbled to a halt, then fled, launching into flight.

The fox chewed through feathers to the meat. Nothing compared to fresh food right out of the flock. As she ate, she thought about Ducky Mart. She had been too unsettled to return since her first encounter with the power lurking within the yellow and purple caves. Seth shivered at the thought of the places. They made his heart thump. Was her avoidance coming from him?

A familiar smell intruded. The Kaylee woman was somewhere nearby with her mate. The fox spotted the cord leading to Kaylee from Ducky Mart.

With a suddenness that made the fox jump back, the cord snapped and flailed. She ran, leaving her goose behind. She found them in moments. A blazing passage in the sky sucked at the two spirits drifting up from slain bodies. Three men were near the bodies. One she recognized from the morgue. Another quivered and talked to himself. The third, an old human, carried upon his spirit the crystal creature the fox had fought with Seth.

The fox growled, getting the attention of the blue creature. It wailed in fear. The fox liked that and added a deeper, throatier rumble. The creature forced the mortal to flee.

The fox glanced up at the passageway. It was shrinking, folding its gleaming mouth in on itself.

Seth cared for these freshly-killed ones, though he refused to admit it to himself.

The fox whined. She couldn't pass through to the higher worlds while still attached to her mortal body. The cord couldn't reach that far.

Could she take her body with her?

The fox spread her spirit around her mortal body and gently tucked it within. Nestled within her soul, her body became inert. The fox examined it, not entirely sure she could restart it when she returned.

Oh well, *she thought,* work that out later. *She gazed at the quickly closing mouth of the passageway – and leaped out of the world.*

The Book of
the Shoot-Out

51

SETH

Chase and Nathan had gone to collect more stuff from the last house, leaving the rest of us to usher in Antoine's first night of freedom. I regretted setting him loose. Not because he stirred up any trouble but because I flinched every single time he moved, remembering him breaking my fingers or swinging a chain at my head.

We scarfed down Chinese food. The fox watched us, licking her lips. I pointed out her bowl of Yumyums but she just looked mournful. Finally she scratched at the door and I let her out.

"That used to be Bedstefar's collar?" Antoine asked wistfully.

"Whose?"

The ex-killer got a faraway look. "My great-grandfather fought in World War One, for Russia. I found his old army coat in my dad's closet. I had the fur cleaned and put onto my tailor-made jacket."

"I didn't know it was a family heirloom. Besides, at the time I thought you were going to shoot me."

"I was. Eventually." He caught my expression and grimaced. "I mean, the phonus was."

As we ate, Eugene and Antoine got into a discussion about his audition shoot and Locke focused on a glass of whiskey. I felt left out.

Suddenly Locke's eyes crossed and he did a header into the tabletop. I figured he'd passed out, but he came up sputtering.

"Bugger. A true believer is born."

"Oh, hell. Where?"

"On the other side of this park." Jutting his jaw toward Galway beyond the windows. "Emile and Kaylee are with him. Them. Charles Moffat and his compatriot."

"His Grace is right there?" Antoine pushed his chair back, eyes wide.

Locke blubbered and belched. "This is an incalculable nightmare. They have dispatched Kaylee and Emile. Now that they have the believer brought back, they no longer required Emile."

"Emile raised someone? Who?" Then the answer popped into my thoughts. "Theo. Chase blew him away at the morgue."

"This is correct," Locke slurred.

"We need to get over there and bring them back."

"Emile has taken care of this himself."

"Oh. Good. But we still need to find Theo. You can track him, right?"

The galaxies in Locke's eyes dissolved, and he had pupils once more. His head thumped onto the table again.

"Locke!" I screamed in his ear.

A snore filled the air, long and rumbling.

I paced. Antoine and Eugene watched, mouths open.

Then I had a thought. I tore my new phone from my belt and hit the button for Emile's number.

"Hello," a smooth voice answered.

"Who is this? Charlie?"

"Do not call me that, Mr. Brown. You will show me respect."

"Respect? For what, your mind-numbing incompetence? You snatched Kaylee and Emile."

"And you wish them returned."

I thought fast. "Yes. That's right. We need them back."

"You have something we want, Mr. Brown. Devan. Is he all right?"

"He's fine. What have you done with Emile?"

"Put Devan on the phone."

"Put Emile or Kaylee on."

Silence. "We have dispatched them."

"Then no deal. I'm hanging up now." No chance of me doing that, but it sounded good.

"Mr. Brown, we are well aware you can return them from Hell itself. I propose an exchange. Devan for the location of the bodies."

I thought about how Kaylee had been after Devan raised her. Odds were good Theo came through equally messed up, so he'd be a handful.

"Okay," I said. "Soon. Now, in fact. Let's meet. In a public place."

Locke sniffled.

A soft laugh. "Bring Devan to the vicinity of Pellier and Whitherwood Streets. Then call this number. You will receive further instructions then. Come alone."

The phone said, *click*.

I had to chuckle to myself about that. I recognized the address. Kaylee's condo. That must be where they wanted to meet.

Antoine looked at me, his arms crossed. "You're going to trade Devan? They'll kill you."

I smiled grimly and marched to the kitchen counter. I tore a sheet of paper towel free and dug out a knife, one of the brutally sharp, brand-new blades Locke had bought us. The blade opened my thumb with a single slice. I squeezed blood onto the towel then tripped a heal.

Antoine stared at the splash of blood. "Some kind of ritual? For good luck? I know guys who do that kind of thing, but I didn't think you were the type."

"I'm not." I carefully folded the piece of paper. "Emile brought Nathan back with just his ear. If they get me, any of my brothers can raise me with this."

"Wow," Eugene said.

Antoine glanced at the other man. Then he said, his voice unsteady, "If you need backup, I can handle a gun. I may not have that phonus thing in me anymore but I can still aim and shoot."

"You can't," Gene said quickly. "We've got company coming, people you need to meet. You know, for your audition."

I looked at Antoine and grinned. "No worries. I'm covered. As long as this is here" – I touched the blood-soaked piece of towel – "I don't have to worry about what happens to me."

He let out a long breath.

"The important thing is Theo," I said. "I need to cap him. Locke will know if they blow me away."

We looked at the comatose Locke.

"Damn," I said. "I need him on his game."

"Maybe strong coffee?" Gene offered.

Back in school, I used to dip into Mom's whiskey. I'd get plastered for half the night, and when she drove up, I'd drop a heal on myself. Alcohol is a fun poison, but it's still a poison.

I touched Locke's neck and set off a heal. What was the worst that could happen?

My phone rang. It was Hilda. I hit the button. Her voice boomed out: "WHAT THE FUCK DID YOU DO?"

Then my phone turned into a turkey drumstick.

"Locke, cut that out. Hilda will be here any moment."

Locke hovered in the living room, feet dangling inches above the floor. Red horns had grown from his temple. "THIS IS BLOODY MARVELOUS. I HAD FORGOTTEN HOW IT FEELS TO MANIFEST."

"You need to stop. Right now. Before Jehovah notices."

He flicked a fingernail against one of his horns. It rang like a tuning fork. "IS THIS NOT NIFTY?"

This had to end. I reached up and tugged on his pant leg. "Stop this, dumbass."

"YOU DARE SPEAK TO ME SO?" Galaxies burned in his eyes, though one of them looked wrong, like a cat's eyes where one of the slits had shifted to horizontal.

"If you're going to manifest, does this mean you can clear the booze out of your blood?"

"I AM NOT SURE. I HAVE NEVER FELT THIS WAY BEFORE."

The door flew open. "LOKI. STAND DOWN." Hilda glared at me, eyes burning blue fire, and said in a strident voice, "Do you have any idea what you've done?"

"No." I held up the turkey leg that used to be my phone.

Hilda rose, spreading her arms. Whiteness glared. "LOKI," she roared. She continued in a language I didn't recognize. Locke barked something in return. Then he looked at the floor and lowered himself meekly to it. The drumstick became my phone again. Locke's eyes still glowed, but the fight left him.

"Good." Hilda lowered herself to the floor. "Damn it, Seth."

"What exactly did I do?"

"When you heal a mortal, you widen the connection between the soul and the body, so strength comes out of the soul and feeds the mortal form. But when powers have a body, it's separate from our soul and we have to squeeze a bit of ourselves into it. Think of it as being under pressure. In Loki's case, the heal caused the part of him in this body to spurt into the rest of him. So instead of his soul healing his body by getting rid of the alcohol, his state of mind in this body has been fed back into his higher form."

She snorted. "You got him drunk – all of him."

I chewed that over. "His chopra is tanked? Oh. Crap."

"Oh crap is right. The only reason he isn't comatose is you purged the booze from his mortal self. His chopra would pass out otherwise."

"Wow," Eugene said, sipping his Ducky Mart cup while he and Antoine looked on.

I glared at them then looked back at Hilda. "How do we sober him up?"

"Give him time," she said with a glum shrug.

"'Til morning? We don't have that long."

"It's his soul that's drunk. He operates on a different time scale. He could be this way for decades, or even a couple of centuries."

I blinked. "Hilda, we need him on his game."

"I'm tempted to leave you to cope. You did this to him."

"I didn't know –"

"That really doesn't change much." Hilda frowned. "What's happening here, Seth?"

I told her about Theo.

"A true believer." Hilda sank her hands into her coat pockets. "I've never heard of one of those before." She shook her head when I started to speak. "Jehovah is a different aspect of the godhead, with his own rules. Odin and his pantheon don't work the same way; that's all. Go on."

"Moffat and Cobber think I'm prepared to trade Devan for the location of Kaylee and Emile's bodies. But we already know Emile has brought them both back himself. My problem is Theo; I need to send him across again fast. But right now Locke is too useless to detect him."

"Thataway," Locke gurgled, gesturing around us. "It is thataway."

I explained my plan to Hilda, and showed her my stored blood. She nodded, impressed.

I collected Devan from his cell in the basement, locked him up with pink furry handcuffs – he didn't know you could release them by touching a lever nestled in each cuff – and told him we were giving him back to Moffat. He spared a glare for Gene and Antoine on his way to the car.

52

KAYLEE

"Emile, couldn't you have left well enough alone?"

"Love, I just thought it was simplest –"

"Don't call me 'love.' I'm not your girlfriend. We're friends with benefits. Hell, we aren't even friends. I could have gone into a glorious afterlife. Now you've screwed that up."

We are drifting along the tunnel. Emile is naked, his body a perfect cartoonlike animation. Mine is thinner than I recall, breasts slightly, pleasantly, larger and higher. How much of this is wishful thinking?

"Please, love. You just need to relax," Emile says.

"Relax? I could have stayed dead this time."

"Gr. Gr."

The sound comes from behind us. Turning my head causes my whole body to rotate. Seth's fox lopes toward us on an invisible surface, her tail a thick fan of fur jutting straight up.

"It's dead too now?" I mutter.

"I'm not sure."

The fox trots up to us and makes a snarling sound. Her gaze reaches past us. We turn to look. There ahead lie two suns, too bright to stare at. I shade my eyes. We drift apart.

"Hey, wait," Emile says. "You're going the wrong way."

It's true; we are each drifting toward a different fire.

"Moffat shot you." I point. "That'll be the way to the Styx. I'm not going there. I'm going back to heaven. If I'm going to get dragged back to the world, at least I'll get a taste of it."

"That's not a good idea. Ever seen someone try to quit smoking or get off drugs? One hit, and they're messed up again."

I laugh. "I don't care. I'm going back there, thank you very much. There isn't a damn thing you can do. Enjoy your time at the beach."

The fox growls. Then pounces, catching my wrist in her jaws. I feel no teeth. The touch is gentle.

"Hey!" I shriek. "What are you doing?"

She backs off, dragging me.

"Let me go!" The pathway to ecstasy lies before me, but the fox pulls. As my arm stretches, my body snaps to it. The animal drags me toward Emile.

"I don't think it wants you to leave me." Emile drifts toward the glowing hole on my left. The fox backs toward it, my arm in her mouth. I kick at her. Her eyes narrow and she makes a rumble in her throat. Teeth grow, pressing into my wrist. A flash of redness, blood of the soul.

Then Emile and I tumble into a blaze of whiteness.

I sprawl amid warm sand. A sky of unblemished azure fills the world above. I lie here, drawing breath after breath.

"Kaylee?"

It is Emile's voice in my thoughts. I keep counting breaths, aware that breathing really is a comforting formality here. My heart doesn't beat. The air smells of lilacs.

The fox's snout fills my vision. I flinch. Beyond her, Emile's perfect face appears, staring over the animal's ears. I shift onto my side, lift myself to my feet. Sand. Stones along the bank of a broad length of water that is not quite water. A thought of water. A belief in water. On its far side, dark, rocky hills reach for sky.

"The Styx?" I whisper.

"I guess so."

"Gr."

I want to cry, beat my fists on the sand. "Damn it, I wanted funland again."

"This is for the best, I think, love."

I turn my back on Emile and stare across the river. "Wait. This isn't right. The Styx is supposed to have souls in it. Figures writhing in the water, that sort of thing."

"And Charon's boat, yes. I remember that much from the Discovery Channel. Maybe Charon retired."

"Somehow I doubt the afterlife includes a pension plan."

The familiar grip of a resurrection clenches my belly, roiling and clawing and dragging me back toward life. I double over, discovering Emile doing the same thing.

I gasp. "What –?"

The world turns flat, like a three-dimensional scene compressed into a photograph. Then it hurtles away, enveloping us in darkness. A snarl reaches us across vast darkness. The fox appears in the middle distance, racing along as though on an unseen pathway, her body a lean, undulating mass of muscle lunging toward us. Then we are falling . . .

My eyes flew open to an imperfect sky. Then something dark flickered across my vision and a warm wetness stroked roughly across my cheek. I sat up. The fox backed off.

"Good God, cut that out." I wiped my face on my arm. My white sleeve came away pink. I stabbed a finger at the fox. "That's disgusting. That's my blood."

53

SETH

Kaylee's condo. Again. I parked outside twenty minutes after escaping Hilda's snarkiness and punched Emile's number up.

Moffat sounded less sure of himself. "Hello, creature. Do you have Devan?"

"He's here."

"Good. Are you at Miss Jerrel's home?"

"Near enough."

"Excellent. Set your phone to its speakerphone mode."

Moffat's voice came from the bottom of a well. "Do you have your phone set properly, Mr. Brown?"

"I do."

"Devan, are you there?"

"Your Grace? It's me. I'm with the demon."

A long sigh. "Devan, child. Are you well?"

"Yes. They tried to tempt me, Your Grace, but I didn't falter."

"I knew you were strong."

"They have Antoine and Eugene. Their souls have been corrupted."

"You have no idea," I said.

Moffat sniffed. "They are lost to us, then. Mr. Brown, drive south along Pellier Street. I will give you directions as you go."

We neared red lights a couple of blocks down. A row of stores on the left, the inevitable Ducky Mart on the right, and a used-car lot farther along.

"We're at the light," I said.

"Proceed to the next set."

We carried on past the car lot, past a mall I didn't recognize.

"We're nearing the next set of lights."

"Good. Turn left. Devan, if there is any deviation from my directions, I want you to tell me so."

"Yes, Your Grace."

We waited until the light changed, Devan chattering happily with the bishop.

"Left again," Moffat said moments later. "You should find yourself on Thorne."

"That takes us back the way we came."

"Your powers of observation serve you well, demon. Tell me when you near the lights."

"Okay, we're there."

"Excellent. Turn left on Trembey."

"Done. I have green."

"Good, good. You should see a Ducky Mart just beyond the intersection."

My belly turned to stone. "Ducky Mart?"

"We await you at a table inside."

THE BISHOP

The angel had withdrawn to a distant, shrill presence in my mind that would surely beget a headache in due course. I wondered why it should withdraw in a secret house of the Lord. But then, Lucifer himself was a fallen angel; perhaps God had made both angels and demons vulnerable here. A brilliant ploy.

Without the angel of death badgering me, I could think matters through more carefully. We would have Devan back. The Seth demon couldn't cause trouble here in its weakened condition. Only a few of the demon's brethren remained. It would take time to finish and would be harder with them warned, but we could do it.

I could wield the weapons myself. I had drawn the blood of the demons called Nathan and Emile. Soon Theo would be ready to rejoin me and Max in the fight. He knew now that the Lord walked with us and salvation could be his.

Theo had grown calmer when we brought him into the Ducky Mart. He merely murmured prayers as he nursed the towering mug of coffee before him. Max had grown twitchy.

"Can't you hear that?" he asked in a low voice. "Like whispers."

"Relax. Seth Brown will be here soon." I grasped his arm. "You will do nothing to the Seth creature. Leave him alone. Our goal is to get Devan."

Max turned wide eyes upon me. A calculating look passed over his face and subsided. "Leave him?"

"We retrieve Devan and then depart. That's all."

We watched the demon's white Toyota pass by with Devan in the passenger seat. My heart swelled in expectation. Max gave me a nod: no one followed. When the demon informed me it had reached the lights, I told it where we were.

"Look, Charlie, there's a park across the street. How about we get together there? Bring Max and Theo."

"No. We meet in Ducky Mart. Join us with Devan."

"Don't you find the decor rather harsh? All that yellow and purple hurts my head."

"Join us, demon, or you will not find the bodies of Mr. Chantal and Miss Jerrel until they are too long dead to be recovered."

"Maybe I'll just take Devan down to the river and finish him off. How about that?"

I smiled. "Doing so will bring on the wrath of the Lord his Father. Your only hope is to bring him to us."

"Theo with you?"

"Theo is not your concern. But yes."

"The park will be quieter. You outnumber me, obviously. It'll be more secluded."

"Demon, you waste time. Bring Devan now."

"You know there are security cameras in there, right? If you try anything, the cops will know all about it."

"Park your car and bring Devan in here. I have no patience left for this."

We waited. For a few minutes, I thought perhaps the demon had fled with Devan. Then his car edged into a parking stall.

Max slipped his hand into his jacket, but withdrew it when I touched his shoulder. The creature opened the passenger door. Devan stood up, holy wrists bound together with fuzzy pink handcuffs.

54

SETH

The hardest thing I've ever done was step into that Ducky Mart. Devan, on the other hand, looked giddy; he could see Moffat sitting at a table, sucking back a coffee. Did Moffat and Max know I could be permanently killed in Ducky Mart?

I pictured those spots of blood I'd left at the house. Probably useless. If I died here, the trip would be one way and Ducky Mart's afterlife likely involved garish colors and cute rubber duckies. Solution: don't die.

I reached into my pocket, using Devan as a shield, and worked my thumb into the pin ring of the grenade there. A sharp jerk freed it.

Factoid: It isn't enough to just pull a grenade's pin; you have to let the handle release before it can deliver a bad day. I repeated this thought to myself. It wouldn't do to forget.

Cobber, Moffat, and Theo sat at a table near the back wall. They weren't alone. Behind the front till stood a young woman whose name tag read, *Hi! My name is Adele! Please be patient. I'm new!* At the till at the back, before the rows of coffee makers, paced a guy with a little ducky badge on his yellow T-shirt. It just read, *Braydon*.

He smiled. "Can I get you anything?" Then he saw the pink handcuffs on Devan and gave me a funny look.

"Later," I said. No customers in the place. The only innocent bystanders were the staff.

Moffat rose. Cobber stayed put, eying me hungrily. Theo sat there with his palms together. He appeared to be crying softly. When I neared, I heard a quiet prayer.

"Stay where you are," I told Moffat.

He ignored me, moving forward. "Devan. It is so good to see you."

I dug into my memories of what Antoine and Gene had told me. Moffat hired crooks and used an ex-porn star as his driver. Cobber was a former attorney who strangled a client. Not much there I could use.

Moffat motioned at the table. "Join us. Let us be clear, demon. I simply want Devan back. You may leave whenever you wish, unharmed."

A muscle jumped under Max's left eye. He clearly hadn't expected Moffat's offer.

Devan and I sat down. Moffat looked at the handcuffs. "The key, please."

I laid it on the table.

Moffat lowered his voice. "Of course you have a weapon. Pass it over."

I took the grenade out of my pocket and held it under my hand, giving them just enough of a view to recognize it.

"Demon, that's unwise. Your talents fail in this place."

"Maybe."

Moffat laughed. "You're a terrible liar. The Lord has consecrated this place. We can destroy you and your kind here with impunity." The bishop held out his hands. "Besides, you want to your fellow creature, I presume. As a show of good faith, you will find Mr. Chantal and Miss Jerrel on the service road at the southeast end of Galway Park."

"Are you sure Devan isn't just like me?"

Moffat's smile twitched at the corners. "Our faith is strong. Devan is the one true son of the Lord. You demons will be cast back to Hell."

Max grinned. He suddenly looked relaxed. "You have no advantage here, do you, Mr. Brown?" He opened his dark suit jacket, revealing his pistol.

"Our Lord is the light of the world," Theo added helpfully, his eyes bloodshot and glazed.

"Your Worship," Max said, his voice clear now. "Please take Devan and Theo with you and leave. Mr. Brown and I have business to attend to."

Devan fumbled with his handcuffs, working the key.

I gulped down the part of my innards that tried to crawl up my throat. "Maxi, if you're hurt in here –"

"I have lived with the expectation of death as finality for all my life. You apparently have not. Devan has brought me back twice, but why should I fear death even now?" His face split into a broad smile. "I have seen what awaits. Besides, Mr. Brown. I'm actually good at what I do. You've just been supremely lucky."

My heart thumped like the pistons in an old truck.

Max's forehead furrowed. "Do you hear someone whispering? 'This place is sanctuary.'"

"No, I don't." Moffat rose. "Max, come along now."

Max gazed up at him. Moffat stared him down. Max drew a long, exaggerated sigh. "Very well. Mr. Brown, you can live a while longer."

Devan got the cuffs free and dropped them onto the table. He rose, glowering at me. "You will burn for your sins."

"Come along, Devan, Theodore." Moffat gripped Theo's arm. Max got up then, his palms spread.

A gleam of hope. I could let them go. I could walk out of here.

But Theo could bring on Armageddon just by stepping out of this place to where my old man could sense a True Believer. One prayer too many and . . . game over.

Damn. "Theo," I said evenly, my gaze on Max. "I'll send you back to heaven if you take Max's gun away."

Theo blinked. A beatific expression filled his face. Max's mouth formed an O as Theo turned on him.

I leaped up. Moffat tugged at Devan's arm. I stumbled back, letting Devan's body fill the space between Moffat and me, and ducked behind a metal panel that separated aisles, grenade clenched in my hand.

Max and Theo were thrashing around on the floor behind the table. I poked my pistol in Moffat's direction and discovered the flaw with using Devan as a shield between us: I couldn't get a clear shot at the bishop. Moffat scrambled for the door, Devan behind him. I squeezed a shot through the glass. The woman at the till shrieked and ducked down.

Max pummeled Theo. As soon as he got the other man onto his back, his pistol thumped, quieter than mine. Theo's feet jerked. Another thump and he settled, motionless.

The door swung shut behind Moffat and Devan. Shit. My luck bottle had just poured out its last drop.

I dug out my phone and punched Hilda's number. She answered immediately.

"Hilda," I gasped.

She didn't give me a chance to speak. "Seth, what the hell have you people been doing these past few days? There's a film crew setting up in the living room. Prissy Hardsuckle just autographed my tank top. And isn't Antoine Maverick the guy who tried to kill you?"

"Hilda, look –"

"They've written Nathan up as the set doctor. He's signing papers saying everyone has had their STD shots and checkups. That's fraud; I could bust the lot of them."

"Can you quit whining and save my fucking life?"

"What are you –?" came a voice from the back. A pair of suppressed pistol shots sounded. I heard a grunt and the thump of a body falling. Peering around the aisle, I saw Braydon flat on his back with blood forming a puddle around him.

Pulling back, I could see Moffat outside. He turned toward me, face contorted in rage, pistol in his hand. I threw myself around the aisle. Moffat's weapon didn't have a silencer, so it made as much racket as mine. Bullets pierced glass and slammed through the paneling that separated aisles. I tumbled straight into Max's firing line. A bullet thumped into the wall above me.

"Hilda. The Ducky Mart. Pellier and Trembey. Moffat and Cobber shooting at me. Call the cops. Call Homeland Security. Do something."

A moment of silence as she chewed on that. "We're on our way." The phone clicked off.

I crouched and flung the grenade up and over. It bounced off the ceiling and made a rattling sound on linoleum. A mumbled curse and pounding feet. Then the bomb cracked off and flung a wave of air through the building, rattling ceiling panels free, shattering windows, taking out lights, plunging parts of Ducky Mart into dimness. Smoke filled the air.

THE BISHOP

The voice of the angel roared into my thoughts the instant I reached the sidewalk outside the store. <<Kill him!>> My weapon swung up toward Devan.

No! My resolution pressed the angry voice back.

The angel sounded conciliatory for a change. <<Look around you, Charlie. Theo's dead and even Devan can't bring him back now. Max is having the time of his life in there, in full view of at least two cameras. You're finished. The best you can hope for now is to wipe out one more demon and become a martyr. Leave Devan, he can get along without you.>>

Inside Ducky Mart, the Seth creature cowered near some bread. In despair and rage, I fired. The creature ducked behind a cabinet. I crept along the side of the building, peering in for any sign of movement or exposed flesh. Liquid joy filled my veins.

Thunder swept through the shop, shattering windows. I stumbled back and fell, scraping my knee upon the sidewalk.

<<Brilliant!>> the angel shrieked in my thoughts. <<Get moving. You've got him cornered.>>

Ecstasy and power filled me.

<<That's the spirit.>>

My knees creaked as I stomped on broken glass and leaped at the frame of a destroyed window.

<<Wait, this isn't what I meant, Char–>>

I landed awkwardly inside the ruined building. The moment my feet touched the linoleum, the voice of the angel retreated, leaving me with a vision of Devan struggling in his innocence to make his way in the world. Perhaps I had no chance of escaping without facing prison. But I could still be his mentor.

Damn you, Angel. I turned back to the outside world.

SETH

Hoo-boy, a second chance. The bishop blinked as if not fully aware that he had come hopping back in here. He turned to flee.

It's awfully unsporting and impolite to shoot someone in the back. But I'm not saying don't.

55

KAYLEE

"Gr," the fox called impatiently. Emile made a face at her.

We'd walked for what felt like an hour. Without my phone, I had no timepiece. I gave Emile the silent treatment. He didn't respond with the usual vacuous comments intended to fill an uncomfortable void, so it didn't appear to be working. He had his hands in the pockets of his dress pants. Dried blood splattered the front of his white shirt, but most of it had run down his back. If he weren't looking so cheerful, he'd be a mess. In my case, blood had dried against my face and head, gluing patches of my hair together.

The fox ran ahead, then returned to us yipping. The path came to an arching bridge. Emile glanced at me, brow cocked. Then he stepped down beside the bridge to the little stream. He crouched and scooped water onto his head and face. He lay down then, ignoring dirt gathering on his white shirt, and dunked his head in the stream. It carried away the blood.

I crouched beside the water and washed my face and head. The water felt like ice against my neck and ran in a chilly rivulet down my spine.

The path brought us to a street: Matchbox Place. The fox raced ahead again when we came upon a driveway. I noticed a van, white with faded lettering across its door, parked outside the house next to a familiar SUV.

Emile gave me a glance and a grin then jogged to the SUV. "It's definitely Locke's. His jacket is on the seat. The keys are in it, even."

The house sprawled before us with huge wide windows on the main floor and towering vertical windows on the upper. Chase had mentioned his uncle picking up a mansion for a song. But this was incredible.

I forgot my anger with Emile. We laughed and bounded up the steps. He flung open the door. A glare like a set of spotlights hit us, that characteristic blue-white hue used for video shoots.

"Quiet on the set," a voice barked. "Shut that door. Oh, God, that better not be the Witnesses again."

Moments later Emile and I sat on the porch step in the kind of silence that can only be shared by two people who have walked in on a porn film being shot in a friend's living room.

Emile spoke first. "That woman. With the . . ." He held his hands out in front of his chest.

"That's Melody Melons."

"You've seen her before?"

"Yes."

"You don't suppose –"

"They're fake."

"You're sure?"

Between *Thongs and Dongs Four* and *Five* she . . . swelled."

"Oh."

Silence returned, broken again by Emile.

"What do you suppose Antoine was wearing? Besides the ball and chain?"

A flash of leopard print shot through my mind. "I have no idea."

A moment later Eugene emerged and sat next to us. "We weren't expecting you."

"I gathered that," I said.

The fox yipped.

Eugene said, "Oh, yeah. Seth's in trouble. Locke and Hilda took off in a hurry."

The fox bared her teeth and growled.

"What happened?" Emile and I spoke up simultaneously.

Eugene spilled the story. Seth had left to trade Devan for Theo, who had become a true believer like me. Armageddon could be coming over the hills at us right now.

"I need a phone," I said.

Eugene passed me his, and I keyed in Seth's number. No answer. I tried Locke.

A female voice answered. "Yes?"

"Who am I speaking with?"

A momentary silence. "You called me. Who're you?"

"That phone belongs to Locke, not you."

"That'll be Detective Langella," Eugene said.

"Who the hell is –?"

The voice on the phone interrupted. "Is this Kaylee? We've met, sort of. You were expiring in the back of Seth's car while he raised Quentin from the dead."

"Oh. Hi," I said with an odd feeling of embarrassment. "What's going on?"

"Loki and I are en route to the Ducky Mart near your condo. Pellier and Trembey, I believe?"

Dread filled me. "Seth plans to meet Moffat in a Ducky Mart?"

"He is already there. He knows what he's doing."

"You think *Seth* knows what he's doing?"

The fox leaped straight up, spun 180 degrees in flight, and hit the ground at a run. I stared after her.

Emile rose. "Where is she going?"

"Quiet on the set!" came from behind us.

"Sh," Eugene said.

I gave him a glare. "We're taking your phone."

"Hey!"

I ignored him. Emile pointed at Locke's SUV. "Shall we?"

"We'll need a camera van too." And a change of clothes, I thought, and a shower. I keyed in the number and put Eugene's phone to my ear. Emile had the SUV running when I reached it, and I had Urma on the line, patching me through to the editing room.

Bobby Hale answered. I told him curtly to pass the phone to someone else. He didn't like that. I didn't care. Emile slammed the SUV into gear and spun tires as I gave orders to Deco Franklin.

"Don't talk to Tony before you go," I told him. "Just get moving."

"Yes, ma'am."

56

THE BISHOP

A gunshot wound is a remarkably peaceful way to die. I lay on my chest, almost unaware that I had legs. Devan knelt beside me, moaning and crooning.

He will save me, I told myself through a haze. *The devil's creatures can't win.*

Blood crept across checkerboard linoleum. My body grew cold. Darkness enveloped my vision, narrowing to a black tunnel.

With shocking abruptness, sensation returned to my legs. I picked myself up – and found myself rising, unchained by gravity.

I flexed my fingers. A decade of arthritis had evaporated from my joints and knuckles. The spots on their backs had vanished. I ran my palms over my face and head. My chin felt smooth, though I hadn't shaved for two days. My hair remained.

<<Ack.>>

The voice came from behind me. I blinked and turned, not entirely sure how I managed to rotate my body as I floated.

A beast with blue skin and angular joints towered over me. Its mouth bristled with crystalline teeth.

<<Ouch. I pulled something during the shift.>>

"What are you?"

<<I'm Rain-of-Blood.>> I recognized that voice; it had lurked in my mind for two days.

"You don't look like an angel."

<<I'm not one. I've been telling you that since I landed in your skull.>> The creature sighed. <<I hope we can find a way back.>>

"Why would you want to go back?"

<<I'm a bringer of bloodlust and death. I can't very well carry out my destiny as a phantasm.>>

The walls of the tunnel around us took on a combination of yellow and purple, the colors shifting in disorienting swirls. At the end of the passage, whiteness blazed. <<I think we go that way.>>

"Are you sure?" I asked.

<< Do we have a choice?>>

The instant we passed into the white glare, a surface appeared beneath us. My feet settled onto unblemished black and white linoleum.

"Hello," a voice said. We looked around, the creature beside me twitching its head this way and that.

The figure began as a shadow in vapors. His body thickened, until we found before us a young man in a yellow shirt and black slacks. The logo of Ducky Mart lay above his heart. His skin was charcoal black, face round and hairless – but in an instant his skin lightened to that of a Caucasian man with a thin shock of red hair covering his head. "Welcome. We have a great deal to talk about."

"Who are you?" I stammered.

Rain-of-Blood recoiled. <<A god.>>

The figure tilted his head. "Thank you. Call me DM." His features shrank into themselves and a narrow nose emerged beneath round feminine eyes. The body shifted into that of a short, young woman. "I'm the power who created this world around us. Yes, the place is monotonous. But with a little imagination –" Three couches appeared, heavily upholstered in black leather. "They're very comfy."

A shout behind me drew my attention. I turned to find Theo stomping toward us. "It's all wrong. I want the other place, the good place."

DM's body grew taller, features twisting into a slender Asian man with shoulder-length dark hair. He glanced at Theo and rolled his eyes. "What a whiner."

I swallowed. "This can't be Heaven."

"No," Theo wailed, "it's Hell! Or worse!"

DM snapped his fingers. Theo hurtled away across the vast plain of flooring until he vanished in the distance. "That'll keep him busy; it's a long walk back here. And you're right, this place isn't Heaven or Hell. Hell doesn't exist. As for Heaven, you really don't want to go there. Believe me."

THE FOX

Seth had gone inside a Ducky Mart. That made things both easy and hard. The fox pondered as she ran. She charged headlong to the street, then veered onto the grass and dug claws in. The move halted her less than a body span from the traffic. She glanced right and left, watching for a gap.

There. The cars were not moving in either direction. The fox bolted. A car rolled out from a side path, the fox leaping across before it. The car screeched and slowed as the fox bounded on. Ahead lay caverns, glass sides joined together in what humans called a "maul."

When, *the fox wondered,* did I start thinking in human ways? *She now understood that a stone-with-eyes was a car, and had even begun to picture the sound "car" as one of the roving caverns. Language had once been sounds and smells. This concept of "words" had slipped into her mind when she wasn't paying attention. Embarrassing.*

The fox slowed and glanced about. Part of the glass wall had the bird shape on it. There were humans walking across the stony terrain where their cars had been left in the hot sun. None were coming this way.

Bear-crap, *the fox thought.*

Then a squeak drew her attention. A female human with a large drink in her hand emerged from the cavern. The glass wall began to swing shut.

The fox leaped. The closing wall caught her side, tumbling her through the gap. She rolled and scrabbled to her paws.

A thousand pathways opened here, invisible to natural eyes and nostrils. One bore the soul-scent of the man, laced with fear.

Behind a counter stood a thin woman. "Hey," she said. Her eyes began to burn with yellow fire. "Ah, hello again."

The fox snarled, then sniffed once more for the scent. There. The fox wrapped soul around body and leaped at the passageway.

A voice behind her roared: "GET BACK HERE, FUZZ-BALL!"

57

SETH

"Congratulations, Mr. Brown," Cobber yelled.

"Fuck off."

Cobber continued. "You're doing remarkably well, Mr. Brown."

"Thanks."

"It will be a pleasure killing you."

"Ditto, Maxi."

Devan had hunkered down beside the bishop's body, bawling and blubbering with absolutely no sense of family dignity.

"The cops are on their way, Maxi. You'll never get out of here if you don't go now."

A laugh. "I've been to prison before. I am a survivor. Perhaps this time I shall settle for a mental-illness plea."

"Didn't you try that after you strangled your client?"

A brief silence, then a strained note appeared in his voice. "My client lacked respect."

Footsteps crept along the aisle to my left. I poked my pistol out and cracked a shot off.

"Well done, Mr. Brown," Max called out. "However, you missed."

His silenced bullet made a thud in the metal paneling behind me.

"You may be interested in this, Mr. Brown. I am using a suppressor, so I've selected subsonic ammunition. Thus, I have considerably less range than you, and cannot shoot through these metal shelves. Isn't that fascinating?"

Why are you telling me this, moron? I wondered, easing along the aisle in the direction of his voice.

"Perhaps you're wondering why I am enlightening you," Max said. "I do savor a good contest of wills. You have utterly failed to provide that, so I plan to dispatch you with haste. However, I think knowing your weapon is somewhat better than mine gives you a fighting chance. Or at least the delusion of one. Perhaps you can provide a little amusement toward the end."

I turned onto my stomach and shuffled toward the end of the aisle. I could tell he had moved closer. Maybe just an aisle over.

A lump pressed into my side. I felt my jacket pocket and found the other grenade. I took a deep breath, eased it out, tugged the pin free, and tossed it up and over the aisle. A dull thump off the ceiling. Then a single clop sound as it hit the floor.

A muttered curse and a laugh. Then my grenade hurtled back over the aisle barrier, bounced twice, and rolled under the shelves in front of me.

"Oh"

– On my feet, racing along the aisle, keeping low.

– "bloody" –

Into the open, thump of suppressed pistol fire slamming into the till counter ahead of me.

– "hell!"

I leaped up and over the counter, colliding with the till and plowing it onto the floor before I tumbled into the arms of brand-new staffer Adele. She babbled something that could have been a foreign language.

Thunder shook the building. An entire set of shelves jumped into the air and took out a chunk of ceiling. I raised my pistol as a wind howled through. Chunks of ceiling and bags of Doritos flew about.

Footsteps. I cracked a shot into the ceiling. The footsteps stopped.

I waited, trembling. Adele yammered something in ShitYerPantsian.

"Would I be mistaken in suggesting you don't have any more of those toys?" Cobber called.

I laughed and lied. "Four more."

"I doubt that. You lack the pockets for them."

Footsteps again, quieter. I twisted, shoulders aching from my tumble into the alcove. In front of me squeaked a little door on hinges. I nudged it with my foot, and a bullet thumped into it. I kicked hard. The door swung open upon Cobber, standing like a TV show cop, gun clasped in both hands. I fired. He leaped aside. I kept shooting and shoved the door open again when it threatened to close. Beyond lay the assistant manager. I leaned to the right and saw the front door. Devan was trying to drag Moffat out by one ankle.

"You do have a remarkable supply of dumb luck, Mr. Brown. Surviving our encounter at Ms. Jerrel's condominium. And of course the bomb in Graeme Thunderbird's apartment. Speaking of which, Mr. Brown, however did you live through that? We knew you were visiting him. Poor Theo timed the explosive carefully to ensure you would be in the apartment."

That recalled a vision of huddling in Graeme's bathroom while the building shook around me and the door buckled as though it were about to cave in.

"I was giving birth to a lawyer at the time," I called.

I had time to reload my pistol before he got it.

Boy, did he get it.

"Yousonofabitch!" Cobber bellowed, his voice like a jackhammer. Footsteps pounded toward us. I fired into the ceiling in his direction. Suppressed gunfire dug into the paneling on the other side of the till. Then louder gunshots; the psychopath had taken the silencer off his gun.

"Mr. Brown," came Cobber's heavy, breathy voice. "I am not going to merely kill you. I am going to do it slowly. I am going to watch your eyes as your life drains away. I may even pry one of your eyeballs out with my pistol muzzle, just for my own amusement. I am going to enjoy every moment of your end."

I'd found his Achilles' heel.

"Adele," I said, "know any lawyer jokes?"

She stopped moaning and gazed at me. "You're in the middle of a gunfight and you want lawyer jokes?"

A scraping sound. I poked my pistol out and laid out four shots. Running steps and a smashing sound. "You have no idea how much pain you're going to feel!" Cobber yelled.

I popped another shot in his direction and said to Adele, "I'm the good guy. That psycho out there will happily kill you. Just listen to what he wants to do to me."

"You're shooting at him. I'm just hiding."

"I don't think he's going to care about the distinction here. He used to be a lawyer before they disbarred him for choking a client to death. If we can drive him off the rails, maybe he'll run out of bullets and I can finish him. Lawyer jokes. Please."

Adele thought a moment and shouted, "What are ten thousand lawyers at the bottom of the ocean?" A pause for effect. Then, "A great start!"

Bullets slammed against the wall above us. I poked my gun up and fired blind three times, spacing the shots out. That emptied another magazine. I had two left. Damn.

"Cobber," I called. "You can just leave. If you stick around, the cops are going to nail you. I hope you have a good lawyer. Better than you were."

A pistol shot cracked.

"Cobber? Is that his name?" Adele asked.

I nodded.

She cleared her throat. "Mr. Cobber, a monk, an accountant, and a lawyer go bowling together –"

A grunting sound reached us, silencing Adele. The assistant manager, Braydon. Not dead obviously. I nudged the little door open. He struggled to sit up, wiping his face with his sleeve. "Ugh."

A couple of gunshots barked. He flinched and flopped back down into his blood pool.

I popped up from the alcove. Max stood over the body, muttering to himself.

I squeezed my trigger. My shot took him in his side. He turned in surprise, and I put one through his chest. Then another. He flinched, looking annoyed, so I added another. He rocked on his heels. I kicked the door open, stepped out, and blasted him again.

"Well," he said, and his lips frothed with blood. "This is . . ."

He didn't finish. I put another bullet in his chest, and Max toppled like the Leaning Tower of Pisa finally giving up its war with gravity.

For good measure I stepped over him and shot him in his head. My hand trembled, so the bullet didn't pierce his left eye as I'd intended. His head rocked side to side then stopped.

Silence. Except for the thud-thud-thud of my heart.

Then the sirens penetrated. I looked up. Beyond the smashed windows were rows of blue lights.

Adele came up beside me and stared at Max, her face green. She looked over at Braydon. "Is he dead too?"

"Yes." Nobody lost that much blood and got up afterward. I lowered my pistol. Mom wouldn't be impressed with her son getting carted off to prison. I'd shot Moffat and Cobber. My pistol would be linked with the morgue shootings, too.

Still, I felt great. Armageddon? Not gonna happen on my watch. I shut my eyes and drew in a long, pleasurable breath.

The gunshot distracted me. Not so much the sound as the lancing pain through my right arm and the spray of blood from my shoulder. I stumbled and turned around.

There stood Devan, pistol in hand. The gun had come from Moffat. But the glare in Devan's eyes, that look of someone embracing his inner wacko, that was all Devan. The bishop's blood drenched his white shirt and soaked the knees of his pants. He looked like an intern at Vivisections 'R' Us.

THE FOX

The fox ran, slowed at a crossroads in the paths that formed the substance of the Ducky Mart god's realm. She sniffed plasmic air. Blood-smell from the man. And terror. The fox bent her nose to each path, chose the strongest, and scrambled along the roiling surface.

A figure loomed before her. A human male this time, with the customary black cloth on his lower parts and yellow covering his upper body. His eyes flashed with plasmic fire like the sun glaring from piss-holes in snow. He flung his arms out and bellowed, "YOU SHALL NOT PASS!"

The fox drew back, snarling, and readied herself to leap.

The god lowered his feet to the passageway's floor. "Oh, calm down. I've just always wanted to do that. Have you seen Lord Of The Rings?*"*

The fox growled.

"Probably not." The god stroked his chin. "This would have been easier if they had taught you Morse code, like Chase suggested."

That brought the fox up short.

The god shrugged modestly. "Yes, yes. I've had a seat at the table with your little band of malcontents, thanks to Kaylee. She's one of mine, you know."

The fox growled, impatient.

"Wait. This is important, if we're both going to survive this. Just listen . . ."

The Book of
Ducky Mart

58

KAYLEE

A police blockade got in the way as Emile and I neared my home. I recognized Flora Bingham directing traffic off Pellier Street. Farther on, amid police cars with flashing blue lights, were two large gray trucks, Summerton's Emergency Tactical Response Division.

I called Deco. "Where are you?"

"Almost at the intersection of Pellier and something. The place is crawling with cops."

"Get set up as close as you can."

Farther on past the ETRD vehicles was an NBC truck and the local CNN affiliate. I actually considered bolting out of the car there and then, but I had no cameraman and blood had dried all over my shirt. I'd be the story in no time, rather than covering it.

Emile took us a block over, around the police, and into my condo's parking garage. I leaped out and headed for the elevator before he rolled Locke's SUV to a stop.

He raced me to my condo. I cranked the shower on, peeled off my clothes, and threw myself into the spray. Emile joined me, all business despite his manhood brushing against my hip. Seconds later we raced into the bedroom to gather clean clothes. He took less time, going for black slacks and a white shirt, almost exactly what he'd just discarded. I put on my blue skirt, cream blouse, and matching blue jacket. Cool and professional.

I wondered what was happening down at Ducky Mart. My God. Seth was up against Max Cobber – a professional killer.

Do you trust Seth? My inner voice asked.

I don't know. He's as crazy as Cobber. No, wait, that isn't true. He shot Quentin during our meeting, but he knew Quentin could heal himself. His heart is in the right place. And he's done surprisingly well against people who spent a great deal of time mastering the fine art of death and mayhem. So I guess I do.

Oh, well, thank you, my head said.

"Get your laptop," I told Emile. He gave me a quizzical look. "The story is on it," I said. "We'll need it. This is going to be huge."

He scooped his laptop bag up from where it hung on one of the dining chairs. I took the camera we'd swiped from Bobby Hale's truck. We headed for the lobby.

I worked through the logistics of the shoot while we walked, and came to an unsettling conclusion. Gritting my teeth, I called the station.

"Hi Urma."

"Kaylee? Tony is ready to crucify you."

"Put me through."

"Are you sure?" she whispered. "He is out of his mind."

"That's normal. Give him to me."

"You're taking your life in your hands." The phone clicked. A pause. Then thunder.

"Jerrel? You are beyond fired. Someone is shooting up a Ducky Mart here, and we're running a story about poisoned soda crackers in Iowa. Every station in the city has scooped us. Even some dick-wad with a cell-phone is on the scene and streaming video to YouTube."

"It doesn't matter. We have a story they don't. Bishop Moffat is inside there."

"I'm sick of your bullshit. Jesus, the YouTube guy is interviewing a cop. This is a disaster, and its name is Kaylee fucking Jerrel."

"Tony, shut up. Before we're done, we'll own this story."

"If you don't have an amazing story, Jerrel, you're totally fired. You can try blackmailing me, but you'll still never work again. I'll bury your career so deep in Screwup Cemetery that you'll never find it."

"Bishop Moffat is dead," I said.

Emile turned a quizzical look to me. "What makes you think – ?" he whispered, but I waved him to shut up.

"Moffat is dead?" Tony said in a tiny voice.

"Yes, and I'm the only journalist who knows that."

"You're sure."

"Yes." I pictured Moffat sprawled inside the door to Ducky Mart, a pool of scarlet around him. "Tony, we can run my story."

We reached the scene and I spotted the Channel Forty-eight truck, Deco Franklin walking back and forth like a desperate tiger in a cage.

"And have the Catholic Church sue us," Tony said. "Sure. Your job is to get on the air and tell this city what the fuck is going on there. Get out there and do it."

The uncomfortable thought I'd had earlier lurked at the edges of my mind.

"Do you want my story, Tony? I can take it to CNN. Sam Lloyd is over at their truck; I can talk to him right now."

"Goddamn it, you shot that on our equipment."

"After you fired me. Feel like tying the story up in court? Good luck finding a judge willing to do that. No, Tony, CNN will broadcast it, and you'll look like a moron. Or we can preview it today and air it tomorrow and watch it go global." And make my career. I didn't add that, pretty sure he didn't want to hear it.

Tony sucked in a breath; I pictured him counting to twenty. "You can't put this together all by yourself."

"You're right. I have my guy here ready to do the editing with me."

"And while you two are handling that, who is doing the on-air coverage? The tooth fairy?"

The disturbing thought I'd had earlier wandered over and rubbed itself against my leg.

"Send Simone," I said, my mouth dry. "I'll cover until she gets here."

SETH

Devan trembled. Or maybe it was my vision doing it, thanks to the machine-gun thump of my heart as the agony of a bullet wound throbbed through me.

I popped a shot in his direction. It punctured a sign near the window reading, *Get your Root-Beer Vat, $5.09!* Devan hadn't had any practice at being shot at, so his eyes popped wide and he scrambled behind an aisle panel. Meanwhile Adele screamed and cried, real horror-movie shrieks, one after the other dissolving into burbling. I fled to the back of the shop, cradling my arm and trying not to trip over Max's body. In seconds I dropped behind the counter.

By instinct I laid a heal on myself. Tried, at least. Forget about my healing power waking up, it didn't even turn over in bed.

Once down with my back to the shelves, I got a look at my wound. Blood soaked my sleeve and splattered my gray jacket. The hole in my arm was nearer the underside than the top. All that torn meat was ugly as hell. I tried another heal. Nothing – except the wound spat a blob of scarlet. I'd never seen so much of my own blood.

I kept my lunch down and dug out my phone. I had to cradle phone and gun in the same hand. Unnerving to point a pistol at your own head while making a phone call.

Hilda answered immediately. "Hello. We're still hearing gunshots."

"No shit. I need help in here. Cobber is down but now Devan has Moffat's gun. I'm shot."

Silence.

"Hilda?"

More silence.

"I can't heal this."

Footsteps, tentative, outside the cubbyhole I had bolted into. I held up my pistol and fired over the counter, hoping Adele had buggered off.

A curse from Devan. "You killed him," he moaned. I worked the pistol muzzle over and fired once in that direction. He shut up.

"Look," Hilda said, "we can't just stroll in there. To begin with, Summerton PD are all over the place. They'll storm the place soon. If you toss your gun aside, they won't shoot you."

"Devan will."

"Tell him to put his down too. If you both surrender, it'll go much easier."

"Did you miss the part about him going bat-shit?"

"I can't come in there. I'll be cut off from my chopra."

"Hilda, do something. I don't want to die in a Ducky Mart."

59

THE BISHOP

"What do you mean, I don't want to go to Heaven?" I demanded. "Heaven is my reward for service to God. The Lord said –"

The abomination in its yellow shirt shook its head. "Please don't quote. So many who come through my doors have minds full of quotes about this or that. It's enough to drive one mad. Look, Heaven and all the other worlds where you mortals get swept into when your bodies end, they're storehouses. Souls are shipped off to them and given something mindless and repetitive to do. All that bliss? It's a lot of wheel-spinning."

DM eyed Rain. "Hades is one of them. Look at the story of Sisyphus. He had the job of rolling a stone to the top of a hill, whereupon it would roll back down and he'd have to do it again. That one is pure legend, but whoever first imagined it thoroughly understood the afterlife under the godhead's control. Sisyphus wouldn't have lasted two centuries."

Rain-of-Blood straightened up. <<That's not right. Zeus himself said –>>

"Oh, bother, here we go again." DM motioned over his shoulder where a sign had materialized: *No-Quoting Zone*. "The godhead doesn't want souls to run free. Some may one day rival it. It's afraid of competition. Any competition."

"The Lord fears nothing," I said. "And you're no god."

"I never said I was. He did." nodding toward Rain.

Rain shook his entire body. <<What do you mean, Sisyphus wouldn't have lasted? I've pushed thousands out of the world. They had Charon waiting to take them across the Styx to the afterlife.>>

DM snorted, a sound that became a laugh when he morphed into the shape of a young black woman. The only constant was the uniform. "Let's play show-and-tell." A window like a video screen materialized behind him, enormous. "Have a look here. Charlie, this is Heaven, where you're so eager to go."

Bodies floated, their limbs splayed. A faint cry issued from them. They gleamed, backs and necks arching as they drifted before a background of shifting colors. "All these people are caught up in bliss. Raw, orgasmic joy. This one back here?" DM pointed at a figure, little more than a silhouette. "I've been watching this poor woman for years. She's bored with all the bliss. Even perpetual joy gets monotonous, given time. She's fading into nothing. Soon she'll be gone."

A second screen materialized. DM gestured. "Rain, here we have the river Styx." The view swept over the broad watery expanse. A little boat lay on its side, a thick rope binding it to a post. "That's Charon's ferry. Charon has been gone for centuries, as near as I can tell."

<<That can't be right.>> Rain choked.

"Let's have a look at Hades itself."

Rolling hills. A figure wandered along, clad in rags.

"Recognize him?" DM asked.

A gasp issued from Rain. Blue claw-like fingers made a scraping sound as they slid against each other. <<I pushed Antoine into shooting this man years ago.>>

"All he does is wander around the hills. Doesn't need food or water. He tried cutting off his arm four years ago. It grew back instantly. Hades is huge so the denizens rarely run into each other. He hasn't seen another soul for about five years. He might last another couple of decades, poor thing."

Rain slumped into a couch, blue face pale.

DM sat on the armrest. "I'm sorry. Anybody you pushed across more than a hundred years ago is gone. Pfft. Like a fart in the hurricane of eternity."

KAYLEE

Deco, camera on shoulder, had popped a button on his shirt. His paunch now threatened to burst out into full furry view. I held the mic and stared into the lens as Michael at the station did the intro. My earbud picked it all up, including Tony in the control room sucking air.

Emile sat on the back of the satellite truck, laptop on his knees.

"What can you tell us about this situation, Kaylee?" Michael at the station said in my ear.

"A witness has informed me that Bishop Charles Moffat is inside this Ducky Mart and has apparently been shot. We don't know yet of any other casualties, but this altercation appears to be related to the destruction of a Ducky Mart convenience store near the university two days ago. In that incident three young men died."

"And Bishop Moffat is connected?" Michael asked. His voice had picked up a scratch. I felt for him. Tony'd probably told them I had lost my mind. If I melted down live on the air, Michael could expect his career to choke also as the front man.

"I've been pursuing this story for several months. My investigation revealed that Bishop Moffat is connected to the murders of no less than fourteen boys and young men going back at least a decade."

"Jesus," Tony said in my earbud.

"So your investigation links the bishop to this alleged hostage-taking?" Michael said.

"Absolutely."

I'd learned years ago the trick of looking at the camera lens and talking directly to it while processing what peripheral vision showed me. Locke and a woman in gray pants and tank top made their way toward us, Locke shuffling while the woman held his arm to guide him.

Another Channel Forty-Eight vehicle rolled in. Simone in a company car.

At that moment Michael said, "Kaylee, we're going to a break now. We'll connect with you in a few minutes."

Simone lurched the car to a stop next to Deco's truck. She wore spike heels and a ridiculous narrow dress she could barely move in. Her mountain of hair wobbled.

"Kaylee?" she squealed.

"I have a story to prep." I gestured at Emile. "You're taking over the live updates."

"Where is the script?"

"There isn't one. This is real news. The story is happening around us. We're going out and getting it." I pointed. "You can start by talking to the police over there."

Her heavily painted lips quivered. "I can't just walk up to them and start asking questions."

"That's your job, Simone. Go ask Flora what she knows about the situation inside: who is doing the shooting, whether they can see the bishop's body. She'll blow you off; keep at her. She'll send you packing at least twice; then she'll give you something good to make you go away. She makes a great source. Go."

Simone looked ready to burst into tears. "Well, fiddle-faddle." With that, she minced off.

I turned to Emile. "Are you ready to send something to the station?"

"I think so. Five minutes of our Moffat interview."

"Way too long. We need a sound bite. This is just to give the late-night viewers a taste. Forty seconds. We'll assemble the whole story for broadcast tomorrow."

"Oh, okay. Give me ten minutes to pare it down."

"Ha! Funny. You have three."

60

THE BISHOP

There was no time now to brood about the reality of being dead.

"Rain," I said to the blue creature grieving on the couch, "this demon is lying to you. It's in league with Lucifer."

DM laughed grimly. "I don't serve Lucifer, Charles. And those so-called demons you've been killing? Maybe you should meet some of them." Three smoky forms solidified into the shapes of vaguely familiar young men. "Sorry to interrupt, guys. I need you to meet someone."

One of the men glared at me. "Aren't you the asshole who blew us up in Ducky Mart?"

"Jerome, please."

"My girlfriend has been crying ever since she got the news. My poor mom and dad had to go to the morgue and identify me. Fuck you."

"If it helps, Jerome, Laci is one of mine. She'll join us when she shuffles off her mortal coil."

"But what will I be then?"

DM smiled. "Anything you like. Eternity awaits."

I stared the abomination down. "You're granting these creatures eternity?"

One of the demons shrugged. "That's not how this works. Am I right, DM? You don't make us immortal, we start out that way. Heaven, Nirvana, all the rest, they just wear souls down until they wither away."

"Precisely, Mark. That way lies true death. When you lose your mortal form, you're more susceptible to dissolution. The trick to immortality is to keep yourself interested – learn and grow. Slackers die."

Rain-of-Blood threw himself to his blue hoofed feet. <<All those people. No, that . . . no.>>

"I truly am sorry," DM said, "I know it's a shock –"

"Don't believe this creature, Rain," I said. "It's trying to manipulate you."

Rain-of-Blood ignored me. <<They were only supposed to cross over on Charon's little boat. Just some fun.>>

"Just some fun," the Ducky Mart creature said. "Murdering people."

<<Pushing them across to the shores of the Styx, where Charon could take them to Hades. Hades isn't at all like what these mortals think of as Hell. For the deserving, it was supposed to be paradise.>> The blue creature beat its fists on the sides of its head. <<It's not supposed to be like this.>>

"If it's any consolation, up until that little animal attacked you, you were bound to the godhead. It dictated your desires. Only when you were severed from it did you have a chance to think for yourself. I suspect that's why you are beginning to feel remorse. The old you wouldn't have cared less."

<<I used to be part of this godhead thing and never knew it?>>

"That's right."

Rain grunted and wiped his eyes. <<That doesn't make me feel better. I've had loads of experience with self-loathing. All those killers I rode, or pushed into their profession. Lots of them were real messes by the end. When they departed the world, I thought they had eternity to recover.>> He shook his head mournfully. <<Is there anything I can do to bring

those people back?>> A flicker of hope passed across a face chiseled in sapphire.

"Sorry. They're gone. There's nothing anyone can do about that."

Rain convulsed, a sob breaking from crystal lips.

"There might be something you can do to help prevent it," DM said.

The angel squared its shoulders. <<What can I do?>>

"Teach me your talent."

"There it is," I bellowed, stabbing a finger at the abomination. "Rain, this monster wants you to teach it how to murder people."

Jerome laughed out loud. "Listen to the kettle judge the pot. You've been killing people for years. That blue creature just gave you an excuse to get your own hands bloody instead of hiding out while your assassins did the dirty work."

DM smiled. "Charles, what I want is actually the opposite. My chain of stores has expanded around the globe and I've gathered all sorts of new converts. Some of them are real wackos." DM's features shifted, becoming Max in a Ducky Mart uniform. "This guy is out of his gourd. But he's part of me and all that conflicting psychosis has a nasty effect. I start feeling like mayhem might be kind of fun and, frankly, I don't want to go there. But it's hard keeping that kind of insanity under control."

"Wait," I cried. "Do you mean to say you possess Max? You really are a monster."

DM shrugged. "Yes, I do possess him, though not the way you mean. I possess him in the same sense that you possess toes." His gaze swept to Rain. "Before they drive me as batshit crazy as they are, teach me how you twist their minds. So I can twist them sane again."

61

KAYLEE

Simone did better reporting on the scene than I'd expected. Part of me hated that. Another part thrilled at her professionalism. She stood before Deco, mic clenched in hand, her steely gaze on the camera lens. "We now know the police have moved in on the building, Michael, but we cannot say whether they have made it inside."

I dragged my attention from her to Emile's laptop screen. He rolled the clip.

"That's good," I said, ten seconds in. "We'll send that."

I tugged my phone from my belt and brought up Tony's number. He answered without a ring.

"We've got a segment of the interview," I told him without preamble. "Let's run it. I'll do the intro."

Tony grunted. "I'm really not sure about this. We are so far out on a limb –"

"It's not going to break, Tony. Trust me."

"Trust you?" his voice squeaked.

"Yes. Or I'll screw your career."

62

SETH

Damn. Just couldn't bring myself to pop lead into Devan, even after four opportunities. He was my brother – my nut-job, hide-him-in-the-attic brother – but still family. Sending him to Ducky Mart hell, or heaven, or whatever, didn't feel right. So I fired wide and over his head to discourage him from getting close.

I was thinking about this, listening to my heart bang away in me, when Adele screamed. A long, piercing, blubbering kind of wail, followed by, "Braydon's moving."

"Stay low. If he's just wounded –"

"He's getting up. He looks confused."

A gunshot took out another glass jug of coffee beans above me. Now I smelled like Ethiopian Dark, Organic Colombian, and blood. Devan hadn't run out of ammunition yet. When he had shot off eight rounds, I thought he'd emptied out, but then he cracked a couple more.

I crawled over to the little swinging door and sprawled on my side to peer underneath. Adele knelt next to Braydon's body. He struggled to sit up in a bloody puddle. How the hell did someone survive that much blood loss? Damn lucky.

Or maybe not. Max Cobber's legs started to move too.

Then came a groan. "Interesting," Max said.

A cold wave rolled through my spine. I sat up in time to hear racing footsteps. Scrambling to my knees, I poked my pistol over the counter to see Devan running straight at me. I popped one off past him. He squeaked and bolted left among what was left of the potato chips.

I crouched down, nursing my arm, and held my phone to my cheek.

"Hello, Seth, my boy," Locke's slurred voice answered.

"Listen carefully. Max Cobber shot the assistant manager."

"That is terrible. Sorry chum, I cannot interfere."

"Now he's waking up."

"Ah, a fortunate thing, then."

"So is Max."

"Mr. Cobber is alive?"

"Yes, Locke. He's coming back. I shot him in his chest and his head. Right below his eye. Now tell me, how is it that people are getting resurrected in here without help from us?"

"I cannot answer that."

"Locke, get in here and help me. The Ducky Mart god is at work. Cobber is about to join Devan, and together they're going to whack me. Understand?"

Footsteps, kind of hobbling. I switched the phone to hands-free and set it on a shelf under the counter. Then I popped up and looked around.

Cobber peered down at himself. "This suit is a mess."

"Max!" Devan shrieked.

Max looked around. "Ah, Devan. And where would Mr. Brown be now?" He bent down, out of my sight, and rose, shaking blood off his pistol.

I cracked a shot at him. He looked up, startled, and ran in Devan's direction.

"Locke, get your ass over here," I pleaded. "Cobber isn't even hurt now. I'm so screwed."

"I am terribly sorry, old chum."

"I'm up against a fucking power in here."

"Yes, well. I cannot bind to my chopra in there."

Footsteps. I held my pistol up and fired. A chorus of retaliatory bullets crashed against the wall above me.

"Locke," I said, "when I get murdered and sucked into whatever nightmarish afterlife a god who runs convenience stores creates, I'm going to tell him you're the biggest trouser-loaf in the whole multiverse. And I'm going to keep on saying it for all eternity."

63

KAYLEE

Emile's fingers glided over the keyboard, uploading my video to Tony. "You know, I always pictured myself as more Clark Kent-slash-Superman than Jimmy Olson."

"Quiet," I said, peering at the screen.

"Yes, Lois." He smiled.

The green upload bar crept to its end and flashed *Transfer Complete*. I gestured to Simone. She didn't look at me, but a subtle shift in her shoulders told me she understood.

"Michael," she said, "our colleague Kaylee Jerrel has been investigating the events that led up to this incident for some time. Kaylee?"

I stepped to her, into the camera's view. "Simone, as you said, I've been investigating the activities of Bishop Charles Augustus Moffat for the past few months. I have a segment of an interview I conducted recently. We are assembling a documentary, which will run in the very near future on precisely this topic. Michael, I think we have that clip ready?"

"We certainly do, Kaylee. Would you tell us about it?"

"This is part of my conversation with the bishop about his alleged involvement in the killings."

The clip rolled. I listened to Moffat squirm and babble. That felt great. Simone made a sound in her throat. She had a look on her face that lived somewhere between power and elation.

When the clip finished, we were back on.

"That's a remarkable story, Kaylee," Simone said. "You make some strong accusations there."

"Yes, Simone. Of course, my investigation has tied Mr. Moffat to these killings and amazingly has led us to the events unfolding tonight in Ducky Mart."

"Truly astonishing."

There came a string of curses off to my left.

"Yes, it is," I said, glaring at Locke. He looked agitated; the woman beside him tried to hush him. Not a stylish drunk, obviously; more like the high-school kid who discovers he's an asshole when drinking and loves it. "We have tied the bishop and his people definitively to eleven murders and there may be more."

Locke made a snorting noise.

"That is incredible, Kaylee," Michael said, "Can you tell us – ?"

"Michael, I'm getting a great deal of noise nearby, I'll need to move to a different location."

Relief filled his voice. "Of course. The chief of police is announcing a press conference regarding the current situation. We'll come back to you in a few minutes."

The light on Deco's camera went out. I stormed over to Locke. "What the hell are you doing? I'm trying to broadcast here. If you need to yell and carry on, go somewhere else."

"I cannot go in there like this," Locke moaned, wobbling, oblivious to me.

"What's he on about?" I asked.

The woman rolled her eyes. "He can't hold his liquor. And Seth is probably not going to survive this."

"Detective Langella?" I asked.

She nodded. Across her tank top in barely decipherable handwriting was, *Prissy was here!!!*

Locke whined, "It is my fault. And there is nothing I can do. As soon as I cross its threshold, I shall be severed from my chopra."

"You mean you can't go into Ducky Mart?"

He nodded, arms flailing. "This is a nightmare."

"Leave, then."

"I cannot abandon Seth. It is unseemly."

"You don't have a choice," Detective Langella said.

Locke uttered a string of curses.

"Quiet," I said, wondering what the police detective thought about his crazy rambling. "I don't need that on my broadcast. If you can't go in there without your chopra, then why don't you call it down here and take it with you? Just do something, anything that gets you the hell away from my camera. I'm trying to do a news segment here."

My rant ended when I saw the expression creeping across Locke's face: revelation morphing into conviction.

"What?" I demanded.

"Oh, my," Locke said, his voice clear now, and full of wonder.

"Oh, shit," Detective Langella said.

Oh, frack, a voice in my head said.

SETH

My bullet gash throbbed. I tugged my belt out of my pants and wound it around my arm. That looked like it worked in movies, but just sent agony pulsing up my arm. I checked my resources: one phone, four bullets in my pistol, three empty magazines in my pockets – I'd hung onto them figuring I might reload them with the ammo back at Chase's house. If I lived that long. Without going to prison. Maybe I could throw things and hit Devan or Max in the temple, in that sweet spot where one good thump makes a bad guy drop like a wet rag.

I glanced over the counter. "Hey, Max. Still there?"

"Yes, Mr. Brown. How are you feeling? Devan tells me your right arm is injured."

"He's wrong. I'm fine. Never better. Max?"

"Yes?"

"Know what lawyers use for birth control? Their winsome personalities."

"You little –" And there he was, stomping out from behind an aisle panel. I lifted my pistol. Dizziness rippled through me. Then a hand caught Max's collar and dragged him back. I fired wide. When I tried to crouch down out of firing range, my legs stiffened and I slumped against the wall.

Light glared. The tunnel, I thought; I'm dead. The glow grew into brilliance. A shape emerged within it, legs together, arms spread. Then another, a form like a horse with a woman on its back. And the light swelled brighter still.

The building shook, coffee beans rattling behind me.

I wished I'd called Mom to say good-bye.

The glare illuminated the panel Max hid behind, silhouetting him, as though the intensity of the light carried it right through the metal. An easy shot, if I had any strength left. But the gun refused to hold steady.

The light swelled again, and a third figure hovered above us. An explosion of thunder. Then something collided with my chest and threw me back against the jars of coffee beans. I fell sideways, arm roaring with pain. Death shouldn't hurt so damn much.

A figure hovered over me, dark now that my eyes were used to the eruption of light. Eyes like bloody orbs glowed.

My eyes focused on a little black nose.

"Gr," the fox said cheerfully.

THE FOX

The fox gazed at the hovering powers. Tendrils of plasm roiled through the air around them. They reminded her of white bears roaring at each other. Or humans planting their feet and clenching their forepaws.

Remember, *the fox told herself:* You're just a dog. You're a dog. You're a dumb, harmless dog. *She glanced about in embarrassment, then sprawled and licked her crotch.*

The Book of
Linoleum

64

KAYLEE

Locke disappeared. Not with any flash or excitement. Reality simply changed its mind about Locke's being here and deleted him. Detective Langella glared at me, cursed, and deleted herself from next to the spot formerly known as Locke.

I stared at the two empty spots. The usually unflappable Deco squeaked, "Kaylee. They . . . gone."

"Who?"

"Them." He fluttered his fingers in the direction of empty space.

I shook my head. "Seeing things, Deco? The stress is getting to you."

He gaped at me, then looked about as if to make sure no one else had disappeared.

I knew Locke had mysterious talents. But what the hell was Detective Langella anyway? An archangel?

A Valkyrie, actually, said my inner voice. Then from the direction of the police blockade came the sound of an explosion, which distracted me enough to keep from pondering obvious questions like, how did I know that?

Emile's breath erupted in a rush. "It's started."

"What?"

"Armageddon."

"Are you sure?"

He swallowed. "Uh, well, no."

"Okay then. If we're doomed, we can't do anything about it, so we may as well assume we aren't."

He opened his mouth. I stabbed a finger at his laptop. "To work."

He turned his gaze to his screen and started typing again. Then Simone came running up.

"Kaylee," she gasped. "The cops were, like, *seconds* from going in there, and then something blew up. I think I'm going to be sick."

"Don't," I said in drill-sergeant mode; it seemed to be working on everyone else. "Get on the air and do your job."

Her cameraman stared off in the direction of Ducky Mart.

Simone's hair wobbled. "Deco," she said, her voice grating. His head whipped around. He gulped and hoisted his camera onto his shoulder. Simone picked up her mic from the cord looping around his arm. A brief horrified look at me, during which her cheeks bulged up alarmingly.

Oh, no, I thought. Don't screw it all up now.

The camera light glowed, and Simone transformed from wet rag to pro.

"Michael, we have breaking news here in Summerton. Several explosions have been heard coming from the Ducky Mart beside us. Police were planning an assault on the convenience store – were, in fact, mere moments from going in when the explosions began. They are now holding back, anticipating further developments." At that moment the sky lit up. Simone, newly crowned ice queen, turned and shaded her eyes. "There goes another blast. Police are now openly using the word 'terrorists' to describe the people involved. However, at the moment we know little about them, with the exception of what Kaylee has told us." She glanced at me, a question in her eyes. I shook my head. Simone cleared her throat. "We'll be back with Kaylee for more details in a few minutes, Michael."

The camera light went dark, and she leaned over and gasped for breath. "Oh, God."

"He could turn up anytime," Emile muttered.

SETH

Blood seeped out of my bullet wound, running down to my elbow. Meanwhile the interior of Ducky Mart glowed, a glare of white light causing hard, angular shadows over the countertop. I struggled to my feet. The fox yipped at me.

I turned, bringing my left arm up to block the light since my right wouldn't cooperate, and stared straight into Max Cobber's pistol.

"Good-bye, Mr. Brown," Cobber said pleasantly.

Then his pistol leaped out of his hand and the smile fled his face. Devan, behind him, held Moffat's pistol in the air, cop style with both hands. His pistol tugged in his grip. He fought the pull, holding on to the weapon until it twisted free.

Someone was looking out for me. Locke, I figured. I raised my own pistol and sighted between Cobber's eyes. He looked offended. Then my own weapon leaped away. It flew end over end until it reached . . .

Braydon, the assistant manager. Blood had splashed over his yellow cotton shirt, gathered around the holes in his chest. Beside him stood Adele, who stared at him in astonishment. No fear there; whatever chemicals cause fright had been boiled out of her brain. My pistol reached Braydon and joined its colleagues in slow orbits around him.

Braydon's eyes burned with yellow flames. Possessed by a power. The god of Ducky Mart, I presumed. We were screwed.

The light in the room glared brighter than daylight and cut right through me. I had no shadow; just whiteness all around.

"Ah," Locke bellowed, filling my guts and soul. "ALL BECOMES CLEAR NOW." I tried looking up and had to shield my eyes. Locke hovered at the center of a silver Bat Signal, his body canted to one side as though he couldn't bring himself upright. Beside him floated Hilda. In the white glare surrounding her body, I could make out the shape of a figure on the back of a horse.

Locke's gaze settled on Braydon. "I SHOULD HAVE KNOWN. YOU CRAWLING COLLECTION OF MAGGOTS."

"Could we perhaps take this outside?" the Ducky Mart god asked. I pictured them squaring off in the street, surrounded by all the rubberneckers in Summerton. Then the floor tilted. The windows all turned black. The cop cars, the flashing blue lights, the occasional sweeping spotlight, all gone. An eruption like fireworks lit up outside.

Adele babbled something. Beyond where the broken windows used to be lay huge, swirling shapes, like those pictures taken from Hubble. Blazing, spinning spirals.

Hilda looked around, wide eyed, her massive horse-shape turning, twitching this way and that. "Shit." Not a word let out in full god-speak. More like an under-the-breath mutter, amplified to near deafening volume.

"Galaxies," Adele murmured, turning around to take it all in.

The Ducky Mart god sniffed. "Universes, actually."

"YOU HAVE A SIMPLE CHOICE, ABOMINATION," Locke said. "GIVE UP YOUR POWER – OR MEET YOUR END HERE BEYOND THE WALLS OF THE LOWER WORLDS, LOST AND FORGOTTEN."

"Locke," I said, struggling to breathe. "I've been shot."

Cobber tittered.

"TERRIBLY SORRY, CHUM," Locke boomed. "I MUST CONTEND WITH THIS ABOMINATION. I AM SURE YOU WILL BE FINE."

The Ducky Mart god cleared his throat and rose into the air until he hovered at the same altitude as Locke. The pistols orbited him like planets. "Abomination?" he said. "Is that what you call anything that isn't part of your godhead?"

"YOU KNOW WHAT WE ARE. SO YOU KNOW YOU CANNOT STAND AGAINST US."

"Wait," I said. "Locke, you mean he isn't part of the godhead?"

"PRECISELY."

"I thought that wasn't possible. What is he?"

Locke gave me a look as though I were bug, as though the question was insane.

"MORTALS FORM THE ECTOPLASM OF HIS BEING." Locke's god-voice oozed contempt. "DUCKY MART IS *PEOPLE!*"

Braydon guffawed. "What Charlton Heston here is trying to say is: I am the accumulated conscious minds of a significant portion of the coffee-drinking, doughnut-nibbling public. I'm impressed that you realized it so quickly. I only figured that out a decade ago."

I laughed out loud, which hurt like hell. "How could you not know what you are?"

Braydon looked down his nose at me – literally. "You mortals are seventy trillion amoebas flying formation. You needed how many millennia to catch on to that?"

"YOU ARE AN ABOMINATION!" Locke boomed.

I almost fell over, just out of general wooziness. The fox yipped like a mutt.

Braydon held his hands up. "Why must anything that isn't part of the godhead be destroyed? I've been across the barriers between worlds, out into the frontiers of the multiverse. I've seen the wreckage of the other powers. Your vaunted godhead fried them into oblivion."

"POWERS MUST BE KEPT IN CHECK. WE INDULGE THOSE THAT HAVE NOT YET BECOME MIGHTY. BUT IF THEY DO, THEY MUST ACCEPT THE CAGING OF THEIR POWER OR BE CULLED BEFORE THEY THREATEN THE GODHEAD. SO IT MUST BE." Locke spread his arms, and huge crimson tendrils licked out across the room. Cobber and Devan crouched. Adele curled up in a heap on the floor, head between her knees.

Braydon crossed his arms. "I am a composite of mortals. Not just any mortals, twenty-first century mortals. That means I am familiar with seeing gratuitous special effects used to trowel over chasmic holes in logic. You're making a ridiculously circular case. 'Powers must be destroyed before they threaten the godhead.' From what I've seen, the godhead has been the threat. It's insane, fragmented into a thousand aspects, and since you're part of it, you're hardly the best judge of what should be allowed to live in peace. I speak for those who make up my spirit. Even the psychopathic ones like Max." Cobber straightened up, murder on his face. "And now that I've seen what you do with their souls, I will not permit it."

"IDLE WORDS. CHOOSE: DESTRUCTION OR THE CAGE."

My head swam. I could feel blood leaching into my jacket. "Wait. Before we get to the carnage, Locke, what does he mean? What happens to souls?"

Braydon beat Locke to the answer. "Know where powers come from? Consciousness. When you become self-aware, your mind weaves itself into the fabric of the multiverse, the plasm. Some minds fade away because they don't revitalize themselves by learning and changing. Those that stay interested grow into powers. If they get big enough, the godhead gets worried. Near as I can see, ages ago it hit on the idea of catching spirits and locking them up. That's what Heaven is for. And Hades." He turned deliberately then and faced Hilda. "And Valhalla."

Hilda stiffened. "Valhalla?"

The god nodded. "Why do you think you and the rest of the Valkyrie clan specifically target heroes, mortals with a backbone, curiosity, determination – those who make a difference in the world? They're the ones most likely to cause trouble if you let them evolve into powers."

Hilda's blazing body darkened. I made out her face – her human face. She looked like someone had just told her she'd spent the last millennium murdering people she thought she'd been rewarding.

Her god-voice boomed. "LOKI?"

65

KAYLEE

"Kaylee, tell us more about the connection between Bishop Charles Moffat and the incident unfolding now," Simone said, and held her mic to me.

"Well, Simone, three young men who worked together at the Ducky Mart near Summerton University two days ago apparently fit the group the bishop chose to target – males aged twenty-one born between April 3 and April 8. Apparently Moffat was present to observe the work of his assassins when that Ducky Mart was bombed. We followed him from there to the Church of Mary the Virgin downtown, where we conducted the interview you saw part of in the footage we've broadcast."

"And now the bishop's alleged henchmen are at work in this Ducky Mart outlet?"

"It appears so, Simone."

"A fascinating story."

She droned on but I couldn't follow. The voice in my head distracted me It said: Kaylee, it is time.

Time for what? I thought. The voice didn't sound like me now.

I'm coming out of the closet, so to speak, so I may as well do it in a big way. Tell the people this.

The voice spoke further.

That's ridiculous, I told it.

Across this world thousands are tuning in to this incident, some as far away as Johannesburg, all streaming the news of a bizarre terrorist act in a Midwestern city. Some will record your words and release them on YouTube. Word will spread. You will be more famous than you could have imagined. Have faith.

Simone was just finishing. "...two different Ducky Marts in as many days. Back to you, Michael."

"Michael, before we go, let me add this," I said quickly. "A truly astonishing fact related to these incidents is: in its thirty-year history, Ducky Mart has never before experienced a violent crime such as a robbery – or any crime at all, for that matter. Not even a single shoplifting charge has ever been laid. In spite of having over a hundred thousand outlets, some in the roughest of cities, Ducky Mart is possibly the safest place in the world to work or go for a cup of coffee. Remarkable."

Tony bellowed in my ear. "What the hell are you spewing?"

Michael squealed and caught himself. "Yes. If true, that is remarkable. Well. We'll take a break now."

The camera light went out. Simone looked confused. Tony blew up. "What the fuck? No crime? Are you out of your skull? That is statistically impossible!"

"It happens to be true," I said quietly.

"Know what, Jerrel? You just killed your story. You may as well have said the CEO of Ducky Mart is an alien. You are fired fired fired!"

"Tony," I said. "It is true."

"No, it isn't. But thank you, Jerrel, for showing our viewers you're a flake. Now get off my channel."

Simone looked ready to fill an airline bag. Deco had a wary look in his eyes.

I popped my earbud out and tossed it to Deco. Emile peered at me over the lid of his laptop. He closed it and eased it into his carrying bag. Then he came to me.

I hadn't felt this tired in years. He put his arm around my shoulder. I let him lead me away.

"Why did you say that?" he whispered. "It isn't possible."

"But it's true. And they will air my story. Not tomorrow. But soon. Let's go home."

"Home?" He nodded toward the police blockade. "What about – ?"

I smiled up at him. "I'm tired."

A muffled sound like an explosion underground reached us from the direction of Ducky Mart beyond the police cordon. Emile stopped. I tugged on his arm. At last he relented. We walked along Pellier toward my condo.

Thank you, the voice in my head said.

I'm crazy, I thought. It's all been too much. I've finally cracked.

No, actually. You haven't.

Right. I'm debating my own sanity with a voice in my head.

66

SETH

I almost forgot the whole agonizing bleeding-to-death thing. Hilda looked just as wired up over what Braydon had said as I was. The fox, meanwhile, scratched her chin with a hind paw and yawned. Her nonchalance was starting to piss me off.

Braydon held his hands out. "Look. There's a reason why you have phrases like 'soul destroying' for talking about repetitious bullshit. It really is soul destroying. You spin your wheels for a few decades until the last particle of consciousness has worn itself down to a nubbin. Destruction of the spirit."

That couldn't be. Immortality was immortality, full stop. Locke would know. We looked up at him and waited in expectation.

The hovering bat signal said, "THAT IS THE WAY IT MUST BE. FREE POWERS COULD CAUSE UNTOLD DESTRUCTION."

Hilda blanched, which said a lot since she already blazed with white light. "YOU MEAN IT'S TRUE?"

"OF COURSE." Locke sounded as though the question amazed him. "THE GODHEAD IS THE KEEPER OF THE MULTIVERSE. IF THAT MEANS THE DESTRUCTION OF A FEW BEINGS HERE AND THERE, SO IT MUST BE."

Braydon snorted. "Does the godhead still believe that? From what I've seen, in the old days, it shot first and asked questions never. Now parts of it are changing their minds." He made a sweeping gesture that took in Hilda, which surprised the hell out of me. "Even you, Locke; you came here with a line about cages or destruction instead of skipping straight to the mayhem. You've been the godhead's enforcer for a long time, haven't you? Remember when you went in and blasted away without any thought? Why don't you do that now? Besides, there are beings more powerful than me in the multiverse; they're no threat to you or the rest of the godhead, if you leave them alone."

"THIS IS RIDICULOUS," Locke thundered. "MORTALS ARE PETTY CREATURES, AND YOU ARE A PRODUCT OF THEM. GIVE THEM POWER, AND WHO KNOWS WHAT KIND OF MESS THEY WILL SPAWN? AS FOR THESE BEINGS YOU SPEAK OF, I WILL SIFT THE FRACTURED PLASM OF YOUR SOUL AND EXTRACT YOUR KNOWLEDGE. THEY WILL BE HUNTED DOWN AND GIVEN THE SAME CHOICE YOU FACE HERE. THE CAGE OR ANNIHILATION. CHOOSE NOW."

Devan decided to throw in his nickel worth of BS then, so he piped up with, "Sinners should be destroyed." He moved away from Cobber, who looked rather gleeful at all the talk of destruction. "When my father brings his wrath upon them, I will stand at his right hand."

Braydon shook his head. "What magazines have you been reading?"

The fox, curled up near my feet, rolled over and rubbed her back on the linoleum. She had been useful back at the house when Antoine's phonus tried to kill everyone, but now she seemed more interested in licking her paws.

My legs gave way. I slumped against the counter and put my back to it. I knew which side of this fight I wanted to be on. Even dying. I looked up at Hilda, who clearly wavered in her loyalties. She hovered closer and closer to the floor.

I had one card to play.

"You," I said as clearly as I could. "Godlet, demigod, whatever the hell you are."

Braydon turned to me, eyebrows cocked.

"Locke's chopra is drunk. It's only his sober human side that's keeping him conscious."

"Oh, really," Braydon said.

"CHUM, YOU NEED TO KEEP YOUR MOUTH SHUT." Locke flickered a glare at me, then turned his attention to the young god. "THAT WILL DO YOU NO –"

The convenience-store god attacked. Fire cut across the space between Braedon and Locke. The flames hurtled past Devan and Max. Devan scampered away as if his butt were on fire. Max backed off, arms shading his eyes.

The Ducky Mart god looked downright tranquil while fire jetted from his hands. The flames washed against Locke's chopra. The bat-shape flinched, and his floating human body jerked back from it.

Hilda floated some distance away. She yelled something but didn't step in. She sounded like the Valkyrie/higher-power equivalent of a schoolteacher pacing back and forth while barking at two kids in the process of beating holy hell out of each other.

Meanwhile Locke roared, a nuclear explosion sound that went straight through my guts. His bat-wing body swelled.

Braydon unleashed a second blast. Tongues of reddish white fire flared across the gap and washed against Locke's wings.

The god aimed for Locke's mortal body. Locke's higher self shook but held its ground. The bat shape grew, and its huge wings curved around the Ducky Mart god's body. The convenience store god flung tentacles of flame at the massive gray shape. You could see ripples pulsing through Locke's higher form, but aside from that, the blasts didn't make any difference.

The store around us vanished. Suddenly it was bare black and white linoleum under me. Miles of it in all directions.

"WAIT!" Hilda yelled. "LET'S TALK ABOUT THIS."

The fox scratched an ear. I wanted to yell at her, tell her to do something. But the noise of the dueling powers dug into my belly and shook my vital organs like the loudest rock concert you've ever heard.

Adele ran to me, muttering something unintelligible. Cobber crouched beside a table that had faded into a translucent mirage. The noise crawled inside me like something alive and solid.

Braydon floated up, lancing fire at Locke's growing bat wings. The bat shape swelled and curved, inexorably arching around Braydon; behind the bat wings hovered Locke's mortal body, arms out as though he were on a cross, hands in fists. He grinned like a kid.

The wings almost enclosed Braydon. Explosions like flash bulbs and lightning erupted, light spilling around the wings. And far back from the fight hovered Locke's mortal body, his gaze intent on the bat shape of his higher self, the cord between him and his chopra glowing like white-hot wire.

Max Cobber scrambled to where Adele, the fox, and I sat. He knelt and leaned close. "Hello. Assuming we survive all this, I want you to know I will hunt you down and choke the life from you with my bare hands."

I grabbed his collar with my good hand and laughed in his face. "A lawyer and an accountant go bowling together and the lawyer says –"

Cobber's face contorted, one eye swelling like a cue ball. He reached for my throat.

"Gr." The fox rolled onto her paws and glared. Cobber loosened his grip on my neck. He wore a lopsided "who, me?" smile.

The fox snarled and moved toward him, teeth bared. I let go of Cobber. The room spun.

My hand landed on the fox's back. It was like when we were fighting the phonus and Locke touched me. I saw tendrils of power: a huge web of silver arcs burst out of the god, vanishing at points all around us. So many, they ran together into a fog. Thin lines jutting out from Locke's and Hilda's higher forms, piercing the wall of Ducky Mart. There were even almost invisible lines from myself and Devan. Our own connections to the godhead, where our own power came from.

A tendril, almost invisible, ran from Max Cobber to the god of Ducky Mart, now almost out of sight behind the folding bat wings. Another cord ran from me to Locke.

And one more: a thin spiraling tangle of power from my chest . . . to the fox. A connection between us. I hadn't seen it before, not when Locke had touched me. That meant Locke couldn't see it.

Then I noticed how Locke's human body drifted even farther back from his chopra, a much thicker cord taut between them.

The fox jumped back from me, glaring. Then the expression in her eyes softened. Deliberately, in a very unfoxlike way, she winked.

A jolt of revelation shot through my brain about why the fox had been pissing me off so much. She wasn't just acting like a dog. She was overacting.

The fox didn't so much leap as hurtle. A blur of whiteness, an arrow flung at the space between Locke's mortal body and his higher self. A colossal explosion erupted like a mushroom cloud without a stalk. Waves of power poured from it, slamming through body and brain. The undulations threw Cobber off his feet, flinging him into me. My arm had nasty things to say about that.

A scream, long and echoing, trailed off into a whimper. Then a voice, impossibly loud but utterly calm, thundered across linoleumland.

"I TOLD YOU THERE ARE BEINGS MORE POWERFUL THAN ME, MOTHERFUCKER," the god of Ducky Mart boomed. "DID I MENTION *ONE OF THEM IS HERE WITH US?*"

67

Above the infinite checkered floor came a flash and the sound of something huge blowing up. A massive fox shape burst from the center of the explosion and landed on the floor in front of me. Huge, with a mouth full of teeth like steel blades and blood red eyes the size of soccer balls.

It shrank, and the fox yipped a greeting as a human shape fell out of the sky. Locke's body came to a stop on his back. He lay there, sucking air in gasps. Above us hung a gray smudge, unmoving. Like a stain on a window.

"WOW," Hilda said.

Braydon hovered over Locke, arms crossed.

"Oh, bugger," Locke breathed. He rolled onto his side and shifted to his knees. "This. Is. Not. Possible."

"YES, ACTUALLY, IT IS," the god said. "YOUR CHOPRA IS SLEEPING IT OFF."

"You cannot do this. It is not right."

The god smiled. His voice softened. "It's the way it has to be. You were dangerous. Now go away." And Locke vanished. Poof. Actually, not even a poof. He was just gone.

Hilda turned on the god. "WHAT DID YOU DO TO HIM?"

The god shrugged, unconcerned. "We've cut his mortal form from his higher self. And from the godhead. As for where he is, we recently opened a convenient new location at the Changi Airport in Singapore."

I lifted my limp arm into my lap. "Shit, this hurts."

The god fixed his gaze on me. "You came very close to ruining everything. If Locke had realized how vulnerable the connection between his mortal body and his chopra was, we would all have been screwed."

"I was trying to help."

"We didn't need help. We're gods."

"Oh. Sorry." Then I thought, *We?*

Braydon sank to the floor and put his hands in his pockets. He turned first to Hilda, then to Devan, and finally back to me. "You three. We cannot allow you to leave, not as you are. You are all bound to the godhead."

"I'm dying," I managed to utter.

The Ducky Mart god shrugged. "This is true of any mortal. But life waits for you on the other side. The dying is the hard part."

The fox said, "Gr?"

I laughed, which hurt like blazes. "I'm okay with dying. But can I get a last phone call? I want to say good-bye to Mom."

My vision clouded. My head swam. My legs felt cold. Too late.

Reality rolled back, just before the end. Ducky Mart shimmered into existence. Purple and yellow tables.

Down the street from my apartment in Cove City stood the majestic Cove Hotel with its tall, distinctive windows. Beside it towered the steeple of St. Andrews Church. Right now I could see the windows of the hotel and that spire catching moonlight on its cross. I figured my brain had thrown the comfort switch, deciding that being in a Ducky Mart back home would be more pleasant. I had to agree. The fox rubbed against my left shoulder. My subconscious had included Devan in my death-throe hallucinations, so he paced back and forth, mouthing something that looked like swearing. He kept rubbing his temples with his palms.

I shut my eyes and let my head drop. Time to go, I figured. Maybe the god of Ducky Mart would be better than my old man.

The world darkened as though someone shut off its lights, one by one.

68

I didn't die after all. This was good. Waking up in bed with a woman old enough to be my grandmother wasn't any afterlife I'd have chosen. My bedmate wore green pajamas. She had a plump nose and red cheeks and a blonde perm showing gray at her temples.

I sat up, bones creaking, and looked around. My own bedroom. In my own apartment. On the chair across from me, a heap of laundry threatened to tumble over. I'd meant to deal with it the day before I flew out to Summerton to chase my brothers' killers. My arm had a white bandage around it. It didn't look nearly big enough for the wound.

"Gr?"

Eyes like blood peered at me from under the chair. The fox emerged and stretched.

I checked my clock radio. Seven AM.

"Hello." Grandma rubbed her eyes. "How do you feel?"

"Uh . . ."

"I'm Dr. Carlson. Call me Megan."

"Oh."

Megan lifted herself up and moved her feet to the edge of the bed. "I . . ." Her eyes unfocused. "On my way home from work I got paged. Sort of. I work at the Lion's Head Hospital. A voice in my head told me I had a patient waiting for me. At Ducky Mart. I go there every day before my ER shift."

A switch went on in my brain, and the reason for the green PJs became obvious.

"A voice," I said.

Dr. Carlson gave me a pleading look. "It sounds insane, doesn't it?"

"You should have seen my life for the past week. Does the voice have a name?"

Her eyes unfocused. "It says it hasn't made up its mind yet. But Braydon and Adele say hi. Does that make sense?"

"Believe it or not, yes." I lay back and winced.

"Good. You have a minor bullet wound. More of a scrape, really."

"Minor? What about all that blood?"

"You really didn't lose much. A good dry-cleaner can probably get it out of your jacket sleeve. I have a friend who can do artful things about the bullet-hole with a needle and thread." She smiled warmly. "Don't worry; plenty of people are squeamish about blood. There's a surgeon at the ER who faints at the sight of his own, even though he spends his days up to his armpits in other people's." She touched my arm and studied the bandage. "I'm obliged to report bullet injuries, but the voice . . ." She tapped her temple and trailed off. "It insists I shouldn't mention this to anyone."

"I guess that's a good thing."

"Your friend is asleep on the couch. He's rather rude, isn't he?"

"My friend?"

"The wiry fellow. He had blood on his clothes – rather a lot."

"He's here?"

Sure enough, Devan lay unconscious on my loveseat. The fox growled, but it didn't sound like a threat or warning. In fact, it sounded like, "Ah, what can you do?"

Devan wore my *Noise Tour* T-shirt from the Tailored Genes' concert that had tried its best to deafen me two years ago. He had snuggled into my sleeping bag. A bowl of my Cheerios sat next to him on my coffee table.

"The voice wants to know if you can keep him for a while," Megan said.

"Keep him?"

"He has a job waiting at the Ducky Mart down the street. With benefits after six months. It's a hair above minimum, but it's a start."

Devan made a mumbling sound and opened his eyes. He raised himself on his elbows and scowled at me.

"You have got to be kidding," I said. "I need a coffee before I have to face this."

I filled a cup at the kitchen sink, cold water splashing my hand, and took it back to the living room. I nudged it over to coffee and lifted it to my mouth.

Cold. And still water.

"Damn."

Devan laughed bitterly. "Your dog did it. To both of us."

"Gr!"

I glared. "Don't call her a dog. Apparently the god of Ducky Mart wants to hire you."

"I am aware of that."

"How does it feel to go from Messiah to coffee jockey?"

Devan looked ready to cry. I felt like hell then. "Sorry," I said. "Look, most people live their lives without our … heritage. We just need to get used to it."

"Used to being like them? We're nothing now."

That was the last straw. "You little shit," I said. "Look. Look at my arm. You did that. You shot me. And now you're whining that you can't turn water into Pepsi anymore? When I snatched you, you said this was the start of your forty days in the desert. Did you think all it took was being locked up with a bunch of guys who fed you three meals a day, let you watch all the TV you wanted, and listened to your smug bullshit? Guess what: now you really have to sacrifice. Like the rest of humanity." I looked mournfully into my cup. "I don't even have a coffee maker."

Megan turned a bright smile to me. "Ducky Mart does a great Colombian roast."

I stormed over to the closet near the doors. "I'm going for a walk." I grabbed my long, woolen coat from the closet and shoved my left arm into the sleeve then shrugged my right shoulder into it.

"Your keys are here," the doctor said.

Back at the coffee table, I stared at the pile of stuff. The keys to my rented Camry. And three empty magazines for a Kimber pistol. "Oh, shit." I picked up my phone and the keys to my car, leaving the rental's keys on the table. "I'll have to courier those keys back to Chase."

Megan coughed. "I'll be going to Ducky Mart for my morning coffee. I can drop them off if you like. Chase can pick them up at the outlet near Galway Mall. The voice says don't call Chase quite yet because – No, I'm not saying that!"

I stared. Her face had turned scarlet.

"Oh, come on," she said, then listened to her own head. "The voice says the . . . film shoot didn't finish 'til two in the morning."

After Megan took off with the Camry keys, I left my snarky half-brother moping on my couch. The fox followed me into the corridor and down the hall to the elevators.

I hoped Garcia, the manager, wasn't around. He'd get bitchy about my "dog."

We walked, the fox padding along happily. "So you're a god."

She looked up at me and cocked her head. "Gr."

My arm ached as we wandered Riverbend Drive. "I don't have my powers anymore."

"Gr."

"You did that, didn't you? Slashed the cord between me and my old man."

"Gr."

I glanced at the fox, trying to figure out if I should be angry. That needed more thought.

"I can't keep you in my apartment; my landlord would kick me out. But Mom's acreage has a pond on it. You'll have to get used to people calling you a dog. Most people are going to think you're a pet."

The fox made a yipping sound and scampered ahead. She came sauntering back moments later, tail straight up, tongue lolling.

I was filling air, listening to myself talk to distract myself from the obvious. No more free coffee, no more insta-fix for a cut finger. I was normal. It occurred to me after crossing half a dozen intersections that I could get killed at any moment. Picturing a car running me down, I veered into Astrid Park, away from the street. You can see the river from its south side and the mouth of the bay to the ocean. I wandered along the paths and found a bench, where I sat and hugged my coat around me.

I started a long, hard think to get my bearings. Five or six hours ago, I'd been holed up in a Ducky Mart five hundred miles away, figuring a psycho named Max was going to shoot me. Or Devan was. Or the police. Now I was alive and well, except for the "minor" bullet wound.

"I could use a week of sleep."

"Gr."

"You too?"

"Gr." Yawning.

"I guess fighting a part of the godhead is kind of wearing, huh?"

"Gr." She hopped onto the bench and leaned against me. I touched her head. The film rolled across my vision. Beside me sat her spirit, enormous, her living body at its core. I was partly inside the silhouette of it, sitting there like that. A

looping strand of power wound out from me into the fox.
The fox's spirit looked down at me with scarlet eyes, then
rested her intangible chin on my head. Warmth spread down
my neck and into my wound, driving the ache away and
fighting back the chill of the morning.

It felt and probably looked ridiculous. I didn't care; no
one else could see it anyway. Anyone looking at us would
believe I sat here with my little white dog. Normal. Just
living my life, doing my job. I'd have to go back to that in a
few days. The bills wouldn't pay themselves.

"You'll like my mom."

FOX

This is the life, *Fox thought, peering through long grass at the
geese. She didn't feel particularly hungry, but chasing geese
into flight was even more fun than running lemmings into a
river.*

*Weeks had passed since Seth had brought her to his
mother's home. The woman provided Harry's All-Natural
Dog Chow, which tasted like real food and moved through
her like food should.*

*Her ears rose to a familiar sound: the distant closing of the
door to the woman's cavern. The man had come for his
weekly visit.*

*Fox herself saw him most days. She had learned to move
through this world by wrapping her soul around her body
and drawing it with her, no longer dependent on DM's
intangible passageways. She could reach the city with hardly
an effort of will.*

*She walked often with the man, though lately he depressed
her with his self-doubt and whining internal monologue
about the loss of his gifts.*

*She shook her head in a far too human way. Right now,
there were geese. Fox leaped through the reeds and hit the*

water. Five birds splashed wildly, wings beating air and water. She yipped at them, driving them into a frightened frenzy. They rose in confused spirals, figured out which direction they should go, and lanced toward the east in a V.

Fox watched them a moment longer before scrabbling out to shake water from her coat. Sighing happily, she wandered back toward the house.

Even in a war, *she thought,* there is always time to chase a goose.

The Book of Revelations

69

CHARLES

Weeks of what should have been my exaltation in Heaven passed in the Hell that was the abomination's home. The beast turned it into a stylish Cape Cod house with a perpetual fire in the hearth and legions of books on shelves. Outside lay endless plains of linoleum. I had attempted to leave but couldn't walk far enough for the house to be completely gone from my sight. Nothing ever lay before me except more miles of flooring. So I turned around with a heavy heart.

The three demons were gone. I saw them leave days ago with DM. It could be in as many places as it wanted to be, so I'd gone inside to find the fiend in a comfortable chair by the fire, book open in its lap. "For the last time, no."

"You released the others. Why won't you do that for me?" I pleaded. "You have an obligation to let me go."

The abomination turned a grim face to me. "Your own beliefs view suicide as a mortal sin."

"Heaven is not suicide."

"Actually, it is."

The abomination rose and turned to the fire. "I wonder how long he'll be like this. Sleeping it off, I mean."

Above the fire hung a gray smudge, framed in dark oak as though it were a piece of modern art: *Still Life With Mud Puddle*. The archdemon Lucifer, reduced to hotel art.

"DM, you're clearly very powerful. I'm pleading with your moral side."

"It's my moral side that won't let me sentence you to death, even a blissful one." The creature, now in the form of a plump woman with ponytails, waved at the chairs. "Have a seat." The abomination settled in beside me. "I'll make you the same offer I made to Jerome and the others, the same offer I make to everyone who is part of me when they leave the living world. I can teach you how to travel among the higher worlds. How to hide from the godhead. Until you're ready to learn that, you're stuck here. You are capable of living forever if you learn and grow."

"You expect me to let you corrupt me!"

"No. I expect you to grow. It will take decades to teach you to leap from one world to another. But consider this. After you learn to travel among the higher planes, you can get yourself to your specific Heaven if you wish. You can then dive into all that bliss and let yourself waste away.

"All you have to do is decide you are ready to learn how to become much more than you are now. New ways of thinking, new ways of perceiving the multiverse around you." DM shrugged. "While we wait for you to come to terms with that, you'll have me for company. There's plenty to read. If you prefer television, you can have it. But not reality TV. That will destroy your soul faster than a couple of decades in Heaven."

I sighed in dejection. "Please? Can't you just –?"

"I'm sorry, Charles. You have eternity ahead of you. You can spend it here with me – or out there among the worlds. Now stop moping and get on with afterliving."

70

ALL NEWS ALL DAY!

"You're watching *In the Morning* here on Channel Forty-Eight. Now, Simone, you made some interesting remarks about our colleague Kaylee Jerrel earlier. Please, tell us more."

"Certainly, Skip. For those just tuning in, we've been discussing Kaylee's apparently outrageous claim that the entire worldwide chain of Ducky Mart convenience stores had never had a holdup or any other violent incident –"

"With the exception of the incidents last month, of course."

"Exactly. My point is, some journalists heard that claim and immediately did what good reporters do: they investigated. I'm sure they assumed this was Kaylee's Dan Rather moment –"

"Referring, of course, to Rather's infamous story about George W. Bush and the National Guard, which ultimately turned out to be false."

"That's right, Skip. As we now know, there wasn't a single police report mentioning violent crime in a Ducky Mart store anywhere in the world before last month. When you consider some of the locations of Ducky Mart outlets –"

"Belfast, Kosovo, New York City."

"Absolutely. With outlets in places like those, it's quite incredible to contemplate that there has never been violence in a Ducky Mart. Even the head office of the chain has been amazed at this discovery. It stretches credulity. In fact – dare I say? – it's miraculous."

"Exactly the right word, Simone."

"But I think the fundamental point that has to be made here, Skip, is that a hard-news investigative journalist made this discovery. This wasn't even the story she was pursuing; it was an ancillary detail. But she discovered it and made a point of checking it out. In this age of Internet bloggers and so-called citizen journalists, it took a professional reporter just doing her job to uncover this."

"Absolutely true. And a reminder to our viewers, Kaylee Jerrel's fascinating, disturbing documentary, *The Deadly Bishop*, airs Tuesday after the ten o'clock news. Thank you for joining me, Simone. And before we go, I must say your new hairstyle is spectacular. Short is certainly in this year."

71

KAYLEE

The night after Tony called to plead with me for my footage, I found myself staring at the ceiling, unable to sleep. Emile snored gently beside me. He had such a cute snore.

I eased myself out of bed and fumbled in the light from the window until I found clean clothes. Then in the dining nook, I bundled up my laptop and stepped into the corridor with my bag slung over my shoulder.

Soon I drove past the remains of the Ducky Mart where Bishop Moffat and a pedophile called Theo Cessler were found dead with pistols nearby. It seemed almost anticlimactic for the police, after all the shooting and explosions from inside the shop, to discover they had a scrawny runt and a senior citizen as the perps. Both were dead, apparently having juggled grenades before shooting each other. The two staff members, Adele and Braydon, said they had spent the entire shootout hiding behind the counter, getting showered by coffee beans.

By remarkable coincidence, the store's high-tech security system was down for maintenance that night, so the cameras caught nothing. Ducky Mart Inc.'s North American director of security apologized.

I turned at the Lector Avenue intersection and carried on until I reached the Ducky Mart near the Shell station.

Somebody had changed the fluorescent bulb I had reported months ago when it started flickering.

I collected my bag from the trunk of the Mustang and headed for the doors. Beneath the sign, I hesitated. Braydon and Adele were in the central kiosk. Other staff members were at the back.

Braydon and Adele looked my way at the sound of the door chime. I gave them a warm smile. Braydon came over to the near side of the counter. "Hey, Kaylee. How goes it?"

"Great. My show is rolling. Check it out on Tuesday, after the late news."

Braydon frowned. "I work that shift."

"Me too," Adele said.

I moistened my lips. "Has anything come back to you yet?"

Adele flickered a smile. "I kind of hope it never does. My boyfriend says it hasn't even touched my sleep."

Braydon shrugged. "I startle whenever I hear a car backfire." He rubbed his chest. According to Seth, he'd been shot repeatedly. Being part of a god has its perks, though unlike Seth's brothers we could heal or resurrect only if we got hurt inside a Ducky Mart.

Braydon brightened. "The usual?"

"Please. And if you aren't too busy, I'd like to talk to you."

"Have a seat."

I paid for my coffee and took it to my usual table in the back corner. He joined me, tugging at the waist of his official yellow polo shirt.

When he sat, I leaned forward and whispered, "I know what you are."

"Excuse me?"

"Seth told me. I want to talk. Not to the voice in my head. I want to talk to you. Now."

Braydon blinked. "The voice in your head? Kaylee, are you all right?"

I stared for a moment longer then blushed. "Never mind."

He rested his elbows on the table and smiled uncertainly. Then his eyes began to smolder. "JUST PULLING YOUR LEG. LET'S TALK."

His voice boomed. I gasped and looked around. No one else seemed to notice.

"Can you cut that out?"

"Sorry. What can I do for you?"

"You used me. That bit about no crime in Ducky Mart ever."

"It was true."

"I know. But you still used me."

"I'm not sure what your point is."

I drew a long breath. "Seth says I'm part of you."

"You are. There are millions like you. Cells in my body. That's actually a terrible analogy. Your toenails are made of cells, but you have no compunction about clipping them. I, however, don't discard my component parts." Braydon, as avatar for the god, drummed his fingertips. "Unfortunately some of my cells are a bit on the squirrelly side. I've instituted a program of correcting their imbalances."

"Fine. Look, I just wanted to say, no more talking in my head. Okay?"

The god smiled. "Done."

"If I want to talk to you, I'll just come down here."

"Deal. And if I need to speak with you, I'll phone."

"You can do that?"

"I am a god."

"Right." I sipped coffee, enjoying the heat flowing over my tongue. "So what's happening? Seth and Devan are . . . normal."

"They needed to be separated from the godhead; they know too much." The god frowned. "I would appreciate it if you wouldn't discuss anything we talk about with Emile. He is still joined to the godhead through his power. In fact, I need to be careful what I say to you. Fox and I left your connection to the godhead intact. It's helpful to have you feeding what you know of me into it. You're my hotline to the Big Bad.

"The godhead is aware of me but appears quiet. I suspect we have seen the first skirmishes in a protracted conflict."

"How can you fight it? It's been around for billions of years."

The god nodded. "Longer. It predates time. In fact it invented time – accidentally, at least, what with setting off the Big Bang. I don't think it really understood what it was doing when it did that. Seeing its future laid out before it is what drove it mad. That's why it had to fragment. Each of the aspects is relatively sane, in its own way. But the totality is wacko."

"You've only been here for thirty years. Aren't you outgunned?"

The god shrugged. "I have the combined experience of millions of mortals. Your remark about zero crime in my shops went viral on YouTube. I am amassing new followers daily. However, it won't be enough, not for open war." Unexpectedly he smiled. "But there won't be open war if I can help it. The powers that came before me fought the godhead on its own terms. I won't make that mistake. I have something I think it wants very badly, though it may not be aware of it yet."

I put my cup down, eying him with my brows raised.

The god chuckled and said, "Therapy."

72

BRYNNHILDA

Hilda Langella, full-time police detective and part-time Chooser of the Slain, waited in the arrivals lounge of the Cove City International Airport, sipping a mug of Ducky Mart Misto Americano. One great thing about her change of allegiance was the free coffee for life. As an immortal, that meant a lot of free coffee.

The sign indicated Singapore Airlines flight 671 had landed. She browsed a newspaper. When the tidal wave of arriving passengers began, she folded the paper under her arm and made her way through the Saturday-afternoon crowd. Men and women in business attire, rumpled after ten hours in the air, wandered past with occasional families.

She almost missed him in the crowd. He wore a gray shirt, not his usual purple. A wave to catch his eye earned her a scowl. He pushed through the crowd to her side.

"Get me out of here. I had a small child behind me, crying and burping and whining the entire way across the Pacific."

"At least you made it, Loki."

"My name is John Locke for the duration of this incalculable horror that is mortality. Two bloody weeks in the consulate in Singapore getting a bloody passport. Bloody hell. I should have created a hell. I could have filled it with bureaucrats and customs officials." He gave her a glare. "Any word on when I can . . . rejoin myself?"

Hilda motioned to him to follow. "DM says when you shuffle off your mortal coil, preferably at the end of a long life, I am to bring you to him. He will see about joining you to your chopra. Which, by the way, is still unconscious. It'll probably be that way for a century or more. Even dead, you may have a long wait."

"Bugger." Locke glared. "Bloody nightmare."

"You get used to it."

"I cannot imagine." Locke glanced at her as they strode into the afternoon sun. "Is your new patron not concerned about the godhead learning secrets through you?"

Hilda hesitated. "Seth's fox trimmed me as well. I volunteered."

"To be mortal?"

"It cut my cord higher up than you. My link to the godhead is severed, but I'm still bound to my chopra. I'm free but with my power."

Locke gazed at her with those intense dark eyes. "You are betraying all that you are."

"I never signed on to take souls to their deaths." Hilda sighed. "Locke. John. Have you considered that maybe this new god has a point? The thing we emerged from spent so long alone that it became afraid of anything sentient. And we have been bound to it. You like to think you are the most free of us, the one who can traverse the barriers between the higher worlds. But have you ever thought you may just be bound up in its neuroses like the rest of us?"

Locke spat, "I used to be someone."

"You still are." They reached her convertible in visitors' parking. "Get in. I'll take you home."

"Home?"

Hilda raised her brow. "Your house. Remember? The ocean view? The Mini Cooper?"

Locke leaned against the car, wiping sweat from his face with his palm. "Bugger. How do people cope with a memory like this? Mortals are two misfiring neurons away from dementia or psychosis." He fumbled in his pocket. "I did wonder what these keys were for."

73

MAX

"I wish we could have you handle this in court," said the senior attorney in the legal department of Ducky Mart Inc., wholly owned subsidiary of the Kiseiiki Corporation. He set the paper down.

"It's a simple case, sir." Max shrugged. "Frankly, Bean's Coffee House doesn't have a legal leg to stand on regarding unfair competitive practices. They can whine about their customers abandoning them for us, but that's not our problem."

Edgar laughed. "Tell you what. I'm going to fax this over to them."

"Sir, this is an internal document. You'll be giving away our legal strategy."

"Of course I will. It's a brilliant piece of work, Max. Now if I were charging a client my rate in private practice, I would keep this to myself and let it unfold in court. As it is, we won't get paid extra for courtroom time. So I'm inclined to tell them exactly how we'll kill them in front of a judge, what our assorted weapons will be, and how there isn't a damn thing they can do. Case closed."

"Yes, sir." Max nodded while thinking, One day I'll go west and I'll find Seth Brown and I'll strangle him and watch the life ooze out of his eyes –

Fingernails on a chalkboard grated in his mind. *Enough of that. Settle down.*

Max smiled at Edgar as best he could through the galloping headache.

Edgar sighed pleasurably. "We've never had a law librarian with courtroom experience. You're an enormous asset to the firm, Max."

"Thank you, sir."

Edgar left him alone in the broad room that served as Ducky Mart Inc.'s records office and law library. His domain. He couldn't work out how the god had landed him the job. The voice in his mind back in the Summerton Ducky Mart had simply said, "When you leave here, you'll find yourself on Fifth Avenue, New York City, in the lobby of my head office. Take the elevator up to reception on the second floor."

He discovered his résumé was on file along with documents about his prison time and a letter from the CEO herself insisting Maxemilian Cobber would be a valuable addition to the company's legal team as an adviser in the assorted zoning cases, lawsuits from convenience-store and coffeehouse chains, and contract negotiations with wholesalers.

Weeks ago, he had expected to go down fighting.

Dejected, he forced himself to start reading the stack of papers Edgar had brought. When noon arrived, he strolled down the hall to the lunch room and found his brown bag in the fridge. As usual, he found the room empty. Everyone else in the legal department either ate at their desks or followed some random schedule of their own making.

Max sat and unwrapped his turkey sandwich. Then the first of the voices spoke up.

Can we do another lesson now? I'm still not clear on those emotional adjustments.

<<Okay. You need to keep a grip on the adrenal glands. Also, don't let the testosterone run away on you. That stuff's a bitch to clear out of the system.>>

"Shit," Cobber moaned.

<<Okay, here we go. These three lawyers go golfing together . . .>>

Cobber squeezed his sandwich into a pulpy mass of mayonaise, lettuce, and deli meat. Then the phonus twisted his giggle dial, and it was all he could do to keep from rolling on the floor.

I see, the god said. *Let me try.*

Max shut his eyes and struggled to keep upright. The golfing-lawyers joke was pretty good, he thought dimly. He felt certain a part of himself – a fundamental part – was dying a spectacularly horrid death. But right now he couldn't manage to mind.

The Second Book of Seth

74

Day 27 since my return from Summerton.

Jessica eyed the bandage on my right arm. "So, what happened to it again?"

"I fell."

"On what?"

"Something sharp and awkward."

"Can you lift boxes yet?"

"Nope."

She gave me a scowl and stalked off. I went back to typing book orders in. My new doctor, Megan, had told me I could stop using the sling but to do absolutely no lifting. She stopped by every couple of days to clean and dress the wound. It was an ugly monster on my upper arm, looking like a mouth with all the teeth pulled out and lips sewn shut.

Just weeks ago, the thought of getting hit by a bus while crossing the street would have made me laugh. But now the walk home from Wordwings, my four-block commute, gave me the willies. If I survived an accident, I'd have to call one of my half-brothers to heal me. If I died. . . . Like any mortal, I shook that thought away.

When I got home, the roommate I'd been saddled with was sitting on the couch chewing on a drumstick from the rotisserie chicken I'd bought yesterday. Devan was watching *Pulp Fiction*. Again.

"Dev."

"Yeah?"

"Remember that invention I showed you?"

He gave me a glare.

"It's called a vacuum. Using it does suck, but it gets your sandwich and cookie crumbs out of my carpet. Give it a try."

He shrugged.

"There's more to life than working in a Ducky Mart and watching television. Go out and get yourself a girlfriend."

He looked at the carpet. "I'm supposed to keep myself pure. For the end times." Devan sounded less and less sure every time he said it.

My phone chimed. I glanced at it. Norm was calling. I sighed and answered. "Hey."

"Hey dude. Wing night. You coming?"

I hesitated. Joining my half-brothers used to be fun. But someone would ask about the bandage on my arm. Unless I wore a long-sleeve to keep it hidden. And Norm loved my coffee. He'd be bound to ask me for a mug.

"I can't. Work's been busy."

"Look, man, if you're short of cash –"

"I'm not."

"Then catch the bus and get down here."

"Okay. Sure."

"Cool."

I clicked off with a tight sensation in my chest. "I'm going out."

Devan didn't take his eyes off the screen. Travolta and Jackson shot some college kid. I grabbed my jacket and shoes. At the bus stop, I realized there was no way I was going to the pub to see the gang. I swiped my pass over the scanner aboard the number 38 bus heading downtown instead. There had to be something good on at the Cinaplex.

I never made it.

I got off the bus on Cedar Street and walked past a sushi place, a banking machine, and a hairdressing salon. On a little ledge by the salon stood a row of photos and plastic flowers. Even a teddy bear. Some kind of memorial. I glanced at the photos as I walked by. Then stopped in mid stride, staring at a smiling face with dark hair brushed over the left side of her head. Rachelle.

I stepped back. There were marks in the bricks. Bullet holes had been mortared over. This must be where she'd died protecting her brother. I didn't even know I'd reached for my phone until it lay against my ear, ringing.

"Hello, Seth," Hilda answered.

"I'm downtown. Rachelle died on Cedar Street, right? That's where you collected her."

"Rachelle. Yes."

"You took her to Valhalla."

A sigh that sounded like resignation. "That was my job."

"We need to do something about her. You heard what DM said: Valhalla and Heaven and the rest are soul slaughterhouses. She'll die of monotony up there."

A laugh. "*We* need do something?"

That hurt. "I don't have any powers anymore. But you do. You could get her out."

Another long sigh. "You cost me a bet, you know."

"Huh?"

"Fox swore you'd be back in action. I figured, without your healing power, you'd turn wimp and stay safe at home."

"Even without my powers I can still do something." I winced. "Answer phones, maybe."

I listened to Hilda's breathing. Here it came: *Let the professionals handle it, sonny.*

"Seth," she said at last, "you can be slow at times. You don't have your powers because you're no longer joined to your father. Get over it. There's another god you are bound to. She's young, as gods go, but precocious. And she *likes* you. We have work to do. Now get down here."

My phone clicked.

"Gr?"

I turned. The fox stood there, steps away.

I shivered. "Can you read my mind?"

She canted her head as though saying, "Dumb question." Her tail waved.

"Hilda wants to talk at her place. I have no idea where she lives."

I lifted my phone. The fox yipped and leaped at me.

"Shit, what – ?" I put my arms up out of instinct as a bundle of white fur and teeth and blood-colored eyes flew at me.

The fox vanished. So did downtown Cove.

Rows of houses surrounded me, little ranchers with built-in garages. Lawns mowed into abject submission.

I spun around at a sound behind me. Something ticked against concrete. The fox looked as though she'd just landed.

The nearest house had a narrow driveway leading up to white aluminum-siding walls. There was a cute yellow trim around the windows. Hilda's little white convertible sat in the driveway.

The valkyrie cop stood on the step in a blue tank top and black jeans. "Come on in. We don't have all night."

I swallowed and headed up the walkway, the fox padding along beside me.

"So we're rescuing Rachelle?" I asked, glancing at the four-legged god.

"Gr," the fox said.

Hilda nodded. Her eyes flashed blue with power. "She's a start."

The End

If you enjoyed this tale
of convenience store gods and heroic bookstore clerks,
please post a review on Amazon, Goodreads,
or your favorite online site.

Reviews are the single strongest way to ensure an
independent author can keep on writing
the books you love to read.

Read on for a peek at

THE FROG OF WAR

ARMAGEDDON BOYS ⚡ BOOK TWO

The Book of Chase

I

Suds tickled my ankles as I tried to make bathwater support my weight. Not one of the half brothers I'd talked with could do this. We could heal and resurrect and turn water into more interesting liquids. It just made sense for walking on water to be part of the package.

I'd hoped another attempt at this would stop me thinking about my girlfriend. My sort-of girlfriend. My is-she-my-girlfriend-or-not.

My friend who I wished was my girlfriend taught herself to write music for my birthday two months ago. She set her laptop on her coffee table and woke up music software. A slow-rolling explosion of guitar and violin erupted over us.

"I call it 'Chasing Chase'," She said shyly. "One part Mozart and two parts Sex Pistols. It's not done yet." A moment later: "Are you really crying?"

"Of course not," I said, wiping my eyes.

"You're tearing up."

"Nope," I sniffled, the music digging into my gut and making my heart swell.

We snuggled on the couch as she laid out musical staves on her screen and deftly added notes. Taylor spun them out into heartbreaking cello riffs as I watched and listened, my fingers running through her hair. It was the color of burgundy wine, silky in my hands. Her wall clock chimed 9 pm and she broke off. "Chase. I need to study." Out the door I went.

Last week we walked hand in hand around Galway Park, ending up snuggled in front of the TV in my living room. Nine o'clock came. "Gotta go," Taylor said. I started hating clocks, on general principle.

I thumped my knuckles against the side of my head to drive out the memories, focusing on the bathwater. Setting my right foot on the surface, I hopped up with the other. Once more to the bottom. I stumbled, struggling for balance.

I swore, wishing Mom hadn't kept secrets from me. I'd missed a lot of practice time. She'd let me grow up thinking my dad had been some pimply junior high kid. Mom had skipped the part about a voice in her head saying, "You're pregnant, blah-de-blah, Second Coming, blah blah." I only found out my origin last year when I learned about my half-brothers.

Once Seth showed me he could turn water into coffee, I threw myself into figuring out what I could do. Experimenting in the back room at BARC distracted me from the dogs whining in their cages. I carefully sniffed a bottle of chloroform from a distance and fumbled its lid back on while my head swam, then filled a soda can with water from the tap. "Chloroform," I said. "Chloroform. Chlo-ro-foooorm. Um, trichloromethane. Cee-aitch-cee-ell-three."

I thought about the smell of chloroform. I opened the bottle again and dipped my fingertip in, and rubbed it on my skin to get a feel for it. Nothing.

Dejected, I sat on a stool and gazed into the can. It was too bad. Chloroform might be fun. When my co-worker, Ryan, washed in the little restroom, he always used a damp cloth on his cheeks, neck, and forehead. I pictured myself snapping my fingers to tweak the moisture on the cloth. Imagined Ryan looking at me cross-eyed as he slid to the floor.

I guffawed, setting the dogs barking. Then nearly passed out myself from the sweet smell oozing from my can of former water.

Walking on water wouldn't be the same kind of visual, I suspected. I ran my toes through the water as I thought. Freezing was a way for water to take weight. Picturing myself skating might work, but the warmth around my feet distracted me.

As I reached for the cold water tap, the ceiling of the bathroom opened. A tunnel of blazing white sucked my naked self straight upward, parts flapping like a lawn flamingo in a howling storm. Above my head spread a green field with rolling hills. My body flipped over and I fell, screaming the whole way down. I landed on grass and stopped dead with no sense of impact.

Gasping, I turned full circle. A smell of fresh-cut lawn filled the air. Some distance away, a tall wall of stone held a huge wooden gate snugged into a frame of boulders. A ululating cry came from far away as a figure leapt across the sky, spiraling toward me. When it neared, I made out a woman upon a white horse.

"SON OF JEHOVAH!" Her bellow echoed across the heavens.

They flew like an insane bee until they slammed into the ground before me. The horse vanished, leaving the woman behind. She was all black leather and metal bits. Silver-white hair moved by itself to encircle her face.

"You're a valkyrie," I said.

The woman stopped short. "What?"

"A valkyrie. And isn't that Valhalla?" I pointed at the wall.

She blinked. "How would you know this place?"

"I met your sister, Hilda. She is your sister, right?"

"Yes. How do you know Brynnhilda?" The valkyrie glared at me, then rubbed her temples. "Never mind, that's not important. My name is Kara. You work for me now. You are seeing a woman called Taylor Corin."

"Um. Not for long."

"*What?*"

"I'm breaking up with her tonight."

"You will not –" Kara blinked like a strobe. "Why are you considering breaking up with her?"

"I've already considered –"

Thunder echoed above.

"Um, I'm considering it because. . ." A lump formed in my throat. Bartender syndrome kicked in. I hadn't even told my roommates about this, but having a stranger to talk to made it somehow easier. "We've been together four months. You'd think after that time – Look, I'm not some kind of sex fiend. When you get romantically involved, you expect the relationship to progress into the bedroom. But by ten every evening she's out the door. It. . . hurts."

Kara pursed her lips. "Have you tried talking to her?"

I felt ready to burst into tears. "I can't say, 'I'm breaking up with you because you won't boink me.' That sounds like I'm trying to twist her arm. It's gross."

"Well, yes, that's true. But you could –" Kara looked at the ground and shook her head as if shifting mental gears. "Hang on, I didn't bring you all the way up here to give you relationship advice." Her body blazed white. She rose, legs together, arms out. Full-on god mode. "Mortal, you will not break up with her!"

"But –"

"YOU WILL NOT!" Her voice reverberated across the hills.

I crouched, hands in front of my face. The light was so bright I could see the bones in my fingers. "Okay, okay!" Discovering I couldn't end it with Taylor tonight, after all, made me feel like I could fly. Like the crazy valkyrie.

"I DON'T CARE WHAT YOU DO TO REMAIN WITH HER. OBSERVE HER AND REPORT EVERYTHING YOU SEE."

"Everything?"

"IF I SUSPECT YOU HAVE HELD BACK, YOU WILL SUFFER PAIN LIKE YOU HAVE NEVER KNOWN!" The white fire surged and vanished. She stood on the grass before me once again. "You'll find me in your phone's contacts list. Under K."

"You want me to spy on her. That's not right."

Whiteness blazed.

"Um. Fine."

"Call me as soon as you have something. Now go away."

The tunnel sucked me into the sky. I flipped over almost immediately. Far below lay my bathroom, the only thing visible from here. Down I went, landing with no sensation of a sudden stop. I stood, trembling, in warm water.

A string of notes surrounded me like auditory fireworks. My ringtone, Taylor's composition. Transferred from her laptop in a university coffee shop when I proudly showed her my sleek new phone.

As Seth would say: Well hell.

2

I didn't get to my phone in time. The message icon glowed so I put the phone on speaker.

"Hi Chase. You're coming over tonight, right? I'm making dinner. Lamb. I hope you like lamb. And I. . . We need to talk. There's just. . . you know, stuff. See you at five. Bye."

Red flags popped up in my thoughts. Talk? What did we have to talk about? I'd been planning to talk about how I was dumping her. Maybe it was going to be the other way around.

I sat at the dining table, towel around my middle, and shivered. Kara couldn't fault me for getting dumped instead, could she? My stomach tied itself in knots.

I drove to Taylor's apartment in my work van, the BARC logo on its side peeling with age. The interior always smelled like old, wet dog, so I kept the windows open. I parked outside her building and eyed her rusty Honda. The bumper looked ready to fall off.

Usually, when I hit the buzzer to be let in, Taylor pretended she didn't know me and grilled me on what I wanted in her building. An annoying, endearing game. This time she let me in without a word. I walked up the three flights rather than taking the elevator.

She threw the door open and stood still for a moment, a smile flickering across her face. Then she threw herself at me and kissed me. "Brilliant timing. Dinner is ready."

Taylor had put on a long, flowing dress. I'd never seen it before. Very much not her usual jeans and tank.

She saw me looking her over. "Don't you like it?"

"Um. It's great."

"Come in."

I followed her into her little apartment. She had set up her square table with two plates, and a spread of neatly sliced meat, mashed potatoes, and sautéed snap peas.

"This is wonderful," I said.

"Thanks." She flicked her hair back. "I had to ask my dad for his lamb recipe. It turned out pretty good. I hope. It could be burnt for all I know."

I eyed the pink flesh as I sat. "I don't think you burned it."

"Good." She picked up a wine bottle and poured a glass for each of us. Her hand quivered.

"Um, Taylor? What's going on?"

She looked up, startled. "What do you mean?"

"All this. And your message about needing to talk."

She looked down, fumbling with her fork. "Well, yes. I've been thinking a lot. It's time –"

"Are you dumping me?"

Her fork fell from her fingers. "Is that what you want?"

"What? No! But –"

"Good!" Relief shot through the word. She waved her hands. "Stop. Just let me say this. Just shut up."

"Okay."

"That's not shutting up."

"I – um. Sorry."

Taylor clenched her fists. "I need to just spit it out. Throw it out there."

Silence. I leaned forward. "Um –"

"I want to sleep with you."

The world appeared to blink in surprise.

"You. . . what?"

"I'm sleeping with you. I got protection and everything. So. We're sleeping together tonight. There. I've said it."

I tried to figure out what words to push out next. "Can you say that in a way that doesn't sound like you expect it to be a chore?"

Taylor's face crumpled. "Oh God, I so suck at this."

"Do you need a sex therapist?"

"Huh? No! I'm – I've been told. . . Never mind. I mean this." She gestured between us, fingers fluttering like butterflies. "This conversation. I never know what to say. Then it all goes to hell. But there are things about me you need to know. This is so complicated."

"Yeah, I guess it is. I don't even know what it is, but it already sounds complicated."

Taylor glared.

"I mean," I continued in a hurry, "I thought maybe you were secretly Mormon and couldn't have sex until you were married and didn't want to tell me about it."

Taylor scowled. "That's not it. But every guy I've ever slept with has bolted like a scared rabbit."

"You've slept with assholes and you think I'll be another of them?"

"I don't think you're an asshole. Maybe they ran away because it was the smart thing to do. I don't know. All I know is. . ." Taylor stopped babbling. "I sleepwalk."

I studied her eyes, waiting for the punchline. "And?"

"That's it. I sleepwalk. Actually, that's not accurate. I sleep-shower. And I sleep-order-pizza. And sometimes I sleep-read – I've found books on my Kindle that I don't recognize. And I sleep-channel-surf. Once I think I even sleep-wrote-notes-to-myself. I couldn't read them. The pages were full of weird little triangles and squiggly lines. Written with my favorite pen."

"Um."

Taylor stared and waited. "Is that all you can say?"

"I'm not sure what to say." I chugged back half my wine glass. "If you're afraid of me being with you when you fall asleep, we could, um, make love in the afternoon."

"Yes, and we could cuddle up afterward and maybe fall blissfully asleep. Then my other half could wake up and throw you through a wall."

"*Throw me through a wall?*"

"Shit, I shouldn't have said that. It only happened once."

"You threw your boyfriend through a wall while unconscious?"

"Marcus wasn't my boyfriend. I was at this party and I fell asleep. I woke up outside with a monster headache, walking home in the dark. I learned later that he liked slipping drugs into girls' drinks. The story went all over my school, especially the part about him flying through a wall. But I think that was embellished. It was a thin wall and I'm not that strong. He wasn't seriously hurt. Well, broken arm."

"Holy crap!"

Taylor buried her face in her palms. "I've ruined things, haven't I?"

"I . . . No. Not necessarily. I mean, it's a shock, that's all." I drained my wine glass. "Have you seen a shrink about this?"

"Once. He hypnotized me." Taylor rolled her eyes. "Afterward he told me I was fine and don't come back. While sort of hiding behind his desk."

I reached for the wine bottle. "I have an idea. Let's not get, um, intimate."

Taylor looked up with stricken eyes.

"I just mean, right now let's not . . . you know. But, maybe I could stay here tonight. I could meet your sleepwalking self, and, I don't know, see if she's okay with us."

Taylor gazed back. "Are you sure?"

"Yes. Um. Great. Lamb?"

"What?"

"Let's eat. You put a lot of work into this meal. Then, maybe we could watch a movie."

Taylor stared, an expression on her face that bounced between fear and hope.

"Do you really like the dress?" she asked in a faint voice.

"Yes. It's gorgeous. You're gorgeous."

"I hate it. My Mom bought it for me years ago. Flowerprints aren't my style. I only wore it because it comes off easily."

* * *

We made out on Taylor's bed but agreed I should sleep on the couch.

"Hey, junior." Something pushed against my shoulder. I woke to find toes touching my chin.

"Sweetie," I said and rubbed my eyes. Taylor stood before me in a black bra and tye-dyed wraparound skirt. She planted both feet on the carpet and raised a brow.

I peered up at her, smiling. "Couldn't sleep?"

"Let's have a look at you."

My heart crashed against my ribcage. "Um, Taylor?"

"No."

"Oh. Um. You're her? Just, asleep?"

She set her hands on her hips, moving like a gunfighter from an old Clint Eastwood movie. "You don't know me. But I know who you are. Son of that upstart creep from the godhead." Her eyes ignited with green fire.

"Oh, shit."

The monster running Taylor's body grabbed my shirt and hauled me up. "Silence, little one. I won't harm you. Unlike that creature you're bound to. Through you, it could learn about me. I can't allow that."

"Um, wait," I wailed in panic. "I won't tell anyone."

"True enough." Taylor lifted me by my neck. Her eyes flared.

Agony seared through my head. The world tumbled into darkness.

*   *   *

I woke up on the couch, a dull ache in my temples. Taylor sat at the kitchen table, elbows either side of her laptop. I eased my feet to the floor. My shoes were next to the door. Taylor or the thing that possessed her had her back to me. In the dim light given off by the screen, she wore headphones. With luck she wouldn't hear me move.

"Tea," she said.

I froze.

"I said, tea. Make some. Decaf Earl Grey. I want Taylor to get a decent sleep, after all."

"Um, okay."

"She hates it when you say 'um'. She's too polite to tell you." The Taylor monster turned. Her eyes were normal now. No fiery green lights. "You're wondering if I'm going to throw you through a wall."

"It crossed my mind. We talked about it last –"

"I was there, remember?"

"Um, you know what happens to her when she's awake?"

"You have my blessing, if that's what you're looking for. Just be good to her. I'm tired of all the evenings when she's heartbroken and lonely, watching romcoms while devouring chocolate walnut fudge ice cream. Those emotions bleed into me and I spend the night getting misty-eyed over Netflix. Then I have to go out running to burn off the calories."

"What are you?"

"That's none of your business."

I put Taylor's kettle on and, trembling, tossed a teabag into a cup.

"Make it a pot," the Taylor monster said. "I'll be busy all night."

"Taylor will be a mess in the morning if you don't get some sleep."

The monster laughed. It wasn't Taylor's laugh. Not even close. "The only one losing sleep here is you." The creature looked away, as though staring into the distance. "Taylor is currently dreaming. It borders on nightmare. She has you on repeat play in her head. You're running away endlessly. From her."

"Um. Oh."

"You can quit saying 'um' now."

"How long have you. . . possessed her?"

"What you don't know won't hurt you. When you're done with that tea, you may as well go to bed. You'll wake up next to Taylor."

"I don't think I'll be able to sleep. And I don't want to wake up next to her. She'll think we got physical while she was asleep. That's just a step up from date rape."

The creature blinked. "Aren't you the gentleman."

I brewed tea and set cup and pot next to her, glancing at the laptop screen. Wikipedia. Something about Sumeria. A map.

The creature closed the screen. "Time for you to nap again." It gestured. The world departed.

3

Footsteps beside me.

"Aaaah!" I bolted upright and pressed my back into the couch.

Taylor set a mug on the coffee table. She wore purple pajamas with frog pictures all over them. I recognized Ribbit the Frog from a kids' TV show.

"Taylor?" I squeaked.

Her throat danced. "Are you okay?"

"Yeah."

"Did you sleep okay?"

"Um. I mean, yes." Aside from being choked while some demon thing fried my brains.

Her eyes looked haunted. "Did I?"

"You were up."

Fear gave way to intrigue in her gaze. "Did I say anything? What was I like?"

"You –" *You have a monster inside you that likes tea.* "The other you is okay with us."

"What did I do?"

"You spent a lot of time on your laptop, looking up something on Wikipedia."

Taylor raced to her computer and opened the screen. The machine glowed to life. "Damn. The browser history is clear." She sank to the couch next to me. "It's always clear."

I thought of glowing green eyes. "The other you remembers what happens to you during the day."

Taylor sighed. "It's so weird. I must be a split personality."

It's not a personality, it's a power, I thought. *Personalities don't give you the strength to pick someone up by his throat or set your eyeballs on fire.* Those words refused to come. I'd have to explain how I knew what a power was, and that would lead to the whole 'I'm one of the Messiahs' thing. My brothers all said it killed relationships to mention it. Come to think of it, maybe I should tell Taylor. Or, I could just stay shut up. I really didn't need two different powers coming after me.

"I'm making pancakes. Want some?" It hurt to see the desperate, hopeful look in her eyes.

"Sounds great."

"You don't have work today, do you?"

"No. But . . . I need to take care of some stuff at home."

"If you're free later would you like to come over?"

"Um, maybe. I mean, yeah, I guess."

She was silent as she set pancakes on plates. We ate. Her tongue darted out to moisten lips, as though she wanted to say something.

The pancakes might have been good. I didn't taste them. Part of me kept wondering if I could make a run for the balcony and leap over the railing. Her apartment was only on the third floor. A heal would take care of any broken bits.

When I finally got myself out of there, I fled to my van. I drove a few blocks, put my phone in the cradle on the dashboard, and keyed up Kara's number. I got voicemail.

"Um, Kara. Call me. Please. I need to talk. Taylor's got a power inside her. I can't do this."

I drove, white-knuckled, toward home. The phone buzzed, and I hit hands-free. "Kara."

"You called."

"She's possessed. Some kind of demon."

"I'm aware."

"I can't go back."

"As a matter of fact, you can."

"No, actually, I can't."

"Pull over."

"How do you know I'm driving?"

"Never mind. Pull over."

I found a parking spot outside a gas station and stopped the van. "Okay, I'm –"

The van's ceiling opened and the white tube sucked me away to the gates of Valhalla. I landed hard this time, the impact thrumming through my guts. Kara's introductory ululating cry sounded beneath dark clouds. She spiraled down and landed before me.

"I did not say, 'Do this unless you get scared.'" Kara smoothed black leather sleeves and crossed her arms.

"Well, I am scared."

"Pee your pants then. The warmth will make you feel better."

"That's not funny. The thing takes control of her when she's asleep. It picked me up by my throat!"

"Like this?"

"Urk."

Look for Book Two, THE FROG OF WAR,
in February 2019